The Sweet Gardenia

A NOVEL

EUGENE HARKINS

Lulu Publishing Services rev. date: 05/19/2022

PART I

CHAPTER I

※

West Coast of Africa

It was a moonless midnight in August and the very heart of the rainy season in the year of Our Lord one thousand eight hundred and fifty-two. *The Wandering Maiden*, a sleek 250-ton schooner of the Baltimore Clipper class, lay at anchor off the Bight of Benin on the West Coast of Africa. Sixteen-year-old Billy McHugh stood at the rail, peering down at the African traders in their native canoes as the crew offloaded the trade goods.

"Hop to it, Billy! We've no time to squander," shouted First Mate, Patrick McHugh, who was also Billy's father.

"Yes, sir," said Billy, who ran over, picked up a crate of tobacco and ran back to the rail, dropping it into the waiting arms of the African traders.

Before they set sail from Charleston, Billy overheard his dad telling Captain John Sturgis and Second Mate, Tom Moran, not to show him any favoritism:

Don't treat him any differently," Patrick had said. "Make him earn his wage.

That was fine with Billy, for he was excited and anxious to prove he was up to the task on this his first time at sea.

The Wandering Maiden was loaded with kegs of rum, *aguardiente*, tobacco, muskets, powder, bolts of blue clothing, cowry

1

shells, and iron bars, all of it taken on board weeks before in Charleston. As he continued offloading the goods, Billy caught a glimpse of Captain Sturgis, pacing back and forth on the main deck, a tense, worried look on his weathered face. Sturgis had good reason to worry. For suddenly the night sky lit up with the pinkish-red glow of a rocket flare. Everyone stopped and watched as the bright light particles floated slowly down, illuminating the unlawful scene. Boom! The thunderous roar of a thirty-two pounder split the still night air. Seconds later, the deadly missile hit the water with a hiss just off the starboard bow. Boom! A second blast thundered forth, the heavy ball entering the water off the port side toward the stern.

"It's the bloody British," Sturgis cried, rushing to the rail and lifting his glass. "Cast the goods overboard! Hurry! We can't afford any extra ballast."

One of the crew was lugging a keg of rum and hesitated, staring at the Captain in disbelief.

"Heave it over. Now!" Sturgis bellowed.

This time the man obeyed, watching as it fell on a native canoe, capsizing it. Billy was carrying a heavy crate of muskets and did not hesitate, tossing it over the side, barely missing the canoes and eliciting hostile shouts from the African traders.

"You heard the Captain, hop to it, mates," yelled Patrick. "Over the side with them, all of them!"

The crew hurriedly jettisoned the trade goods, rushing then to raise the anchor and unfurl the sails. It started to rain, and within seconds, it was coming down in sheets. The wind howled and blew hard, buffeting and filling the Baltimore Clipper's sails, and she quickly got under way. Suddenly, another rocket flare lit up the sky followed by another cannon blast. Sturgis lifted his glass again and spotted the Royal Navy frigate about a half-mile off their port side. Lightning flashed, zigzagging across the sky, thunder followed rendering it difficult to distinguish between the thunderclaps and the cannon blasts

Patrick knew that Captain Sturgis was retiring and that this was to be his final voyage. Sturgis had been on this dreaded coast countless times during his long career. Indeed, McHugh had been with him on many voyages. He recalled Sturgis' words in the Charleston tavern on the eve of this one. *I've had enough. This abominable business has sustained me financially but cursed me spiritually, and I want out. This will be my final voyage, Patrick.*

Patrick also knew that if the Royal Navy caught them, they would take them to Freetown, Sierra Leone and confiscate *The Wandering Maiden*. They would throw them all in chains, try them, find them guilty and possibly even hang them. Of course, they would have to catch her first, which was not an easy task, because *The Wandering Maiden* was built for speed and had a first rate crew. And thanks to the crew's quick action, she was now well under way and flying with the wind.

A seasoned mate named Barney was at the wheel. Patrick McHugh stood next to him studying navigation charts when Billy walked up.

"They can't catch us now can they, Dad?"

"Not as long as this wind stays strong," Patrick said. "But you better get back to your duties, Billy."

"By my reckoning' we're outta cannon range," said Barney. "They aren't gonna catch us now."

"Thank God for that," said Captain Sturgis, who suddenly appeared, looking a little calmer.

Unfortunately, it didn't last long as blood-curdling screams and the loud banging of chains erupted from the bowels of the vessel, where hundreds of Lucumi and Kongo slaves had been stacked and packed like cordwood.

"I knew they were too quiet," said Captain Sturgis. "Hurry, get below and nip this in the bud, Patrick."

Patrick called out to the fearsome mate called "Big Ben," and together with two rugged mates and the ship's translator, they rushed below deck. Patrick had warned Billy to avoid the slave hold, but when he saw them all going below, his curiosity got the better of him, and he followed behind at a safe distance so as not to be seen.

They stood at the entrance to the slave hold, assaulted by a stench so horrid that it caused all but the strong and hearty to back off. Big Ben, however, stepped in boldly, shouting, cursing, and cracking his cat-o'-nine. The translator and the two mates followed behind him. Patrick remained at the entrance, watching as Big Ben made his way along the narrow wooden planks between the rows of human ebony, cracking his cat-o'-nine on the pitiful black bodies lying there naked in chains. Big Ben was indifferent to their plight, unmoved by how the shackles rubbed off their skin and dug into their raw flesh. He had stacked and packed them so tightly that they couldn't stand or stretch, able to sleep only when exhaustion had overtaken them. He knew that often they could not make it to the "mess tubs," burdened by the other slaves chained to them, thus having to relieve themselves where they lay amidst their own feces and urine.

"*My God!*" gasped Billy, straining to keep from throwing up at the sight and smell of them. This was the first time he'd seen the horrid conditions in the slave hold, the first time he'd witnessed the suffering and cruelty that these Africans were forced to endure. Soon he had seen enough, and he slipped away and went back up on deck, horror and disgust contorting his handsome, boyish face.

It took some doing but Big Ben was able to calm down the slaves, aided considerably by the translator, who told them in their native dialects that they were being taken to a land of plenty, a paradise, where they would lead a much better life. And by the time Big Ben climbed the stairs to the main deck, the frenzied shrieking of the slaves had become just a pathetic, mournful moan.

2

When the dawn broke that day, the Royal Navy frigate was nowhere in sight. The sea was calm, and although the winds had weakened, *The Wandering Maiden* maintained a sprightly speed, which Second Mate Moran estimated at some eleven or twelve knots. Captain Sturgis, exhausted by the ordeal of the night before, was asleep in his cabin. The Africans remained quiet.

Young Billy was thrilled to be making this voyage on *The Wandering Maiden,* a voyage which his mother, Bonny, had sought to deny him. Patrick had spent most of Billy's school years at sea, and he saw this as an opportunity to spend some time with his son and exert some fatherly influence. When Patrick told Bonny that Billy was coming with him, she was mortified.

I forbid it, Patrick! I will not let you take my Billy on a slave ship.

He needs to spend some time with me and with other men, Bonny. The lad needs to get some calluses on those soft hands of his. Billy had overheard it, and when Bonny burst into tears, Patrick rushed to comfort her. Billy then feared that she would get her way and he would never get to go to sea.

Billy was an only child, and his mother was overly protective, hovering over him, babying him. She was afraid to let him ride a horse. She rejected several of his closest chums, whom she had decided were ill-mannered and bad influences. She had forced him to take piano lessons which he hated and for which he had no talent. And worse yet in Patrick's mind, she had made him sit down to tea with her lady friends after school, ostensibly to observe and learn proper etiquette and manners. Patrick, however, was resolved to take Billy, and Bonny had no choice but to relent, resolving to revisit the issue when *The Wandering Maiden* returned to Charleston.

When the crew first set eyes on Billy, one mate was heard to remark:

He's a handsome lad all right, but he sure as hell don't look much like his dad.

Patrick had overheard the remark but took no offense.

He takes after his mother, tall like her and he's got her blue eyes and wavy brown hair. Why Hell, the only thing he got from me was this cleft chin," Patrick had said, rubbing it and smiling good-naturedly. *Once he starts shaving he's going to have the same problem I have with slips of the razor.*

As a cabin boy, Billy had to run back and forth throughout the ship, toting lumber, nails, and barrels of tar for sealing the leaks, and pots of boiling water for the ship's surgeon. Billy learned that a cabin boy was something akin to a seagoing factotum whose duties encompassed every imaginable task. Occasionally, but only occasionally, he would get to visit and sit for a spell in his dad's comfortable First Mate's cabin, sometimes even snatching a morsel of the better food served to the officers by the ship's two cooks. But for the most part Patrick and the officers and crew of The Wandering Maiden hewed closely to the pledge not to show Billy any favoritism.

Being of good humor and strong of heart, Billy chose not to focus on the negative aspects of shipboard life, of which there were many. Instead, he embraced the excitement and adventure of his first time at sea. He had a few episodes of queasy stomach and loss of balance, but in a few days, he got his sea legs. And in spite of the twelve to fourteen hours of shipboard duties assigned to him each day by the crew of *The Wandering Maiden*, Billy thrived in his role as a cabin boy. Though only sixteen, he could easily lift the heavy water jugs and double-time them to the thirsty sailors and the slaves when they were up on deck. He took the time to talk to the crew, even the fiercest-looking ones, the ones whom others, both on board and ashore, avoided at all costs. His desire to overcome his inherent shyness may have helped in that regard, because many of the crew perceived it as charming. Though they kidded him and made common fun of him, they seemed willing to cut him some slack, instinctively sensing that in spite of the wide gap in background, education, and social standing, here was a lad who at heart was something of a kindred spirit. There was of course some element of restraint from the crew because Billy was the son of the First Mate. Billy quickly grew to like most of the crew, and much to the delight of Billy's dad, who had overheard the scuttlebutt, the crew liked Billy as well.

There was, however, one crewmember, which Billy avoided and with whom he felt more than just uncomfortable. It was well known that Big Ben was a decidedly mean man, and along with his cat-o'-nine, he carried a chip on his shoulder. He had a loathing of anyone of a higher social standing than he, and Billy McHugh certainly fit that bill. Big Ben was for all intents and purposes a sea-going scoundrel, who looked and acted every bit the part. He was big and slovenly with a thick black beard frequently infected with scum, the remnants of food particles trapped there from his ravenous eating. His clothes were dirty and smelled like the devil. He'd been caught more than once trying to break into the rum closet. He must have succeeded occasionally and purloined his own private stock, because at times he appeared to be drunk. Captain Sturgis would have booted Big Ben off *The Wandering Maiden* long before, had it not been for the fact that he was thought to be the best of the lot at reading the actions and controlling the behavior of the slaves.

Billy ran afoul of him when he had stopped and watched as Big Ben whipped Javier, another cabin boy, punishing him for failing to empty the slaves' mess tubs. Billy had done nothing more than watch for a few seconds like many of the crew. But Big Ben had shown hostility toward him, threatening to tie him to the mast and give him a good hard flogging. The next evening Billy managed to slip away to the First Mate's cabin and mentioned the incident to his father. Unbeknownst to Billy, Patrick had learned about it moments after it occurred, which he did not reveal to his young son, not wanting to show too much concern. Patrick had, however, spoken to Second Mate Moran and ordered him to monitor carefully any interaction between Big Ben and Billy.

Every day after the evening meal, the crew got their daily allotment of rum, and they gathered on deck to relax, smoke, and spin yarns of their shipboard adventures. Billy would sit and listen with great interest as each one endeavored to outdo the other. They were surprised and impressed that the son of the highly respected First Mate would choose to mix with the common tars rather than the other cabin boys. At first sight Billy appeared to be a young and tender lad whose soft hands and easy life made him unfit to do the hard work aboard ship. But it turned out that he was made of tougher stuff and did more than just pull his own weight. Even the few times when he had to dump the slaves' mess tubs, he was able to steel himself up for the repugnant task, hold his breath and carry out the order without so much as a veiled complaint.

3

Big Ben cracked his cat-o'-nine as he herded the slaves up the stairs and on to the main deck. He need not have whipped them to get them topside, so anxious were the poor devils to simply get some fresh air to breathe and some space to stretch their stiff and battered bodies. Twice a day they were brought topside to be fed, exercised and looked over by the ship's surgeon, a forty-year-old native of Charleston trained in veterinary medicine. They segregated the men from the women. If there were to be a slave rebellion, it would be the men to initiate it. Patrick McHugh, as a rule, stationed additional guards on the barricade with their guns and cutlasses at the ready.

The crew gathered around to watch the goings on. There was always something to see, something unexpected, sometimes good and sometimes bad, but always exciting. Indeed, it was a form of entertainment for the crew.

"Hop to it with those water buckets," shouted the Second Mate.

Billy began filling the cups for the thirsty Africans, many of whom had difficulty grasping them with their manacled hands. He could not help but feel sorry for them. Unlike the rest of the crew, he was new and not hardened to the horror and cruelty, which these Africans had to endure. He watched as they gulped down the water and looked up at him with sad eyes and forlorn expressions as they begged for more. As Billy doled out the water, the ship's surgeon went down the lines of slaves, touching and feeling their bellies, limbs, and backs, examining their overall condition. From time to time, he would stick out his tongue, signaling them to do the same. Some slaves had raw flesh wounds from the constant rubbing of the chains. Those he took aside and applied palm oil on the wounds.

"Best we take off the chains, and let them move around a bit, lest infection set in. Some of these wounds look pretty bad," said the ship's surgeon.

"Post some extra guards on the barricade," said Patrick.

Moran ordered Big Ben and two others to hop to it. The big

man scowled, for he was accustomed to leering longingly at the slave women on deck. Swallowing a mouthful of curses, he turned and walked off, rubbing his filthy beard. The surgeon finished examining the slaves, and then looked around for the ship's fiddler.

"Get that old albatross up on deck," he said. "They need to dance and expend some energy."

Of the hundreds of slaves in the hold of *The Wandering Maiden*, there was one woman for every two men and two children for every woman. Don Fernando de Castilla, the wealthy owner of *La Dulce Gardenia*, a large sugar plantation southwest of Havana, had requested that ratio in his charge to Captain Sturgis. Losses were inevitable, but Sturgis felt confident there would be no more than ten percent. Sickness, especially dysentery and the bloody flux, would take their toll, as would accidents and suicide. Slave suicide was quite common on slavers, and jumping overboard to drown or be eaten by sharks was the usual practice.

4

The Wandering Maiden sailed ever westward toward her final destination in Cuba. The crew finished their evening meal and were lounging on deck. They sipped and savored their daily allotment of rum and smoked their tobacco, joking with each other as the western sky exploded in a brilliant sunset. Most of the older crewmen sat with their backs against the rail, their legs extended as they spun out tales of their past exploits. The younger lads stood, leaning against the rail, discussing how they would spend their time and their wages when they got to Cuba. One of them boasted of a spot in Havana with the sauciest señoritas. Billy listened with great interest.

Below deck, all was quiet. Some attributed it to the translator, who had been telling the slaves that their long journey would soon be over. Others believed that the slaves were simply exhausted and hadn't the will or the energy to resist their captors any longer.

"Just two more sunsets, me lads, and we'll be off o' this *Wandering Maiden*. And that's when I shall do me own wanderin' with me own maidens," quipped one enthusiastic tar, evoking some hearty "hear hears" from his shipmates.

"And just you wait, me boy, till ye see those lovely maidens in Havana," said another; the prettiest things you'll ever see and quite coquettish," he said, conveying to all that he spoke from experience.

5

Captain Sturgis sat in his cabin, staring down at the ledger books atop his ornate mahogany desk. There were administrative and financial matters to attend to, losses to tally, wages to calculate and profits to compute. He sent for Bill Wrett, the able-bodied seaman who also served as the ship's accountant, to go over the books. It was one more thing that he disliked about his "abominable business," as he termed it. He stared down again at the ledgers, and the more he tried to contemplate and appreciate the huge profit he would earn from this voyage and the comfortable retirement it would provide, the more it all suddenly seemed unimportant and anticlimactic. The long-awaited joy and excitement of retirement that he anticipated had all but vanished into thin air. He pushed the ledgers aside now and frowned. Reaching for the bottle of brandy, he poured himself a full glass, stood up and peered out the open porthole. The sun shone brilliantly, casting magnificent silver flashes of shimmering light on the calm blue water. It was a beautiful sight to behold, and he felt suddenly relaxed, wondering whether he would miss the life at sea that had been his career and his lifeblood.

There was a knock on the cabin door.

"You may enter," the Captain said, turning and walking back to his desk. It was Bill Wrett, carrying some books and papers.

Wrett was a pale thin man whose eyesight had faded over the years and whose spectacles helped only some, failing to correct the twitch in one of his eyes.

"I'm ready if you are, Captain," Wrett said, standing in front of Sturgis' desk, his demeanor expressing a lack of self confidence.

"Have a seat," said Sturgis. "Will you join me for some brandy?"

Sturgis' mood was already brightening from the effects of two full glasses.

"No, Captain, I think I'll decline for now, if you don't mind."

"As you wish. Have you got the final losses?" Wrett looked down at his ledgers.

"I think so, Captain." "Looks like it's twenty-three as of today. That includes numbers 61, 116 and 118 that died just after breakfast, according to the ship's surgeon. They threw them over the side—amazing how fast them sharks arrive. Anyway that makes twenty-three."

Sturgis poured himself another half-glass of brandy.

"Have you done the wage calculations?"

"Yes, sir, I have."

They spent the next two hours going over the ledgers, and when they finished, Captain Sturgis asked Wrett to send Patrick McHugh up to see him. McHugh appeared ten minutes later, took a seat and accepted Captain Sturgis' offer to share some brandy. Sturgis handed him one of Wrett's ledger pages with the First Mate's share underlined.

"That's your share, Patrick, which takes into consideration the losses up till now. It shouldn't vary much from that."

McHugh looked at it and smiled approvingly. Sturgis had informed McHugh that he would retire after this voyage, and had offered to sell him *The Wandering Maiden*. They had agreed on the price, subject only to a thorough inspection in Havana. McHugh saw immediately that his share of the profits was sufficient to cover about seventy-five percent of the purchase price. Patrick agreed to pay the remaining twenty-five percent in gold coin.

"Tell me, Patrick, you know how fond I am of this vessel. What are your plans for *The Wandering Maiden*? Are you going to continue in the business or start hauling some of that cotton out of Charleston to England? I'm told you can now get a full hold of woven goods to carry back to America."

"I haven't yet decided, Captain. I don't have to tell you that there's big money to be made in this business. There's huge demand in Cuba, Brazil and the United States. But this is one helluva risky business. If the Royal Navy had caught us, we would be in a cell right now in Freetown awaiting the hangman's noose. Then there's my wife who wants me to get out of this business, says it's too dangerous. But the truth is, Captain that I haven't yet decided."

That evening Patrick McHugh called his son Billy to his cabin and told him that he would be purchasing *The Wandering Maiden*. Billy had heard the rumor, so now it was confirmed.

6

Billy was on deck as the crew brought the slaves topside for a final inspection before the vessel entered Havana Harbor. He looked at them, feeling the same pity and guilt that he had felt during most of the voyage. At the same time, however, he brimmed with excitement and anticipation, knowing that they were nearing Havana.

"There she is, mates, the El Morro Castle," said one veteran seaman. "It's the entrance to the Havana harbor."

Billy couldn't stop thinking about the sites he would see and the adventures that awaited him in Cuba.

The crew washed and oiled the slaves, then fed them their heartiest meal of the entire journey. For the past week, they had been given more and better victuals, more time above deck to breathe the fresh air and to exercise, all of which was designed to make them appear healthy and robust to their purchaser, don Fernando de Castilla.

When the slaves finished their meal, they were ordered to stand. The loud crack of a whip was heard from way back in the slave huddle. Big Ben had swung his cat-o'-nine down hard on the back of a slave who had refused to stand up.

"Put down that bloody cat, Ben!" shouted Second Mate Moran, an angry expression on his face. "There is to be no more whipping. You hear me, Ben? You understand?"

Big Ben scowled and walked off.

The interpreter was busy telling the slaves more stories about the island paradise they were about to enter. Some smiled, a few even began to sing and dance. But the vast majority were un-smiling and stoic. Billy, however, was wide-eyed excited as *The Wandering Maiden* sailed past the El Morro with its imposing, centuries-old fortifications and armaments. Soon they were in a wide and beautiful harbor with the sprawling city of Havana in the background. They dropped anchor, and an Assistant Harbor Master came on board. Sturgis paid the customary bribe, reducing the port tax and eliminating any question concerning the unlawful cargo. A few hours later *The Wandering Maiden* was safely moored at dockside. Captain Sturgis sent a messenger to don Fernando de Castilla, informing him of their arrival, and then he and the ship's officers retired to his quarters. Billy remained on deck with the rest of the crew, keeping watch on the slaves.

The scene at dockside was alive with frenetic activity, and Billy tried to take it all in. Street merchants hawked their goods and delicacies. A constant parade of carriages came and went. Exotic-sounding languages echoed all around, a result of the diverse mix of African slaves brought to the island over the years. Overseers barked out orders, at times stinging their slaves with whips as they loaded and unloaded vessels.

Later that afternoon don Fernando de Castilla came aboard *The Wandering Maiden*, accompanied by an entourage of plantation overseers, physicians, and translators. He was a tall, distinguished-looking creole gentleman with olive-colored skin. His thin, well-barbered mustache created an air of roguishness about him, and in spite of Havana's heat and humidity, he was formally dressed in black waistcoat, trousers, and top hat. He appeared to be a man in his fifties, and every aspect of his dress and appearance reflected his aristocratic standing. From the moment he stepped on board all eyes were upon him. The slaves followed his every movement, aware that here was the fearsome White Chief who would control their destiny.

Don Fernando walked about the deck with his entourage, accompanied by Captain Sturgis, to get a feel for the condition and quality of the cargo of slaves. Then, he turned things over to the physicians and overseers, after which he and Sturgis went to the Captain's quarters, where Patrick McHugh and Bill Wrest had already gathered. After some pleasantries and good brandy, Sturgis informed don Fernando that he was retiring, and that his First Mate, Patrick McHugh, would be purchasing *The Wandering Maiden* and would take over as her new master. To work out the details, don Fernando extended an invitation to Patrick to accompany him to *La Dulce Gardenia,* his largest sugar plantation and estate, where he could familiarize himself with its operations and discuss their future relationship. Patrick asked if he could bring his son Billy.

"By all means, please do," said don Fernando.

Billy had already made plans for shore time in Havana. Before *The Wandering Maiden* arrived in Cuba, the other cabin boys had offered to show him the sights. Billy wanted to walk the principal plazas and view the beautiful señoritas who paraded by in the early evening as described by his shipmates. For the first time in his life, he had seen naked females, exotic black slave girls and crewmen lying with them. However, Patrick had to disappoint him. His decision was not based upon the need to protect Billy from the sins and vices of Havana. Rather, he was certain that a visit to don Fernando's sugar plantation and estate would be a unique and valuable experience for Billy, one that would serve him well in the future.

CHAPTER II

Cuba Captivates Billy

The next morning a carriage arrived at their hotel, and a messenger entered and paged Patrick McHugh. They were met by Victorio Arquídez, the Chief Overseer of don Fernando de Castilla's estate and sugar plantation, *La Dulce Gardenia*. Victorio Arquidez was a sturdy-looking mulatto with a bushy mustache who spoke basic English. He had a casual, rustic manner about him, in both dress and demeanor, which Billy immediately noticed was quite distinct from that of don Fernando.

"...And I hope you are having a comfortable stay in Havana," said Victorio, as Patrick and Billy stepped out of the morning sun and climbed into the carriage.

"Yes, thank you, Victorio," said Patrick. "The accommodations were quite comfortable."

"We will go now to the railroad," said Victorio. "It will take us to the plantation. You know it is the first railroad built in Cuba and it is first in all of Spanish America."

Billy was looking out the window, where the city had already come to life. Carriages rolled past, pulled by one and sometimes two horses. Men on horseback galloped ahead. Male and female slaves walked along the road, the females carrying heavy loads on their backs and heads. The males were chained together and marched along by overseers, their whips at the ready.

They drove past neat geometrically shaped plazas, some with bubbling fountains and majestic statues. Tall palm trees, taller than those Billy knew from Charleston, lined the roadside. Some carriages were parked beneath them, and well-dressed men stood talking, gesticulating and smoking long cigars. Victorio described the sites as best he could in his broken English, while Patrick responded with questions and comments. Billy continued focusing on the people and the activities out his window, all of which had him spellbound. They stopped at a crossroads to allow a line of oxcarts loaded with sugarcane to pass.

There was a church and an adjoining building nestled within a cluster of palms, where adolescent dark-haired girls dressed in blue and white uniforms were lining up. Billy watched the girls with great interest, as saintly looking nuns shepherded them into the church. Patrick and Victorio nodded and smiled at Billy, acknowledging that they too had been adolescents. They waited for the oxcarts to pass, and then headed off again. Soon they arrived at the railroad depot, where they saw several wagons loaded with slaves parked alongside the steam locomotive and railroad cars.

"Some of these slaves are from *The Wandering Maiden*." said Victorio. "But most are from a vessel that arrived last week."

"How many sugar plantations does señor de Castillo own, Victorio?" Patrick asked, recalling don Fernando's statement that he could use as many slaves as Patrick could procure.

"*La Dulce Gardenia* is one of four. There are others with more plantations, but it is the size of his that makes the difference. Don Fernando's land holdings are vast."

Both Patrick and Billy noticed that the steam locomotive and railroad cars were smaller than those in the United States, as was the gauge of the track. There was only one passenger car; the other cars were for slaves and freight.

"This railroad was built for the sugarcane. It will stop at many plantations before we arrive at *La Dulce Gardenia*," said Victorio.

They had some time before departure, and Victorio escorted them to the passenger car, which was only half-full. Among the passengers was a stout slave woman dressed in a white uniform, holding a white child. She smiled when Patrick and Billy entered the car. Seated opposite her was a white man in his late twenties, flipping through a thick ledger book. He looked up at Patrick and Billy and smiled slightly.

"I had a letter from your mother, Billy, sent in care of señor de Castilla. She misses us very much and hopes that we'll be home soon and in time for the harvest."

Billy looked at his father, managing a forced smile, knowing his mother would insist he return to school. He had been hoping to make one more voyage on *The Wandering Maiden*, especially now that his dad was to be its owner and Captain.

"We will be carrying more than one hundred slaves to *La Dulce Gardenia*," Victorio said, as he sat down with them.

Billy asked about the name of the plantation. Patrick knew a little Spanish and was about to answer, but then waited for Victorio to explain it.

"'Gardenia' is the same in English, *no?* It's a *flor*, I mean, a flower. And '*Dulce*' in Spanish means 'sweet.' So in your English it would be 'The Sweet Gardenia.'"

"So, the word 'gardenia' is the same in English," Billy said.

"Yes, and the spelling is the same in Spanish and English. The pronunciation, of course, is different. Am I right, Victorio?" Patrick asked. Victorio nodded yes.

The steam locomotive came to life with loud staccato huffing and puffing. Black smoke belched from its stack, and the train began pulling away slowly from the depot. As it picked up speed, the noise diminished, eventually smoothing out and assuming a steady rhythmic clicking as it rolled along the tracks. Within minutes, they heard another strange sound, almost musical, with its own rhythmic quality.

"It's the slaves, singing, chanting," said Victorio. "They are amazed at this train. In their languages, they call it 'a magical beast' that can pull heavy loads. They say the train is the white man's rhinoceros or hippopotamus but so much stronger. Therefore, you see this train may confirm for the slaves what they were told of a new life in the 'island paradise.'"

The train passed through miles and miles of sugarcane cultivation. Billy stared out the window wondering what it would be like to live in Cuba, to be Cuban, to speak Spanish, to live on those plantations, and to go to school there. Most of the people he saw were black slaves, loading or driving oxcarts, bending over in the fields and cutting the cane with machetes. At one point, they passed an open-air carriage, bordering the railroad tracks, with two young women dressed in what looked to Billy like formal attire. The girls waved as the train passed. Billy smiled and waved back, wishing the train had been going slower so he could get a better look. He then turned his attention to the conversation that his dad was having with Victorio.

"…But tell me, Victorio, what do you think about the United States' new offer to purchase Cuba?" Patrick asked. "I read an article saying that the issue has come up again this year in our presidential election. The United States is now willing to pay more than $100 million dollars, which was what President Polk offered back in 1848. That's a lot of money to reject, don't you agree, Victorio?"

"You are right, señor McHugh. It is a great deal of money, but not quite as great as the Spanish pride. As for me, I would not favor it. Excuse me for saying so, señor McHugh, because your country is a great country, but our two cultures are so different that it would not be successful."

Victorio's expression took on a look of unease, and Patrick wisely decided to drop the subject.

"How much longer before we arrive, Victorio?" Patrick asked.

"Very soon now," said Victorio, as Patrick reached over and rubbed Billy's unruly mop of wavy brown hair.

"Are you enjoying the ride and the scenery, Billy?" he asked.

"I sure am. I can't wait to get to *La Dulce Gardenia* to see more," he said, straining with the Spanish pronunciation.

Victorio took a cigar out of his shirt pocket after offering one to Patrick, who politely declined.

The train began to slow, coming to a stop alongside a water tower and a row of low-slung structures. Several carriages were stationed alongside, one of which stood out from the rest with its elegant black-lacquered exterior and rich silver trim. Patrick and Billy stepped down from the train, and Victorio led them over to that luxurious carriage, where they were welcomed by don Fernando de Castilla, the *gran patrón*.

"Welcome to *La Dulce Gardenia*, señor McHugh," said don Fernando, smiling broadly and flashing a handsome set of white teeth. "Oh, and this is your son, Billy, a good-looking boy you have here. Welcome to you both. *Bienvenidos* as we say in Spanish. Now, let me introduce you to my son, Felipe, and my new grandson, Antonio."

The young man whom they had seen on the train walked up carrying the baby, the black nursemaid following behind. Patrick and Billy were introduced to Felipe de Castilla. Don Fernando was just beaming as he leaned over and kissed his new grandson.

"I also want to congratulate you señor McHugh on the purchase of *The Wandering Maiden*. Captain Sturgis told me that the vessel will be in very capable hands."

Don Fernando's charm and grace were on full display as he beckoned for Patrick and Billy to step into the elegant carriage. Felipe and the nursemaid walked over to another carriage, which would take them to the Main House, where Felipe resided together with his wife and two sons. Don Fernando then mounted the carriage and they got under way.

2

"Let me give you an idea of the layout of the *La Dulce Gardenia*," don Fernando said.

"There's a ring road that encircles the plantation. We have a spur railroad for transporting cut cane to the factories and for carrying our slaves to the cane fields and the main railroad depot."

"Victorio told us that *La Dulce Gardenia* is only one of your many plantations. How do you manage all that?" Patrick asked.

"The way any good businessman does. I have good people who work very hard and are rewarded for it," responded don Fernando.

Billy sat quietly staring out the window for the most part; listening at times to the conversation and staring at don Fernando. He admired his distinctive appearance, the fact that he looked nothing like his dad, whose chalky-white Irish skin had darkened very little after all his years at sea. *These Spanish people sure do have a special look, and they act different from people in the United States.* Billy was struck with a strong desire to speak Spanish, to understand these people, to enter their exotic world and become a part of it.

"…Also, I've been wanting to ask you, señor de Castilla, where did you learn such fine English?" Patrick asked. Don Fernando paused for a second and smiled.

"Thank you for the compliment, señor McHugh. I owe it to

my father. He sent me to school in your country. I spent my high school years in a private school in Providence, Rhode Island. The climate was difficult for me, and I must admit that I was quite homesick at first. But I am grateful that he sent me. I am very fond of the United States of America. Indeed, I was disappointed when Spain turned down your President Polk's offer to purchase Cuba back in 1848. I think it was a mistake. The Spanish pride gets in the way. Cuba is one of Spain's last great possessions. Their once vast empire has all but disappeared."

Don Fernando lit up a cigar after offering one to Patrick, who politely declined. Billy smelled the rich aroma and watched as don Fernando puffed on it contentedly. The driver pulled back on the reins as they rounded a curve, revealing a crossroad, on each side of which was a virtual botanical garden of tropical vegetation. Don Fernando pointed.

"If you follow that road, you come to the De Wolf plantation. They are from Providence, Rhode Island, you know, where I went to high school."

"Yes," said Patrick, "and they have come under heavy criticism from our northern abolitionists."

"Such a shame," said don Fernando with a slight frown. "There is no doubt that the United States is a great country, the wonder of the world, but there is still a great deal of ignorance amongst your people. You, being from South Carolina, understand that Cuba as well as your southern states could not survive without slave labor."

Billy would have liked to say something about don Fernando's statement, but he wisely let it pass.

The carriage slowed and then turned onto an entrance road leading to the Main House of *La Dulce Gardenia*. Tall majestic royal palms lined both sides. The sweet sound of tropical birds wafted through the air, somehow surviving the rush of dissonant sounds, emanating from what looked like a factory building. Don

Fernando explained that his factories were equipped with the latest steam-powered machines imported from England.

The carriage pulled up to the Main House and came to rest on a wide and beautiful pinkish-gray plaza which looked like granite. A fountain bubbled up close by, and colorful tropical birds fluttered in and out to drink and bathe. The Main House itself was a truly magnificent structure, similar in size to the cotton and rice plantations which Patrick and Billy were familiar with in Charleston, but unique in expressing the culture, style, and atmosphere of the tropics. A black, wrought-iron lacework door some ten feet in height added a touch of elegance. A Mediterranean style red tile roof covered the many different levels, offsetting the whiteness of the house; all these distinct features lent a tropical atmosphere to the stately dwelling.

"My, I've never seen such a beautiful house," Patrick exclaimed as Billy looked on in awe, glancing then at the house slaves who suddenly appeared out of nowhere.

"Thank you, señor McHugh. My father built it thirty years ago, and so far we've had three generations of the de Castilla family living here."

The slaves took their luggage and carried them inside as don Fernando ushered Patrick and Billy into a spacious tile-floored room filled with tropical plants and multi-colored flowers. He led them out some French doors to a central square covered with the same distinctive granite-like surface as the plaza in front.

"Follow me," said don Fernando as he led them over to some tall, bushy palm trees and bid them to sit and partake of some refreshments.

Two coal-black slaves appeared with pitchers of juice, sliced mango, and papaya fruit.

"Just relax here a while. You must be weary from all your

traveling," said Don Fernando as he sat back now and puffed on his cigar.

"I'm used to traveling," said Patrick. "Of course, my normal mode of travel is by ship."

Billy suddenly noticed that two young girls had emerged from a doorway at the other end of the courtyard, one of whom looked almost as fair as he, with light brown hair. The other had a lovely suntanned appearance and long dark hair. Don Fernando looked up and waved as a young woman carrying books appeared behind the two girls.

"*Sofia, Margarita, vengan aca, por favor,*" (Sofia and Margarita, come here, please) said don Fernando, changing then to English. "There's my youngest daughter Sofia and her English teacher. She has an English lesson every afternoon at this time. I would like to introduce you so you can talk to her, and I can judge how well she's doing."

The girls approached and Patrick and Billy stood up.

"This is my daughter, Sofia, and her English teacher, Margarita."

They smiled shyly and curtsied. Don Fernando put his arm around his daughter and kissed her tenderly on the cheek, but he never acknowledged the other girl's presence. Billy was surprised and disappointed as the other girl was strikingly beautiful.

"Sofia, this is Mister McHugh and his son Billy. They recently arrived in Havana and will be staying with us a few days."

"I'm delighted to meet you, young lady. How do you do?" Patrick said. "This is my son Billy."

Billy smiled at Sofia, and then turned to the dark-haired girl, disappointed that she had not been introduced.

"Your father told me that you're studying English, Sofia. Do you speak any other languages?" Before responding, Sofia put her arm around the dark-haired girl.

"This is my friend, Dolores. She is also studying English, and sadly, I sometimes think that her English is better than mine."

Dolores curtsied and smiled. Billy was relieved. "But please, tell me if I'm pronouncing your name correctly. Is it señor 'Mick, Mick-Hiyou'?"

"Yes, you said it well, Sofia."

"Thank you, Mister McHugh. Now to answer your question, I also speak French, and of course, I speak Spanish"

"My, my, three languages, that's very impressive, young lady."

Patrick was taken with Sofia's poise and seeming maturity. He had often heard that girls from the Spanish American countries were more mature for their age than their American or English counterparts, and that they married at a much earlier age.

"How old are you, Sofia, may I ask?"

"I'm sixteen and Dolores is fifteen," Sofia replied.

Billy was surprised. He would have guessed that Dolores was the older of the two, because she had large breasts, which delighted and excited him. He could not keep his eyes off her.

"Your English is very good, Sofia, you have hardly any accent just like your father. How long have you been studying English?" Patrick asked. Sofia looked to Margarita, who said it had been about three years.

Billy spoke up for the first time.

"Maybe I could learn some Spanish, Dad," he said, turning to him. "I could bring some books with me on our next voyage and practice with Javier and Jorge."

"Billy is referring to two Spanish-speaking cabin boys whom he sailed with," Patrick explained. "Well, yes of course, Billy. I'm sure you could learn Spanish. You've always been a very good student."

"He can begin right here in Cuba. Margarita can get him started," said don Fernando

"Well, it's been quite some time since I've taught our mother tongue," said Margarita. "But yes, I can get him started."

"Marvelous," said don Fernando. "I'm sure by the next time we see Billy here in Havana he'll be speaking like an *habanero*. But you run along now Sofia and study your English," said don Fernando, kissing his daughter Sofia again on the cheek.

"Yes, papá," said Sofia, turning then to Patrick. "It was a pleasure to meet you, Mister McHugh," said Sofia.

She pronounced his name perfectly this time.

"And a pleasure to meet you as well, Billy."

Billy smiled, reached out and shook Sofia's hand. He looked then to Dolores, unsure of what to do or say. Somehow finding the courage, he reached for her hand. She smiled shyly and reached for his, which caused Billy's face to blush a crimson red. It could not have gone unnoticed, but no one said a word.

"I'll have Mario Luis show you to your rooms," said don Fernando, ending the awkward silence. "I put you in separate rooms and hope that's acceptable."

"Yes, of course. That will be fine," said Patrick.

A tall, wiry old slave appeared and picked up their luggage, bidding them to follow him. He led them to an elegant winding staircase, where large and elaborate crystal chandeliers hung from the ceiling, and portraits of beautiful dark-haired women and stern-looking men hung on the wall.

3

Billy awoke suddenly from his nap as someone was knocking on the door. Still half-asleep, he got up, walked over and opened the door.

"Get cleaned up and dressed, Billy. There's to be a dinner in our honor in forty-five minutes." Billy noticed that his father was already shaved and dressed in more formal attire.

"I'll get ready right away," Billy said.

He walked slowly over to the water basin, and as he washed the last of the sleepiness from his eyes, some lingering scenes from his dream flickered across his consciousness.

He was in his tiny quarters on The Wandering Maiden. Sofia and the lovely Dolores were present and they were speaking Spanish. He joined the conversation, speaking the language effortlessly and fluently as though it were his native tongue.

As he prepared to go down to dinner, he savored those dream scenes, recalling the promises he'd gotten earlier that day, that Margarita and the two girls would give him Spanish lessons.

Patrick and Billy walked down the staircase and were ushered into a spacious dining hall. There was a large oval table set with the finest silver, crystal wine glasses, and vases filled with multi-colored flowers. Don Fernando stood at the entrance and introduced them to his wife, doña Teresa de Castilla. Doña Teresa was in the grips of middle age, having lost her slender figure over the years. She was, nonetheless, still an alluring woman with clear white skin, jet black hair and large expressive eyes. There was an air of sensuality about her, heightened still more by her full, pouty lips discreetly painted with red lip rouge.

She must have been a spectacular beauty in her youth, Patrick thought.

"Now, señor McHugh, please have a seat right there next to my husband and your son next to you. Yes, that's good."

Doña Teresa slid effortlessly from English to Spanish and back again, but unlike her husband and daughter, she spoke accented English.

"…Soledad y Felipe, *si ahi,* next to Billy. Yes, that's good."

Next to arrive were Don Fernando's older son, Arturo and his wife, Daisy, followed by his older daughter, Constancia and her husband, Ricardo. When everyone was seated, a bevy of slaves appeared, carrying large kettles of soup, bottles of wine, and plates of exotic dishes. Just when it seemed that the fare could not possibly get any more sumptuous, two slave women appeared carrying a roasted pig, which they placed in the middle of the table, its head still firmly attached and its mouth agape. Don Fernando smiled broadly and announced that they were to be treated to a dinner of "*lechón,*" a typical Cuban delicacy reserved for holidays and special guests. He then stood, turned to Patrick and proposed a toast.

"Heres to "a long and successful relationship with our new American friends."

Everyone raised their glass and drank to it, after which there was some polite applause.

A slave in a white uniform and hat appeared, whom doña Teresa announced was their cook, Francisco, known by his nickname "Pancho." He began carving the roast pig and passing plates of *lechón* down the line until everyone had a large helping. As they ate and drank, all the while engaging in lively conversation, four black musicians appeared and began to play.

"It's a danzón," explained don Fernando, "a typical Cuban dance of Spanish origin." Billy tasted the *lechon* and smiled with delight at its rich flavor.

"*Oiga, Billy, le gusta el lechón?*" Sofia asked, smiling and using the Spanish polite *usted* form of address. ("Billy, do you like the lechón?").

"I like it very much, Sofia. Now, how do I say that in Spanish?" He asked. Sofia turned to Billy, and in mellifluous Spanish:

"*Me gusta mucho, Me gusta mucho.*" All eyes now turned to Billy, awaiting his response.

"*Me gusta mucho,*" responded Billy.

"Your pronunciation was very good," said Sofia.

Billy was about to thank her for the compliment, when he spotted the beautiful Dolores entering the room with a baby in her arms. A slave woman followed behind her, carrying a little cradle. Dolores looked nervous and out of place. She walked over to Soledad and gently placed the baby in the cradle. Billy followed her every move, spellbound by her extraordinary beauty.

But why didn't don Fernando introduce her? Is she a slave? But she's not black. She's not even a mulatto, at least not like the ones in Charleston. She's just a little darker than me, but that's probably from the tropical sun.

"Antonio has had some colic," said Soledad. "I hope he's finally over it now."

"Won't we wake him if he stays here with us?" asked Daisy.

"Oh, no, you need not worry about that," said Soledad. "Once he goes to sleep nothing seems to wake him. He's like his papá," she added with a chuckle.

Soledad's husband, Felipe, smiled and the others laughed. Both Billy and Patrick were amazed that everyone seemed to speak such good English, and they complimented them for it several times during the dinner.

The desserts and coffee were served, then the brandy and cigars, and that's when the talk turned to politics.

Tell me, Mister McHugh," said Arturo de Castilla, "have you followed the writings of John L. O'Sullivan, the American journalist who coined that phrase 'Manifest Destiny'? He's also written a lot about Cuba and..."

"It wasn't O'Sullivan," interrupted Felipe. "It was the Jacksonian Democrats who popularized 'Manifest Destiny.' O'Sullivan was the one who persuaded President Polk to make Spain an offer to purchase Cuba."

Felipe's brother, Arturo, looked annoyed. He did not like being interrupted and corrected by his younger brother, and he glared at him for a moment before lighting his cigar.

"I've heard of O'Sullivan," said Patrick, "and I like his fine Irish name. But I didn't know that he was pushing our presidents to purchase Cuba. I have to confess that you Cubans are much more knowledgeable and better informed than I as to the politics. It's because I spend so much time at sea, and it's hard to get caught up when I'm back in port."

Billy sat there listening intently to the exchange.

"As Cubans, señor McHugh, we have no choice. We have to be well informed. Our business and our economic and political future depend upon it," said don Fernando."

Don Fernando paused and poured Patrick a glass of brandy, then poured himself one and passed the bottle to Arturo. Felipe would have to wait his turn, but he didn't have to wait to speak.

"It was totally predictable that Spain would turn down Polk's offer. They will never give up Cuba voluntarily. It's a matter of pride. The only way the United States will get it is to take it by force."

Patrick recalled hearing similar words from don Fernando's Chief Overseer, Victorio Arquídez.

"All right, that's enough politics for this evening," said don Fernando.

"Why don't you and our guests retire to the library, *mi amor*," interjected doña Teresa, who along with the other women, had had very little to say during much of the evening. "You can take your brandy and your cigars, and you'll be more comfortable there."

"Yes, you're right, *mi amor*," said don Fernando, "and I apologize for dominating the conversation. I'm sure you and the other ladies had some interesting things to relate to our guests."

The de Castilla family got up now, said good night, and left the dining room. Don Fernando and Patrick McHugh headed for the library.

"I have to confess that I was interested in what your sons were discussing," Patrick said, "because the political and economic situation here in Cuba is going to directly affect whether I can continue to deliver the African slaves that you need for your plantations."

"Well, you're wise to be alert to the political situation. It's essential. I'm sure you're aware that Cuba has become directly entangled in the political debate over slavery in your country. If Cuba joins the Union by purchase or by a filibuster operation, it will enter as either a free state or a slave state. And each side fears that the other side will prevail. We need slaves, señor McHugh. We can only cultivate sugar cane with slave labor. It's the same with your southern states that cultivate cotton and rice, isn't it?"

"Yes, it is. I've tried to keep up with the politics, but as I told you, I'm at sea most of the time and lose contact with what's happening at home. You Cubans are really much better informed than I am."

"What really troubles me is the growing abolitionist fever in your country, so now I'm against Cuba becoming part of the United States," said don Fernando. "It's perfectly obvious to me that we're better off remaining under Spanish rule. And I believe that Cuba will remain under Spanish rule for a long time to come, because Spain depends upon Cuban revenues"

4

Billy walked toward the spiral staircase, about to retire for the night. He didn't feel tired and wondered why, settling on the view that it was the highly enjoyable dinner and conversation. He'd been stimulated and was still bursting with energy.

"*Como estás*, Billy?" (How are you, Billy) He turned and saw Sofia standing there with a wide smile on her face. She poked him jocularly on the shoulder. "Would you like to go see the garden?"

"I'd like that very much," Billy said, smiling back and following her toward the front door.

"We'll start your Spanish lessons tomorrow, but I can start teaching you a few words right now. Can you say '*jardín*,' which is 'garden' in English?"

"*Jardín?*" Billy repeated the word.

"Very good, Billy, your pronunciation is excellent."

"Thank you, Sofia. I am very happy to hear that. I just love the sound of the Spanish words."

Sofia led Billy out to the main entrance and on to the plaza, where they were bathed in the brilliant light of the moon.

"It's the biggest and brightest moon I have ever seen!" Billy said.

"Isn't it just magnificent?" said Sofia.

They began walking down a path that wound around to the back of the sprawling, multi-level mansion. There they entered the garden, and Billy's nostrils and senses were filled with a delightful scent.

"What is that sweet smell?" He asked.

"Isn't it lovely? It's our gardenias," said Sofia. "They're in full bloom." She stopped and picked a large specimen and held it up to Billy's nose.

"Grandfather named this sugar plantation *La Dulce Gardenia*--(The Sweet Gardenia) because of the gardenias that grow wild here."

"You are so lucky to be living here on this beautiful tropical island, Sofia."

"Yes, but you too are lucky, Billy, to be living in a wonderful country like the United States of America."

Sofia smiled then playfully tried to put the gardenia in Billy's hair. Billy backed away, laughed and took it out of her hand, and placed it in her hair.

"It looks much better on you," he said.

They walked along the path and came to a clearing with a gazebo in the center.

"What is it like to live in Charleston, Billy?" He was about to respond when Sofia exclaimed.

"Oh, look! It's Dolores with her white cat Neva!"

Billy looked over and saw the lovely Dolores sitting on a lawn chair with a white cat on her lap. They walked over, and Sofia broke into a girlish giggle, calling out then in Spanish:

"*Mira quien está conmigo!*" (Look who is with me). Earlier that day after the girls' English lesson, Sofia had referred to Billy as "*el mas bello muchacho del mundo* (the most beautiful boy in the world). Dolores didn't reveal her own opinion, but every time Sofia mentioned his name, Dolores blushed, eliciting some playful teasing from Sofia.

"What are you doing out here all alone, Dolores?" Sofia asked. Billy stared at Dolores, admiring her beautiful long, dark hair which glistened in the moonlight. He hoped he would not blush again, but it was going to be a struggle.

Sofia took the gardenia out of her own hair and stuck it in Dolores's hair.

"*Que hermosa!*" (How beautiful) Sofia exclaimed. "It's even whiter than Neva."

Suddenly, the cat jumped off Dolores's lap. Dolores grabbed for its tail, but it slipped away and ran off into a thick clump of gardenia bushes. Dolores jumped out of the chair.

"Neva, Neva," she screamed. "Neva!" Dear Lord, please don't let the dogs get her, please!" she pleaded.

"Don't worry, we'll help you find her," said Sofia. "Come on, Billy. She ran into that clump of gardenia bushes."

"At least it's easy to see her in the moonlight," Billy said.

"But it's not any easier to catch her," said Dolores, who was frantic and began running faster. Suddenly, the harsh sound of barking dogs pierced the still, moonlit night.

"Did you hear that? We better find her, those dogs can get out," Dolores said, tears in her eyes.

"Where are they? They sound pretty close," Billy said, running closely behind Dolores.

"They're in a kennel in back of the overseers' house. It's just over that row of slave quarters," Sofia said.

"There she is! I see her," shouted Dolores.

They looked up and saw the cat running through the open door of a dilapidated shack. Dolores stopped running, turned and started walking back to the gazebo.

"Aren't we going to go over and get the cat?" Billy asked.

Neither of the girls responded and began speaking in rapid-fire Spanish. He couldn't understand what they were saying, but he could tell that it was something important.

"Good night, Billy," said Dolores, smiling shyly. "I'll see you tomorrow at our Spanish lesson." Billy was noticeably disappointed and watched as she walked off.

"She has chores to do," said Sofia, aware of Billy's disappointment. "Let's sit down for a while and enjoy the moon."

"Why didn't Dolores go get the cat and bring it back with her?"

"Dolores's mother lives in that shack, and Dolores knows her mother will take care of it. This happens all the time. The cat gets out and runs off to the slave quarters, where she's treated to a second dinner."

Dolores's mother is a slave? What about Dolores, is she a slave too? Is that why don Fernando didn't introduce her, why he totally ignored her?

Billy leaned up in his chair not sure if he really wanted to ask the question. He took a deep breath.

"Is Dolores a slave?" The words came out in a muffled voice.

"Dolores is something in between," Sofia said. "Her position in the de Castilla family is undefined. She's not really a slave, but she's not really free nor a family member either. You like her, Billy, don't you? I can tell," said Sofia.

Billy was reluctant to acknowledge it, fearing he might hurt Sofia's feelings. She'd been flirtatious with him.

But how could she have missed the way I blushed in Dolores, presence? How could anyone have missed it?

"Can you tell me more about her, Sofia?"

"If you wish, Billy. Everyone here at *la Dulce Gardenia* is familiar with her origins and background, and I don't think Dolores would be upset to learn that I told you about her. It's not as if I'll be revealing any secrets. So, let's see, where shall I begin? My grandfather, don Francisco de Castilla, was the original patriarch of the de Castilla family here in Cuba. Dolores's mother, Beatriz, was don Francisco's loyal and trusted house servant. When don Francisco passed away, Beatriz continued to work in the Main House, serving my father, don Fernando and our family. Everyone knew that Beatriz had the best slave job on the plantation. Her room was in the nicest part of the Main House, and she had access to all the good food and comforts. But all that changed, when it became known that Beatriz was pregnant."

"What did Beatriz look like?" Billy asked.

"I don't know, Billy. I was an infant at the time. But I can tell you that Beatriz is a mulatto. Now, after I was born, my mother went to Spain to visit her cousins. The following May, Beatriz gave birth to a baby girl, a very light-skinned baby girl. People said that she bore a striking resemblance to don Fernando and rumors spread. She was a beautiful child, and Beatriz named her *Felicidad,* which in Spanish means 'happiness.'"

"And that baby girl was Dolores," Billy said.

"I'll get to that, Billy." Sofia said. "When my mother returned from Spain, she confronted my father, accusing him of infidelity and the immoral act. He insisted he was not the father, but my mother believed otherwise and so did mostly everyone else. As for me, it was unclear, though everyone believes that Dolores and I are half-sisters.

Why is she telling me all this? But I asked her to tell me, didn't I? It's very personal and private. Wouldn't Dolores want to keep it private, and even if she wouldn't, would she want Sofia to tell me?

Billy could not resist and wanted to hear the whole story.

"If don Fernando is not her father, then who do you believe is, Sofia?"

"Well, I was given another possibility by the oldest and wisest female slave on *La Dulce Gardenia.* Her name is Angelina, and by reputation and practice she's said to know things that no one else does. Some say it's black magic, others that it's intelligence. No one really knows. But Angelina says that Dolores's father was a handsome, white machinery salesman from England, who spent several months on the plantation installing steam-powered equipment."

Is it possible that Sofia is telling me all this to discredit Dolores and make me more likely to show her more attention?

"I learned that my mother had demanded that Beatriz be thrown out of the Main House. Beatriz was turned over to Victorio Arquídez, who put her to work in the cane fields. On the advice of Father Ignacio, our parish priest, Mother took the baby into the house. When it came time to baptize her, Padre Ignacio refused to baptize her 'Felicidad,' insisting that the name would be a sacrilege, clothing the child with an undeserved cloak of good fortune.

The more appropriate and proper name would be 'Dolores,' to reflect the true nature of her unfortunate birth. The word *"dolor"* in Spanish, Billy, means 'pain.' And from that moment on she has gone by the name, Dolores, though I know her mother, Beatriz, still insists on calling her Felicidad. Well, we had better be getting back. Mother might be worried, and your father told you to get to bed early, Billy."

As they walked back to the Main House, Sofia tried to teach Billy some more words in Spanish, but he was unable to concentrate, his thoughts fully focused on the lovely Dolores and all that he had learned about her.

5

Dolores entered the slave quarters carrying a basket of fruit. There was the usual smell of the field slave all about the dank, ramshackle dwelling. Her mother was bent over the crude hearth stirring a large pot of yams. Beatriz was indeed a mulatto, the brown-colored offspring of a Lucumi slave woman and a white Spanish overseer. She was slender with large breasts and a prominent posterior, characteristics that did not go unnoticed by the men folk of *La Dulce Gardenia,* black and white alike.

"Buenos días, mamá. I brought you some fruit. Maybe tomorrow I can bring you some meat."

"Don't step on the cowry shells, Felicidad."

"Don't worry, mamá, I see them."

I wish she wouldn't put so much trust in these Santería practices. She'd be so much better off trusting in the Catholic Church where her true salvation lay.

"I wish you would come to mass with me, mamá. It would be very good for you."

"I've told you many times, Felicidad. I don't trust the Catholic Church. They think they can trick me into giving up my religion by teaching that my *Obalos* are one and the same as their saints."

The Church had tried but failed to convert the Africans to Catholicism. What they got was an uneasy compromise that gradually took hold in the form of an amalgamation of the African gods with the Catholic saints.

"Look at how the cowry shells landed when the Santero threw them, Felicidad." Dolores had pleaded with her mother to call her Dolores, but she continued to call her Felicidad.

"Do you know what they predict, what they say? You see the black shell? It is predicting my doom and my death. It is already the second time that they landed face down. They don't lie, Felicidad. Do you see them? Do you see them?"

"I see them, mamá, but I don't believe them."

Dolores went over and kissed her mother tenderly, tasting the tears that rained down her wrinkled face. They embraced and Dolores burst into tears, mixing with her mother's as they sobbed together in a sad duet of despair.

"You see don Fernando and doña Teresa every day, Felicidad. You must speak to them. I am not a young woman. I can't do the work of a field slave any longer. I have bad rheumatism and the pain is severe."

There was a hissing sound from the crude hearth, and Beatriz turned and went over to the pot of yams she'd been cooking. She picked up the ladle, but it fell out of her hand. She grimaced, and her face contorted in pain.

"You see how I suffer? You must do something to help me, Felicidad!"

Over the years Beatriz had tried everything to return to the good graces of the de Castilla family and end her banishment from the Main House. She'd even tried acquiescing to the constant sexual demands of Victorio Arquídez, but all her efforts had been for naught.

"I will ask Auntie Panchita to come over with some herbs, and she can rub down your shoulder with palm oil, mamá. And I'll ask Panchito for some more meat for you, but I must return to my duties now, mamá. Oh, and please, if Neva gets out again and runs over here, keep her inside until I can come and fetch her."

As if to emphasize Dolores's words, the rough, raspy sound of barking dogs erupted from somewhere beyond the slave quarters. Dolores closed her eyes and shuddered as the barking continued.

"Please, Felicidad, you must speak with don Fernando and doña Teresa about my condition. I can't endure much more of this."

Dolores had tried in the past to intervene on her mother's behalf, but her shy efforts had little or no effect. Dolores's status was inadequate to convince the Master and Mistress to end Beatriz's banishment. Dolores truly felt her mother's pain and pondered a different approach.

Maybe Sofia will help. She's very close to her mother, and it was doña Teresa who was responsible for mamá's removal from the Main House.

Dolores kissed her mother good-bye and turned to leave.

"Be careful, Felicidad! Don't tread on the cowry shells!" But it was too late. Dolores kicked the mat, and the cowry shells went flying in every direction.

"I'm so sorry, mamá. Can we put them back where they were?" Dolores asked, bending down and picking up a shell.

"Just leave them. The Santero must return now and throw them again."

Dolores walked out the door, and Beatriz went over to her chest and took out the velvet pouch. Then she bent down and picked up the cowry shells and put them back in the pouch. When she stood up, she saw Victorio Arquídez standing in the doorway, a bottle of rum in his hand and a sinister smile on his face.

"You don't look sick to me, but you do look sad. I'm here to make you happy," he said as he went over, grabbed her by the buttocks and pushed her down on the floor. "Stay there and don't move," he said, taking a big swig of rum.

"No, please, don Victorio in God's name, I am not well."

She struggled to get up, but he took hold of her arm and twisted it behind her back. She grimaced in pain.

"Please, don't. I beg you don Victorio! You are hurting me."

But he was not to be deterred, and he reached down now, tore off her crude dressing gown and began fondling her large breasts with his dirty, filthy hands. Then he dropped his pants and pounced on top of her. Finding it difficult to penetrate her, he stuck his fingers in his mouth and retrieved some spit, rubbing it on her private parts and penetrating her, taking his pleasure like a wild animal of the forest. Beatriz had little choice but to acquiesce, knowing from experience that it was useless to resist. He was the Chief Overseer on this vast plantation. She was a defenseless slave, and he had absolute power over her.

She suppressed the desire to scream, closed her eyes, clenched her teeth, and endured the pain and humiliation as best she could. Her only consolation, and a pathetic one, was knowing that it would all be over in less than a minute. Victorio finished, casually pulled up his pants and tossed her the dressing gown.

"Get dressed. You're coming with me to the cane fields."

"No, the hospital excused me for three days. I cannot work, don Victorio," she said, sobbing.

He grabbed the bottle of rum, took a swig, then wiped his mouth with the back of his dirty hand. Beatrice wept, slowly and mournfully as she dressed. She made her way back to the hearth, where she discovered that the yams were burnt. She snuffed out the remaining embers, and then turned to don Victorio.

"Have you talked to don Fernando and doña Teresa?" she asked, the tears still flowing down her face.

"I told you, when the opportunity presents itself. Come over here," he commanded gruffly.

She walked over slowly, reluctantly, and stood before him, fearful that his passion might rise once again. He handed her the bottle with one hand and fondled her buttocks with the other. But when he tried to pull her down and kiss her, she pulled back from him, showing him only minimal abeyance by taking a swig of the rum.

"I'll rid you of that defiance in the fields soon enough."

"I cannot work there any longer, don Victorio. The hospital has confirmed that. You promised that you would talk to the Master and Mistress on my behalf, but you have not done so."

"The opportunity has not yet presented itself," said the Chief Overseer. "Now, if you were to talk to that cute little daughter of yours about my needs, it might just then present itself."

Beatriz shuddered and glared at him with hate in her eyes.

6

Patrick and Billy walked along the delightful garden path and came upon the charming patio bar split off from the rest of the Main House. A bevy of attentive slaves seated them and began serving a sumptuous breakfast of soft-boiled eggs, freshly baked bread, papaya, mango, freshly squeezed orange juice and coffee.

"You're going to notice the difference between this coffee and the coffee we drink on the ship, Billy. This is homegrown, and the sugar is also. Cuba is a bountiful country and a beautiful one as well. I'm told the beaches here are some of the most beautiful in the world," said Patrick.

"Can we go see them, Dad?"

"There's not enough time, Billy. We're leaving tomorrow. The crew's being rounded up and we're taking on provisions for the voyage back to Charleston."

A look of extreme disappointment formed on Billy's handsome face. "We'll do it on our next trip," Patrick said.

As they were finishing their breakfast, Billy looked up and saw Sofia approaching. She trotted up like a frisky little filly and greeted them both warmly. Margarita was behind her.

Where's Dolores? Why isn't she with them? Will she be there for my Spanish lesson?

"*Buenos días!*" Sofia said. "You chose a perfect day to have your breakfast out here. It's one of my favorite places on the plantation."

Two male slaves brought some more chairs, placed them around the table, and Sofia and Margarita sat down. They wore riding clothes with high leather boots.

"*Listo a comenzar sus lecciones, Billy?*" (Are you ready to begin your lessons, Billy?)

"I'm ready whenever you are," Billy said, excited at the prospect.

"Looks like you two were horseback riding," said Patrick, smiling and greeting them both.

"Yes, we were, Mister McHugh," Sofia said. "Margarita rode Rubio, a palomino, and I rode Medianoche, an Arabian stallion. He was sluggish today, and Rubio was quick as the wind and surefooted. Margarita easily beat me on the jumps."

"That doesn't happen very often," Margarita said.

"Maybe you would like to join us tomorrow, Billy," Sofia added.

"I'd love to, but my Dad just told me that we're leaving tomorrow."

"So soon!" Sofia said, looking at Patrick. "We were thinking of taking him on an excursion to the mountains and then to a lovely beach."

"We would love to stay longer," said Patrick, "but I'm afraid both business and family are calling us back. Maybe next time."

Billy frowned and shrugged his shoulders.

"You have to see our mountains and beaches. If not this time, then certainly next time. They are very beautiful. You can even see snow on the highest peaks, and the beaches are breathtaking with beautiful, clear, azure water..."

As Sofia spoke, Billy listened closely, studying her. He liked her well enough, but he had no desire to hold her, to kiss her.

"All right, Billy, I have some business to attend to, but I'll be leaving you in good hands. So learn some Spanish. I'm sure it will serve you well in life." Patrick said good-bye, got up and left.

"Where is Dolores this morning?" Billy asked, trying not to sound too interested.

"She went to get our books, but she will be there for your lesson," Sofia said.

They walked back to the Main House and out onto the courtyard, where Billy had seen the two girls and Margarita the day before. They entered the room at the end of the courtyard, and there she was. Dolores rose from her chair and smiled shyly. She wore a red, taffeta dress, her slender waist set off by a black satin sash, and her long dark hair adorned with a gardenia.

"*Buenos dias*, Billy," she said, smiling shyly. Billy felt his face flush and his heart race as he stared at her simply spellbound. Sofia had a much different reaction.

"*Que hermoso vestido Dolores! Pero por que ahora y por que aqui?*" ("What a beautiful dress Dolores, but why now and why here?"). Billy didn't understand what Sofia had said, but he heard the annoyance in her voice.

"*Estaba haciendo alteraciones para Soledad y no le presté atención*

*que ya era hora de la leccion de Billy. Cuando me di cuenta no quise
llegar tarde y corri aqui vestida como me ves."*

("Billy, I told Sofia that I was making some alterations on this
dress for Soledad, and I lost track of time. When I realized it was
time for Billy's lesson, I ran down here wearing Soledad's dress so
I would not be late.")

Sofia seemed to accept Dolores's explanation, but she still looked
a little surprised and embarrassed by the stark comparison of how
they were dressed. Dolores was aware of Sofia's discomfort, and it reminded her of a painful incident at Sofia's *quinceañera* a year earlier.

*There were more than one hundred guests who attended. An or-
chestra played all the latest European waltzes and polkas, and there
was a bevy of young men ready to dance and celebrate this very special
day for Sofia. Doña Teresa instructed Dolores to circulate amongst
the guests with a tray of champagne. She was wearing a simple white
muslin dress, but when she appeared, all eyes fell upon her. When
she'd finished serving the champagne and had put the tray down, a
handsome young man rushed over and asked her to dance. She told
him she was working and could not dance, but he persisted, grabbing
her arm and pulling her out on the dance floor, where he waltzed
her around to the delight of everyone in attendance. By the time the
dance ended, there was a line of suitors waiting for the chance to
dance with the lovely Dolores. The general appearance that emerged
was that Dolores had upstaged Sofia on her quinceañera, the most
important birthday in the life of a Cuban girl. It was, however, purely
unintentional. Sofia was obviously hurt and embarrassed and rushed
out of the hall to the plaza, trying to conceal the tears running down
her face. Dolores rushed to her side, overhearing what some of the
guests were saying.*

"*Sí, ella es muy hermosa, pero tiene sangre de negro.*" (Yes, she's
very beautiful, but she has black blood).

In the days and weeks that followed, those words took on a

new meaning for Sofia, helping to assuage the hurt she had felt from the stark realization that she was not a beautiful girl and would never be a beautiful woman. Though society places great importance on a woman's physical appearance, Sofia knew that a woman's family and bloodline were also important.

Though Dolores was strikingly beautiful, she could never hope to marry a white upper-class gentleman of Havana society. Yes, she could pass for white, but everyone knew that she was the daughter of a mulatto slave woman and had *sangre de negro*. The most prominent gentlemen of Havana society would undoubtedly want her for their mistress, but they would not want her for their wife.

"...All right, we're here to teach Billy some Spanish, so let's get started with some simple phrases," said Margarita.

"Buenos dias, Billy. Como está usted?" Now you say, '*muy bien, gracias, y usted?*' Billy repeated the phrases as best he could, but his mind and his heart were permanently distracted by the presence of this strikingly beautiful Cuban girl.

7

Patrick and don Fernando paused in their discussions and took their lunch at the delightful patio bar. Though the sun was high in the sky, the slaves had arranged the tables and umbrellas under a shady clump of palms, where it was cool and comfortable.

"As I mentioned to you earlier, señor de Castilla, I have exhausted all my available funds on the purchase of *The Wandering Maiden*, and obtaining credit by way of a ship's mortgage is out of the question."

Patrick looked at Don Fernando, who pulled two long black cigars from his shirt pocket and offered one to Patrick, who declined.

Patrick watched as don Fernando lit the cigar and puffed on it contentedly, obviously savoring its rich taste.

"…So, what I would propose señor de Castilla is that for our first venture together you advance me the funds, at the current rate of interest, of course, with which I can provision the vessel, purchase more slaves in Africa and pay the crew."

"That would be agreeable. I will provide the funds. However, I would want a discount on the price per slave on your subsequent voyages, presuming, of course, that this first venture is successful and our relationship continues. And I have every reason to believe that it will."

A slave in a white uniform appeared and refilled their cups with coffee.

Don Fernando stopped puffing on his cigar and looked directly at Patrick, waiting for his reaction. Patrick sipped his coffee, and it was a few seconds before he responded.

"I think that can be arranged. How about ten percent?"

Don Fernando smiled slightly then looked away and began puffing again on his cigar. Then, with a sudden detachment and a business-like crispness in his voice said, "I would propose a discount of twenty-five percent. After all, you've got a market price here in Cuba of better than ten times what you pay in Africa. That's a hefty profit margin in any man's book. Wouldn't you agree?"

Patrick smiled, realizing that he had just seen the real don Fernando de Castilla, the one beneath that lustrous veneer of charm and grace that came with his role as the gracious host.

"With all due respect, señor de Castilla, you are forgetting that from the day that I set sail for the Coast of Africa to procure negro slaves for your plantations, I'm putting my vessel, the lives of my sailors and indeed my own life at risk."

Don Fernando looked at Patrick, a slight and sly-looking smile on his face.

"The market price of slaves in Cuba and also in my own country, is based upon those very real risks. I don't have to tell you that the British are still capturing vessels, sometimes sinking them. I run those risks, and the market price is fully justified."

"All right, Mister McHugh, I hear you. Let's make it fifteen percent." Don Fernando picked up the coffee pot. "Would you like more coffee?"

"No, thank you, señor de Castillo," said Patrick. "I'll give you a fifteen percent discount on the second voyage. If there are subsequent voyages, we'll make it ten percent." Patrick took on a serious countenance, which changed to a smile with don Fernando's response.

"My American friend, you've got yourself a deal." He reached for Patrick's hand, and they shook on it.

Don Fernando then called out to a tall rangy slave standing near the kitchen, telling him to bring a bottle of French brandy and two glasses. The slave approached and placed the bottle on the table. Don Fernando then filled their glasses.

"Here's to a long and successful business relationship, Mister McHugh."

"And here's to a long and warm friendship between us, señor de Castilla."

After a few more moments of small talk, don Fernando squashed out what remained of his cigar and smiled at Patrick.

"This is the hour in which we Cubans rest before assuming our other tasks and challenges of the day. So, if you will excuse me, I will take my leave of you for the next hour or so."

"By all means," said Patrick. "Maybe I should do the same."

Margarita, and the two girls completed Billy's Spanish lesson.

"…And this is yours to keep, Billy," said Margarita, handing him the book of Spanish Grammar they had used in the lessons.

"Thank you so much, Margarita. I'm going to put it to good use."

"I think Sofia has something for you as well," said Margarita.

Sofia smiled at Billy, reached over to the chair and picked up a large black leather-bound volume with ornate gold-colored lettering. She stood up, lifted the heavy volume and handed it to him.

"It's a Spanish dictionary, published in Madrid by the *Real Academia Española*, which is the official authority on the Spanish language."

"It's heavy and really beautiful," said Billy. Thank you so much, Sofia," he said as he opened it and began thumbing through it.

"I know you won't be able to understand it now, but if you work hard with your Spanish studies, you will eventually be able to use it," Sofia said

"I have to excuse myself now," said Margarita, "but before I go, I want to suggest, Billy, that you try to obtain a Spanish language newspaper in the United States and find some Spanish speaking friends to practice with."

"I think there are some Spanish-speaking folks in Charleston," Billy said as he stood up, thanked her for the lessons and the grammar book.

A house slave entered the room and spoke to Sofia.

"My mother wants to see me upstairs, Billy. She usually insists that I take the afternoon siesta," Sofia said, frowning. "But I'll see you at dinner, Billy, and perhaps after dinner we can meet again at the gazebo to wish you a *bon voyage*."

Billy stood up and watched with anticipation as Sofia left the room, realizing that this would be the first time during his visit that he would be alone with Dolores. There was a moment of awkward silence in which the two adolescents smiled shyly. Billy fought hard to suppress his blushing, but it burst out in full scarlet bloom, Dolores was merciful and sought to help him, breaking the silence.

"Will you be returning to Cuba with your father, Billy?"

He managed a smile, but his face remained a crimson red. He had never before had a problem with blushing, but then again he had never before seen the likes of Dolores and never before felt such an overwhelming attraction.

"I hope so, I mean yes, I think I will," he said, stumbling badly with his words, aware that his mouth and throat had dried up. He tried to keep talking, having decided that it was the only way to temper his love-struck condition. "My dad bought the vessel, and he's gonna keep sailing it…"

He's blushing so badly. It's worse than when we first met in the courtyard.

But Billy kept talking, telling her about *The Wandering Maiden* and her crew, describing The Bight of Benin and his adventures on shore in Africa. Dolores listened with interest, smiling, commenting, and before long his blushing subsided.

"…And do you go to school here, Dolores?"

"No, Billy, Sofia has teachers who come here to the plantation, and I sit in with her lessons. The teachers are very good, and I have learned a lot."

He tried to get her to talk more about herself, but she was reluctant. Dolores managed to change the subject, smiling and pointing to the dictionary.

"It's a very beautiful and elegant volume, Billy. Sofia was so sweet to give it to you."

"It's the perfect gift for me now. I just hope I can learn enough Spanish to use it."

"We could write to each other, Billy. That would help your Spanish."

It came out of nowhere, and he was speechless, finding it hard to believe what he had just heard her say.

"We could write mostly in English at first, but I could also write some in Spanish to help you..."

Patrick McHugh suddenly appeared in the doorway.

"I need to talk to you, Billy, and you better begin packing."

Patrick could not have missed the look of extreme disappointment on Billy's face at the intrusion.

8

After the dinner party that evening, the de Castilla family bid good-bye to Patrick and Billy, wishing them a safe voyage back to Charleston. Patrick went to join the men for brandy and cigars in the library and turned to his son.

"Have you finished packing, Billy?"

"Yes, I'm all packed, Dad."

"Well, try to get a good night's sleep. We have a long day tomorrow."

Unlike the last time, Billy had no desire to accompany his dad to the library. And as he walked toward the staircase, he noticed Sofia was following behind him. Once his dad and the others were out of sight, they both smiled, turned and headed toward the plaza.

"I'm supposed to have a chaperone," Sofia said. "It's one of our strange Spanish customs and a terrible nuisance and bore. Usually it's Constancia or Daisy. I was lucky last night and escaped. I will try to do the same tonight."

They walked down the garden path that skirted the Main House, admiring the moon that illuminated the way. When they entered the orchard area and walked past the flowering gardenias,

Billy felt Sofia's hand reaching out for his. It surprised him, and he gently pulled his hand back. But he reconsidered, and a second later reached out for her hand. Sofia smiled with delight. As they approached the gazebo, Billy let go of Sofia's hand and looked to see if Dolores was there.

"Oh, look. It's Dolores and her mother," Sofia said.

As they drew near where the two were sitting, Billy immediately noticed the woman's darker complexion. Beatriz looked nervous and out of place. Neither Dolores nor Sofia introduced her, and seconds later, she got up and walked off towards that ramshackle slave dwelling where Dolores's cat had escaped to the night before.

"*Como estás, Billy?*" Dolores asked, using the familiar form of address, which did not go unnoticed by Sofia. "I was going to introduce you to my mother, Billy, but she's in a lot of pain, suffering from a shoulder injury."

Dolores glanced at Sofia to remind her to speak with don Fernando and doña Teresa about liberating Beatriz from the backbreaking work in the cane fields.

"*Estóy muy bien, gracias, y tú?*" Billy responded to Dolores.

"*Le ensenaste a tutear*! (You taught him the tu form?) Sofia asked, unsmiling, looking directly at Dolores.

"No, Sofia. No lo enseñé." Dolores said (No, I didn't teach him.).

"How did you learn to *tutear*, Billy?" Sofia asked.

"After our lesson today, I went back to my room and studied the grammar book Margarita gave me. It wasn't that hard."

"We're very impressed, aren't we Dolores? If he keeps studying like that, he could be fluent the next time we see him here in Cuba."

"Now, that's something I'd sure like to accomplish. I love the Spanish language and your Cuban culture, and I'll never forget that Spanish guitar we heard tonight. I can't stop thinking about it."

"When do you think you'll be returning to Cuba, Billy?" Sofia asked.

Billy smiled, looking at both girls and then shifting his smile to Dolores.

"I don't know exactly when, it depends upon my parents, especially my dad. But I want to come back soon, very soon."

"We're very sorry you have to leave tomorrow, aren't we, Dolores." Sofia said, smiling at Billy.

Her smile suddenly disappeared, when she looked up and saw her sister, Constancia, approaching."

"Mama wants you to come back right now, Sofia," said Constancia.

"Oh, no, please, Constancia, tell her I'll be back in a little while. We're saying good-bye to our American friend. I won't be long."

"Mamá told me to bring you back Sofia, and I must obey her."

Sofia looked both disappointed and embarrassed.

"I'll have to say good-bye to you Billy and bon voyage. It was wonderful to meet you, and I hope you can stay longer next time."

Sofia offered Billy her cheek to kiss, but he was not familiar with the custom and just reached for her hand.

Once again, Billy found himself alone with Dolores, and his mind conjured up moments of bliss, sweeter even than those he had experienced earlier that day, when she had suggested that they begin a correspondence. He pictured holding her hand, slipping his arm around her shoulders and holding her close, and maybe, just maybe, a kiss on the lips. But his romantic musings were interrupted by the harsh sound of a barking dog, which seemed to be getting louder and closer. Dolores grimaced and covered her ears with her hands. They saw the white cat run out from the gardenia bushes.

"It's Neva," Dolores cried leaping to her feet. "She's out again. Hurry, we must catch her or the dogs will..."

Just then, they spotted a bloodhound chasing the cat. Fortunately, Neva was able to scamper up the nearby tree. Seconds later the bloodhound caught up, jumping and barking ferociously at the base of the tree.

"Don't worry, Dolores. I'll get her," Billy said.

Dolores was crying uncontrollably and ran off to her mother's shack. The bloodhound continued to jump and bark ferociously, and the terrified cat hissed, meowed, and climbed ever higher. A moment later Dolores ran back out, accompanied by an old slave carrying a ladder.

"Hurry, Bartholomew, hurry please," Dolores yelled.

Bartholomew placed the ladder against the tree, but when he tried to push the bloodhound away with his foot, it growled menacingly and bared its teeth. The old slave got no more than a few steps up the ladder before it bit down hard on his leg and pulled him down. Bartholomew fell to the ground, and the bloodhound was all over him, sinking its teeth into his leg and backside. He screamed for help, his arms and legs flaying about like a rag doll.

"Get off him! Get off him," Billy yelled, waving his arms and trying to push the dog off with his foot. The bloodhound let up a little but then bared its teeth and growled menacingly at Billy.

"Stay back, Billy, these bloodhounds are vicious," Dolores said.

Suddenly, to their horror, they saw another bloodhound run to the tree, then another, and all hell broke loose. They encircled the old slave and pounced on him like a pack of hungry wolves.

"I'll run back to the Main House and get help?" Billy yelled.

"There's not enough time, Billy. Oh, God, please help us!" Dolores cried, tears running down her face. Bartholomew screamed, and they could see the blood, oozing through his pants as the bloodhounds tore him apart. Billy was filled with fear, but he could not just stand by and let the dogs kill the old slave. He tried again to intervene, kicking and screaming at the vicious canines.

"Don't, Billy!" cried Dolores. "They'll attack you. I'll get help."

No sooner had the words left her lips, when Victorio Arquidez appeared out of nowhere, shouting loud, harsh commands that the bloodhounds obeyed. They backed off, and the Chief Overseer chased them back to the kennel. Bartholomew was carted off to the hospital, and Neva came down from the tree. Dolores took the cat back to her mother's shack. Moments later she returned with her mother.

"I saw him standing behind the gazebo, watching, as those bloodhounds tore poor old Bartholomew to pieces," said Beatriz. "I told you, Felicidad, Victorio Arquídez is the devil himself, the meanest, cruelest man on this plantation. You have to save me from him, Felicidad, save me before it's too late."

"I'm trying, mamá; I'm trying hard. I asked Sofia to speak with doña Teresa…"

"I heard that devil telling the men who carried Bartholomew off to the hospital that he had consumption. He said it was good that the bloodhounds had finished him off, because he couldn't work anymore in the cane fields and couldn't perform any other useful function on this *ingenio*. (sugar plantation)

Billy sat down at the gazebo still in a state of shock from the horror he had just witnessed. He had seen such horror and cruelty on *The Wandering Maiden* as well, a vessel now owned by his father; a vessel that engaged in slave trading, an evil and illegal practice that was his family's chief source of income. He wondered whether he could return to sea and carry on the dirty business of capturing Africans, taking them to far off places to be tortured and exploited; only to be killed when no longer of any use to their Masters. He knew for certain that slavery was an evil and inhuman practice, and that he could never again be indifferent to it. But he also realized that if he did not return to Cuba, he might never see Dolores again.

He looked up and saw her approaching, her countenance expressing sadness and despair. She sat down next to him

"I know it's hard to believe, Billy, but what we just saw is common practice here on *La Dulce Gardenia* and all over Cuba. My poor mother and thousands of others like her suffer untold horrors on this island."

"I'm so sorry that you have to live in such conditions, Dolores, but maybe you could come and live in the United States and..."

She immediately burst into tears, and he realized he should not have said it. He reached out now for her hand, seeking the right words to comfort and console her, no longer afraid that he might blush.

"You made me so happy, Dolores, when you told me we could write to each other."

A trace of a smile emerged on her lovely face, and her tears dried up. He looked into her beautiful dark eyes sparkling in the moonlight, and a chill ran up his spine. His heart raced and his whole body tingled. He had been longing for this moment, and he gathered up his nerve, put his arm around her and kissed her. It was just a little kiss, a sweet and innocent little kiss. But to Billy, it was the most wonderful and beautiful moment of his life. And although he reminded himself as he lay in bed that night that he was just an inexperienced sixteen-year-old, still he felt with all his heart that he was in love.

CHAPTER III

The Road to Manhood

It was Saturday morning. Billy opened the window in his second floor bedroom and craned out his neck, looking for the postman. It had been a year since his trip to Africa and Cuba, during which time he and Dolores had written each other faithfully.

Where is he? He is always late. Oh, there he is now, finally!

He closed the window, went downstairs and rushed out the door. His mother was coming towards him, holding the letters.

"Any letters for me?" he asked excitedly.

Bonny thumbed through them and took out a pink envelope, postmarked Havana, Cuba, noticing its sweet scent. She frowned and handed it to Billy.

"Just who is this Spanish girl, Billy? I want to know more about her."

"She's my Cuban friend, mama, and she helps me with Spanish. I told you many times,"

He rushed back to his room and closed the door. Opening Dolores's letters had become a ritual. He would stare at the letter longingly, trying to imagine Dolores's sweet words of affection. He would hold them up to his lips and kiss them lovingly, savoring the sweet scent of gardenias and imagining that he was holding her, kissing her. He'd examine the exotic postmark written in

Spanish again and again, reading it out loud, trying to perfect his pronunciation, longing for the day when he could talk to Dolores and write to her in her native language, so she would understand his deep love for her. Only when he had achieved a heightened state of anticipatory bliss would he open the letter.

Querido Billy,

> *It was a terrible disappointment to learn that you would not come to Havana. My heart sunk when I found out about it. I so much longed to see you. We learned that don Fernando purchased slaves locally from don Antonio de Cadiz, and that is why he say he don't need more from your father...*

Billy stopped reading, wondering whether to try to correct Dolores's written English, which unlike her spoken English, was full of errors. But no, he concluded, it would only slow things down.

> *We had a very big produccion of sugar and tobacco this year, Billy, so I' am sure that don Fernando will need more slaves. But I have a conflict, because slavery corrupts every part of life, here in Cuba, and I despise it, and pray every day to the Virgin that we don't need slaves to do the work here. Some day I will tell you everything about it.*
>
> *Thank you Billy for your concern of my mother. Victorio Arquídez still keeps her in the cane fields working. It is very sad for me to see her suffer. She cannot do this work much longer because it makes her weak and she can catch the cholera that is so common here. This past August doña Teresa herself was very*

sick. She was lucky to live. It is just from the grace from God that mamá has not caught this terrible disease.

I have some very good news to say, Billy, almost too good to trust. Mamá confessed to me that don Fernando is my real father. She told me how it happened and how she has suffered for it. Until now, she wouldn't tell me, but she told me that he always has me in his heart and loves me as a daughter. He wants to recognize me as his daughter but because of doña Teresa he doesn't do it. Mama told me that someday he will, but I must be patient...

There was a knock on the door. Billy slipped the letter under his pillow just before his mother walked in

"Billy, I want you to come downstairs and meet somebody. Hurry now and clean yourself up, you hear?" She closed the door and went downstairs.

Billy was annoyed, but he put on a clean shirt and went down.

"Here he is. Emily, this is my son, Billy."

Billy smiled as best he could and shook her hand.

"This is Mrs. Beckett's daughter, Constance."

She was frail but otherwise not bad looking. He sat and listened, trying not to show how desperately he wanted to return to his room and finish reading Dolores's letter.

"Now then, let's have some tea," Bonny said. "Billy, go in the kitchen and tell Becky to serve the tea."

As he started walking toward the kitchen, he brushed past Constance's blue hoop skirt, which caught the buckle of his shoe, lifting her skirt and revealing her nicely shaped ankle. Constance shifted her skirt out of his way with a smile and a swishing sound.

"Who is dat out der wid yo mamá?" Becky asked, brushing

aside some tears running down her face from the onion she was cutting.

"My mom called her Mrs. Beckett. Her daughter, Constance, is there with her."

"Sho, Mizz Beckett. She da wife o da man who own dat clothin sto on Church Street. Aah seen her daughter, she a pretty lil thing."

Billy marveled at how Becky always seemed to know everyone and everything that was happening in Charleston and its environs. The Becketts were Episcopalians and Episcopalians were the ruling class in Charleston. Billy had heard his mother lament that to be an Irish-Catholic in Charleston was an obstacle to one's social and economic mobility. Patrick had taken issue with it, stating that even if it were true, it didn't trouble him in the slightest.

"All right, Massa Billy, tell yo mamá Aah be bringin out da tea in jes a minute o two. Go on back now and talk wid Mizz Constance," Becky chuckled.

Billy walked back to the parlor and was met with a wide smile from Constance Beckett.

"Becky will be here with the tea shortly," Billy said, thinking this was a good time to excuse himself, so he did not sit down.

"Sit down Billy and chat with us a while," Bonny said.

I know what she has in mind, but she's not going to succeed, not if I can help it.

Constance stared at Billy, a cute little smile on her face. Billy sat down brushing against Constance's hoop skirt.

Is she doing this on purpose?

"...And what are your plans after graduation, Billy?" asked Mrs. Beckett.

Billy hesitated before answering, looking at his mother, wondering what her reaction would be to what he was about to say.

"Well, I've been thinking about the Military Academy, but..."

Bonny raised an eyebrow and interrupted him.

"The College of Charleston is the preferred choice," Bonny said.

Becky came in now, carrying a tray with tea and blueberry muffins, as the conversation turned to the social event of the year, Charleston's week of horse racing and its elegant nightly balls and entertainments.

"...Yes, and I'm told there's going to be a Mozart festival. I simply adore Mozart! Don't you? His music is so romantic and touching," said Mrs. Beckett.

Billy sat there, waiting for an opportune time to excuse himself, but it never came. When at last, the tea had cooled and the conversation had wound down, the guests got up to leave. Constance smiled and said good-bye to Billy, adding,

"I hope to see you at the races."

Billy smiled back but remained noncommittal. No sooner had they left than Bonny began probing Billy about Constance. But he kept his feelings to himself and rushed back upstairs to his room.

He reread Dolores's letter from the beginning, savoring how she addressed him in Spanish as "*Querido* Billy." When they first started writing to each other, she used "*Estimado*" Billy, which he learned would simply translate in English to the standard "Dear," carrying no affectionate undertones. But after several months and several of Billy's letters in which he had described how very much he longed to see her, he received his first "*Querido* Billy." When he looked it up in an English/Spanish dictionary, it set his heart a fluttering, especially the part that said: "...and much more than 'dear'; more like 'beloved' or 'darling'..." In every subsequent letter he wrote, he always addressed her as "*Querida* Dolores."

He came to the part in Dolores's letter before his mother interrupted him.

I try with all my heart to respect and have love for doña Teresa. And I pray to God and to the Blessed Virgen and hope that she accept me someday. I know is difficult too for her. I remind of don Fernando's unfaithfulness. Sofia even say if not for doña Teresa, don Fernando would pay to send me to United States for college with Sofia. Oh, how wonderful it would be querido! I would be closer to you.

It is hard to believe that it been more than a year since I have seen you, querido. If I did not have your precious letters, I will not survive. They so dear to me! I read them again and again. I long to see you again!

Buenas noches, querido. I hope see you in my dreams.

As always,
Your Dolores

2

In spite of his strong opposition to slavery, Billy resolved that he simply had to compromise with his conscience and persuade his father to take him on another voyage to Africa and on to Cuba, where he would be reunited with Dolores. But Bonny would have none of it while school was in session. When the school year ended, however, Billy saw an opportunity to take his second voyage. But it never came to fruition, because don Fernando telegraphed Patrick McHugh that he didn't require any more deliveries until the fall, and by that time Billy would be back in school.

The Charleston High School was established in 1839 and had a rich curriculum and a good reputation. The tuition was forty dollars per year. Billy was in his final year. He'd always been a good student and achieved good grades, particularly in his Spanish and history courses where he was the outstanding student in his class.

Bonny McHugh was pleased with her son's academic progress but expressed concern to Patrick about this "Spanish girl" in Havana with whom Billy seemed so infatuated. Patrick advised his wife not to worry and said it would likely pass. But Bonny remained concerned. She wanted her son to court the local planters' daughters who were tutored and refined and could help assure him a place in Charleston's wealthy and prestigious aristocracy.

As for Patrick, he had become much too busy with the myriad problems of captaining and maintaining *The Wandering Maiden* to have time for monitoring what he referred to as "Billy's schoolboy romances." Upon returning from one lengthy voyage and endeavoring to escape Bonny's constant carping on the subject, Patrick had shouted:

"For God's sake, Bonny, let the lad choose his own friends and flames!"

That was when Bonny decided it was time for her to tell Patrick of her shock and dismay when she happened to enter Billy's room as Becky was changing the bedding. Bonny saw the sticky white substance on the sheets and became alarmed, fearing that he had contracted some dreadful disease. *Tain't nothin ta worry bout, Miss McHugh. He jes becomin a man.* Becky had said. Bonny also found a book in Billy's room, something called the *Kama Sutra*. She told Patrick it contained filthy illustrations, and she considered it to be another sign of Billy's growing licentiousness, most probably the result of his having gone to sea with that motley bunch of immoral sailors. Bonny insisted that Patrick have a talk with Billy and that he be made to go to confession at Saint Mary's Roman Catholic Church.

Patrick finally agreed and on Saturday morning, he and Billy rode into town to get a haircut. Some time later they were back on the street with fresh haircuts. They headed to the General Store, passing by the hitching post where they had left their carriage. Patrick told the old slave to keep watching it and that they would be returning shortly.

Bonny usually did the shopping, but since Patrick and Billy were in town for haircuts, she asked them to pick up some things. They stood at the counter while Patrick paid for the goods.

"Good afternoon, Billy. How are you today? Oh, and is this Mister McHugh? We haven't met before, sir. I'm Emily Beckett and this is my daughter, Constance."

Mrs. Beckett shook Patrick's hand and smiled, while Constance, true to her name, stared constantly and admiringly at Billy.

She looks a lot better than the last time I saw her. Maybe it's the rouge on her cheeks and lips.

But in what had become the norm for Billy, whenever he saw a pretty girl, the image of Dolores would flash across his mind and he would inevitably conclude that the other girl was sadly lacking in comparison

"I'm very pleased to meet you, Emily," said Patrick. "Bonny has told me a lot about you, and she wants to plan an evening with you and Mister Beckett."

"Yes, I hope we can get together soon," said Mrs. Beckett.

"Will I see you at the races, Billy?" Constance asked with her biggest smile ever.

"I'll be there," Billy said. "My friend Charlie Flynn and I go every year."

Patrick and Billy walked back to their carriage, where they found the old slave awaiting his remuneration. Patrick gave him a one-dollar silver coin, which produced a wide smile and a string of blessings. As they drove back home, Patrick turned to his son.

"Billy, your mother wanted me to talk to you about a few things. She said she found a book in your room."

Billy felt a wrenching knotting up in his stomach, which he managed to disguise when the carriage hit a deep rut in the road.

"Do you know what I'm referring to?"

Billy turned pale. Patrick pressed him: "Do you?"

Billy still didn't respond, looking straight ahead.

"I'm talking about a book called *The Kama Sutra*. Where did you get it?"

There was nowhere to run and nowhere to hide. He could not deny that he had the book. Patrick tightened up on the reins and looked sternly at his son, waiting for an answer and an explanation.

"I got it from Javier on *The Wandering Maiden*," Billy stammered. "He told me he got it in Bombay. He had two of them and, uuh uuh, he sold me one. He said it was just some kinda ancient Indian book about male and female…"

"Well, your mother seems to think that it was filthy and disgusting, and she wants you to go to confession this Saturday."

Billy sought some solace from the fact that his father didn't express his own outrage and disapproval of the book but spoke only of what Bonny thought of it. He relaxed a little knowing that his dad, who had had a lifetime at sea, was more than familiar with a sailor's taste in literature.

"Your mother is also deeply concerned about your relationship with this Spanish girl in Cuba. She wants you to start meeting other young ladies more suitable and appropriate to your condition in life, like that nice girl, Constance, back there at the General Store."

At that moment, the trail led them to a section of deep swampy bogs, and Patrick tightened up on the reins, slowing the carriage. Suddenly, the horse reared up, whinnying nervously. It was obviously frightened by something, and when Patrick and Billy looked down, they saw a large snake slowly wriggling across the trail.

"Look at the size of that snake!" Billy said, relieved somewhat from the sting of his father's reprimands, which the distraction of the snake provided.

"It's an eastern diamondback, and he's big all right," Patrick said.

Billy tried to keep the conversation going.

"I saw a snake in Africa, Dad, when I went ashore and that guide took me on a little tour in the bush. I think he called it a 'black mamba' or something like that. The guide said it was the fastest and most deadly snake in all of Africa."

Fortunately, for Billy, Patrick made no more mention of the *Kama Sutra*. But when they pulled up in front of their house, Billy knew that he would still have to face his mother.

3

It was the dreaded day of Billy's confession, and he drove the carriage up to the vacant lot across the street from Saint Mary's Roman Catholic Church.

"Pull it up a little, Billy, but don't get too close to that brown carriage," Bonny said.

"All right, Mama, how's that?" He looked over at the church, feeling nauseous.

"That'll do," Bonny said. "Now let's hurry."

Billy had delayed it as long as he could but his time had run out. He had overheard his parents talking about the *Kama Sutra* book Bonny found in his room.

"You saw those filthy illustrations, Patrick, and I told you what I saw on Billy's bed sheets…"

Patrick had said little, making light of it.

Saint Mary's Roman Catholic Church was established in 1791. The original building was destroyed by the terrible fire of 1838, which ravished much of downtown Charleston. It was rebuilt in a new location on Hassel Street, reopening in 1839. Billy was baptized at Saint Mary's and attended mass there regularly. Unlike many of his young compatriots, he did not mind attending mass. But going to confession that was an entirely different matter.

Billy took his mother's hand and helped her out of the carriage, grateful that she was wearing gloves and would not notice his sweaty palms.

"Come on, Becky, give me your hand," Billy said.

"Ya got yoself a real gennelman fo a son, Mizz McHugh, a real gennelman," Becky said, smiling at Billy as she stepped down. Bonny didn't respond.

They walked up to the elegant portico of Saint Mary's and entered the sanctuary. Billy felt his heart skip a beat. It happened again when they stopped at the figure of the Virgin Mary, where Bonny genuflected and made the sign of the cross. She then dipped her hand in the holy water font, touched her forehead and again made the sign of the cross. Billy did the same then followed his mother down the nave, genuflecting before entering a pew on the Saint Joseph side. Becky went to the Virgin Mary's side of the nave where some Negroes were kneeling and praying. Billy knelt down beside his mother and tried to pray, but the words wouldn't come. Suddenly, it sounded like somebody was whispering. Billy turned and saw his best friend, Charlie Flynn, in the pew behind him. Billy nodded to him. Charlie's face took on a fragile smile, his expression seeming to say, *"We're gonna have to take the medicine."*

Some time passed and soon it was Charlie's turn. Billy watched him get up and walk toward the confession box. Again, Billy tried to pray, this time succeeding. He prayed that it would be Father Lynch who would hear his confession and not Father Bailey. More time passed. When Charlie finally emerged from the confession box, he looked shaken. When he knelt down in the pew behind

Billy and his mother, Billy turned and asked him which priest was in there. Bonny overheard him and cast a disapproving look at both of them. But that didn't stop Charlie from whispering: "Father Bailey."

A tidal wave of fear and panic cascaded over Billy.

What should I say? How should I say it? Am I really going to say it? Should I mention the illustrations? Maybe I won't have to. Maybe he knows about the Kama Sutra, and I won't have to say anything about them, just the title. But remember the catechism? If I don't mention them, will it still be a valid confession?

As he knelt and nervously waited his turn, he pondered these questions long and hard.

Billy watched as his mother got up now and walked to the confession box. He was next, and he was feeling panicky. But luck was with him that day. When he happened to look over to the Virgin Mary's side, he saw a woman leaving the confessional, and there was nobody else in line. So, he got up, walked to the other side and entered the confession box. He knelt down and announced the required words in a faint and shaky voice.

"Forgive me Father for I have sinned. It's been a year since my last confession."

His throat was dry, his palms were sweaty, and his stomach was rolling like *The Wandering Maiden* in a stormy sea. The screen separating priest from penitent provided a measure of privacy and anonymity for both priest and parishioner, but it did little to relieve Billy's apprehension and outright fear.

"What are your sins, my son?"

Billy immediately identified the voice of Father Patrick Lynch, who usually celebrated the 9:30 Sunday morning mass, which Billy regularly attended. Everyone in the parish considered him a kind man and a good priest.

"I've, I've had impure thoughts, Father, and I've, I've..."

It was a term often used in confessions, its meaning widely understood by priest and supplicant alike.

"Did you touch yourself?"

Billy flinched, taken aback by the question. He tensed up, not responding at first. His mouth totally lacking in saliva.

"Take your time, son, take your time."

Billy took a deep breath, hoping the priest would not hear him.

"Yes, Father, I, I, many times…I had a, a…"

"Take your time, son. You need not hurry."

"I had a book, and there were drawings."

"Drawings?"

"Yes, Father, drawings, illus, illustrations, many, many illustrations."

"Illustrations of what, my son? Take your time."

"Drawings, drawings of men and wom, wom, women."

"Were they naked?"

"Yes, Father, naked. They were naked, and …"

"What was the name of the book?"

"It was an Indian book, Father, not American Indian, but from India. It was called Kama, uh, Kama, uh, *Kama Sutra*."

"Where did you get the book, son?"

"From a Cuban boy."

"Do you still have it?"

"No, Father. My moth, moth, mother found it in my room and took it."

"Your mother did the right thing. The book is intended for married couples. When you are older, more mature and have found a girl whom you love, you will receive the sacrament of holy matrimony."

The pure and beautiful image of Dolores flashed across his mind, and for just an instant, his anxiety eased.

"God will bless the marriage, and the Church will sanctify it.

Only then would it be appropriate to read such a book. To read it now will only lead you to sin, and sin again. Keep yourself pure and clean for your future bride. Remember that your body is a vessel for God's grace and love. Do not despoil it with impure thoughts and sinful acts before marriage. Do you understand, son?"

"Yes, Father, I understand. I do understand."

"Now, for your penance, I want you to carry out an act of charity in the parish community. And before you leave the sanctuary, say five Our Fathers and four Hail Marys. Now, in the name of the Father, and the Son, and the Holy Ghost, I absolve you of your sins." Billy could make out the hand motion through the dark screen, as the priest made the sign of the cross.

"Go in peace, my son, to love and serve the Lord. And try not to sin again."

"Thank you, Father. I'll try."

Billy stepped out of the confession box, feeling a deep sense of relief. He looked around for his mother and Becky but they were nowhere in sight. Then, he knelt down in a pew and carried out the easy part of his penance, silently reciting the Hail Marys and the Our Fathers. As he left the church and walked back to their carriage, he felt a sudden rush, an unexpected sense of well being. Bonny and Becky were already seated in the carriage.

"Billy, I want you to go to confession regularly. I told your father there will be no more voyages for you on *The Wandering Maiden*," Bonny said. "I don't want you mixing with the likes of that Cuban boy who got you that horrible book. He's not your kind. Do you understand? He's beneath you. Those Spanish people are not like us, Billy. I want you to start socializing with some of your own kind right here in Charleston. You don't need to go to Cuba to find friends."

Billy understood his mother's thinly disguised message and it was a knife wound to the heart. He had thought about stopping at the Watkins' house. The Watkins were a poor family of share croppers with nine children, and it had occurred to him that he might do some chores for them as the act of charity that Father Lynch had given him as penance. But the sting of his mother's remark destroyed his desire to follow through on it. As Billy drove the carriage back home, an uncomfortable barrier of silence took hold between him and his mother.

4

"...Well, tell him you've already made plans, Billy. Your father and I will be leaving in an hour, and we're going to meet the Becketts. We want you to come along with us, you hear?" said Bonny McHugh.

"I'm going with Charlie, Mama. He'll be here any minute," Billy said, his expression one of disbelief that his mother would try this at the last minute. He knew what she was up to. She wanted him to see that Constance Beckett again.

"I want you to start mixing with a better class of people, particularly now since you'll be starting college."

"I can meet up with you and Dad at the races," Billy said and rushed out, finding Charlie Flynn out front mounted on his sturdy red roan.

February was a festive time of the year in Charleston. It was the start of racing season and a week of excitement that everyone looked forward to with great anticipation. The week of races offered the opportunity to show off the finest horseflesh. It also provided an occasion and a venue for the prettiest ladies and the most handsome and available gentlemen to seek and find romance. There were lawn and garden parties, lavish dinner parties and exclusive, elegant balls. But it wasn't just the landed gentry that celebrated racing week; every level of Charleston society participated.

Schools were closed, and even the Catholic Church sanctioned the festivities, offering a silent dispensation of sorts, so people could let their hair down and give vent to their primeval instincts to enjoy themselves.

"Good mornin', partner," Charlie said, a devilish grin on his handsome face. "You ready?"

"I'm more than ready, Charlie, so let's go!"

"That's the spirit," Charlie said. "Gotta say, you're lookin' pretty good. Might even be an asset and help us find some pretty little things."

"Let's just get to the races, and worry about that later," Billy said as they spurred their mounts and raced off.

It was a sunny day and somewhat mild for February, and when they arrived at Washington Racecourse, there were throngs of people making their way into the park grounds. Luxurious carriages were parked side by side in the adjacent field, guarded by slaves, who, themselves, were dressed in their finest outfits. Touts lined the entranceway hawking their tip sheets. There was a public stable in back of the grandstand where Billy and Charlie took their horses. As they walked back to the grandstand, Charlie nodded in the direction of two young ladies who had just walked up and leaned on the fence, ostensibly to look at the horses. They were beautifully dressed in wide, fashionable hoop skirts and colorful silk tops with plunging necklines, displaying their full and rounded bosoms.

"What say we go on over and introduce ourselves?" Billy didn't respond.

"Come on, partner, you're still not thinkin bout that Spanish girl, are you?" Charlie asked. "She's far away in Cuba, and these girls are right here and now."

Billy had told Charlie about his relationship with Dolores, but Charlie simply couldn't understand why Billy would remain loyal to a girl who was so far away, especially when there were so many pretty and available girls right there in Charleston.

"Come on. We're not gonna marry 'em, maybe just talk a little and have some fun. I don't think your Dolores will mind, especially if she don't know 'bout it."

Charlie walked over to them and leaned up on the fence. Billy followed behind him.

"Good mornin', ladies! Y'all sure do look pretty this morning," Charlie said, smiling broadly. "My name's Charlie Flynn, and this here's my friend Billy McHugh."

The girls smiled back shyly and introduced themselves as Charlotte and Nancy. That was more than enough for Charlie to turn on the charm, and he launched into his full arsenal of sweet compliments and funny stories that made the girls laugh.

Billy said very little and continued to view the horses being paraded in the paddock. When he looked up, he saw Constance Beckett and a plain-looking girl approaching. This time, however, she was almost a welcome sight because he had no interest whatsoever in either of the girls that Charlie was doing his best to charm.

"Well, hello, Billy. I was hoping to see you here. This is my friend Maria del Carmen. She's from Central America, Nicaragua in fact."

"They speak Spanish in Nicaragua, don't they?" Billy said.

"Yes, we do," said Maria del Carmen, smiling at Billy. "All of Central America speaks Spanish."

At first glance Billy found Maria del Carmen to be pitifully plain. She looked like some of the Indians he'd seen in Charleston, with a round face and short, black, straight hair. But when he looked more closely, he saw that she had lovely, dark eyes, expressive eyes that immediately seemed to capture and hold one's attention, in spite of her otherwise plain appearance.

"Do you know any Spanish?" she asked.

"I'm studying it now," Billy said.

"Oh, that's wonderful. Maybe I can help you, and in exchange you can correct my English."

"Oh, but your English sounds very good to me," Billy said.

"Well, thank you, Billy. You are very kind to say that, but I really do need some improvement. Just ask Constance."

"You're right, Billy. Her English is very good," Constance said, wanting badly to join the conversation but finding it hopeless, because Billy had already launched into a long narrative, telling Maria del Carmen how he'd been to Cuba; how he'd begun to study Spanish; and how he very much wanted to become fluent in the language.

"And what are you doing in the United States?" Billy asked.

"I'm here studying at the Joan of Arc Girls Academy."

"And you're living here in Charleston?" Constance heard the question, seeing an opportunity to get Billy's attention.

"She's living with me and my family," Constance said, looking directly at Billy and smiling coquettishly. "Our families have known each other for many years."

Billy smiled and looked at Constance with a new light, noticing that she even looked pretty in her pink hoop skirt and red silk top, revealing an hourglass waist he had not noticed before.

Meanwhile, Charlie continued to flirt with Charlotte and Nancy, touting the finer points of a large black stallion named Midnight, who, he assured them would be the winner in the first race.

"I'm gonna bet him, and y'all would be smart to do the same."

Just then they heard the bugle sound the "call to the post," signaling the jockeys to mount their horses and make their way to the starting line.

"We better hurry," Charlie said, "I'm sure there'll be a line."

And there was. There was a crowd around the betting tables, and after several minutes wait, they still hadn't gotten to place their bets. They heard the starting bell ring, and the horses were off. It was too late; they had missed it. The number seven horse, a grey stallion, led until the three-quarters pole, where Midnight surged to the front, winning easily by more than three lengths.

"Damn! I knew it!" Charlie exclaimed.

But he did pick three other winners, softening the blow, and one of them was a fifteen-to-one shot that filled his pockets with winnings. He was not so lucky when it came to Charlotte and Nancy, whom he later saw in the company of two handsome twin brothers, the sons of wealthy planters. Charlie somewhat jokingly blamed Billy for refusing to join him in courting the girls.

After the last race, the McHughs and the Becketts left to attend a dinner party and formal ball at the luxurious residence of John Alston, one of the wealthiest men in Charleston.

Constance and Maria del Carmen were also to attend a ball that evening, a ball that Bonny had tried her best to get Billy to attend but to no avail. As the two lads made their way back to the stable to retrieve their horses, they came across little groups of revelers who had set up barbecue grills and makeshift bars, selling beer and homemade whiskey. The smell of the meat on the griddle was simply irresistible. Negro musicians played lively fiddle and banjo music lending a fun-filled atmosphere to the day.

"How 'bout we stop for some of that barbecue, Billy? I'm 'bout to die of starvation."

"Sounds good to me. I'm hungry too."

They walked up to the makeshift bar and ordered the meat. Charlie asked for some whiskey.

"How old are you boys?" asked the old-timer behind the bar, who wore a full gray beard.

"Seventeen," Charlie said, "be eighteen soon."

Having heard Charlie's response, the black banjo player immediately began playing and singing a lively tune called "Sweet Sixteen."

"What'll you have son, whiskey or beer?"

"Make mine whiskey," Charlie said.

"I'll have a beer," Billy said.

One whiskey later and Charlie wanted to dance. Billy sat down on a wooden box, ate his barbecue and sipped his beer as Charlie danced with a woman more than twice his age. But after a second beer, Billy too was enlivened and began tapping his foot to the intoxicating rhythm of the banjo player. Long about eight o'clock, Charlie wanted to leave, surprising Billy, because it was uncharacteristic of Charlie.

"You know, there's a place I heard about that I've been wantin' ta visit. Heard 'bout it the last time I was in Michael's barbershop, a place called the Big Brick. Let's you and I go and take a look."

Charlie thought he had been talking in a low voice, but he had been heard.

"Your friend's talkin' 'bout that love nest over on Beresford street. Place's not been open long, but I hear tell it's always busy." Others who heard it also chuckled.

"Ya know, dey allows free niggaas in dat place," said the banjo player.

"Iffen of course dey gots da money," said the fiddle player.

"A Jew lady owns da place. She's a rich 'en, and Aah hear tell she knows da mayor and all da po-lice."

Billy looked at Charlie and said he was not interested and wanted to leave.

"Oh, come on, partner. I heard that just about every lad

studyin' at The Charleston College has been there. And since you'll likely be studyin' at that fine institution, why don't we just ride by and take a look?"

"I'm not going, Charlie. What if someone were to see us there? It would be all over town the next day, and my parents would hear about it."

The old man behind the bar looked at Billy and laughed.

"You needn't worry about that, son. Jest about every planter, merchant, and politician from miles around has been there and been seen there. No one says a word."

"Come on, partner, don't you think it's about time that you be initiated into manhood?" Charlie asked, slurring his words and no longer concerned that others might be listening.

"I'm leaving, Charlie." Billy said as he got up and walked away.

Charlie swallowed the last of his whiskey and reluctantly followed. The old man behind the bar smiled, bid them good-bye and added a final tribute for all to hear.

"They sure are dressed up nice for The Big Brick, aren't they, folks? Look at them fancy pants, waistcoats, and cravats. They won't have no trouble gettin' in, long as they got the money."

Everybody laughed, black and white alike. Charlie smiled, tipped his hat to the crowd and followed after Billy.

As they walked back to the stable to get their horses, Charlie continued to work on him. Billy thought of Dolores. He thought of what Father Lynch had said:

Your body is a vessel for God's grace and love. Do not despoil it with impure thoughts and sinful acts before marriage.

But Charlie was persistent and persuasive.

"All right, Charlie, but we just ride by and take a look, no more."

"Fair enough, partner. Let's go!"

5

It was pitch dark as they rode off to Charleston, but when they arrived at Beresford Street they found it brightly lit by the gaslights. The Big Brick, true to its name, was a large, red brick, three-storied structure, the last house on a dead-end street.

"All right, Charlie, we've seen what it looks like, now let's get out of here."

Once again, Charlie prevailed, and persuaded Billy to take a closer look.

It was an impressive building with a majestic portico girded by four stately white pillars. They walked up, peeked through the window and saw a richly furnished parlor, bustling with activity. A massive crystal chandelier hung from the ceiling, which reminded Billy of the one he had seen at *la Dulce Gardenia*.

"Looks like some of those plantation houses, don't it?" Charlie said.

Billy frowned, but he had to admit it was impressive.

"But I don't see a bar," said Charlie.

"Can't see it from here. But you go inside and you'll see the finest bar in the whole city of Charleston."

They turned and saw a smartly dressed middle-aged woman, standing with her hands on her hips. She had appeared out of nowhere and had large breasts bulging out of a plunging neckline, so low you could see part of her nipples.

"Haven't seen you boys here before. You're not from the Charleston College, are ya? We don't allow them in here anymore. Too much trouble."

"No, Ma'am, we're not," Charlie said, somewhat sheepishly.

"Well, your first drink's on the house, since it's your first time here."

"Let's go in and get our free drink, partner."

"That's right it's free," the woman echoed.

"Come on, we'll just look around, nothing more," Charlie said.

Billy shook his head but then found himself staring at the woman's breasts.

"Ain't nobody here who'll make you do what you don't want to do. I make damn sure of that," She said.

She smiled and came closer, her hoop skirt making a swishing sound as she stepped forward.

Just then, a distinguished-looking older gentleman in a black waistcoat and top hat stepped out the door. He was smoking a cigar and carried a fancy black walking stick with a gold encrusted handle.

"Until we meet again, Grace, my dear," he said, smiling broadly, as he leaned over and kissed her on the cheek.

"You hurry back, Colonel. It's always so nice to see you."

"I shall do that, Grace, but for now I'll take my leave and say good night."

The door opened again and out stepped two pretty, young women. Billy immediately noticed that one of them looked Spanish with long, dark hair, dark eyes, and painted lips. The other had red hair, dewy white skin and looked Irish. Grace looked at them coldly.

"What are you two doing out here?" she asked.

"We just came out for some fresh air, Miss Peixoto," said the red-haired woman. "We've been upstairs with some clients, and..."

"Y'all get a minute of fresh air and then get yourselves back inside," said Grace, interrupting the girl and nodding in the direction of Billy and Charlie, as if to say, here's two more for you.

With another stern look, Grace turned and went back inside.

"We'll be just a minute, Miss Peixoto," said the red-haired girl, smiling obediently.

The dark haired girl moved out of Grace's path, avoiding her stern looking eyes, and once Grace was out of sight, she slipped a gold coin down into her bosom.

"*Ay, Dios mio! No aguanto mas!*"

That caught Billy's attention, and he looked at her now with great interest, deciding to risk it with his limited Spanish.

"*De donde viene usted?*" (Where are you from?)

The girl looked surprised to hear Spanish coming out of the mouth of this handsome American-looking young man.

"*Yo soy costarricense, y tu?*" (I'm Costa Rican, and you?)

"*Yo soy Americano y yo estudio espanol.*" ("I'm an American and I study Spanish).

They spoke for a little while longer until Billy's Spanish vocabulary was exhausted, and he had to switch back to English. Meanwhile, Charlie and the Irish girl, Nelly, were engaged in a conversation of their own. Billy couldn't help but see that she already had her arm around Charlie's waist.

"You're not from the Charleston College, are you?" Nelly asked.

"No, y'all need not worry 'bout that," Charlie said. "We don't like that college none."

Miss Peixoto suddenly appeared at the window, a stern expression on her face, motioning for the two girls to come inside.

"Let's go inside. We won't hurt you, we promise," Nelly said, tugging on Charlie's coat sleeve.

Charlie looked at Billy.

"Come on, partner, you don't need to do nothin. You can just practice your Spanish."

With that, Isabel reached for Billy's hand and began tugging him along. And they followed Nelly and Charlie through the front door to the parlor.

"Look at this, would 'ya. This place's got class all right," Charlie said.

It was spacious and richly decorated with oriental carpets, an elaborate crystal chandelier and some fine looking artwork hanging on the walls. Large velvet-covered loveseats and armchairs lined the walls, occupied by pretty young ladies sipping champagne in the company of distinguished-looking gentlemen.

"This way, boys," said Nelly as she led them down a hallway with risqué paintings of beautiful young women on the walls.

"Vamos al bar, Billy," said Isabel.

"*Si, vamos,*" parroted Billy.

They followed Nelly and Charlie as an array of attractive young females sashayed by, swishing their hoop skirts. Isabel nestled closer to Billy, guarding her client from their come-hither glances and coquettish smiles. Billy was struck with a surge of conflicting emotions: overly stimulated and excited by the proximity of these beautiful young women, yet beset by a nagging sense of guilt and a chorus of admonitions from a harsh Catholic conscience.

"*…and lead us not into temptation but deliver us from evil.*"

The bar was the focus of activity in The Big Brick. There were comfortable armchairs lining the walls occupied by couples kissing and caressing before their inevitable trip upstairs to the privacy of the separate rooms where the girls plied their trade. Grace Peixoto was behind the bar, watching over the money and setting the price for the trips upstairs. Occasionally, she'd pour a drink, but a plump woman in her forties served as barkeep.

"What'll you boys have?" Miss Peixoto asked.

"Don't forget us girls!" said Nelly."

"*Que vas a tomar?*" (What are you having to drink?) Isabel asked, smiling and flashing her dark eyes at Billy, who hesitated.

"Why don't you have a whiskey, partner? It'll help you relax." Charlie said. Billy looked nervous and tense, but the fact that he was able to understand Isabel's Spanish energized him.

"I'll have a whiskey," Billy said.

"Make that two," said Charlie.

Grace poured the whiskey as Isabel began rubbing Billy's back. A chill ran up his spine, a surge of sexual energy shot through his loins and he suddenly felt both aroused and afraid.

"And what about you ladies?" Charlie asked.

"We only drink champagne," Nelly said. The owner smiled.

"The bottle will run you ten dollars gold," said the owner. "But don't forget, since it's your first time here, your two drinks are on the house, so you only pay for the champagne." Charlie checked his funds.

"What the hell! I'm up more than thirty dollars from the races, and I got my allowance today."

Charlie smiled and tossed a ten-dollar gold piece up on the bar. Grace then directed a waiter to set up a table for them against the far wall. A Negro waiter dressed in a smart looking white uniform brought their whiskey and poured the champagne for Nelly and Isabel.

"Here's to a rip-roarin' good time for us all!" Charlie said.

They drank to it and the all-black band broke into a lively French Polka.

"Let's have us a dance, Nelly," Charlie said as he took her by the hand and led her out to the dance floor.

"*Bailemos*, Billy!" ("Let's dance, Billy!") said Isabel, reaching for Billy's hand. He didn't know the word but he got the message.

"*No bail, no bailamos*," he said, trying to get it right.

"*Ven conmigo. Te enseño.*" ("Come with me, I'll teach you."), But Billy stayed put. Isabel changed the subject and dropped the Spanish.

"Maybe you more comfortable, if you take coat off," she said in awkward-sounding English.

"*Si, tiene razones, caliente mucho aqui*," Billy said, unaware that his Spanish was every bit as awkward as her English.

Billy stood up, took off his waistcoat and placed it on the back of his chair. Isabel then moved her chair closer, and as Billy sat down she adjusted the folds in her hoopskirt so that her leg would touch his.

"Billy, Billy," she repeated. "I like Billy name, and you are very handsome boy. Do you have a *novia*?" she asked, reaching for his hand and caressing it.

Billy felt his face flush, and he looked around self consciously, wondering if anyone was looking at them.

"'*Novia*,'" she said, pronouncing it slowly. "You say in English, 'girlfriend,' no?"

"A girlfriend, '*novia*' yes. I have a *novia* in Cuba," Billy said.

That didn't stop Isabel, and she brazenly leaned over, displaying her pert little breasts and began rubbing his chest. Billy didn't know what to do and feared he might lose control.

"Her name is Dolores, and, and, you look, look a little like her," he stammered.

Isabel smiled and continued to rub Billy's chest. He moved his chair away a little and Isabel then stopped rubbing his chest.

Why did you make her stop? Didn't you enjoy it? What are you afraid of?

Isabel drained her champagne and looked around for the waiter to refill her glass.

"Why is the *novia* in Cuba, Billy?" asked Isabel. *Ay, si, ahora entiendo por qué quieres aprender espanol.*" ("Oh, so now I understand why you want to learn Spanish.")

Isabel moved her chair closer again and this time put her hand on his leg and began slowly rubbing his thigh without regard to the waiter who had appeared and began filling her glass with champagne.

"*Hiciste el amor con ella?*" ("Did you make love to her?") Isabel asked with a teasing tone and a sly little smile.

Billy didn't understand, but he did notice that she had used the familiar tú form, which pleased him.

Charlie and Nelly returned from the dance floor arm in arm, joking and laughing.

"And how are you two getting along?" Nelly asked.

"How we getting along, Billy?" Isabel asked, poking him in the ribs for fun, her hand no longer on his leg.

"Just fine," Billy said, turning a little red.

"Let's order some more drinks," Charlie said as the waiter approached. He ordered another whiskey, and Nelly drank down her champagne.

All the while Isabel continued to coo and woo young Billy.

It was obvious that Nelly was way ahead of Isabel in closing the deal. Indeed, Charlie needed little if any convincing.

"Let's go upstairs my dear sweet Charlie," Nelly said, taking him by the hand and leading him over to the stairs. Charlie had a wide grin on his face, and he turned and looked at Billy.

"Why don't you take that pretty little thing upstairs? It will do you good."

Isabel smiled, leaned over and kissed Billy on the cheek. Charlie looked at Isabel.

"Go easy on him, ya hear. He's never been..." Billy was embarrassed and blushed. He reached for his whiskey but found the glass empty.

"Come, Billy. We go upstairs too." Isabel said as she got up and grabbed his hand. But he resisted. An internal debate broke out within him between his acute arousel and his conscience.

"*Que te pasa,* Billy? *No quieres hacer el amor conmigo?*" ("What's wrong, Billy? Don't you want to make love to me?")

She moved even closer to him now, trying to sit on his lap, but her hoop skirt got in the way. She continued to tease and caress him rubbing his chest and his legs, all of which was driving him to a feverish pitch of excitement and desire. But alas the image of his sweet Dolores struck him, and the words of Father Lynch prevailed:

Keep yourself pure and clean for your future bride. Remember that your body is a vessel for God's grace and love. Do not despoil it with impure thoughts and sinful acts before marriage.

By now, Isabel's patience had run its course, and when a gray-bearded older gentleman standing at the bar stared over at her, she made up her mind. He looked old enough to be her grandfather, but he had a look of affluence about him. And when he smiled and waved his hand, Isabel got up and walked over to him without so much as another word or glance at Billy. Billy sat there now all alone.

You are a fool. You should have gone up those stairs with her.

From time to time one of the little lovelies would come up and try to get him to come to terms. But Billy waved them off. He ordered another whiskey, his third of the night, and he sat there waiting for Charlie to come down.

Charlie and Nelly finally came downstairs, having stayed longer than the rules permitted because of Charlie's generous tip. And he simply assumed that Billy had gone upstairs with Isabel for the standard forty-five minutes. Billy, wanting to save face, didn't disavow him of that notion.

Billy had a dream that night, and he remembered it clearly when he awoke the next morning.

He was in bed with his beloved Dolores. She was sweet and tender, as sweet and tender a girl as ever did exist. It was his very first time, his virginal introduction to love making. It was the long-awaited moment, the moment he had lived for. She was God's reward for having waited and resisted temptation. But at the climactic moment for them both, Dolores's image faded, and the image of another beautiful, dark-haired girl emerged, alternating with that of his sweet Dolores.

That was when he awoke.

6

Billy entered the kitchen and found Becky slumped over the table, sobbing uncontrollably.

"These things happen, Becky, and there's not much you can do about it," Bonny said, trying to console her but failing miserably.

"Dey gonna sell ma Julius, Massa Billy. Massa Pringle gonna put 'm up fo sale. Aah jes now found out bout it dis mornin'."

Billy looked into her tear-filled, bloodshot eyes.

"Julius, he on the otha side o fifty now, and dey gonna trow 'em away like he jes some kinda trash. God almighty, what gonna happen to our chillen? How can dey do that, Massa, Billy?"

Billy took Becky's hand and squeezed it gently, not knowing what to say, but trying his best to calm her and sympathize with her.

"I'll get my dad to speak to Mister Pringle, Becky. Let me see what I can do."

"Oh, God bless ya Massa Billy. Aah don't know what Aah'd do iffen dey sell ma Julius. But we ain't got much time. Dey puttin'im up fo auction dis Saturday at the Charleston wharf."

Bonny McHugh had always been strict and distant with Becky. She believed in keeping her in her place, fearing that kindness and gentleness would make Becky take advantage of her. Billy treated Becky more like a friend, even a confidant, without regard to her race, her color, and her status as a slave. He valued Becky's pragmatism and street wisdom and told her things that he would never have told his parents. The moment Bonny walked out of the kitchen, Billy hugged Becky, assuring her that he would do whatever it took to keep Julius nearby.

Julius was Becky's mate and worked on the Pringle family's large estate that bordered the McHugh's land. Julius and Becky lived together as husband and wife with their two sons in a small cabin on the Pringle land. Every evening Becky left the McHugh residence and joined her family, returning in the morning. As was common with slaves, they never formally married. Billy knew that the sale of a slave usually resulted in the breakup of a family, separating the parents from the children.

Billy discussed the problem with his father, Patrick.

"I told her you'd talk to Mister Pringle, Dad, and we'd try to get him to change his mind."

Bonny now turned to Patrick.

"Becky told me, Patrick, that if Pringle sells Julius, she'll buy his freedom. She said she would find a way to raise the money. I don't know if she really has the money, but I don't want to take a chance, Patrick. I don't want to lose her."

Bonny needed Becky to do the housekeeping and general chores so Bonny could continue to live the life of a lady of leisure, attend the various functions in Charleston that she so much enjoyed and entertain her literary friends.

"It's going to be very hard to replace Becky, Patrick, so if Pringle won't budge then I want you to attend that auction and purchase Julius," said Bonny. "There's plenty of work he can do for us right here on our property."

"You mean we would buy him, mama, and he would be our slave?" Billy asked.

"That's right, Billy. He'd be our slave, and we can do what we want with him."

"God, I don't have enough trouble with slaves in Africa and on my ship, now I have to play nursemaid to them right here in my own household," Patrick said, looking more than simply annoyed.

The next day Patrick talked with John Pringle.

"I'd like to help you, Patrick, but I have to sell him. My

overseer has a personal problem with Julius and if I override him he'll quit, and I need him to stay."

On Saturday morning Patrick and Billy rode down to the Charleston wharf where the slave auction was being held. They tethered their horses behind the administration building then walked back to the auction block, where they saw the posters on the wall.

Negroes for Sale—Men, Women & Children
Date: 23 April 1854 Rain or Shine
Place: The Charleston Wharf
Registration Required

They spotted the slaves' holding pen, and Billy could hear their low rumbling, muttering, and intermittent cries, which he had heard on his first trip aboard *The Wandering Maiden* slaver.

Prospective buyers were going from one slave to another, poking their bellies, feeling their limbs and checking their teeth, trying to gauge their value in advance of the auction.

"Let's go over and see if we can spot Julius," Patrick said, adding, "I don't want to hang around here for nothin'."

Billy remained silent, but there was no silence in his mind or in his heart. He knew they had to purchase Julius, but he found that to be more than just distasteful; it was downright inhuman.

There were about a hundred slaves in the corral.

"I don't see him, Billy, do you?"

"No, let's ask those two men," Billy said. It was difficult to distinguish one slave from another. There were two husky white men with whips guarding the slaves. From time to time they would herd a slave over to a small platform where he'd be examined and picked over more closely by a prospective purchaser.

"Say, you got a slave here 'bout fifty-years-old named Julius?" Patrick asked.

The guard looked annoyed by the question and before responding cracked his whip at an unruly slave nearby.

"I don't care ta know their names, mister," said the guard. "We go by numbers, 'round here. You tell me his chattel number, and I will point him out ta ya. Go on up to the agent's office, register and get yo'self a catalogue and a number. Then maybe I'll be able to answer your questions."

"Looks and sounds like a mean cuss, doesn't he," Billy remarked.

"It's understandable. It's the nature of the business, Billy."

They went up to the office and picked up a catalogue. There was a line for registering, and while Patrick waited, Billy thumbed through the catalogue.

"There he is," Billy said.

Chattel # 6—Julius—50 years old. Still in good condition, experienced as a field hand and knows carpentry.

"I found him, Dad." Billy said.

"At least they listed his real age. I was afraid they'd mark him down and try to get a higher price," Patrick said.

As they were walking out of the office, a man dressed in white trousers and waistcoat, with a black cravat and a black top hat, walked in. He looked like a ringmaster at a circus, Billy thought. He was smoking a thick, black cigar. Patrick recognized him immediately as the auctioneer. He had officiated at the horse auction where he'd bought the black mare that Billy rode daily. As the noon hour drew close, people began jockeying for position all around the auction block. The block was constructed of coarse gray stone and had steps on both sides that climbed to a flat platform, with space for four or five slaves standing side by side.

At twelve o'clock sharp, the auctioneer came out of the office, took his position and banged his gavel down.

"All right, folks, we're offering today some one hundred examples of the finest negroes in all the southland. Y'all just look at them and you will see just what I'm talkin' 'bout. Please remember that all sales are final and there are no guarantees. Now, let's get started."

Three negroes were herded up to the platform, their fate, their very lives in the hands of a total stranger, a buyer somewhere in the audience who could be cruel or kind.

"Chattel number one is a family group. There's Thomas, thirty-three and strong as an ox, Martha, twenty-eight, the best cook in Charleston County, and Stewart, twelve, who works his magic with horses, cows and goats. Now, what am I bid for the lot of them?"

"One thousand," shouted a dapper gentleman with a curled mustache in the back of the crowd.

The auctioneer smiled, a slightly sneering, insulting little smile, pointing to the man.

"My friend, a thousand won't even buy Thomas. We're talkin' about a robust family of slaves that will do you good and proud for the rest of your lives. Now, let's get serious. Do I hear twenty-five hundred?"

Silence was the response. The auctioneer paced across the stage now, smoking his cigar, trying to excite the crowd, coaxing and cajoling them to make a bid.

"Two thousand," said a middle-aged gentleman right in front of the auction block. A stylishly dressed young woman, the only female in the audience, accompanied him.

"I've got two thousand. Do I hear $2,500? Come on folks. These are prime negroes. I can't let 'em go for any less than $2,500."

"I'll bid five hundred for the boy," said a stout man next to

Patrick and Billy. The three slaves on the block looked shocked and the woman drew closer to her son who hugged her for dear life.

"Six hundred for the boy," said the smartly dressed, middle-aged man in front after his female companion leaned over and whispered something to him.

The auctioneer looked surprised and disappointed at first but acquiesced and acknowledged the bids.

"All right, I've got $600 for the boy. Do I hear $650. Come on now, $650 and worth every penny. He's a magician with animals. Let me hear $650."

The auctioneer paced excitedly back and forth, losing his hat at one point, while urging the crowd to up their bids.

"All right, we've got $600 once. Come on now, let me hear $650... $600 twice..." He waited for the bid, but it didn't come, and he banged down his gavel. "Sold to the gentleman with the lady for $600. You've got yourself a real bargain, sir."

The woman smiled her approval and gave her benefactor a smile and a little hug.

"Go on into the office, pay the man and pick up your bill of sale. All right, now, what do I hear for the man and the woman?"

The two slaves were both crying. A second later the man regained some control, took on an angry look and turned his back to the audience. The auctioneer signaled to the guard who brought his whip down hard on the slave, ordering him to turn around. The slave turned around and began sobbing pitifully. The slave woman became hysterical as she watched the guard take her son away to an unknown fate.

Billy had remained silent, but internally he was filled with anger and disgust.

"How can they do that, Dad?" Billy asked. "He said they were being sold together for $2,500, and so they wouldn't have to break up the family."

"Just because he said it doesn't mean he has to do it," said Patrick. "They'll do whatever it takes to bring in more money. That's how it works. It's as simple as that. Can you blame them? I'd do the same thing, wouldn't you?"

"No, I would not," Billy said forcefully. "What if it had been Becky and Julius up there with their children? You wouldn't want to see their children sold away, would you?"

Billy's face contorted slightly as he looked at his dad, deeply disappointed by what he had said. "These Africans are people just like us, and they have feelings..."

Patrick interrupted Billy and looked at him with something akin to scorn.

"They're slaves, Billy! Black nigger slaves plain and simple! Don't ever think they're like us! 'Cause they're not! They'll never be like us. You should have learned that as a cabin boy on *The Wandering Maiden*. You know I'm beginning to get worried about you and your feelings about these slaves. I'm in the business, and I know firsthand what these slaves are like. I know how to treat them, and I think it's about time that you learned that as well."

A man standing next to them overheard the discussion and chimed in with his opinion.

"Sounds like your son's one of them abolitionists," he said. "Maybe you oughta send him up nawth with the Yankees."

But in the meantime, the auctioneer was selling the boy's father.

"...All right, now, we got $1,500...$1,500 going once...$1,550 anybody?... $1,500 going twice...Come on folks. Let me hear $1,550..." But silence reigned and the gavel came down hard. "Sold for $1,500 to the gentleman with the red and white cravat."

Minutes later the woman sold for $1,200, after which she collapsed and had to be revived before being dragged away by the purchaser and one of the guards.

"You see, son? I told you. The three of them sold separately yielded $3,300. Now, if they'd sold them in one lot they'd have gotten probably only $2,500, $2,600."

Billy remained silent but inside he was seething. He saw a side of his father that he had not seen before, a side that he had missed when he sailed with him on *The Wandering Maiden*. He was not just indifferent to the suffering of these Africans, he was downright mean and hardhearted.

Chattel numbers two and three went quickly. That brought Chattel number four to the block, triggering a great deal of interest and excitement.

"Here we got Sophie, a sixteen-year-old light-skinned mulatto girl, experienced as a nanny and a wet nurse."

A throng of men moved up closer to the auction block to get a better look. She was slender and lithe with an attractive figure, and unlike most of the other slaves auctioned off that day, she had a smug little smile on her light-skinned face.

"She sho look like a wet nurse, don't she? Jes look at the udders on that lil gal," said a man leaning on the auction block.

Guffaws of laughter echoed throughout the crowd. Patrick smiled; Billy did not. The bidding for Sophie was lively, and when the gavel finally fell she sold for $1,400, which surely had more to do with her desirability as a concubine than her utility as a nanny and wet nurse.

Chattel number five was a twenty-three-year-old man with an outstanding physique. The catalogue stated that he could read and write, which some in the audience commented was a disadvantage that could spell trouble for his master. He went for $1,200. That brought them to Julius, Chattel number six. Patrick and Billy watched as a guard let him up to the auction block, a frightened and forlorn look on his pitch-black face.

"I'm gonna start him off with an opening bid of $400. He's

fifty years old, gentlemen, but he still has years of productive work left in him. Knows carpentry too, and carpenters are in demand right now as I'm sure y'all know. All right, who'll give me $400?"

Someone in the middle of the crowd said "$400."

"Do I hear $500?"

Billy looked at his father, wondering why he hadn't bid.

"Come on, folks. Give me $500."

Finally, Patrick raised his hand and bid $450. The auctioneer frowned then smiled jeeringly.

"All right, I've got a measly $450. Who'll give me $500? He's worth every penny of that, folks and lots more. This man's a carpenter, y'all hear me? A carpenter. Now, who'll give me $500?"

Julius looked out now in the crowd and apparently recognized Patrick and Billy, because his expression brightened. Becky must have told him that they would be attending the auction and would purchase him.

"Come on now, folks. You know he's worth far more than that. Do I hear $500?"

"$500," said a disheveled old man just a few feet away from Patrick and Billy. By the looks of him he'd been drinking. Billy looked at his father.

"Hurry, Dad, and bid or we'll lose him." Patrick's face flushed with anger, unaccustomed to receiving commands from his son. But he bid nonetheless.

"$550 here," Patrick yelled, raising his hand. Billy looked over at the old man, wondering whether he would now bid higher. The old man was staggering about and looked like he was about to topple over.

"I've got $550. Do I hear $600?" said the auctioneer. "Ole Julius here can build you a barn or whatever else y'all might need. Come on now. Who'll give me $600?"

"I will, $600 here," said the old man, dropping his badly-faded top hat on the ground. Billy was frantic.

"You gotta bid, Dad. Come on, hurry!"

But Patrick looked away and said nothing. Billy pleaded with him, but it was too late as the auctioneer banged down his gavel.

"Sold to that fine gentleman for $600."

"Why didn't you bid more, Dad? We came here to purchase Julius, and that way we wouldn't lose Becky. I promised her, Dad, I promised Becky. And you promised mama."

Billy was in disbelief of his dad's betrayal. Patrick glared at Billy, grabbed his shoulders and shook him.

"Shut your mouth, Billy! I'll do what I damn well please. Damn nigger's not worth $100. So just forget about him."

The man who had joked about sending Billy up north with the Yankees overheard them and again added his two cents:

"These niggers ain't nothin' but trouble, son. You oughta be glad your dad didn't buy him. He did y'all a favor."

Billy was still in shock, a shock made worse by the shaking he'd received from his father.

"I've had enough. Let's get outta here. I've got work to do," Patrick said.

As Billy followed Patrick back out of the audience area he heard the auctioneer continuing to bark out solicitations for the purchase of those hapless human beings, and he was struck with a sickening feeling in his gut.

Maybe that man was right. Maybe I am an abolitionist; maybe I should go up north.

Why didn't he bid more? It couldn't have been the price because I know he's got the money. Just plain meanness cause he hates negroes? What am I going to tell Becky? She'll be heartbroken.

For the first time in his life, Billy realized just how different he was from his father, and he felt truly grateful for that.

They mounted their horses and rode out past the auction block. The auction was still in full swing. When they got up to the office, someone stuck his head out the door and called to them.

"Say, Mister, that old man that outbid you for chattel number six couldn't come up with the money. So, if you still want him, he's yours." Billy's face lit up and he looked to the heavens. "Let's go get him, Dad," he cried.

Patrick was silent and stone-faced. They went inside and Patrick signed the papers and paid the price. As they rode home Julius and Billy were all smiles. But nobody's smile was brighter than Becky's as she looked out the window and saw Julius behind Billy astride the black mare.

7

Billy was now in his second year of studies at the College of Charleston. He was a very good student, particularly in history and Spanish. As he entered the classroom, he noticed that Professor Chesterton hadn't yet arrived. The course was British/American Political History of the 19th Century. He took a seat in the first row.

"He's late today," said a student sitting behind him. "Must have gotten caught in that thunderstorm."

As Billy sat there waiting for the professor, his mind wandered. *I wonder what she's doing right now, right now as I sit here in this classroom. It's hard to believe that it's going on three years since that night in Havana when I kissed her.*

Billy treasured the letters they exchanged, sometimes several a week, and kept them hidden so Bonny couldn't find them. He wanted desperately to go back to Cuba to see Dolores again and tell her how much he loved her. However, Bonny had forbidden him to set foot on another ship. Additionally, Patrick's slave trade with Cuba had tailed off as don Fernando de Castilla had found additional suppliers.

Of course, he had to admit that after those first few years, his correspondence with Dolores had begun to lag.

Maybe Charlie was right after all. How many times did he tell me that I was a damn fool to sit and pine for a girl I hardly knew, a girl who was so far away, a girl I couldn't touch, couldn't kiss, couldn't make love to?

Charlie had often told Billy to take Constance Beckett in the woods and "just do it."

Well, he can't now say I didn't try, though it wasn't in the woods.

It was Constance's eighteenth birthday party. There was a bevy of beautiful girls from the Joan of Arc Academy where both Constance and Maria del Carmen went to school. There were scores of young men from Charleston College and the Military College, including Charlie Flynn. Constance's parents had arranged a truly gala affair sparing no expense. There were two separate musical groups—one contemporary and the other classical. There were cases of French champagne and uniformed negro waiters popping the corks and filling the glasses. Dinner was a sumptuous fresh brook trout and escargot. And for dessert they served peach ice cream.

Billy was looking for a place to sit and eat his ice cream when Constance appeared, suggesting they go out on the front porch. Her breasts had filled out, her light brown hair was long and lustrous and her hourglass waist was simply alluring. Billy couldn't keep his eyes off her. When most of the guests had left, Constance guided Billy up the stairs to her bedroom. Gone were the images of his sweet Dolores. Gone were his remonstrations of conscience and the warnings of Father Lynch to save himself for his bride. He watched as she closed and locked the door. She led him over to her four-poster canopied bed. Billy wrapped his arms around her and kissed her long and passionately, his hands straying freely over her breasts. He was aroused and breathing hard and so was Constance. They hugged and kissed and explored each other's bodies, moving inexorably closer to the point of no return when suddenly there came a knock on the door.

"Are you in there, Constance?"

Billy slid off the bed fearing the door was about to burst open.

"Yes, father."

"Come down stairs right now. Your mother wants to speak to you."

Fortunately for Billy there was a tree right outside her window, and he shimmied down and fled the scene.

"Good morning, gentlemen," said Professor Chesterton as he walked down the aisle and placed a stack of books and papers on the lectern.

"I apologize for my tardiness, but let's get started."

Billy loved the course and so did everyone else. It was the most popular course in The College of Charleston. Professor Randolph W. Chesterton was a British ex-patriot and a former MP for the district of West London, renowned for his non-conformity, his humor and his classroom antics. His lectures were peppered with snide, sarcastic jabs at the British Empire and its imperialistic designs and pompous condescending manner, all of it delivered in his distinct and sprightly British English. One of his favorite sourcebooks was Edward Lear's *The Book of Nonsense*, which he frequently quoted from, once likening Queen Victoria to a milkmaid...

8

Billy was up in his room studying when he heard the sound of carriage wheels on the gravel outside. He got up, looked out the window, and saw Julius at the reins of a two-horse wagon loaded with lumber. He decided to go down and talk to him.

"What ya got there, Julius?" Billy asked.

"Got some lumba fo yo mama's greenhouse," Julius said.

Bonny had been pestering Patrick for years to build her a greenhouse, and now she was finally going to get it. Julius stepped down from the wagon and walked back to steady some boards that were sliding off.

"That's a big job, Julius. I hope it won't interfere with your lessons." Billy had been teaching Julius the ABCs.

"Don't ya worry. Ain't nothin gonna interfere wid ma lessons, Massa Billy."

Julius had been making good progress, but when Patrick learned of the lessons, he ordered Billy to stop them. Billy disobeyed, and since Patrick was at sea much of the time, it fell to Billy and Bonny to oversee Julius' activities. In truth, Julius needed little if any overseeing. He was a responsible and dependable man who did his work with skill and pride. In the six months since Patrick had purchased Julius at the slave auction, he had replaced the rotten wood in the barn, built another stall for Bonny's new carriage and replaced the wire in the chicken coop. The value of all that certainly exceeded by far the $600 that Patrick had paid for him. Of late, Patrick had told Julius to clear some scrubland for cotton cultivation that bordered the Pringle plantation. Billy knew that Julius had his heart set on building a little house there for him and Becky.

"Did you find a good spot for your little house, Julius?"

"Aah sho did," Massa Billy. Aah jes hopes yo papa gonna let me build it on dat land."

"He's seen all the good work you've done for us here, Julius, so, I'm pretty sure he will."

The two of them continued to unload the wagon, working side by side.

"When ya goin down ta Central Merica like ya told me?" Julius asked.

"Well, I gotta finish college first, but I am gonna ..."

From that first day that Julius rode home with Billy on the back of the black mare, their relationship grew and flourished. Other than Becky, Billy had had no personal experience with negroes. His voyage on *The Wandering Maiden* engendered in him a profound sense of disgust and pity for the way they were mistreated, for the way they were captured and sold like farm animals; for the cruelty and inhumanity of the institution of negro slavery; and for the common presumption of white folk that negroes were something less than human. What Billy had witnessed at *La Dulce Gardenia* in Cuba only strengthened those feelings. So, it didn't require a great leap of faith for Billy to conclude that slavery was an immoral and evil institution. He also came to understand that although Julius and Julius' kind might be illiterate, that did not mean that they lacked intelligence, something that Patrick himself had come to learn, though he wouldn't readily admit it.

The scrubland bordering the Pringle estate, which Patrick had ordered Julius to clear, had to be surveyed. Mister Pringle hired a surveyor who fixed the boundaries, awarding an additional thirty acres to Mister Pringle in the process. Julius witnessed the survery and told Patrick that it was not done properly.

"It look ta me, Massa McHugh, like da man place his instroment on a slight angle so he capture mo dat land fo Massa Pringle."

A second survey was undertaken and the thirty acres in

question were determined to be part of the McHugh's land and Pringle acquiesced.

Julius was well aware of the burning, contentious issue of slavery. Unlike Becky, who attended mass with the McHughs, Julius attended a local Baptist church. One Sunday the preacher's sermon centered on those hallowed and exalted words of the Declaration of Independence—*that all men are created equal*—and Julius later raised the issue with Billy.

"Iffen all mens was created equal, why den we black folk still slaves?"

It was not simply a rhetorical question. It was a real question, serious and grave, and Billy was deeply touched. Sadly, he had no answer. But Julius knew that Billy truly cared for him, and when Billy put his arm around Julius' shoulder, Julius broke down and cried.

"You'll be free some day, Julius. You'll be free," Billy said.

No sooner had the words left his lips, when he too became teary-eyed.

PART II

Spring 1856–Spring 1861

CHAPTER IV

Doña Dolores

A misty rain fell from a somber gray sky as six black horses with red plumes drew the hearse up to the plaza, coming to rest at the entrance to the Main House. The stark presence of the hearse brought home the dark reality of death's appearance at *La Dulce Gardenia*. The two coachmen, dressed in black uniforms with black top hats, stepped down and went to steady the horses. House slaves stood there, some crying openly, others moaning plaintively. Just then, another carriage pulled up. Victorio Arquídez stepped out, walked to the back of the hearse and opened the door, signaling to the house slaves to remove the coffin.

Hundreds of field slaves had gathered on the lawns surrounding the estate. Though not permitted to enter the Main House, they were paying their respect by means of a chant, accented by the slow rhythmic beating of Congo drums. Another carriage pulled up, and Father Ignacio stepped out and made the sign of the cross. With the appearance of the Catholic priest, the field slaves stopped drumming and chanting their *Santería* rituals, invoking instead the names of the saints they had been taught to worship.

The house slaves carried the coffin to the library and placed it on the large, rectangular, mahogany table strung with black bunting. Bouquets of gardenias had been placed throughout the large room, their bittersweet scent evoking the funereal atmosphere of a mortuary. An organ played a somber dirge as the mourners entered. The lid of the ornate coffin was lifted, revealing the lifeless body of doña Teresa de Castilla, who had died suddenly of cholera. It was a virulent and deadly strain that struck unexpectedly in early spring, killing thousands and falling particularly hard on the island's large slave population.

The family was advised that the body had been thoroughly disinfected and posed no danger of contagion. That information was discreetly disseminated to the public mourners as well. The family supplied the morticians with one of doña Teresa's favorite ball gowns and some of her most precious jewelry. But as much as they had endeavored to conceal the telltale signs of death by cholera, they could not hide the sunken eyes, the withered fingers and lips, and the gray, death-like skin. Don Fernando stood by the coffin flanked by his daughters, sons and son in-laws. Don Fernando himself had been stricken with the cholera but had managed to survive. He rested his hand on the arm of doña Teresa, his wife of more than twenty years. He bowed his head, and though he had never been a religious man, he appeared to be praying.

Dolores stood way back in the room inconspicuously. She was now eighteen years of age, having blossomed into a strikingly beautiful young woman, rendered even more so by her humble and sweet nature. Just months before, don Fernando had formally recognized her as his rightful daughter, bestowing upon her the family name, de Castilla and the honorific title doña. The decision had come suddenly, and although Dolores was thrilled with it, she had not yet adjusted to her newfound status or to her relationships with family members, which were still tentative and evolving.

The library was filled to capacity. Late-arriving mourners had to congregate in the hallway and wait their turn to pay their last respects. Father Ignacio offered prayers for the deceased and the living, sprinkling holy water and invoking the Lord to spare the inhabitants of the island of Cuba from any further outbreaks of the dreaded cholera. When he began to eulogize doña Teresa, Sofia broke into tears. Constancia put her arm around her, trying to console her but to no avail. Sofia left the room sobbing and ran up the stairs past Mario Luis. Dolores immediately left the room, struggling through the mourners and running up the stairs to Sofia's room. She knocked on the door but got no answer.

"Sofia, it's me, Dolores. Please open the door."

There was still no answer. Dolores persisted and finally Sofia opened the door. Dolores threw her arms around Sofia, trying to console her. The room was stiflingly hot and Dolores saw that the window was closed and rushed over to open it.

"Don't open it, Dolores," Sofia sobbed. "The miasma from the slave quarters is what killed mamá."

It was unusually hot and humid for this time of the year, and when Dolores spotted Sofia's Spanish fan on the night table, she picked it up and began vigorously fanning her.

"This room is so hot, Sofia. Please come with me to the patio bar. We can sit under the mango trees where the air is fresh and clean."

"I can't bear to walk past the library. It smells of death, and that's not how I want to remember my dear mother."

"We can go out through the kitchen. Come with me, Sofia, please. You'll be more comfortable there," Dolores said, taking Sofia by the hand.

"Mamá is gone! Mamá is gone forever," Sofia sobbed.

"No she's not, dear sister. You'll see her in heaven some day. You must have faith and live the way doña Teresa wanted you to live."

Dolores could not bring herself to refer to doña Teresa as "mamá," certainly not out of disrespect or rancor but because she feared it might offend Sofia who had always been protective of the closeness she shared with her mother.

Dolores led the way down the stairs and through the kitchen to the courtyard. They walked hand-in-hand down the verdant trail to the patio bar. The humidity hung heavy over the tropical vegetation and fat raindrops dripped from the wet palm trees, alternating with the rhythmic sound of chirping crickets. But the air was fresh and it seemed the right prescription because Sofia's crying subsided somewhat.

Two slave women appeared and wiped the chairs. Another appeared with a pot of coffee and silently filled two cups with the thick syrupy liquid.

"In just a few months we'll be going to the United States to begin our university education," Dolores said, trying to steer their conversation away from death and despair to hope and future happiness.

Months before, and just after Don Fernando had formally recognized Dolores as his rightful daughter, he and doña Teresa took the girls to the United States. They visited Mount Holyoke College in Massachusetts, which had been highly recommended by the leading academics in Havana. Applications were filed and the girls both took entrance examinations. They passed them with distinction and were accepted for the freshman class of 1856.

"No, no, we mustn't go. We'll still be in the mourning period. It would be disrespectful. Papá won't allow it…"

Sofia's words trailed off, and once again she cried hard and long.

"That's not true, Sofia. Constancia told me that papá still wants us to go because doña Teresa wanted us to go. She said papá and mamá did not want the yearlong mourning period dressed in black. Papá showed Constancia their joint will, and the language clearly stated that."

"But I don't want to go to the United States to study, Dolores. All my friends are at the University of Havana, and I want to study law."

If Sofia doesn't go, then I won't be able to go. Please dear Lord, don't let me lose this opportunity to study in the United States. Please, I beg you.

Don Fernando's middle daughter, Sofia, had also undergone considerable change and development but not in the same way as her half-sister, Dolores. She had not ripened physically. She was still the pert little shorthaired girl without the curves, the girl whom young men might befriend but would not want to court. Sofia's change had come as a ripening maturity, intelligence and strong and growing interest in politics and social causes. She had become a strong advocate of Cuban independence from Spain and wanted to join the student movement at the University of Havana. Fortunately for Dolores, don Fernando insisted that Sofia attend Mount Holyoke as planned. Sofia argued long and hard but finally acquiesced, agreeing to obey her father.

2

It was a delightful late-spring morning and the melodic trill of the *tregon*, Cuba's national bird, filled the air around the Main House. Suddenly, a large male alighted on the red tile roof outside Dolores's window. He fluffed up his pretty red and white breast feathers, then pecked at an insect trapped between the tiles. Dolores went quietly closer to the window, attempting to mimic its call, but the bird flew off.

"Oh, *tregoncito*, don't fly away." There was a knock on the door. "Come in." It was Mario Luis.

"A letter for you, señorita, from the United States."

Mario Luis was well aware that don Fernando had recognized Dolores as his rightful daughter and that her status in the family had changed, but he was not yet used to addressing her as *doña Dolores*.

"Oh, let me see. Gracias, Mario Luis."

"*De nada, señorita.*"

Dolores immediately recognized Billy McHugh's handwriting. She hadn't heard from him in quite some time and hoped that he had not forgotten about her. She reached for the silver letter opener given to her by don Eduardo de Cadiz, the son of don Antonio de Cadiz, the *alcalde* (mayor) of Havana. Dolores smiled to herself and opened the letter, noticing the San Francisco, California postmark.

Querida Dolores,

Please forgive my long delay in writing. I'm in California. I came here like thousands of others in the hope of striking it rich. My high school friend, Charlie Flynn, has been here for quite some time and he convinced me to come out and try my luck at prospecting, which he described as the fastest way he knew to make a dollar. Though reluctant at first, the more I read about the California gold strike the more I was convinced that Charlie was right. I had great difficulty convincing my parents, especially my mother, who was against my dropping out of college after only one year. Finally, I decided I just had to go. So I packed my bags and sailed aboard one of those new steamers to Rio de Janeiro, Brazil. From there we sailed around the Cape, stopping in Cartagena, Colombia and then went on to California. I think

I made the right choice to come by ship rather than by land across the continental US as I've heard that Indian raids and accidents have caused much death and destruction. I still think of you often, Dolores, and treasure the memory of those precious days together in Havana. I would greatly hope that we could see each other again in the future.

Here is my new address: William C. McHugh, c/o The Wells Fargo House, 49 Wells Fargo Street, Coloma, California.

Cariñosamente,
Billy

The door opened and Beatriz entered with a limp. Though strictly forbidden to enter the Main House, she often disobeyed when the Master was gone. Dolores was accustomed to her mother entering without knocking and wasn't surprised to see her.

"How are you feeling today, Mamá?" Dolores asked.

Beatriz sat down on the bed without responding.

"What's that letter you have there? Is it from don Eduardo?"

"No, Mamá. It's from my American friend. You remember Billy McHugh from Charleston, South Carolina? He was here a few years ago with his father."

Beatriz frowned, then got up and went over to Dolores's dressing table, where she saw a stack of letters tied with a red ribbon.

"You never told me that you had a serious correspondence with him. He is just a boy, Felicidad. Don Eduardo is a man, a wealthy and prominent man, and I want you to pay him more respect and attention. Do you hear me?"

In spite of Dolores's constant pleas, Beatriz still refused to call her daughter *Dolores*.

"He is no longer a boy, mamá. He's at least a year older than I am."

Beatriz grabbed the letter out of Dolores's hand, but when she saw that it was written in English, she tossed it against the mirror on the dressing table.

"In comparison with don Eduardo de Cadiz, he is nothing more than a boy. I remember how he stood by and did nothing as those bloodhounds tore poor old Bartholomew to shreds. I also remember that his father was a slave trader. That should be reason enough not to get involved with him. Use your head, Felicidad! Every girl in Havana would give anything to be courted by don Eduardo de Cadiz. And you remain aloof, denying him the respect and affection that he deserves."

Dolores had met don Eduardo de Cadiz at a *tertulia* sponsored by *Nuestra Señora de Caridad*, a religious and social group founded by Father Ignacio. Don Eduardo had learned that the family had dispensed with the traditional mourning period after doña Teresa's death, and he sought and received permission from don Fernando to call upon Dolores. He began showing up weekly at *La Dulce Gardenia*. Dolores was reluctant to receive him and if given the chance would gladly have used the excuse of the mourning period to avoid him. But both don Fernando and Beatriz insisted that Dolores receive him, and she finally acquiesced. He was, after all, said Beatriz, "the most eligible and desirable *caballero* in all of Havana."

Don Eduardo came calling with exquisite bouquets of flowers, imported bon-bons, and books of poetry. Dolores was flattered, but despite his wealth and position, she didn't return his affection.

"Mamá, I told you many times that I'm not yet ready to be courted. I first want to complete my education, and now that papá has agreed to send me to the United States..."

Beatriz grimaced, interrupting her daughter and bursting into tears.

"And what about your poor sick mother? I have terrible pain every day and can hardly walk, Felicidad. What am I supposed to do while you're away in the United States? I will be all alone."

Dolores rushed over to the bed and put her arm around her mother.

"Mamá, you know how much I love you, and I will do everything I can to care for you and help you. But I cannot pass up this opportunity. Panchita will look after you, and papá will see that your needs are met."

Beatriz grimaced upon hearing Dolores refer to don Fernando as "papá"

"And I will be home every summer to be with you."

"Will you at least promise me that you will forget about this young American and pay more attention to don Eduardo?"

"The American is in California now, mamá, but it doesn't matter because as I've already told you, I don't want to be courted at this time, not by Billy McHugh, not by don Eduardo, not by anyone. I am going to pursue my education, mamá. I must not lose this opportunity."

Dolores looked at her mother, feeling both love and pity. She knew that it had been hard for her mother. But she believed that her mother would eventually accept the fact that her daughter's life had changed now that don Fernando had recognized her as his rightful daughter. Dolores was now able to mix and talk with the guests at the spring parties. She was more confident and relaxed. She could ask the house slaves now to help her with her hair, prepare her clothes, and help her dress without feeling undeserving. She was no longer simply Dolores; she was doña Dolores de Castilla, a recognized member of the family. Of course there were still those who said that she would never be accepted into the higher ranks of Havana society because of her *sangre de negro*. There were the whispers that don Eduardo would take her for his mistress but not for his wife.

3

It was a bright sunny day and the first Saturday in June, the day that Don Fernando had commissioned the esteemed Spanish artist, Francisco de Aragón, to begin work on Dolores's portrait. A year before, he had painted Constancia's and Sofia's portraits, and they were proudly hung on the spiral staircase beneath the large crystal chandelier. Everyone who saw them agreed that the artist had captured the essence of the two girls down to the last detail. Many of the house slaves were surprised that don Fernando had recognized Dolores as his rightful daughter. But as for her portrait, some thought he was going a little bit too far and were heard to whisper:

"Just imagine commissioning that famous artist to paint the portrait of the daughter of a mulatto slave." Even doña Teresa, had she been alive, may have had second thoughts.

The artist arrived and had breakfast with the family, after which he was escorted upstairs to the *sala de té*. The sala opened through a set of French doors to a spacious terrace filled with gardenias and other flowering plants. While the artist set up his pallet and other equipment, Dolores went to her room to prepare herself. She was accompanied by Constancia, Sofia and Carmen, the upstairs house slave. Moments later there was a knock on the door and Soledad and Daisy entered the room. Carmen was making some last minute adjustments to Dolores's gown, which was of light blue taffeta. It was cut quite low in the neckline and revealed her lovely full bosom.

"There, that's good," said Carmen, standing up and reaching for the hairbrush. "Now we do the hair."

Carmen ran the brush through Dolores's long, dark locks, each stroke bringing out more body and luster.

"Someone go and get a gardenia for her hair," Sofia said, smiling and touching Dolores's beautiful hair.

"I'll go," said Soledad.

She rushed out of the room, returning moments later with a large specimen. Carmen carefully placed it in Dolores's hair for the final touch.

"Here, I brought the necklace," said Daisy, handing it to Dolores.

"Oh, it's so precious," said Dolores. "I have never seen anything so beautiful."

It was a sapphire and diamond necklace set in gold. "Are you sure it's all right that I wear it?"

"Yes, of course, Dolores," said Sofia. "Mamá let me wear her emerald necklace for my portrait, and she would have wanted nothing less for you."

Dolores handed the necklace to Carmen who smiled and fingered the magnificent piece, before putting it around Dolores's neck and fastening the clasp.

Someone knocked on the door. It was Mario Luis, who announced that the artist was ready to begin.

"She needs her slippers," said Sofia. "Where are they?"

"Here they are. I have them," said Carmen."

Dolores slipped her feet into them and stood up.

"Not yet, child. We still need to fix you a little more."

Carmen reached for the rouge and applied a touch to Dolores's cheeks. Finally, she applied lip rouge and added a few more strokes with the hairbrush for the finishing touch.

"Now, dear child, now you are ready."

Dolores looked at herself in the mirror and smiled with delight. Then she closed her eyes and made the sign of the cross, thanking God for all her good fortune.

Francisco de Aragón was a little man in his fifties with a full beard and an imperious air about him. Once in front of his easel, however, he seemed almost elf-like, gesticulating with his brush in one hand and the pallet in the other.

"Take a position several paces in front of me, señorita. Yes, that's fine," said Francisco.

He put on his spectacles, and as the eye of the artist fell upon her, he almost gasped: the perfectly proportioned female figure, the delicate complexion with just the right mix of pigment, reflecting the lushness and passion of the tropics. Dolores felt suddenly uncomfortable being scrutinized so closely and shyly looked away. Francisco clapped his hands, directing her to fix her gaze upon him and to hold it. Focusing now on her eyes, big brown and expressive with long lashes, and then on her long, lustrous dark brown hair draped over her elegant neck and shoulders, and finally on her slightly pouty, sensual and alluring lips. He had to conclude that she was the most beautiful woman he had ever painted. And though he was a man well past his physical capability, she aroused in him a longing, a passion that he'd thought had long since abandoned him.

"Must I stand perfectly still?" Dolores asked.

"No, señorita. Just try not to move too abruptly."

Felipe de Castilla, the younger son of don Fernando, stood at the window in his living quarters. The shades were drawn and he was alone as his wife, Soledad, had taken their little boy to visit the De Wolf children on the neighboring plantation. Felipe's living quarters were one level above the terrace and set back from it some ten meters. Felipe moved the window shade ever so slightly and picked up the spyglass, fixing it on Dolores's well-developed breasts as revealed by the plunging neckline of her elegant blue gown. He adjusted the range and focus. Oh, how she excited him! He had watched her closely from the moment of her pubescence when those first few buds of her breasts had begun to sprout, then blossom. He'd witnessed how her schoolgirl body had begun to develop those lovely sensual curves, the rounded hips and the beautiful buttocks, culminating in a beautiful young maiden of the tropics.

But she's your sister. She's forbidden fruit?

However, he had noticed that his passion for her had only grown since learning that they were half-brother and sister. Indeed, he could feel his passion rising as a result of that thought, and he moved his hand down to appease it. Suddenly, the door opened, startling him, and the spyglass fell to the floor with a bang.

"Oh, don Felipe! I thought you went to the De Wolfs' with doña Soledad, and I wanted to clean the apartment."

Felipe looked at Carmen crossly.

"Get out, Carmen. I don't wish to be disturbed." Carmen hesitated. "Did you hear me? Get out!"

"As you wish, don Felipe."

His lascivious spell broken, Felipe raised the shade and stared down directly at Dolores.

I wonder whether that cabrón don Eduardo has ever touched her. No, I'm ssure she is still a virgin, but I am just as sure that he has been trying his best to deflower her.

4

It was mid-afternoon, and the de Castilla family members were in their living quarters for their customary siesta. Dolores lay on her bed resting, when she heard a faint knock on the door.

"Doña Dolores, don Eduardo has arrived. He is waiting for you in the *sala de té*."

Dolores got out of bed, went over to her dressing table and picked up her hairbrush.

"Thank you, Mario Luis. Tell him that I will be there shortly, and tell Carmen to come to my room, please."

Carmen arrived and began helping Dolores dress. Though Carmen was no doubt a slave and a very black one at that, Dolores treated her like a friend. She confided in her and trusted her judgment. It was only somewhat recently that Dolores felt comfortable enough to seek out Carmen's services. Carmen minded not at all, in fact she favored serving Dolores over other family members. Dolores was kind and considerate to her and to all the other slaves on the plantation. Her attitude toward them had not changed because of her newfound status at *La Dulce Gardenia*.

"Carmen, what do you think of don Eduardo de Cadiz?"

"Well, Doloresita, he is, of course, the son of the mayor of Havana."

"Yes, but what do you think of him as a person, as a man?"

Carmen helped Dolores pull the dress over her head and shoulders and then smoothed out the folds of material in back.

"Well, Dolores, I'm in no position to judge his character. I see him only when he comes here to call on you." Carmen smiled shyly and began brushing Dolores's hair.

"Yes, but everyone says that you are able to read a face and divine a heart, and that's why I am asking you."

"Would that that were so," said Carmen

Carmen picked up the hairbrush and began brushing Dolores's hair until it glistened like the sun on a rippling sea.

"Your hair is so beautiful, Dolores."

"Thank you, Carmencita. It's your brushing that does it."

Carmen picked up the bottle of cologne now and for the finishing touch, sprayed a fine mist on Dolores's neck and shoulders.

"And could you make some tea and bring it to the *sala de té?*"

"Sí, doña Dolores, right away."

Dolores watched as Carmen walked out of the room, wondering why she was so reticent about rendering an opinion of don Eduardo. Dolores then put on her black silk slippers, and promising herself that she would be receptive and attentive to don Eduardo, made her way to the *sala de té.*

"Buenas tardes, señorita, how lovely you look!" Don Eduardo reached out, took her hand and kissed it with great relish.

"Buenas tardes! Why, don Eduardo, you look so different in your military uniform! This is the first time I've seen you wearing it."

Don Eduardo de Cadiz was a man in his late twenties and tall like his father, the *alcalde* of Havana, but of heavier build. He had a rather round face and was clean-shaven with a prematurely receding hairline. Dressed in the gold and crimson uniform of the Queen's Guard, he wore black polished boots and held his three-cornered hat in his hand. Slung at his side was a long shiny sword. He looked every bit the model of the dashing, young military officer.

"Does my appearance please you, señorita?" he asked, smiling and waiting for Dolores to be seated, after which he lifted his sword and took a seat on the divan adjacent to her armchair.

"Yes, don Eduardo, but I hardly recognized you."

He is trying to impress me. And that heavy uniform he's wearing would be more appropriate for Spain, rather than the tropical island of Cuba.

"I came here directly after leaving the *Plaza de Armas*, and before that I was at the Captain General's residence. I have been in uniform all day."

"Oh, and what were you doing at the *Plaza de Armas*, if I may ask?"

Before don Eduardo was able to answer, Carmen entered with the tea. Don Eduardo glanced at her, a look of annoyance on his face at the intrusion. Carmen placed the tea on the table without pouring it and beat a hasty retreat.

"Doesn't she know by now that I don't drink tea?"

"I asked her to bring it, don Eduardo."

"Well, never mind. You asked what I was doing at the *Plaza de Armas*, Doloresita. I am not sure that you would really like to know." She winced at his rendering of her name in the diminutive, affectionate form. It was the first time that he had ever used it and it did not please her.

"Yes, I'd like to know, provided you wish to tell me."

"Well, we had three executions today by garroting, and I officiated at them. You may have read about it in *El Diario de la Habana*. These were the last of Narciso López's co-conspirators. We had been searching for them for years. They were condemned to be hanged, but their lawyers appealed to the Captain General, José de la Concha, and he granted them an appeal of mercy. Garroting is a much more humane form of execution. It's quick and…"

"Oh please, don Eduardo, I don't want to hear any more."

"As you wish, Dolores. That is why I asked if you really wanted to know. Let me talk about something which I'm sure will be more to your liking, Doloresita." He smiled, and she thought she saw him glance at her breasts. "There was a gala ball last Sunday at the Palace of the Captain General. I had mentioned it to you a few weeks back, hoping that you would do me the honor and accompany me. Well, it was simply marvelous. The Captain General made a surprise appearance along with his charming wife, the *Contesa de Zaragoza*…"

Dolores sipped her tea and tried to listen politely but her

thoughts wandered away. She wondered what it was about don Eduardo that she did not like, but couldn't quite put her finger on it.

He wasn't bad looking after all. He was white, upper class and wealthy, everything that mamá admired. But what really bothers me about him is his family's wealth and power, his aristocratic status and his condescending manner toward those he deems beneath him.

It was a painful paradox, because Dolores was now a legitimate member of the wealthy and aristocratic de Castilla family, freely partaking of the status, prestige and benefits that it offered.

"...Fortunately, Doloresita, there will be another gala ball next week, and I would be delighted if you would accompany me."

5

Goaded by Beatriz's insistence and having learned that Sofia would also be attending, Dolores accepted Don Eduardo's invitation to the Military Ball. At first she had little enthusiasm, and her natural shyness caused some anxiety. But as Saturday approached she felt a growing sense of anticipation and excitement. There were necessary but not unpleasant preparations to be completed, including the final touches to the stunning green gown that Carmen had made for her. There was also the selection of dancing shoes, and she had to arrange her hair and decide what jewelry to wear. Dolores was not, as her mother Beatriz would have wished, wondering how best to please don Eduardo but rather how best to present herself in general. This was to be her first formal appearance after all, her debut into white, upper-class Havana society. Sofia had arranged for them to spend the night at her friend's house in Havana, which was not too distant from the Government Palace where the ball was to be held.

Mario Luis peeked into the room.

"The carriage has arrived doña Dolores, and the driver is waiting for you and doña Sofia." Mario Luis had now adopted the new form of address for Dolores.

"Thank you, Mario Luis. I am almost ready." Dolores felt her heart skip a beat and her expression must have conveyed her angst, because Carmen noticed.

"Don't worry, Doloresita, you will be the most beautiful señorita there. Of that I have no doubt."

"But I'm not a good dancer, Carmencita. I haven't learned the new French and English dances, which I've heard so much about."

"My friend, Pablo, serves at the Palace. He worked at the last ball, and he's a very good dancer. He told me that the orchestra plays mostly waltzes and contra-steps. You will do fine Doloresita."

Carmen finished brushing Dolores's hair, then fixed within it a delicate pink and red orchid.

"Now, take a good look at yourself."

Dolores got up from the dressing table and walked over to the floor-length mirror.

"You see, how beautiful?"

Dolores simply had to agree, and she turned now, put her arms around Carmen and kissed her on the lips.

"I just love the gown, Carmencita! You're a master seamstress!"

It was of green silk, adorned with flounces and with delicate white lace around the sleeves and the neckline. Suddenly, Beatriz burst into the room.

"Hurry, Felicidad, or you will be late! The carriage is waiting for you downstairs. Hurry!" As Dolores rushed out of her room, Beatriz asked, "Where did you get that sapphire necklace?"

"It belonged to doña Teresa, and now it is Sofia's. She gave it to me to wear tonight."

Dolores knew that her mother was proud of her and perhaps

even a little envious. And when Dolores walked down the staircase, she captured the admiration and the applause of the entire upstairs crew of house slaves led by Carmen and Mario Luis. When she reached the bottom she turned, smiled, and waved appreciatively.

The driver, dressed in red waistcoat, black trousers and top hat, helped Dolores into the handsome carriage with red velvet seats. Sofia had arrived first and greeted Dolores with a smile and a pat on the shoulder.

"Do you smell that?" Sofia asked. The inside of the carriage had the sweet smell of spring flowers.

"Yes, it's wonderful," said Dolores as she arranged the material of her long flowing evening gown within the confines of the carriage.

Sofia looked surprisingly pretty in an exquisite blue gown. She was invited to the Ball by a brilliant law student in his final year at the University of Havana. Sofia said that he was being primed by the Chief Advisor to the Captain General for an entry position on the Palace advisory staff.

"Don Eduardo must think very highly of you to provide this beautiful carriage," said Sofia. The driver asked if they were ready and they gave him the signal to depart.

"Yes, but you know how I feel about him, Sofia. He's so proud and arrogant that I find it hard to feel any warmth for him."

"That might change in time and as you get to know him better. He is after all quite good looking; not as handsome as Billy McHugh, but certainly he comes from a better and wealthier family. And of course he has political connections that go all the way up to the Captain General."

Dolores was surprised to hear Sofia refer to Billy McHugh whom they hadn't talked about in quite some time.

The carriage hit a rut in the road and both girls were tossed about.

"How is Billy McHugh these days? Are you still writing to him?"

Dolores wondered if Sofia was still jealous that Billy had chosen to write to her.

"Our correspondence has lagged, Sofia, but the last I heard he was in California, seeking his fortune."

"And has he found it? Sofia asked, with a slight tone of sarcasm.

Dolores also wondered whether Sofia had been speaking with Beatriz or maybe even to don Eduardo, asking perhaps Sofia to speak in his favor.

"I wonder what Billy McHugh looks like now? I remember the first time I saw him. I thought he was the most beautiful boy in the world. How long has it been now since we saw him?"

"About four years," said Dolores.

"Then he's now a young man and must be devilishly handsome. You should ask him to send you one of those new daguerreotype images."

They arrived at the railroad depot and boarded the train. The Saturday evening train was much faster than the weekday trains making no stops and carrying only passengers. Slaves and supplies were hauled only during the week. And before they knew it, they were pulling into the Havana station. Waiting for them with another fine-looking carriage was don Eduardo de Cadiz, clothed in his brilliant red and black dress uniform, complete with black sash, three-cornered hat and sword.

"*Muy buenas tardes, señoritas.* How lovely you both look."

He bowed, reaching for Dolores's hand, kissing it with great relish. Next it was Sofia's turn and he kissed her hand but without the same flair. Don Eduardo helped them into the carriage and they departed for the Government Palace.

It was a cool and delightful moonlit night and as the carriage passed by Havana's *malecón,* the moonlight sparkled on the calm water of the harbor. Palm trees swayed in the background from a gentle breeze, lending clear evidence to the tales of the tropical paradise, which thousands of African slaves had been told they would find in their new home on the island of Cuba.

Don Eduardo, however, was not looking out the window at the local scenery. He could not keep his eyes off Dolores, and her close proximity in the carriage necessarily resulted in their coming in contact whenever the carriage hit a rough spot on the ancient cobblestone streets, all to the enhancement of his sensual delight.

The carriage turned up the entranceway to the Palace, passing majestic Royal Palms lining the roadway. There was an overflow of parked carriages from the adjacent plazas heralding a full house for the Military Ball. They pulled up to the security gate, where in spite of don Eduardo's dress uniform, two military guards carefully checked his formal invitation and looked into the carriage.

"...Yes, doña Sofia," said don Eduardo, "They have tightened security here just recently. In fact, there were rumors that the Captain General's life was threatened recently by an unknown group of so-called 'freedom fighters.'"

Sofia had heard the same rumors but in much greater detail from her friends at the University of Havana.

The guards waved them through and the driver dropped them off at the front entrance to the Palace. They made their way through to the final security check at the entrance to the ballroom. As they waited in line, other officers similarly dressed in their black and red uniforms greeted don Eduardo. At first, he appeared reluctant to introduce the two girls but was soon forced to by the dictates of common courtesy. It was easy to see that his fellow officers were dazzled by the stunning beauty and mystery of the beautiful yet unknown senorita.

Don Eduardo introduced her as "doña Dolores de Castilla,

the daughter of the renowned sugar cane planter, don Fernando de Castilla."

Dolores curtsied shyly but properly, experiencing a rising nervousness and excitement.

Don Eduardo introduced Sofia de Castilla accordingly, but she appeared somewhat indifferent to it all, accustomed to being amongst the upper classes of society. It was only after they passed through the security check and entered the ballroom that Sofia came to life. She saw her law student friend---a studious-looking young man whose chin bore the early signs of a beard that had not fully sprouted. Sofia introduced him as Carlos Santiago, the son of don Pablo Santiago, a wealthy maritime merchant and shipbroker.

The Palace ballroom was simply magnificent, majestic in its size and setting. The floor was a silvery-gray Italian marble, partially covered at the entranceway with beautiful oriental carpets shimmering from the light of a line of massive crystal chandeliers overhead. Works by Spain's renowned artists, including El Greco and Velásquez, hung from the walls. High above it all was an atrium-like ceiling of stained glass employing strategically placed gaslights to reflect colorful beams of light throughout the ballroom.

The Captain General himself, His Excellency, don José Gutierrez de la Concha, initiated the festivities with a short welcoming speech, after which the all-black orchestra opened with a lively waltz.

Don Eduardo took Dolores by the hand and walked her on to the dance floor, overhearing as they went: "Who is that striking beauty with don Eduardo de Cadiz?"

Since the first dance attracted only a few couples, Dolores was acutely aware of the many eyes focused upon them. She felt nervous, self-conscious, and uncomfortable being the object of so much attention. When the dance ended, they walked off the floor and joined a group of military officers and their female companions. That was when His Excellency, the Captain General himself, approached and greeted don Eduardo.

"Good evening, don Eduardo. It was good to see you on the dance floor. And who, may I ask is your lovely partner?"

"Good evening, Your Excellency, allow me to present doña Dolores de Castilla, the daughter of don Fernando de Castilla, whom I'm sure you have met." Dolores curtsied and smiled shyly, her nervousness affecting her otherwise lovely natural smile. As the Captain General spoke to don Eduardo, his eyes inevitably strayed more than once to the lovely Dolores.

"Yes, certainly, I've met don Fernando. He's come to the Palace on several occasions and we had some talks. He's a hunter, as I recall, and I am as well. But, tell me, don Eduardo, I was looking for your father, our honorable mayor, is he here tonight?"

"No, Your Excellency, my father was not able to attend…"

Having seen the Captain General conversing on the side of the dance floor, a crowd of people had begun to form around him with the intent, no doubt, of being seen with him and perhaps even joining the discussion. At this point, two extraordinary and shocking events unfolded. Don Ramón Rodriguez, the Count of Calais, a wealthy and aristocratic member of Havana society, and said to be one of the five most handsome and dashing *caballeros* in Havana, approached the group around the Captain General. Smiling broadly and without saying a word, he grasped Dolores's hand and swept her out to the dance floor as the orchestra struck up a traditional Cuban contra step. Don Eduardo's face flushed, and his eyes filled with rage as he realized what had happened. Apparently, he decided that it would be unwise to confront the Count in front of the Captain General, so he looked away, attempting to hide his outrage. The Count meanwhile guided Dolores into the line of contra-step dancers. He was a polished dancer, and although Dolores was in a state of shock and inhibited by her shyness, she moved about as best she could following the Count's lead.

Within moments of the Count's brazen act, an even more shocking event played out. Sofia and her law student friend, Carlos Santiago, were making their way through the throng toward the Captain General. Sofia got trapped by the crowd, but Carlos continued and gradually made his way up to His Excellency. He stopped and smiled, looking as though he was about to say something. Then, he reached down into his billowy trousers, pulled out a dagger and lunged at the Captain General, shouting, "*Cuba Libre Independiente o la Muerte!*" (A Free and Independent Cuba or Death.) Women screamed, the orchestra went silent and mayhem ensued. His Excellency grimaced, while an alert officer standing nearby grabbed the arm of the would-be assassin and arrested the path of the dagger within a hare's breath of the Captain General's chest; receiving for his heroic effort a nasty gash on his right forearm. Several Palace Guard officers nearby wrestled young Carlos to the ground and pummeled him with blows to the face and body. That's when another cry rang out: "*Viva la Madre Patria!*" (Long live the Mother Country--Spain). Carlos Santiago was carried away on a stretcher unconscious, and the ballroom guests were rapidly disbursed by the Palace Guard.

In spite of the chaos and confusion of the assassination attempt, Don Eduardo was still seething with anger for the affront he had suffered at the hands of the Count of Calais. Don Eduardo sent Dolores and Sofia off in his carriage and then sought out the Count. He found him in his carriage across from the entrance to the Palace, surrounded by his usual entourage of bodyguards and admirers. Don Eduardo shoved his way up to the carriage, threw open the door, and unleashed a torrent of curses and insults at the Count.

"How dare you dance with my *novia* without my permission!" he shouted, drawing his sword. Several of the Count's men attempted to hold him back, but he flung them out of the way and thrust his sword into the carriage just inches from the Count's belly, challenging him to a duel. The Count's bodyguards were eventually able to get the upper hand and pushed don Eduardo away from the Count's carriage, whereupon the Count shouted:

"I suggest you speak with the lovely señorita, because she was perfectly willing and pleased to accept my invitation to dance."

The words only increased don Eduardo's anger, and he cursed the Count and pushed his way back up to the carriage door.

"Put that sword away or we'll call the police," shouted one of the Count's companions.

An angry, scornful smile appeared on don Eduardo's face.

"I'm challenging this scoundrel to a duel. If he's too cowardly to accept, then he best prepare to defend himself right here and now." The Count tried again to diffuse the situation.

"There is no justification for a duel. This is simply a misunderstanding. Again, I ask that you speak with the señorita. Besides, I'm not a swordsman."

"Oh, so you're not a swordsman, are you? Well, then you choose the weapon cabrón or I swear on my honor that I will not let this affront go unanswered."

The Count now fully realized the seriousness of the matter and fashioned words bordering on an outright apology. But it was to no avail, for don Eduardo would not relent, insisting that a duel was the only way to settle the matter and assuage his honor.

"All right then, dueling pistols, but you're making a mistake, this whole thing is nothing more than a terrible misunderstanding, I tell you." Hearing that, don Eduardo finally sheathed his sword.

At the first light of dawn, they mounted the hills surrounding

Havana, and don Eduardo prepared to settle the score with dueling pistols at twenty paces. *El Diario de la Habana* reported the story on its front page, second only in importance to the attempted assassination of His Excellency, the Captain General, Don José Gutierrez de la Concha.

Dance at Military Ball Results in Duel

Yesterday at dawn two of Havana's most celebrated personages participated in a duel in the hills of Havana. The incident arose when, reportedly, don Ramón Rodriguez, the Count of Calais, danced with the beautiful young señorita accompanying don Eduardo de Cadiz, the son of the mayor of Havana. The weapon chosen was dueling pistols at 20 paces. Don Eduardo was shot in the chest and taken to the Holy Sacrament Hospital in serious condition. Don Ramón Rodriguez escaped without injury and attributed the entire incident to a misunderstanding.

CHAPTER V

Billy Studies Law

Billy followed Charlie Flynn though the swinging doors of the Sundowner Saloon in Coloma, California. It was late afternoon on a Saturday, and the place was packed. The old man at the piano belted out one of his usual honky-tonk tunes. When he saw the two young men, he nodded, causing a long gray ash to drop off his cigar and fall on the keyboard.

As Charlie and Billy walked up to the bar, the barroom women eyed them but didn't get up from their tables, guessing that they did not have enough gold to make it worth their while. The bartender, a rotund, jolly-looking fellow with a handlebar mustache, edged over toward them, smiled, and wiped the bar with a damp rag.

"What'll it be, gents?"

"Two whiskeys," Charlie said.

"How you boys payin' today?"

Charlie reached down in his soiled denim trousers and pulled out a small leather pouch.

The bartender nodded his head, grinned, and watched as Charlie opened the pouch, stuck his thumb and forefinger in and took out a pinch of gold dust, letting it fall back into the pouch in a fine glittering stream.

"That'll do just fine, but I do the pinchin'," said the bartender

"Your thumb and fingers are a heck-of-a-lot bigger than his," Billy protested.

"I've told you boys before that if you want to avoid all this hassling about who does the pinchin', you can go on over to the assayer's shop and exchange your gold dust for some gold coin, some specie. That'll make things a whole lot easier for you and for me. Now, do you want the whiskey or don't ya?"

"Pour it," Charlie said.

He did, and Charlie drained the glass in one swallow.

"You know, Charlie, half of that gold dust belongs to me, and we both know that you drink faster and spend more than I do."

"All right, so I owe ya a few pinches, agreed?"

Charlie grinned sheepishly at Billy. Later that night as they were walking back to the boarding house:

"You know, Charlie, I've had about enough of this California gold prospecting. So, just give me my share of the remaining gold dust. At least it will cover some of the cost to get me back east."

"Now, wait just a minute, partner. I know it's not been easy for you. It sure as hell hasn't been easy for me. But I told you about my Yellow Creek claim. We're not gonna continue pannin' for gold, partner. Yellow Creek's got gold ore, the real stuff. Stick with me and I'll give you a fifty percent cut. We just gotta let my lawyer sort out a few legal problems."

"Lawyers don't work for nothing, Charlie. How are you going to pay him?"

"Don't worry, we'll work it out. Just give it another year, and we could be goin' back to Charleston as millionaires."

"I've already been here goin' on a year with little to show for it," Billy said.

"Come on, partner, I'll make it worth your while."

"I'll think about it, but only if you promise to start conserving what little funds we have. That means less drinking and less women. You hear me, 'partner'?"

Billy did think about it. He thought so hard that he slept little that night. The next morning they visited Charlie's lawyer, Gilberto García.

"Good morning, Gilberto. This is my partner, Billy McHugh. He's also from Charleston, and speaks some Spanish."

The young lawyer smiled and shook Billy's hand with a firm grip.

"I was going to write you a letter," said Gilberto, "but it's better that you stopped by, Charlie. Please have a seat. I have some new information on your claim."

Billy noticed the lawyer's slight Spanish accent.

"Remember I told you that the main point in dispute between you and this fellow, Barney Stokes, is whether he actually abandoned the Yellow Creek claim?" Gilberto reached back on his desk and picked up a book. "This is the *Tribunal General de Minería* enacted by the Santa Ana administration in 1854, and later adopted by the California legislature."

"*Con permiso, Gilberto, puedo verlo, por favor?*" (Excuse me Gilberto, may I see it please?).

"My, your Spanish sounds quite good, Billy. Where did you learn it?"

"Mostly in Cuba, Gilberto, but I also spent a lot of time in Charleston studying Spanish."

Billy flipped open the book at random and began reading, discovering to his delight that he was able to understand much of it.

"Now, under the *Tribunal General* and the rules adopted by most of the miners in this area, you are required to work your claim. If you don't work it, you lose it. This fellow, Stokes, maintains that he never abandoned the claim. He alleges that he placed a stake at the site and that somebody unlawfully dug it up, which constituted claim jumping."

"I dug up his stake and threw it in the deepest part of Yellow Creek," Charlie said. "He hadn't worked the claim, and just like you said, if you don't work your claim, you lose it."

Billy handed the law book back to Gilberto and sat there listening. It occurred to him that Charlie's venture was even riskier than he had originally thought. Not only was there the risk of actually discovering gold, but there was the additional risk of securing a valid legal claim.

"Did you put your own stake in the ground there?" Gilberto asked.

"I sure did, and I registered my claim right down here on Main Street, just like you advised me to do, Gilberto."

The young lawyer paused for a second or two, then asked:

"All right, but did you create any evidence to show that you were working it?"

"Like I told you before, Gilberto, this Yellow Creek claim is for quartz gold mining. We're talkin' bout finding a mother lode of gold ore. I don't have the money now that it's gonna require, but I'm gonna raise it."

"All right, Charlie, but you need to go up there as soon as possible and do something to prove that you have begun working it. Maybe use a pick and shovel and take some rock samples."

"That's exactly what I'm plannin' on doin'. In fact, Billy and me are headin' up to Yellow Creek as soon as we leave your office."

2

They set out along the south fork of the American River, spending the better part of that first day to reach the rugged foothills of the Sierra Nevada. They stopped at dusk, set up their tent, and built a fire, eating a supper of beans, bacon, and hardtack. They drank a little whiskey, put some more branches on the fire, and settled in for the night. Billy had some difficulty falling asleep and felt the need to talk.

"How long have you known that lawyer, Charlie?"

"Did ya have to start talkin' just when I was gonna drift off? Why do you ask?"

"I don't know. I was thinking that he's probably got a good thing going for him here. I mean, he's not got a lot of investment like these storekeepers, selling shovels and pans and tents. He's got his education and his training, and he's selling his knowledge and his time."

"Oh, so now you wanna be a lawyer? What ever happened to that banana business you were plannin' to start in Central America? Isn't that why you agreed to come out here in the first place?"

"Yeah, I wanted to raise some quick money. You said it would be easy. So far, I'd say you were dead wrong. Do you really believe that we have a chance of striking it rich?"

"You mean to say you doubt it? Of course, we have a chance. Why the hell d'ya think I came all the way out here? Why do you think I talked you into comin' out?"

"I've been asking myself that same question, Charlie. I could understand it better if we had come out right after the big strike in 1848 and 49. But hell, by now all the easy gold's been found."

"Ya gotta have patience, partner. It'll come, you'll see. And as for you becomin' a lawyer like Gilberto, forget it. You're too honest, and besides you ain't got the education."

"I could get it, couldn't I? Ever hear of Abraham Lincoln? He got it, didn't he? He's a lawyer and a damn good one from what I hear. And he's self taught, never went to any law school. I heard he might get the vice presidential nomination. And in case you haven't heard, they say he's gonna run for president in 1860."

135

"Abe Lincoln? He's nothin' but a nigger-lovin' abolitionist. You don't wanna model your life after him, partner. Stay true to your southern roots and upbringin'. Jump on the band wagon. California did. It came into the Union as a free state, but the politics out here sure as hell are suthen."

The next morning they climbed the last of the foothills beneath the high peaks of the Sierra Nevada and came upon the Yellow Creek. They took some samples and headed back to town.

The next morning bright and early they visited Gilberto García's law offices.

"Have a seat, gentlemen. There's something I want to show you," said Giberto.

He opened his desk drawer and took out a document. "Barney Stokes hired himself a lawyer and a good one, Mister Clint Young, reputedly the finest lawyer in California. He drew up this document, entitled 'Quitclaim Deed and Conveyance,' which he maintains will settle the dispute with Barney Stokes over that Yellow Creek property in a fair and equitable manner. It calls for you to quitclaim all your right, title and interest in the Yellow Creek property to Stokes, who will then devise a fifty percent undivided interest back to you. That will result in your both having a fifty percent undivided interest in the Yellow Creek claim. All the profits, costs and expenses are to be shared fifty-fifty." Charlie's face flushed, and he immediately stood up.

"I'll not give that son-of-a-bitch one inch of my Yellow Creek claim! He abandoned it, and I took it up and registered it. You yourself said I did right, Gilberto."

"Yes, but I also told you that the fact that you pulled out Stokes' stake and threw it in the creek could be a problem. There's also the problem that you have established very little evidence that you've begun to work the claim, and…" Charlie shot a cold hard look at the young lawyer, interrupting him.

"Whose side are you on Gilberto?" There was a ring of defiance and sarcasm in his tone.

"I'm on your side, Charlie, but Clint Young doesn't take on a case when he thinks there's a good chance he'll lose it. So that tells me that Barney Stokes' claim to the Yellow Creek property has some merit. And I'm advising you to seriously consider this offer."

Billy, who had been sitting there quietly, looked at Gilberto.

"May I see the document?"

Gilberto handed it to Billy and he began reading it. *So, I would get fifty percent of Charlie's fifty percent, which is twenty-five percent.* As Billy continued reading, he felt a sense of pride that he was able to understand it and appreciate how the words came together with precision. At one point Charlie looked at Billy and saw the trace of a smile on his face.

"What the hell's so interestin' about that document that's got you smilin', partner?"

"I'm smiling Charlie, because the language interests me and because it's a well written document, at least by my reading."

"And how the hell would you know that?" Charlie scoffed "You got no legal trainin'. You're a strange one, Billy McHugh; a rare bird you are."

"Maybe I'll get some," Billy said, a look of confidence and determination on his face.

"Your friend's right, Charlie. It is a well-written document. When Clint Young drafts something, you can be sure that a lot of thinking has gone into it."

"I ask you again, Gilberto, whose side are you on? And how's about you drawin' up a well-written document for Barney Stokes to quitclaim all of his supposed rights to me?"

"How much are you willing to pay him to do that, Charlie?"

"Not one red cent, Gilberto. That Yellow Creek claim belongs to me, and I'm not about to give it up to anyone."

"Does that include me too, Charlie?" Billy asked.

"No, you're different. You and me are in this together. I'm gonna deed you fifty percent of my claim. In fact, I was gonna ask Gilberto to draw it up today..."

They left the lawyer's office without resolving anything.

When they returned to the boarding house, Billy found two letters waiting for him.

"They came in on the steamship *Sonora*," said Sue Ann, the housemother, cook and laundress.

> *My dear son, Billy,*
>
> *I pray that you will soon come to your senses and return home to Charleston to continue your education at the College of Charleston. You were doing so well until that vagabond and ne'er-do-well, Charlie Flynn, filled your mind with gold fever and led you astray.*
>
> *It's terribly hard for me now, Billy. I'm all alone. Your father has been away more than usual, sailing to Africa and Brazil, leaving much too much work for just one poor tired woman.*
>
> *Constance Beckett has been asking for you wondering when you'll be returning home. I've asked her to write to you and gave her your address. She's such a nice young woman, Billy, and she's so fond of you.*
>
> *I'll write more later, but I'm just too sad and too tired right now.*
>
> *Your loving mother.*

Billy picked up Dolores's letter and raised it to his nostrils, noticing only a faint scent of gardenias.

Querido Billy,   *20 de julio1956*

Como estás? Do you like the new life in California? I hope it is good and hope also you "strike rich" so you can start your business in Central America. Since last I've written, there has been some sad news here at La Dulce Gardenia. Doña Teresa passed away from a terrible wave of cholera on the island. We have been in mourning for several months. Sofia especially has suffered greatly from her mother's death. It was so sudden, so tragic and so sad. But there is also some good news. In ten days I will go to United States with Sofia. We both enrolled in Mount Holyoke College in Massachusetts. It is one of the best girls' schools in your country, and I am so fortunate to have this opportunity. It is such a privilege for me to have the chance for college education. I must study hard and be successful.

Sofia and I remember you and often talk about your visit with us when we were all so very young. We both hope to see you again. That will be easier now because we will be in your country much of time. It is also fate, do you think? I do believe in fate. Do you believe Billy?

Here is my new address at Mount Holyoke:

Miss Dolores de Castilla
Mount Holyoke College
50 College Street, Hadley, Massachusetts
USA.

The two letters further supported Billy's decision that it was time to go home.

CHAPTER VI

The Fateful Meeting

It was Tuesday 8 September 1857. The cannon blast from El Morro Castle announced the first light of dawn, revealing the sleek black hull of the *SS Central America* lying at anchor in Havana harbor. She was a handsome side-wheel steamer almost three hundred feet in length. She had arrived the night before from Panama, carrying some six hundred passengers and crew, thousands of pieces of US mail and tons of gold from the California gold fields. Billy McHugh and most of the passengers were returning east after several years in California hell bent on striking it rich. A few had done so and were carrying their wealth back with them; most had not and that certainly included Billy, who was lucky just to have scraped together the money to purchase a steerage ticket. Their journey had begun on August 20th in San Francisco aboard the *SS Sonora*, which carried them to Panama City on September 2nd. The next morning they boarded the new Panama Railroad, crossing the forty-eight miles of Isthmus jungle to the Atlantic coast. Awaiting them in port was the *SS Central America*, which after an overnight stay in Havana, would carry them, the mail and the gold on the final leg of the journey to New York.

The hot humid air of Havana hung over the harbor like a heavy wet blanket, and as the sun rose, the temperature and humidity rose even more. Puffy white cumulous clouds drifted overhead, destined to darken in the afternoon and cool the city with tropical rains. Some first-class passengers came out of their cabins to get a bit of the fresh but humid air. They stood at the rail and watched as a fleet of sturdy lighters rowed by free blacks ferried sacks of mail, crates of gold bullion, and freshly minted gold coins to the *SS Central America*. A white man with a six-gun sat in each such craft to guard against pilferage.

Other small craft pulled up alongside the steamer, offering fresh fruit and local handicrafts for sale, which, when agreed upon, were thrown up to the buyers in exchange for coins dropped to the sellers' waiting hands. A few passengers had disembarked in Havana but many more boarded the vessel. The day before, the captain and crew advised the passengers that there had been an epidemic of cholera on the island and warned that it would be best to stay on board during their overnight stay. Most of the passengers remained in their cabins, heeding the warning or because they were fatigued from their long journey.

At approximately half past seven, an elegant black carriage with luxurious silver trim and red velvet upholstery pulled up to the quay. The black coachman jumped down and opened the carriage door for don Fernando and his two daughters, Sofia and Dolores. The two young women were traveling to the United States to begin their second year of study at the Mount Holyoke Female Seminary in South Hadley, Massachusetts. They both had done exceptionally well in their first year, where they had pursued a rigorous curriculum of science, mathematics, literature, and Latin, which was standard for all incoming young women. Mount Holyoke had striven to establish a female college on a par with the nation's finest male colleges and was well on the way to achieving that goal.

During that first year at Mount Holyoke, Dolores had found it easier to adjust to her new environment than her half-sister, Sofia. She considered herself fortunate beyond belief to have the chance to acquire an education in the United States of America, and she devoted herself to her studies with enthusiasm and passion. Her English had improved considerably and she was genuinely happy. Sofia had a more difficult time adjusting, suffering from home-sickness. She missed her family and her friends at the University of Havana, but nonetheless managed to achieve as many outstanding grades as Dolores.

Sofia, Dolores, and the entire de Castilla family benefited considerably from the girls' extended stay in the US, for the passage of time lessened the effect of the serious scandals they had been embroiled in. Don Eduardo de Cadiz had recovered from the bullet wound he had suffered in the duel with the Count of Calais. As for Sofia's former *novio*, Carlos Santiago, his tragic fate had been sealed, and he was garroted before the public in the Plaza de Armas. The Captain General himself participated in the execution before a crowd of thousands.

"Take those four trunks in back," said don Fernando to his coachman.

"Oh, look. It's a much larger ship than the one we took last September," Dolores said, as she spotted the majestic vessel, *Central America*, that would carry them to the United States.

"Look at that red stripe running all the way from the front to the back."

"Since you're going to be on that vessel, Dolores, you should use the correct terminology," said don Fernando. "Rather than 'front' and 'back' you should say 'bow' and 'stern'."

"Thank you, papá. I'll try to remember that."

"It's a beautiful ship," said Sofia, who until that moment had remained silent. "I wonder what our cabin will be like."

"I am certain it will be more than comfortable," said don

Fernando. "You are traveling first class, and the vessel is only two or three years old."

Suddenly, some loud-talking vendors rushed over, surrounded don Fernando and the two girls and began aggressively hawking their wares. Don Fernando signaled to the coachman, who quickly shooed them away. Not surprisingly, the two girls began to attract attention as they followed the coachman and the porters carting their trunks down to the dock. They stood out in the crowd of mostly work-a-day men. Dolores wore a pretty blue muslin dress and a stylish, wide floppy hat to protect her from the sun. Her slippers were black satin, and she carried the customary Spanish *abanico* with which to fan herself. Sofia wore a lacy blue dress with a white sash at the waist and black silk slippers. She carried a red and black *abanico* adorned with elaborately painted figures of Gypsy men and women. When they reached the dockside, don Fernando ordered the coachman to contract one of many boatmen gathered there to load the trunks and ferry Sofia and Dolores out to the ship.

"I want both of you to work hard on your studies and make your papá proud. I'll be checking on your progress from my sources in the United States."

"You can depend on that, papá," said Dolores, smiling and the picture of joy. Sofia was unsmiling and remained silent.

"Bon voyage, and don't forget to write, my sweets," said don Fernando as he hugged and kissed his daughters effusively.

He helped them into the small craft and the boatman shoved off and began rowing toward the steamer.

They boarded the vessel and were greeted by the second officer and a handsome mulatto steward. The steward showed them to their stateroom, which was located on the main deck in the aft section of the vessel, away from the noise of the paddle wheels, the engines, and the smokestack.

"Papá was right. It's a delightful cabin," said Dolores.

The cabin was spacious and well furnished with comfortable beds, a mahogany table, leather chairs, a water basin with a large mirror above it and a toilet. The floor was covered with attractive carpeting and there were two large armoires for their things. Fresh flowers and a large basket of fruit adorned the table.

"Oh, look, Sofia, we've got a porthole."

Just then there was a knock on the door. It was the porters with the girls' four trunks.

"Shall we unpack now?" Dolores asked.

"No, let's not," said Sofia. "Let's go up on deck and look around. We'll have plenty of time to unpack later."

Dolores noticed that Sofia was beginning to exhibit some enthusiasm for the first time that day. They found their way topside, noticing that smoke was slowly rising from the ship's black funnel.

"Maybe we're about to depart," Sofia said. "Let's ask somebody. There's a steward."

"Excuse me, what time will we be departing?" Sofia asked. The steward pulled out a silver pocket watch.

"It's half-past eight now. We depart in thirty minutes," he said.

They thanked him and started walking toward the bow of the ship, stopping to gaze at the paddle wheels.

"Look at the size of them. They're enormous," exclaimed Dolores.

"And they're half-under water," Sofia said. "They must be at least two or three stories high." They could feel the vibration from the two powerful steam engines that were steadily idling.

As they continued walking toward the bow of the ship, other passengers emerged. The men were dressed in long coats and stovepipe hats, and must have been very uncomfortable in the heat and humidity. The women wore hoop skirts with colorful blouses. Many carried parasols to protect them from the tropical sun. When the two young women reached the bow, they stopped and peered at the long, thin, black extension that stuck out over the water.

"I think it's called a bowsprit," Sofia said. "I read it somewhere."

Just then, they noticed more smoke rising from the stack, and they felt heavier vibrations. They heard some passengers say they were going up to the "weather deck" to watch their departure. Sofia and Dolores decided to follow them. Soon after, they heard the ship's bell ring along with an "All Ashore That's Going Ashore."

The crewmen raised the anchor, the engines revved up and the huge paddle wheels began to turn, churning up the water and creating a white foamy wake as the majestic *Central America* got under way. She turned to starboard and pointed her bowsprit toward the *El Morro Castle* at the entrance to Havana harbor. Soon she was passing its centuries old stone walls and heading out to open sea, where she settled into her cruising speed of more than thirteen knots.

2

Captain William Lewis Herndon stood at the helm with the Second Mate who steered a course for Cape Florida. Soon they would be entering the Gulf Stream, which they would follow all the way to New York, gaining an extra two or three knots. The weather was sunny and clear with balmy breezes and a calm sea. It was Captain Herndon's twenty-fourth trip from Panama to New York, some of them taken on the *SS George Law*, the original name of the vessel when she was christened in 1853. Men of the sea were wary of a ship whose name had been changed, but Herndon was not at all concerned. He was a United States Naval Officer, a decorated veteran of the Mexican War and the Second Seminole

War. He was also famous for his daring exploration of the Amazon River and had written a book about it, which was widely read.

While Dolores and Sofia were exploring the vessel, they came across a party of first-class passengers, one of whom introduced herself as Virginia Birch, the wife of Billy Birch, the well-known and popular American comedian. The Birches had been married just days before departing San Francisco on the *SS Sonora*. As foreigners, Sofia and Dolores were not familiar with Billy Birch.

"Oh, you simply must see him and hear him while you're in the country," said a handsome gentleman in the group. "He's the rage and a very funny man indeed."

As they talked, it appeared that Virginia Birch took a liking to the two young Cuban women.

"Let me see if my husband, Billy, can get you two a place at the Captain's table for dinner tonight," Virginia said with a wide smile.

"Oh, that's so very kind of you," Dolores said. "We would be honored."

"That would be wonderful, Mrs. Birch," added Sofia.

That evening the mulatto steward delivered an invitation for them to join Captain Herndon and his prized guests at the Captain's table for dinner. Sofia and Dolores dressed in their finest evening clothes made of light and airy crepe, trimmed at the neckline and sleeves with an exquisite white lace.

"Let's go up on deck first and watch the sun set over the Caribbean," Sofia said.

"That's a great idea," said Dolores. And indeed it was.

"Look how beautiful," said Dolores as the fiery red ball sank in the western sky.

"Let's make a wish," said Sofia. Both girls closed their eyes and made their wish, neither one willing to reveal what they had wished. "Now let's go down and sit at the Captain's Table for our special dinner," said Sofia.

As they began walking down to the Dining Salon, they noticed that white caps had begun to form on the sea, and the balmy breeze of earlier that day had given way to a light wind. But they paid it no mind and proceeded down to the Dining Salon.

Sitting across the table from the two girls was a newlywed couple, Ansel and Addie Easton. The story went that Ansel had gone west years before and made a fortune selling supplies to the thousands of miners, who needed everything from shovels to long johns. He never once prospected for gold, but he wound up with lots of it. As for his new bride, Addie, she was certainly not a pauper, coming from a wealthy San Francisco banking family.

Virginia Birch had been charged with the task of seating the Captain's guests, and she placed Dolores and Sofia next to her husband, Billy, who turned out to be every bit as funny as his reputation promised.

"...Now that we've finished the main course, I can tell you about them cannibal Indians I came across in Brazil," said Captain Herndon, steering the conversation as adeptly as he did the ship.

The Captain's story brought forth another slew of gut-busting jokes and anecdotes from Billy Birch. That's when the cart full of dishes rolled away from one of the waiters and crashed against the bulkhead.

"Oh, my, we're not going to founder, are we, Captain Herndon?" asked the pretty young newlywed, Addie Easton, with a smile that made it difficult to tell whether she was fearful or just joking.

"Let's hope not," said Virginia Birch.

"It will take a lot more than a rough sea and a strong wind to send this vessel to the bottom," said another guest, a judge, who'd been quietly puffing on his Cuban cigar.

"The sea is always unpredictable, but I assure you *The Central America* is a stout and sturdy vessel," said Captain Herndon, eager to quell any sense of unease at the table. "She's sailed through much worse seas than this one and I'm confident that she'll continue to do so."

After dinner, Sofia and Dolores joined the women who ventured up on deck to check on the weather. As they were walking up the stairs the handsome mulatto steward happened by carrying pillows, heading for the first class cabins. He greeted Dolores with a *"muy buenas noches, señorita, como está usted?"* (Good evening, senorita, how are you?). Dolores responded in mellifluous Spanish.

"I just love the Spanish language," said Virginia Birch. "Billy and I hear it often in San Francisco, but I noticed a different accent when you spoke just now, different than the Californianos. Is it the educational level of the people?"

"That's probably part of it," Dolores said, looking then to Sofia.

"Let me try to explain," Sofia said. "Mexico became independent early in the century. So their culture and the Spanish language took on its own Mexican characteristics. Cuba is still part of Spain and so we have retained more of the Spanish accent and culture. But someday with the grace of God, Cuba will also be free and independent and we will then fully develop our own culture and speak our own style of Spanish."

Dolores smiled proudly, struck with how well Sofia had explained it.

Up on deck the women were greeted by a stiff wind and a salt spray that beat against their rouged cheeks, prompting most to retreat to their cabins for the night. Dolores and Sofia lingered for a while, watching as the ship's bow rose with the swells then plunged into the waves, its bowsprit dipping gracefully.

Back in their cabin, Dolores and Sofia dressed in their nightclothes and climbed into bed.

"It sounds like it's getting worse out there," Sofia said as she lifted the curtain over the porthole and peered out into the swirling darkness. It frightened her and she quickly closed it.

"Maybe we will sail out of it now and it will be clear tomorrow," Dolores said, trying to assure both her sister and herself. They said their prayers and made the sign of the cross.

"*Buenas noches, Doloresita.*"

"*Buenas noches, Sofia.*"

3

Deep down in the bowels of the *SS Central America*, the steerage passengers were rising from their bunks. Few had slept. The heat, humidity, and crying children were more than enough to keep them awake. But then there was the wind howling, the creaking timbers and the waves breaking on the hull. Adding to their discomfort was the nauseating smell of vomit from the seasick passengers, who from time to time would spring from their bunks and run to the head.

Billy McHugh slid down from his upper bunk. He'd slept little more than an hour during the night. He dressed in his soiled shirt and denim pants.

"Where you goin' Billy boy," asked the middle-aged man in the lower bunk.

His name was Cliff Barton. He and his cousin Jack, who occupied the second tier, were prospectors on their way home to Baltimore. They'd been in California since the early days of 1849 and had had the good fortune of finding the easy gold before the hoards arrived. They both wore money belts, which they never removed, loaded down with freshly minted twenty-dollar gold pieces. They easily could have afforded a First Class ticket, but they had elected to travel in steerage to save their gold. Jack had been sick during the night, and when Billy glanced at him, it looked like he was still under the weather.

"I've got to get out of here, Cliff," Billy said. "I'm going top-side for some fresh air. I can't stand this heat and that stench any more."

"You be goin' to breakfast this morning?" Cliff asked. His cousin, Jack, looked at Billy as if he was daft.

"How the hell can anyone even think about food right now?"

"Yes, I'm hungry and I'm going to breakfast," Billy said.

He couldn't help but think that Cliff and Jack were more than just stingy. They were downright foolish and crazy to be traveling in steerage. They could easily afford first class tickets. Billy had seen all their gold coins and bars. He assured himself that if he had all that gold, he certainly would have purchased at least a second-class ticket or better yet a first-class ticket. As Billy climbed the stairs to the dining salon, he thought about the decision he'd made to return home. He was heading back east with empty pockets but it was the right move. Charlie's claim was full of holes. If he had not demanded his share of the gold dust when he did, there would not have been any left to take. Even still, he had to borrow from friends to afford the steerage ticket.

Up on deck the wind was howling, and the sky was dark and turgid with swirling storm clouds. But it was cooler, and the air was fresh, a welcome relief from the dank, smelly steerage section. He walked toward the stern, noticing the smoke and coal ash rising from the tall black stack. He headed for the dining salon and held on to the rail, judging that if he didn't, he'd risk being swept overboard from the strong and sudden lurching of the vessel. The crewmen were going about their shipboard tasks with a calm nonchalance, as though these rough, stormy seas were simply routine. When he reached the paddlewheels, he noticed that as each large swell struck the ship, the giant wheels became fully submerged, covering even their housings. Just then a uniformed officer walked by.

"Excuse me, sir, do you expect this storm to pass or are we going to be in it the whole voyage?"

"We should be sailing out of it soon, sir. We passed Cape Florida, and the weather should be improving."

"How far have we come since Havana?" Billy asked.

"I'd say about two hundred and fifty miles. We're now situated between the Florida Coast and Grand Bahama Isle. So, we're making good time."

When Billy entered the dining salon, the First and Second Class sections were practically empty. Most people eating breakfast were steerage passengers in their roped off section. He had an appetite, for he'd eaten little since boarding the vessel in Aspinwall, Panama, where he'd taken up with Cliff and his cousin Jack. The party had stretched into the early dawn, and he'd had too much to drink. As a result, he'd remained below deck in his bunk, sleeping it off and venturing out only once or twice for a few light meals. When the vessel arrived in Havana, he thought perhaps he could leave the ship and send a telegram to Dolores C/O don Fernando de Castilla, but then he remembered that she was in the United States, attending college in Massachusetts. So he stayed below deck in his bunk, getting the soundest sleep since leaving San Francisco, since the vessel was at anchor, and there was no engine noise or rocking motion.

He finished his breakfast and wandered up to the main cabin, wondering whether he could enter. Seeing just a few passengers inside, he elected to go in and took a seat on one of the sofas. Before long other passengers wandered in. One reported that huge waves were now breaking over the bow. Another stated that if the rough weather continued, his stateroom was likely to be flooded. All the while Billy could hear the wind whistling through the ship's rigging as the ship rocked and pitched with increasing frequency. From time to time crewmembers would enter, and passengers would question them regarding the storm and the safety of the vessel. Their answers were always the same, that the *Central America* was a strong and stout ship and had sailed through many storms and high seas.

"There's no reason to be alarmed," they all said.

But come afternoon, the rains arrived, blown by an even stronger wind, and the women were becoming concerned, questioning their men folk, seeking assurances that the vessel would not founder. Some passengers could be seen taking crewmembers aside and asking them directly about the storm. Some of the crew admitted that they were confronting what looked to be a tropical cyclone, the seasonal kind that strike the Caribbean in September.

As he sat on the plush sofa, Billy suddenly thought he should answer Dolores's last letter. It had been some time since he had received it, and it would help pass the time and take his mind off the dreadful weather. He got up and headed back down to steerage to get ink, pen, paper, and Dolores's new address from her letter. Out on deck the wind and salt spray stung his face and tossed his hair about. The sky was an ashen gray, and the surging wind blew the rain sideways, pelting the vessel with the sound of a whirlwind. With each rise and fall of the swells, seawater flowed over the deck, and walking became slippery and more difficult. When he looked up at the bridge and then at the bow, he saw the crew continuing to point the vessel directly into the oncoming sea and wind in accordance with long-established maritime practice.

He entered the steerage section, trading the sound and fury of the storm for the cacophony of crying children and the moans of the seasick. The smell of vomit was overwhelming; it was all he could do to keep from retching. Cliff and Jack were still in their bunks, both of them pale as ghosts and seasick. Billy asked if he could do anything to help. Cliff made a feeble attempt at a joke.

"Yes, Billy boy, get us out of this storm, will ya please? And get us out now."

"I'd like nothing better," Billy said. He opened his valise and took out his last clean shirt, thinking he'd be less conspicuous as a steerage stowaway in the main cabin. Then he picked up a pen, paper, and a little bottle of ink, and took Dolores's most recent letter from the stack. He bid good-bye to Cliff and Jack, saying he'd be up in the main cabin if they needed him.

As he headed toward the stairs, he saw a young woman carrying two infants; both were screaming. When Billy was side by side with her, the ship lurched violently, and one of the infants slipped from her grip and began sliding down her torso. Billy reacted immediately, angling his feet beneath the woman to break and cushion the infant's fall, and he caught the baby just before it hit the floor.

"Oh, thank God! I don't know how I can ever thank you," said the young woman, bursting into tears.

"The fact that he's safe, ma'am, is all the thanks I need," Billy said.

"His name's Joseph, and this is his twin brother, Michael. They're just six months old as of yesterday."

"You sure have your hands full, ma'am. Let me carry him for you. Where were you headed?"

"I was trying to make my way to the latrine. My sister is waiting there and we were going to change them," said the young mother, drying her eyes with one of the diapers draped over her shoulder.

"All right, I've got little Joseph now, so you just hold on to me and we'll walk together."

They reached the latrine and found the woman's sister waiting out front.

"Thank you so much," said the young mother. "I'm Betty

Caruthers from Wilmington, North Carolina, and this here's my sister, Caroline."

"I'm very pleased to meet you ladies. I'm Billy McHugh from Charleston, South Carolina."

"Well, God bless you, Billy McHugh. God bless you..."

Billy set out again to make his way back up on deck. The wind howled and shrieked in the rigging, and it became harder and more perilous to traverse the main deck. The rain came down sideways, pelting his face with liquid bullets. The wind screamed and pummeled him, obscuring his vision and threatening to sweep him overboard.

4

"How do you feel, Sofia?" Dolores asked, as she climbed down from the upper bunk.

"Terrible. My stomach is worse than it was yesterday, Dolores. The ship was rocking and lurching all night long, and I got sick again. Did you hear me?"

"No, I didn't. I was very tired and fell asleep right away, but the wind and rain woke me up later, and I couldn't go back to sleep. I heard these terribly loud cracking noises. At first I thought it was a dream. I was back at *La Dulce Gardenia* and Victorio Arquídez was whipping some poor hapless slave. But then I realized that I was awake, and that the noise was coming from the ship."

Dolores noticed that Sofia had stopped listening to her. She watched as Sofia lifted the curtain over the porthole, when at that precise moment a huge wave broke over the hull and smashed against the porthole, startling her out of her wits.

"My God!" Sofia gasped, closing the curtain. "We're in a hurricane, Dolores. I'm certain of it. We've been through them on land, and maybe it destroys some sugarcane, but out at sea it could destroy this ship and send us to the bottom along with it."

"Don't worry, Sofia. Remember what Captain Herndon and the judge said? It's a strong ship with an experienced crew. We'll be all right."

Sofia got up suddenly from her bed, stumbled and rushed to the toilet. Seconds later Dolores heard her vomiting.

"Oh, you poor dear. I'm so sorry you're ill, Sofia. They must have a ship's doctor on board. I'll go up and see if I can find him."

Dolores left the stateroom and made her way up on deck, where the strong wind ripped off her bonnet and sent it swirling overboard. It blew her long dark hair straight back from her head as she grasped the rail and walked slowly along the deck. *Sofia's right. This is a hurricane.* Rain and seawater sloshed about the deck; she walked faster and finally entered the main cabin, where she spotted Virginia and Billy Birch sitting on a sofa.

"Oh, Miss de Castilla, you shouldn't be out there in this tempest. Come sit with us and dry off."

"I came up to see if I can find the ship's doctor for my sister. She's awfully sick and keeps getting worse."

"This is a humdinger of a storm," said Billy Birch. "Our stateroom took on water so, we spent the night here in the main cabin."

"Oh, I want to ask that officer about the ship's doctor, excuse me please."

Dolores got up and asked him where she could find the doctor. The officer told her that the doctor himself was seasick. Dolores then sat down again with the Birches. Just then, a man and a woman entered the main cabin each one carrying an infant. They were poorly dressed, soaking wet and disheveled, presumably steerage passengers.

"Oh, my, it looks like that poor couple is carrying twins," said Virginia Birch.

"As if this storm isn't enough," added Billy Birch.

For as long as she lived, Dolores would never forget what happened next.

"Oh, Billy, I'm so glad you're here. I want to introduce you. This is my husband, Roy Caruthers. Roy, this is the young man I told you about, Billy...uuh, I'm sorry, I've forgotten your last name."

"McHugh, ma'am. Billy McHugh."

"Yes, Roy, this is Billy McHugh, the young man who caught little Joseph when he tumbled out of my arms."

Dolores couldn't believe what she had just heard, but when she looked over, her eyes did not lie. She saw the boy, now a man, whom Sofia had once described as "the most beautiful boy in the world." It was her Billy all right, her Billy McHugh. Her face flushed, her heart raced and she broke out in goose bumps as she gazed at him wide-eyed and spellbound. Virginia Birch couldn't help but notice Dolores's state of excitement.

"Do you know those people?"

"I know that young man," Dolores said, beaming. "We met in Cuba years ago, and we've had a long correspondence."

"Well, aren't you going to go over and say hello?"

"I want to let them finish their conversation," said Dolores, finding it hard to control her excitement.

"He's a fine looking lad," said Billy Birch.

Dolores waited with heightened anticipation for the right moment. She watched as Billy sat down next to a box-like compartment marked "Life Vests". He took out a pen, paper and the little bottle of ink and began to write. Dolores excused herself, got up and started slowly walking over to him, her heart now racing.

"*Billy! Billy! Soy yo, Dolores!*" (Billy! Billy! Its me, Dolores !) He turned and looked up, astonishment the only way to describe his expression. His heart fluttered, he dropped the pen, almost spilling the ink.

"*Dolores! Eres tú? Eres tú!* (Dolores! Is it you? It's you!) He got up and embraced her, and as he did so, the ship lurched, causing him to hug her even tighter. When the vessel steadied again, they stood gazing longingly into each other's eyes, neither one willing to break the embrace.

"This is truly unbelievable, Dolores! Do you know what I was doing at this very moment? I was writing you a letter And the next thing I knew I heard your voice, looked up and there you were. Tell me I'm not dreaming, because it's hard to believe this is real."

"You're not dreaming, Billy, but maybe I am," Dolores said, her beautiful dark eyes filled with tears of joy.

"Do you remember, Dolores, you told me once you believed in fate? Now I understand."

"But what are you doing here on this ship, Billy?" I thought you were in California."

"I have so much to tell you, my sweet Dolores, but my head is spinning, because I still can't quite believe this is real."

He took her by the hand and they sat down on a sofa and gazed at each other lovingly. Billy felt tears of joy welling up in his eyes, and an irresistible urge to kiss her; to kiss her like that first tender kiss in Cuba years before on the eve of his departure. He put his arms around her now and kissed her tenderly. Dolores sat there nestled in his arms; neither one spoke for fear of awakening from what simply had to be a dream for it was just too wonderful to believe it was real…

They awakened from the spell and began to talk and catch up on the details of there new lives.

"…So, you were returning east from California and that's why you're on this ship?"

"Yes, I'm going home to Charleston, Dolores. I've decided to study law."

"Sofia and I are returning to Mount Holyoke College in Massachusetts to begin our second year of studies. I wrote to you about it, Billy."

"So, Sofia is with you!?

"Yes, Billy, she's back in our cabin and awfully seasick. Oh, and I must be getting back to check on her. I fought my way up here to the Main Cabin to search for the ship's doctor, and instead I found you. "It's still hard for me to believe, Billy, even though I'm sitting here right next to you..."

Virginia and Billy Birch got up to leave, and Dolores called out to them. They came over, and she introduced them.

"It's a great pleasure to meet you Mister Birch," Billy said. "I've read about you in the San Francisco papers."

"I hope it was favorable. Some of those audiences out there were pretty demanding and rowdy too."

"It was much more than just favorable, sir. I really hope to get to see you on stage some day."

The Birches walked off. Billy Birch continued to hold on to Virginia, as the *Central America* continued to lurch about violently.

"They are very nice people, Billy, and even though my English is not perfect, I found Billy Birch to be very funny."

"Your English sounds very good, Dolores. I don't hear any accent at all now."

"Pero, que tal tu español? Sigues estudiando?" ("But how is your Spanish? Are you continuing to study it?").

"Seguro que sí." (I sure am).

"Billy, I must go back now to check on Sofia."

"I'll go with you, Dolores, It's very slippery and dangerous out there."

"I made it here all right, Billy, but the wind blew my bonnet overboard."

He was not about to let her go back by herself, and he put one arm around her waist and the other around her shoulders, sheltering her as best he could.

The wind whistled, and the rain pelted them. But the paddle-wheels continued to turn, and *The Central America* plowed directly ahead and into the storm.

Dolores knocked on the door to her cabin.

"It's me, Sofia. I'm so sorry I couldn't find the doctor, but guess who I did find. He's standing right here next to me? Are you decent?"

"I'm in my nightgown."

"Billy McHugh is here with me."

"What? Billy McHugh! I thought he was in California striking it rich."

"*Hola, Sofia, cómo estás?* (Hello, Sofia, how are you?" Can I just say hello to her, Dolores?"

"She's not feeling well, Billy, and she's not dressed."

"*Hola, Billy,* how did you come to be on this ship? Were you in Cuba."

"Yes, Sofia, but only overnight. I'm returning from California via the Panama Railroad acoss the Isthmus. I boarded this ship in Colón."

"I'm hoping this seasickness will be over soon, because I can't wait to see you, Billy."

"Can I see you again later today, Dolores?" Billy asked, almost pleadingly.

"I want to stay with Sofia, Billy, and get some rest myself."

He did not want to let her out of his sight, fearing that he might awaken from what was after all just a dream. But when

Dolores moved closer and they came together in a warm *abrazo*, he knew then for certain it was real.

As he walked away, the image of his beautiful Doloresita flooded his mind, but it came with some troublesome anxiety.

She's even more beautiful now than I remembered. What if she's found another love? There must be scores of men in Cuba and now in the United State who would do anything and give anything to have her for their wife.

5

Dawn broke over a lead-colored sky and an increasingly hostile sea. It was their fourth day out of Havana, and the waves were now towering over the *Central America,* crashing down upon its bow, flooding seawater over its decks and washing up against the first and second-class staterooms. The wind howled, reaching speeds in excess of seventy knots. It buffeted and rattled the unfurled sails high up in the rigging, producing a hideously high-pitched whistle that echoed all throughout the vessel. Wanting to avoid panic, the Captain and crew continued to assure the women that there was no danger; but even some crewmembers were beginning to doubt their own assurances. By now, everyone knew that they were firmly in the grips of a full-fledged hurricane.

There was little change throughout the morning, but early that afternoon the Chief Engineer discovered water building up in the bilge. He got the pumps going and thought that would remove it. The water kept accumulating, however, and he sent his men searching the ship for the source of it. Sometime later, they discovered a leak around the shaft supporting the giant starboard paddlewheel. In addition, as the water rose in the ship's hold, she began to list to starboard, which in turn triggered an even more serious problem. The *Central America's* massive steam engines were fueled by anthracite coal. Tens of boiler room mates pushed a continuous line of wheelbarrows filled with coal from the ship's bunkers to its boilers, fueling the vessel's voracious appetite. The tilt to starboard was making it more and more difficult to push them up the steep incline and carry the coal to the boilers. It got so bad that Captain Herndon ordered all waiters, stewards, mess men, cooks and other non-essential personnel, to form a bucket brigade to hand-carry the coal to the engine room. However, it soon became apparent that the effort was insufficient, and the steam pressure gradually dropped, causing the paddlewheels to turn more slowly. There was a separate problem with the port paddlewheel, which was barely grazing the waterline as it turned, because of the vessel's increasing list to starboard. That was why in addition to her steam engines and paddlewheels, the ship was fully rigged with sails to provide an auxiliary source of power.

By mid-day, it was clear that the situation was worsening. There was no letup in the fury of the storm and no progress made in stemming the leak. The water rose in the engine room, sloshing around the boilers, hissing and dampening the coal fires. Captain Herndon had no choice but to order all male passengers to assume bailing duty. They collected buckets and water pitchers from throughout the vessel and formed three separate bailing lines. They passed from hand to hand the heavy buckets and pails of seawater and dumped them overboard. By now, almost everyone had abandoned the staterooms and steerage compartments and congregated in the main cabin and the dining salon.

Most of the food onboard had been lost to the rising water; all that remained were soggy bread and biscuits. The women gathered what little there was and brought it to the men who continued to bail, trying desperately to keep the vessel afloat. Bailing continued all day and into the night. The men were exhausted but they kept at it. From time to time some would stop and collapse on deck, rest for a spell, and then, spurred on by the women, resume their positions.

Billy McHugh was one of the first to take his place in the bailing lines. But before he did, he struggled back to Dolores's cabin, unaware that she and Sofia had gone to the main cabin.

Dolores found Virginia Birch and asked if she had seen Billy McHugh, the young man whom she had introduced her to the day before. Virginia said she had seen him earlier, but that he must be out there somewhere in the bailing lines.

The women and children filled the main cabin. They were all alarmed that the *Central America* was in peril of sinking. As if to confirm that, the steady pulsing sound of the engines suddenly ceased. Without the engines, they could no longer steer the vessel head on into the storm. They still had the sails, but when they tried to unfurl them, the hurricane force winds ripped them out of their boltropes and tore them to shreds. With no fire, no steam, and no sail to power her, the *Central America* drifted off course to the southeast and lay helpless against the monstrous waves that now came crashing down on it broadside. In spite of those ominous setbacks, the courageous men kept bailing, exerting Herculean efforts to keep up with the ever-rising water level in the hold. Nighttime came and there was no letup. There was now an estimated twelve feet of water in the engine room and no longer any hope of restarting the engines. Passengers had had little if any sleep or food in twenty-four hours. Some of the husbands and wives had met briefly during rest periods from bailing and vowed to tie themselves together and go down as one spirit.

Captain Herndon had now concluded that the vessel was going to sink. He sent up rocket flares and drew down the *Central America*'s flag, had it turned upside down and raised again, an international sign of distress. He gathered the officers in the wheelhouse and told them to prepare for abandoning the ship. Capt Herndon ordered the women and children to be loaded first into the lifeboats. He made no effort to save the many tons of gold.

"It would only weigh us down and make rescue operations more difficult." Herndon had said.

At dawn the next day, they spotted a vessel about a mile off their starboard side. Herndon was convinced that other vessels would learn that *The Central America* was in peril and would come to her aid.

6

The Norfolk Sentinel September 19 1857
Survivors of SS Central America Arrive in Norfolk

More than 150 survivors from the SS Central America arrived in Norfolk yesterday aboard the bark Marine out of Boston and the Ellen, a Norwegian sailing vessel. The Central America sank on September 12th in heavy seas off Cape Hatteras, sending some 450 souls returning from the California gold fields to a watery grave (A partial list of survivors appears on page 2). In addition to the heavy loss of life, the vessel sank with tons of gold destined for the New York banks, causing a worldwide panic amongst the already weak international financial community.

Dolores and Sofia were loaded into a lifeboat and picked up later by the Norwegian sailing vessel, *Ellen*, that took them to Norfolk. They checked into a local hotel. Dolores frantically turned the pages of the *Norfolk Sentinel*, her eyes scanning the names of survivors; past the Js, Ks and Ls, coming finally to the Ms.

101 MORRIS, Ed	Boston
102 MARVIN, Mrs.	
103 MALONE, E.P.	Wis.
104 MOORE, Edward	
105 McLean, James	seaman
106 McCOY, M.	
107 McHugh, Billy	*Charleston, SC*

. . .

"There he is. Thank God," Dolores said, as she made the sign of the cross, then hugged Sofia. He might still be here in Norfolk, Sofia. We must try to find him."

"He might be, but he might already have departed for Charleston," said Sofia. "And at this late hour I'm not sure we could find him. Don't forget, Dolores, we have a train to catch tomorrow morning, and if we miss it, we'll also miss the connection to Boston. I know how anxious you are to see Billy, but I think we must first try to reach papá and let him know that we are safe. I'm sure he knows by now that the *Central America* has sunk, and he'll be worried sick."

"You're right, dear sister. It was wrong of me not to think of papá first!"

"You couldn't help it, Dolores. You're still in love with Billy, and you spoke with your heart."

Dolores felt a surge of emotion. She smiled, though she feared she might cry and reached for Sofia's hand. It was the first time Sofia had acknowledged that Dolores was in love with Billy, ending what had once been something of a rivalry for his affection.

Just then there came a knock on the door. Sofia opened it and saw a man in uniform with an envelope in his hand.

"I have an overseas letter for Sofia and Dolores de Castilla. Would you sign here, please?"

"It's from papá," Sofia said.

La Habana 18 de setiembre 1857

Dearest Sofia and Dolores, Thank God you are both safe! I learned of the tragic fate of the Central America last week, and have not slept since then. The blessed news of your survival reached me only yesterday via the Times-Picayune, a copy of which was brought to me from the good ship Morning Light out of New Orleans. I have never felt such relief and joy in my life as when I gazed upon the list of survivors and saw your names! I went to mass and thanked God for our good fortune.

I sent a draft in the amount of $500 for each of you to the Bank of New York, so that you can buy new clothes to replace the things you lost.

Please write as soon as you are able, and let me know if there is anything else you need for the new year at Mount Holyoke.

God Bless you both!

Your loving papá.

7

Billy stepped off the train at Charleston Station, wearing the workers' trousers and shirt given to him by the Sisters of Mercy in Norfolk. He and four other men had spent five hours together in the raging sea, clinging to cabin doors that had been thrown off the ship minutes before *The Central America* went down. The men were picked up by the schooner, *Happy Season*, arriving a half-day after the bark *Marine* and the Norwegian sailing vessel, *Ellen,* had delivered the women and children. Billy spent a full day in the hospital and was treated for exhaustion and multiple contusions on his back. The Good Sisters gave him a few dollars and released him, whereupon he went directly to the railroad station and purchased a ticket to Charleston. That left him penniless and hungry for the long train ride home. Had it not been for the kind young woman who had boarded the train in Charlotte, he would have gone without eating that entire day. She had a basket of fried chicken and biscuits, and the sight and smell of them had poor Billy staring at her and practically drooling. She couldn't help but notice and kindly offered to share the meal with him. Her name was Alice Endicott, and she was on her way to Fayetteville to visit her aunt and uncle. Billy told her about *The Central America*, how he had tried to jump from the vessel at just the right moment, to escape the suction created by the vessel's descent. He'd held his breath until his lungs were at the bursting point before finally bobbing up to the surface. He saw one of the vessel's cabin doors floating nearby and swam to it, joining a makeshift flotilla of four other men, clinging to debris. They stayed grouped together as best they could to make them more noticeable to the rescue vessels; five hours later, they were picked up and taken to Norfolk. Billy told Alice how grateful he was just to be alive. He told her how men and women abandoned their fortunes, throwing sacks of gold coins and bullion onto the deck without second thoughts, before entering lifeboats or jumping into the sea; the value of gold having instantly paled in comparison to the value of life itself.

When the train arrived in Fayetteville, Billy said good-bye to Alice, settled back and tried to sleep but to no avail. His mind was too active and excited, and in spite of his efforts, he could not quiet it.

He thought first about Dolores and Sofia. He'd seen their names amongst the list of survivors in the Norfolk papers, thank God! And he'd managed to save the letter with Dolores's address that he'd taken from the stack in his valise. It had gotten thoroughly wet, but he was still able to read it. He thought about his parents. He had wanted to send a telegraph, telling them he had survived the disaster, but he hadn't the money. It also occurred to him that they would not have had any reason to know that he had left California; he had mailed his last letter to them the month before and had not mentioned it. He thought about Charlie Flynn and wondered if he had done right by him. They had little money, and Charlie was drifting and going nowhere. He thought about continuing his education, having made up his mind that he wanted to study law.

There were few passengers in the car. One was reading a thick book, while the rest were absorbed in their own thoughts and concerns. Eventually, aided by the steady rhythmic clicking of the train on the tracks, he fell asleep. Hours later, he was awakened by the train's shrill whistle, followed by several loud huffs and puffs from the steam locomotive as it slowed and came to a shrieking stop.

"Charleston, Charleston Station," shouted the coachman.

Billy stood up, perhaps too quickly, because he staggered slightly before grasping the seat handle.

"Don't forget your luggage," said the coachman to the departing passengers.

"I don't have any," Billy said, smiling. The coachman smiled back, apparently expecting an explanation.

"It's a long story," Billy said.

There were quite a few people on the platform, but most were boarding. Billy looked around as though he were waiting for someone to greet him. He saw several carriages standing by for hire and approached one, only then remembering that he had no money. It was just too long to walk, so, undeterred, he explained his predicament to the coachman, assuring him he would get the money from his parents upon arrival.

Off they went down King Street. Billy stared at the buildings and shops, which all looked familiar but strangely smaller and less significant. He looked at the passersby, waiting for the first face he recognized, wondering if anyone would recognize him. But no one did. He was struck with a wave of melancholy and pondered what would become of him now that he was "home."

It had been almost two years since he had left Charleston and a lot had transpired since then.

When they neared the border between the Pringle estate and the McHugh land, Billy's mood changed. He saw the slaves bending low in the rice fields. Some looked up, recognized him and waved. Billy smiled and waved back, directing the coachman up the narrow dusty road then onto the gravel path leading to his house. When the carriage came to rest in front of the house, he saw Julius sitting in a wagon hitched to the black mare. Julius looked up and shouted excitedly:

"Massa Billy! Massa Billy!" Julius jumped from the wagon and rushed to greet him. Bonny McHugh and Becky were in the kitchen and heard Julius' words. Bonny's face lit up as she rushed outside:

"Billy! Oh, Billy! You're back!" Her eyes filled with tears, and she rushed to embrace him, smothering him with hugs and kisses. "Your father and I have missed you dearly. We hope you are home for good."

"I am, Mama. I want to complete my education."

Bonny smiled but could not help but comment. "You should never have gone out to join that vagabond Charlie Flynn."

Becky walked over shyly now and reached for Billy's hand. That was not good enough for him, and he threw his arms around her and hugged her warmly. All the while Julius stood there beaming.

"All da way out ta California and back again. Ya sho is special, Massa Billy!"

CHAPTER VII

Lincoln's Election Means War

Billy walked into Michael's barbershop, took a seat and picked up the crumpled newspaper.

The Herald Tribune November 10 1860
Lincoln's Electoral Triumph

Abraham Lincoln was declared the winner of the November 6th presidential election and will assume the office as the 16th president of the United States on March 4th, 1861. While winning only 40% of the popular vote, the rest being split between candidates Breckenridge, Bell and Douglas, Lincoln captured 180 electoral votes, winning 18 states and swamping the combined total of 123 electoral votes for the other three candidates. The South was swift to denounce the election results. South Carolina immediately announced that it would convene a convention in Charleston next month to enact an ordinance of secession.

"Where did you get this New York paper, Michael?" Billy asked, as he put it back on the table and picked up the *Charleston Mercury*.

"Ole Buck O'Neil brought it in yesterday. Everyone's come in here's read it and got steamed up. Aah'm 'bout ready to throw it out. The Mercury's got it right. We're not about to be a part of any black republican regime," Michael said, all the while continuing to shave the elderly man in the barber's chair.

"You're damn right, we're not!" said a burly bearded man with a scowl on his face, who was waiting his turn.

The Charleston Mercury November 13 1860
Black Republicans Claim Victory
South Carolina Will Secede

The "Palmetto State Flag" flew proudly throughout the streets of Charleston and around the State as word spread that a convention will be convened next month to formally secede from the United States of America. Similar announcements are expected shortly from other southern states, namely, Mississippi, Alabama, Georgia, and Louisiana. Mister Abraham Lincoln and the black republicans can claim all the victories they want, but, Ladies and Gentlemen, we're not going to be a part of it. The Confederate States of America are about to be born.

A lively discussion broke out, and except for the dissenting (though silent) opinion of Billy McHugh, it was unanimous that secession was the right course of action for the proud State of South Carolina. It was unusual for Billy to withhold his opinions, especially now that he was about to be admitted to the Bar. Three years earlier, he had returned from California and undertaken to study the Blackstone's Commentaries on his own. He had also taken some courses at The College of Charleston. Most importantly, however, he had had the opportunity to read law under the guidance of the esteemed South Carolinian lawyer and statesman, James L. Petigru. Billy's affiliation with James Petigru was not merely a stroke of luck, though it certainly was that. Professor Randolph W. Chesterton of the College of Charleston, was a personal friend of Petigru's and recommended Billy as a law clerk. The Petrigru family had tragically lost their three sons in childhood and early adulthood, and when James Petigru met Billy, he took an immediate liking to him and offered him the clerkship. Petigru was quick to recognize Billy's potential and set him to work on some important cases. He also involved him in his political dealings with the South Carolina legislature.

Petigru was one of a few influential South Carolinians who opposed secession. It was not surprising that his young protégé, Billy McHugh, would also oppose it. Billy was already ideologically aligned with the Republican view and believed that President Elect Lincoln had it right when he advocated leaving slavery in place where it already existed but prohibiting its spread into the new territories. Billy thought it a fair compromise and an accommodation to the South. He thought it a mistake for South Carolina to secede from a Union that had provided peace, prosperity, and security for over eighty years. It was a position espoused by Professor Randolph W. Chesterton as well.

From the very first day that Billy returned to Charleston after the sinking of the *SS Central America,* he resumed his correspondence with Dolores. Their chance meeting aboard that ill-fated vessel had rekindled the flame, and unlike the later years of their adolescence, when distance and time apart had cooled their affections, their letters took on a renewed intensity and passion. The image of Dolores's incomparable beauty haunted Billy. He was convinced that it was his fate to be united with her. Dolores herself had intimated that years before.

When Dolores's letters were late, Billy would fall into a state of melancholy. Petigru and the other lawyers in the firm could not help but notice it. Bonny McHugh noticed it as well.

Billy continued to reside at home with his parents. Bonny was happy to have her son home again and doted over him. She did, however, chide him for having lost Constance Beckett, who had become engaged to a handsome and dashing young beau from the Military Academy. Billy's relationship with his father soured. Patrick continued to sail *The Wandering Maiden* to West Africa, purchasing slaves for resale in the Americas, mainly to Brazil, Barbados, and Jamaica. Though Billy was dependent on his father's income and support, at least until he was admitted to the Bar, he was not reticent in expressing his views.

There was one particularly contentious incident involving Becky and Julius. Billy had just returned home for the day from the Petigru chambers and saw Julius and Becky working in the back yard. When he went to talk to them, Julius asked about the election of Abraham Lincoln and whether the new president would abolish slavery. Unbeknownst to Billy, Patrick was upstairs at an open window listening to the conversation, in which Billy expressed his abolitionist's views. Julius and Becky were heartened by Billy's words. Julius asked Billy whether abolition would cover slaves such as he and Becky, who were slaves for their whole lives before any abolition might be enacted. Billy told them not to worry and that they would be freed. Patrick was furious, and threatened to throw Billy out of the house if he ever heard another word from him on the subject. After that incident there were few words exchanged between father and son, even at the dinner table.

A cold, hostile atmosphere took hold whenever they were in each other's presence. Bonny tried her best to bridge the gap between them, taking each to task for his "unchristian-like behavior." But all her efforts were in vain; the estrangement of father and son persisted and indeed worsened.

On December 20 1860, the State Convention met in Charleston, drafted and passed unanimously an Ordinance of Secession.

> *AN ORDINANCE to dissolve the union between the State of South Carolina and other States united with her under the compact entitled "The Constitution of the United States of America."*
>
> *We, the people of the State of South Carolina, in convention assembled, do declare and ordain, and it is hereby declared and ordained, that the ordinance adopted by us in convention on the twenty-third day of May, in the year of our Lord one thousand seven hundred and eighty-eight, whereby the Constitution of the United States of America was ratified, and also all acts and parts of acts of the General Assembly of this State ratifying amendments of the said Constitution, are hereby repealed; and that the union now subsisting between South Carolina and other States, under the name of the "United States of America," is hereby dissolved.*
>
> *Done at Charleston the twentieth day of December, in the year of our Lord one thousand eight hundred and sixty.*

With the enactment of the ordinance, South Carolina became a new and independent republic to great public acclaim and jubilation throughout the State. Celebratory festivities erupted throughout the City of Charleston. There were parades, bands played martial music, and there was spontaneous singing and dancing in the streets. President Elect Lincoln, though hesitant to go public before his inauguration, stated privately that if the three forts in South Carolina were taken, i.e., Fort Moultrie, Castle Pinckney, and Fort Sumter, Federal force would be used to retake them. He also stated that if Buchanan surrendered the forts, "he ought to be hung." As tensions heightened, Colonel Robert Anderson secretly moved his Federal garrison from Fort Moultrie to Fort Sumter, which he deemed more defensible. Then, on December 27 1860, the 27th South Carolina militia took Forts Moultrie and Castle Pinckney. Talk of war abounded as the secessionist movement rapidly spread throughout the South.

2

In June of 1860 Dolores and Sofia de Castilla graduated with honors from Mount Holyoke College. Don Fernando brought the entire family with him to the United States to attend the ceremonies. His older daughter, Constancia, and his two daughters-in-law, Soledad and Daisy, the wives of Felipe and Arturo, were reluctant to join their men folk; the memory of Sofia's and Dolores's close brush with death aboard the *Central America* was too fresh in their minds. But don Fernando insisted, and the entire family went as he wished.

Within a short time of their return to Cuba, Sofia had taken up again with her friends and compatriots at the University of Havana. Unlike her sister Sofia's easy adjustment, Dolores's return to Cuba was difficult and problematic. She had no community of friends and colleagues to rejoin, no cause to champion. She had benefited greatly from her four years as a student in the United States. From the day don Fernando had officially recognized her as his rightful daughter, her life had greatly improved. The free soil of New England, coupled with the liberal education she received at Mount Holyoke, had been liberating for Dolores. She had made close friends and had become completely fluent in English. She had greater self-esteem and was more outgoing. One of her teachers, a Miss Mildred Stone, had encouraged her to concentrate on literature, which Dolores delighted in and for which she seemed to have a particular affinity. She had even written some short stories in English, one of which had caught Miss Stone's attention and admiration for its style and originality.

Dolores's mother, Beatriz, though back in the good graces of the de Castilla family and residing in the Main House, had fallen gravely ill. Her rheumatism had worsened and she suffered from an advanced case of consumption. The doctors said her illness was terminal. Dolores begged don Fernando to send her mother to the United States for further treatment. But in addition to the cost, an unprecedented expenditure by a master for a common slave, Beatriz would not agree to leave the island. She had become resigned to her fate and wished to die on Cuban soil, where she had spent her entire adult life.

As for don Eduardo de Cadiz, the son of the mayor of Havana, he was no longer Dolores's unwanted suitor, having married the youngest daughter of the De Wolf family on the neighboring plantation. When Dolores told her mother of her continuing relationship with the American, Billy McHugh, she informed her that he was no longer part of his father's slaving operation and had become a lawyer with a distinguished law firm in Charleston. Beatriz had no reason now to oppose the relationship and gave Dolores her blessing.

It was a sad realization for Dolores that her mother's days were numbered, and Dolores spent every one of them at her mother's side. In those last few days, Beatriz talked about her African mother, who had told her as a child that when she died, her spirit would return to Africa from whence it had been stolen. Beatriz wanted her soul to "fly to Africa" to be reunited with her mother's, and she asked Dolores to summon the *Santero* to minister to her now and at her death. Father Ignacio would have been mortified, but Dolores obeyed her mother's wishes and smuggled the *Santero* into the Main House, bringing him to her mother's bedside. The *Santero* began to chant and Beatriz fell into a trance, mumbling what appeared to be words in the *Yoruba* language. The instant she departed, a tranquil smile appeared on her face, and though Dolores did not believe in *Santería,* she was confident that her mother was at peace.

Just before Christmas of 1860 and through the good offices of Miss Mildred Stone of Mount Holyoke, Dolores received a letter from a Mister William Meadows, Headmaster of the James Madison Academy, a private high school in Washington for children of members of Congress. The school was inviting her to interview for a teacher's assistant position. Dolores was thrilled, and she wrote an immediate response, saying she was interested in the position and would be in Washington for the interview. Don Fernando was opposed to her going. The United States was in turmoil over the issue of slavery and the secession movement of the southern states. A civil war was a distinct possibility. But it was too good of an opportunity to lose, and Dolores was adamant. In the end don Fernando acquiesced, realizing that Dolores had made up her mind and was determined to go. What Dolores had not told her father was that Billy McHugh had been spending time in Washington.

3

"Come over here a minute, Billy," said Mister Petigru, his haggard face obscured by the stacks of law books on his desk.

Billy stood before the veteran lawyer whose law firm proudly bore his name: James L. Petigru & Partners. Petigru was now in his sixties and had been given the charge of codifying the laws of South Carolina by the State Legislature. He was no longer actively practicing law, spending most of his time on the codification project. He did, however, take on some matters for close friends and colleagues. His services continued to bring in fees for the firm to everyone's benefit.

"I want you to go down to the Town Hall and run a title search on this fifty acre plot bordering the Alston Estate."

He handed Billy a Plat and Map, a Warranty Deed, the Last Will and Testament of one Warren P. Sterling, and a Codicil.

"I think there may be a missing Quitclaim Deed that would settle the matter once and for all."

Billy took the documents, and as he turned to go back to his desk, he saw the newspaper deliveryman drop a copy of *The Mercury* on the chair next to Mister Petigru's desk. The headline read:

GOVERNOR PICKENS: WAR IS IMMINENT

On February 4 1861, representatives of seven southern states—South Carolina, Mississippi, Georgia, Alabama, Florida, Louisiana, and Texas—met in Montgomery, Alabama. And on February 8, they declared the formation of the Confederate States of America. Jefferson Davis was named provisional president and Alexander Stephens vice president. The representatives gathered there declared themselves the First Congress.

The news of the coming war seemed to render everything else of little importance, including the title search that Pettigrew had told Billy to do. As he walked back to his desk, he saw more copies of *The Mercury* on the desks of the other lawyers, most of whom were standing now, talking agitatedly and gesticulating. Billy knew their sentiments. They were pro-secession and pro-slavery. James Petigru, however, was pro-Union and anti-slavery; he and Billy were the only ones.

Billy walked out into the Carolina sunshine and dutifully went to the City Hall. In less than two hours, he found the missing Quitclaim Deed. He found it crunched at the bottom of the property records cabinet between two Warranty Deeds. It had gone overlooked in previous title searches. When Billy returned to the office and informed Mister Pettigrew that he had found the Quitclaim Deed, Petigru was more than pleased.

"I knew I could count on you. I wish we had more young lawyers of your kind in this office, Billy, and I've decided to raise your salary starting next month."

Billy smiled appreciatively.

"I'm very grateful for the confidence you've placed in me, Mister Petigru, but there's something important that I need to speak to you about. I've decided to move to Washington."

He told Petigru about Dolores, how he had met her years before in Cuba and how they had fallen in love. He told him that recently she had gotten an assistant teacher's position at the Congressional School in Washington.

"Not only that, sir, but I don't in good conscience believe I can stay here in Charleston and support the Confederate States of America. My allegiance is to the United States of America."

"I understand how you feel, Billy."

"And sir, I'd like to ask if you would be willing to write me a letter of recommendation. I'm sure it would be very helpful in finding a position."

James L. Petigru's connections reached all the way to the White House. President Elect Abraham Lincoln was a personal friend of James Petigru, and Lincoln respected his status as the highly regarded "Unionist of the South."

"I'm sorry to hear that you will be leaving us, Billy, but I understand your reasons. That is where your heart and your conscience are leading you, and that is where you must go. As for the letter of recommendation, I will be happy to write it for you. I know a firm where you would be very well placed, both for you and the firm."

A few weeks passed during which Billy made plans to depart for Washington. He delayed telling his parents until the last minute.

In the meantime, CSA President, Jefferson Davis, ordered Brigadier General Pierre Beauregard to take charge of the volatile situation in Charleston. Beauregard arrived in Charleston on March 3 1861, and the very next day Abraham Lincoln took the oath of office and became the 16th president of the United States of America. Lincoln vowed to "hold, occupy and possess the property and places belonging to the government." To Charlestonians, the message was clear; it meant war. Lincoln, however, still wished to avoid war if possible and sent his good friend Ward Lamon on a secret mission to Charleston to meet with none other than James Petigru. Petigru told Lamon that "peaceable secession or war was inevitable." Lamon also met with Governor Pickens, who told Lamon that any attempt to re-supply Fort Sumter would mean war. On March 29, President Lincoln ordered a naval expedition to do just that—re-supply Fort Sumter. Lincoln made one last attempt to avoid the conflict, personally drafting a letter to

Governor Pickens, in which he stated that if re-supply was not resisted and the fort was not attacked, there would be no effort "to throw in men, arms, or ammunition." The letter was read by Governor Pickens and General Beauregard, neither of whom backed down.

On April 12, Beauregard opened fire of his batteries on Fort Sumter. The War had begun. Thousands of shells fell on Fort Sumter for a day and a half, destroying it completely. At approximately 2:30 pm on April 13, Major Anderson raised the white flag and surrendered Fort Sumter. The Stars and Stripes were lowered, and the Stars and Bars were raised to the joyous shouts of thousands of Charlestonians. Spirits were high; an air of confidence reigned throughout the city of Charleston that "our southern boys will whip them Yankees in no time at all." Elaborate parties and balls were celebrated throughout the city. Officers appeared in their handsome and newly sewn uniforms to the delight of the ladies, who were dressed in elegant ball gowns and bedecked with jewels and corsages. They ate, drank, and danced until the wee hours. Yes, it was to be a grand and glorious time for all, a time of heroes, honor, and courage in defending the newly minted Confederate States of America.

4

Billy had already packed one valise and was filling a second with his clothes and personal belongings. Bonny stood in the doorway. She was now in her forties. Wrinkles had taken root on her once pretty face, and her hair was streaked with gray. Her countenance revealed a profound sadness as she watched her Billy pack. In her mind, Washington was just as far away as California, maybe even farther. For this time, Billy was a grown man and a lawyer, resolute in his decision to leave Charleston. She knew not when or if she'd ever see him again, for the nation was at war.

"Must you go today, Billy?"

Tears formed in Bonny's eyes. She tried to brush them away before he saw them.

"Your father is expected home any time now, maybe even to-day. Can't you at least wait till he's back home?" Billy continued to pack without looking at his mother.

"I'm sure he would want to see you before you go." Billy closed the valise then turned and looked directly at his mother.

"We'll all be better off, mama, if I'm not here when he returns."

"Your father deserves more respect than you give him, Billy. He's worked hard to provide a good living for both you and me."

"I don't like his line of work, mama, and I don't like the way he treats people, especially black people."

Just then Becky appeared and stood behind Bonny, holding a pair of Billy's trousers, which she had just finished ironing. Becky and Julius had learned that Billy was going to Washington and had secured a position with a respected law firm. They were happy for him, but were saddened that he was leaving.

"Here yo trousers, Massa Billy. Sho is a sad day fo Julius and me ta learn ya leavin." Becky passed Billy the trousers and tried to smile, but it was a feeble attempt that failed.

"Thank you, Becky. I can always count on you." Billy took the trousers and hung them over the door of the armoire.

"We sho gonna miss ya, Massa Billy. But we sho is proud dat you now a lawyer, and dat you be goin to Washington where da new president, Abraham Lincoln hisself, is now in da White House."

Bonny looked at Becky sternly.

"Go back down and finish that ironing, Becky."

"Yezz, Mizz McHugh."

"I'll come down and talk to you before I leave, Becky," Billy said.

This time Becky's smile was warm and genuine as she turned and obediently went downstairs to do her ironing. Bonny sat on the bed, and there was an awkward pause as Billy looked around the room, checking for things he might have forgotten.

"I know you're going up north to meet that Cuban girl. I can never remember her name."

"Her name's Dolores, mama, Dolores de Castilla. How many times do I have to tell you?"

"You're not planning on joining the army and fighting for the Yankees, are you? Your father would never forgive you."

"No, mama, I have no present plans to fight for anyone, other than my clients. I'm going to Washington to be with the woman I love. We've been separated since the time we met eight years ago, and this is the first chance we've had to actually be together."

Bonny reached for Billy's hand and began stroking it.

"What kind of a girl is she, Billy? What are her parents like? And are you sure that she's the right girl for you?"

"Why didn't you ask me all that before, mama? Why did you have to wait till now, just when I must leave? I would have told you how wonderful, how kind and gentle, how beautiful she is, and just how much I love her. She comes from a very good family, and…" They heard the sound of wagon wheels on the gravel. Bonny went to the window.

"It's your father, Billy. He's back."

Patrick McHugh had been gone for months, delivering African slaves to Brazil. Bonny rushed downstairs to meet him. Billy looked out the window and saw his father paying the coachman. Julius had run out to tote Patrick's luggage. Billy hesitated at the window, wondering whether to go down and face his father or wait until he came upstairs. As he walked down the stairs, he heard Patrick greeting Bonny.

"Bonny, my love, I can't tell you how good it is to see you!"

He lifted her off the floor and twirled her around a few times, then hugged and kissed her repeatedly. Billy waited until they'd finished their embrace, then he walked over slowly and stretched out his hand.

"Hello, Dad."

Patrick smiled and shook his hand. "Well now, Billy, what are you doing home so early from Mister Petigru's chambers? Or is it that all you lawyers have joined the cause to whip the Yankees?" Billy was unsmiling

"I'm leaving, Dad. I got a position with a firm in Washington, and I'm leaving today."

Bonny knew what was coming and walked out to the kitchen.

"You're what! You're goin' to *Washington* with all the rest of them nigger-lovin' *abolitionists*!" He dragged out the word with disdain, glaring at his son contemptuously.

"I knew it! I damn well knew this was coming! Bonny, where are you? Come in here, Bonny!"

She walked in from the kitchen. Becky and Julius peeked out and listened.

"Did you hear what your son just told me? He's goin' up north with the Yankees!"

"Yes, I know, Patrick. He told me, but please, it's not what you think."

"We're at war, and he's goin' north, at a time when the South needs every one of its native sons to fight and protect our newly declared freedom from Yankee oppression! Why he's nothin' more than a traitor to our cause. He's yellow, Bonny! I'm ashamed to call him my son!"

Billy stood there quietly, looking at his father, waiting for the right moment to respond. Patrick's face suddenly turned a scarlet red. He cocked his fist, and trembling with rage took a step toward Billy. Bonny tugged at Patrick's arm, trying to pull him back.

"No, Patrick. He's not going north to join the Yankees; he's going up north to be with that Cuban girl." Billy looked at his mother and frowned.

"She has a name, mother! Her name's Dolores, and that's right, Dad, I'm going to Washington to be with her!"

Patrick, still fuming, backed away slowly, then turned and began pacing back and forth.

"You know, Bonny, I never told you before, 'cause I wanted to spare you the pain, and I'm damn sure that he didn't tell you. But that Cuban girl's a nigger! Her mother's a mulatto and a common field slave." Bonny looked shocked and turned to Billy as though he owed her an explanation.

"Now, ain't that right, Billy boy! Why don't you tell your mama about your Cuban girl!"

"She's every bit as white as you are!" Billy shouted back. "Don Fernando de castilla is a Spaniard."

"I tell you, Bonny, she's a nigger, a light-skinned nigger but a nigger nonetheless! Her mother's a nigger, a low down dirty field slave! So it don't matter that her father is Spanish. She's a nigger, and she'll always be a nigger. And if he's foolish enough to marry her, their children will be niggers. And I damn sure don't want no nigger blood in our family. Now get out of my sight, Billy! You're no longer my son! I'm disownin' him, Bonny. I want nothin more to do with him!"

Billy looked at his mother, his eyes pleading for her understanding. He then turned to his father.

"Can't you understand, dad? I love Dolores? I've been in love with her since the first day we met in Cuba years ago. You were there. You knew how I felt about her."

"And what about us, Billy? What about your father and mother? Do you love us? We're your own flesh and blood! Do you love your hometown, your birthplace, the state where you were brought up and spent most of your life? We're your people, Billy, and you're bringin' shame on us and the good name of McHugh. Why, the whole Goddamn town will know about it by tomorrow. You're abandonin' your home, your heritage, and your country in a time of need!"

Patrick was furious again. Billy saw the veins in his neck and forehead pulsing with rage.

"GET OUT! I can't stand to look at your sorry, nigger-lovin' face! You're no longer my son. GET OUT AND DON'T COME BACK! DON'T EVER COME BACK!"

Bonny started sobbing. Billy walked over and put his arms around her. Patrick stood there shaking with rage. He gave Billy one last threatening look then turned and walked through the kitchen and out the back door to the yard, rushing past Becky and Julius and glaring at them with misdirected hostility.

"Can I take the mare and have Julius drive me to the railroad station?"

"Don't leave yet, Billy. Let me see if I can talk to your father. I know he didn't really mean what he said."

"No, mama, talking to him now won't do any good. Now I need to take the mare."

"We're at war," Bonny sobbed. "You might not be able to return to Charleston, not even to visit us. Couldn't you bring Dolores here to Charleston?" Billy didn't respond.

"All right, Billy, take the carriage, but you better leave now before your father comes back. You can't tell what he might do."

Billy ran to the kitchen and told Julius to hitch the mare to the carriage. He hugged Becky and said good-bye, then rushed upstairs for his two valises.

Bonny stood on the gravel patch, crying, as Billy prepared to leave, aware that she might never see him again. Billy kissed and hugged her, said good-bye and climbed into the carriage next to Julius.

"Billy, please come back as soon as you can." Bonny cried even harder now.

"I promise you, I will."

Billy's eyes filled with tears as he motioned for Julius to depart. No sooner had they started riding off, when Patrick McHugh appeared from behind the house yelling and shaking his fist.

"Julius, you halt right there and climb down from that carriage! I don't want that yellow traitor usin' any of my property ever again. You stop, Julius or I swear I'm gonna whip you like you've never been whipped before."

Julius' first instinct was to obey his master, and he pulled back on the reins and the carriage slowed. But Billy grabbed the reins, whipped the mare and the carriage sped off down the trail.

5

When they reached the main road, Julius took hold of the reins again, a worrisome expression on his coal-black face.

"Hold her steady, Julius, and take us down to the Washington Depot. Drive in behind the station and drop me off in back."

The carriage suddenly hit a rut in the road and jostled them. Billy's valises came loose and looked as though they might fall off. Billy told Julius to pull over, and Julius brought the carriage to a halt. They got out and secured the valises. When they got back in the carriage, Julius turned to Billy with desperation in his eyes.

"Ya gotta take me up nawth wid ya, Massa Billy. Ya heard yo

papa what he gonno do ta me iffen Aah goes back der. Take me wid ya, Massa Billy. Aah won't be no trouble to ya."

Julius' plea came as a surprise to Billy, but it shouldn't have, because the two of them had often talked of Julius' freedom.

"What about Becky and your two boys? You can't just leave them here."

"Becky and me's been talkin and plannin fo a long time ta go up nawth where we can be free. We done saved some money too, and iffen da boys can't come by demselves, we can buy der freedom."

In spite of his sympathy for Julius' plea, Billy was suddenly troubled, thinking that Julius' presence might hinder his own efforts to reach Washington. Julius would be a runaway slave, and Billy would be aiding and abetting his escape. Moreover, he would be stealing his parents' personal property.

"Are you sure you're ready to go north, Julius? It will require a big adjustment on your part. You'll be without your family and friends. What will you do in the north? You don't have work and you don't know anyone."

"Aah can wuk as a carpenter, and we knows some free black folk der in Washington. Dey say dey can help us git settled and all. Please, Massa Billy, Aah begs ya. Take me wid ya. Aah cant go back and face yo papa."

Billy remained silent, and his face took on a worried look.

"Aah can pay fo da train, Massa Billy."

"It's not the money that I'm worried about, Julius. There are some legal questions, including the *Fugitive Slave Act*. And this is now the Confederate States of America, and if they suspect what we're doing, they'll stop and arrest both of us."

A sad look covered Julius' face.

"Iffen ya can't take me wid ya, den Aah'l go on down to da

wharfs, hide maself and board a ship, but Aah'm not goin back der wid yo papa, Massah Billy. Aah jest can't."

They entered Charleston proper and headed down Chapel Street toward Alexander, passing groups of newly assembled volunteer troops, most of them still without uniforms and carrying what looked like outdated muskets. Women lined the sidewalks, applauding and raising cheers as the men were marched off for some basic military drill to the glorious and uplifting sound of Dixie.

The melody tugged at Billy's heartstrings, evoking pangs of guilt and regret. The words *coward* and *traitor*, which his father had hurled at him earlier flashed across his mind, stinging him as hard now as they had then. And as much as he hated to admit it, he felt suddenly ashamed.

What about James Petigru, a distinguished gentleman and a superb lawyer who shares my beliefs and feelings? He's not abandoning his homeland; he isn't going north to join the enemy of the south. And what about my parents, especially my mother? Will she be safe?

As for Julius, Billy felt responsible. He'd taught him to read and write, nurtured him, filled him with hope that some day he'd be free. Well, now was his chance, his chance to be free, and he couldn't in good conscience let him down.

"All right, Julius, you're coming with me." The smile that burst forth on Julius' face was wide enough to reveal all his molars.

"God bless ya, Massa Billy. Aah always done knowed Aah could count on ya."

Billy smiled and put his arm around Julius' shoulder.

"From now on, Julius, I want you to call me *Billy*, just plain Billy. No more 'Massa' Billy. You got that?"

"Yessuh, Billy, no mo Massa, no mo Massa." Julius was just beaming.

They reached the Washington Depot, and Billy reminded

Julius to pull the carriage around to the back of the station. Julius pulled up under a tree at the edge of a grassy field and stopped. They jumped down and Julius grabbed Billy's valises.

"No, Julius, I'll carry one and you carry the other."

"Sho nuf, Billy."

Billy had no choice but to leave the carriage and hope that his mother would retrieve it.

"Let's go," Billy said.

The depot was abuzz with activity. Troops were lined up awaiting transport to destinations not yet revealed. Sweethearts and relatives stood at their side. Vendors scurried about, hawking bouquets of flowers, little leather diaries, and other mementos to mark the glorious day their boys marched off to defend the newly proclaimed Confederate States of America.

They entered the station, which was crowded with both white and black folk. It was never an easy matter to distinguish a free black man from a slave, and that was in their favor. Billy walked up to the counter and purchased two tickets to Fayetteville. North Carolina had not yet joined the Confederacy but was expected to do so presently. It was considered friendly territory. And there were several railroad routes to Washington.

As they waited for their train, they sat down on a bench outside near the tracks. A steam engine with several passenger cars pulled into the station. Billy watched without paying close attention to the passengers who were disembaking. Then all of a sudden, there he was, Charlie Flynn, his blond ruffled hair blowing in the breeze and a wide smile on his face. It was Charlie all right, noticeably thinner but unmistakable.

"Sit there, Julius! I'll be right back. I see an old friend of mine." Billy ran over just as Charlie was helping a pretty young lady step down from the train.

"Charlie, Charlie!" Billy yelled. Charlie turned and when he saw Billy, his face lit up.

"Well, I'll be damned if it ain't my old partner, Billy McHugh. How'd you find out that I was on this train?"

Billy decided that it would be easier not to disabuse Charlie of that notion and let it pass.

"What are you doing back here in Charleston?" Billy asked. "I thought you were going to stay in California and bring in that Yellow Creek claim no matter what."

Charlie laughed, then turned to the young lady.

"This here's Agnes, Billy. She's a sweet lil thing I met in Savannah. Say hello to my old friend and partner, Billy McHugh, Agnes. We went to high school together, and Billy was with me in California for a spell."

Agnes smiled and shook Billy's hand, listening while Charlie spun out more information about his old high school friend.

"Did that Yellow Creek venture fizzle out on you, Charlie, or was it the War that brought you back home to Charleston?" Billy asked.

"Both! I'm damn sure gonna join up. Got my eyes on the cavalry. I'm not about to let no Yankees dictate how I live my life. How 'bout you?"

Billy hesitated, and Charlie filled the void.

My dad wrote me that you were readin' law in some big important firm here in Charleston, so I suppose you're gonna be an officer, am I right? Hey, maybe we'll get to be in the same outfit. I recall you're pretty good with a horse."

Billy's smile faded.

"Well, Charlie, yes, I'm now a lawyer and a member of the Bar. And, ugh, I know you're not going to like what I'm about to tell you." Billy paused for a moment.

"Let's have it, partner."

"I'm going to Washington."

Charlie looked aghast.

"You're what?

"I'm going to Washington to…"

"This is no time to be goin north, partner. We're at war."

"…be with Dolores. She's in Washington now. She graduated from Holyoke College in Massachusetts and…"

"She's a Yankee!"

"…got a teaching position at a high school there, and I'm going up to be with her. I'm taking the train to Fayetteville, and from there on to Washington."

"You're goin up there with that nigger-lovin' Abraham Lincoln! Don't tell me you're plannin' to fight for the Yankees! I'm not sure what I'd do if I was to meet you on the battlefield partner."

"No, Charlie, I'm not going to fight for the Yankees, and I'm not going to fight for the south either. I'm a lawyer, and I have no desire to fight for anyone except my clients. James Petigru, the senior partner of his law firm here in Charleston, got me a position in Washington."

Agnes turned to Charlie and excused herself, saying she had to get going home. Charlie bid her good-bye and said he'd be calling on her soon.

"The train to Fayetteville will be leaving soon, Charlie, so we've only got a few more minutes. Why don't we sit down a minute together."

"Well, I've got to wait for my parents. I'm sure they planned on meetin' me here," Charlie said, but he reluctantly followed him.

"Have a seat, Charlie. They'll be able to see you over here. Uh, Julius, this is Charlie Flynn, an old friend of mine. We were in California together. My dad took Julius on a few years back, Charlie. I think you had already left for the gold fields." Julius extended his hand but Charie looked away.

There was an awkward pause, and Charlie's expression turned serious. Billy tried to keep the conversation going, but without much success. Charlie kept looking around for his parents, but it may have been a ploy, for the atmosphere had turned noticeably chilly. Gone was the friendly teasing and banter between the former best friends. They were now in different camps, and it didn't matter that Billy was going north to be with his beloved. He would still be up north with the Yankees, the enemies of the newborn Confederate States of America. So, it was a welcome relief for them both when Charlie's parents appeared on the station platform. Charlie saw them, stood up, and waved. There was little left to say, and when Billy extended his hand to Charlie, he got no response.

PART III

Spring 1861–Spring 1862

CHAPTER VIII

The Marriage

It was a lovely, warm spring day when Billy and Julius arrived at the B&O Station in the nation's capital. When Julius stepped off the train, he got down and kissed the ground. It was not an uncommon occurrence for a slave who had just become a free man, and only a few took notice. Tears of happiness ran down Julius' cheeks, and he reached for Billy's hand and shook it.

"Aah'l neva foget what ya done fo me, Massa Billy!" Billy smiled.

"Remember, Julius, no more Master Billy, just Billy."

"No mo Massa, jes Billy, jes Billy!"

"That's better, Julius."

They picked up the valises and walked out to the street. The crocuses and tulips were in full bloom, and the sweet scent of honeysuckle filled the air. Songbirds sang and chirped, delighting in the marvelous spring weather. Open air carriages passed by, pulled by prancing, spirited horses. Billy hailed a carriage, and they rode off. Julius asked to be dropped a few blocks from the station where he was to look up his Washington contacts. As for Billy, he planned to stay a few days at the Willard Hotel until he was able to find a flat, preferably near his new job. They agreed that Julius would contact Billy at the hotel if he had any serious problems.

He gave Julius the address of his new law firm and told him to contact him in a week or ten days to assure he had been settled.

There were still very few signs of the war that had erupted at Fort Sumter a few weeks before.

"Tell me, Mister, what's the feeling here in Washington about the outbreak of hostilities down in Charleston?" Billy asked.

The coachman turned and glanced at him nonchalantly.

"Why, the whole damn thing's nothin' but a tempest in a tea-pot. I can't see any reason why we should fight a war over some damn niggers. If them southerners wanna have nigger slaves, let 'em. It's none of our damn business. And we sure as hell needn't fight no war over it."

Billy listened quietly, wondering whether the man was expressing a commonly held view.

"Hell, I think this Abraham Lincoln's largely responsible for all this political turmoil that's now turned into hostilities. We'da been a helluva lot better off in my opinion if Douglas or even Breckenridge had been elected. This Lincoln's too damn moralistic."

The Willard Hotel was full of activity. Carriages arrived and departed carrying well-dressed men smoking cigars. Negroes scurried behind them, toting valises, trunks and all manner of other articles. Newspaper boys, both black and white, had set up their stands just outside the hotel doors and noisily hawked their papers. Billy bought a newspaper. The headline read

Union Troops Prepare to Defend Washington."

He checked in and was shown to his room. He was tempted to take a nap but decided not to. Instead, he freshened up and went down to the dining hall for a lunch of tomato soup, oysters and pot-roast. He carried all of his savings with him from Charleston and opened his billfold now to assure that the Willard food and lodging expenses wouldn't exceed what he'd budgeted. He still had to find more permanent lodging, and it would be a while before he would draw his first paycheck. After lunch he went back to the front desk and asked for directions to the Congressional School, which Dolores had written about in her last letter. The clerk said it was on Pennsylvania Avenue, not too far from the White House and within walking distance.

He set out for the school, and bought a pretty bouquet of pink and white camellias along the way. He arrived at the school after a short walk. It was an attractive three-story stone building with a wooden stand in front demarking the James Madison Academy. Billy entered the building and made his way to what looked like an administrative office, where he stopped and introduced himself. He asked to see a Miss Dolores de Castilla. The receptionist told him to have a seat and returned moments later with a light-skinned negro woman, who introduced herself as Patricia Winslow, the assistant to the headmaster, William Meadows.

"Yes, Mister McHugh, what can I do for you?"

Billy stood, smiled and shook the woman's hand, feeling a little uncomfortable and awkward carrying the bouquet.

"I'm here to see Miss Dolores de Castilla. I'm her fiancé."

"I didn't know she had a fiancéé," Miss Winslow said.

"Well, our engagement is not yet official," Billy said, somewhat taken aback by her comment, "but we have known each other for many years."

"We do not generally permit visitors to our faculty during school hours, Mister McHugh." At that moment a tall distinguished gentleman entered the administrative office.

"Oh, Miss Winslow, there you are. I need to talk to you about..."

"Excuse me, Mister Meadows, this is Mister McHugh. He's

come to see Miss de Castilla, but I told him that we do not permit visitors during school hours."

"Oh, those are lovely camellias you've got there. I picked some just this morning in our garden. My wife and I are amateur horticulturists in our spare time."

"They are lovely, aren't they, sir? I was just telling Miss, uh… that I'm Miss de Castilla's fiancé." Mister Meadows smiled and looked at Miss Winslow.

"Oh, I think we can make an exception, Miss Winslow. Why don't you accompany Mister McHugh to Miss de Castilla's office. I'm sure she will be very happy to see him. Where are you from, Mister McHugh, if I may ask?"

"I'm from Charleston, South Carolina, sir. I left just a few days ago."

"Oh, my, did you have any difficulty? I mean in light of the fact that we are at war with the new Confederate States of America."

Mister Meadows' expression turned serious as he waited for Billy's response.

"No, sir, there was no trouble. I came by way of Fayetteville, and the train ride was relatively smooth."

"Well, I'm very glad to hear that. Are you planning on staying in Washington, Mister McHugh?"

"Yes, sir, I'm a lawyer, and I have a new position with a firm here."

"Well, it's a pleasure to meet you, and I wish you all the best here in Washington. Miss Winslow will take you now to see Miss de Castilla. Good day."

"Good day, Mister Meadows and thank you for your help."

Billy followed Miss Winslow along a corridor and up a flight of stairs to the second floor and past an assembly hall. He glanced through the window and saw a full gathering of students attending a lecture. He followed her past another hallway, and she soon stopped outside an office, knocked and then walked away. A second later the door opened, and there stood Dolores, enveloped in brilliant sunshine streaming in through the large window. No less brilliant was the smile on her face when she saw who it was.

"*Ay, Billy, eres tú! Que divina sorpresa!*" (Ay, Billy, it's you! What a divine surprise!) Billy threw his arms around her and kissed her on the lips.

"You should have told me, Billy. I could have made preparations. When did you arrive?"

"Just today, my love."

He handed her the flowers, then picked her up and spun her around, kissing her madly before placing her down on the desk. "I am so happy to see you, Doloresita!"

"And I'm thrilled to see you, Billy. It's such a wonderful surprise, and how did you know that I love these beautiful Washington camellias? They are in full bloom now and just lovely. I'll put them in water."

She walked toward the door with Billy following her, not wanting to let her out of his sight. But she told him to wait and returned with the camellias in a vase that she placed on a table next to the window.

"Look how beautiful!" she said. Billy smiled.

"And look how beautiful *tú eres, mi amor.*" Billy threw his arms around her again and kissed her with abandon. Because his back was to the door, he did not see the janitor walking by carrying a wastebasket. However, Dolores saw him, and he was peering into the room with an impish grin on his face. She broke the embrace, walked over and closed the door.

"I am very new here and they are still evaluating me, Billy. Some of them can make things difficult."

"I think I just met one of them. That Miss Winslow was reluctant to let me see you, but Mister Meadows said it was all right. I thought maybe she was jealous, because you have a *novio* and I'm sure she doesn't."

"No, that's not it, Billy. She's just very strict about the rules. She told me once that the students report any problem or discrepancy they notice to their fathers, who are representatives or senators. That could make it difficult for all of us here. Oh, but Billy, my love, we can only talk for a few minutes. I have to teach a class. Why don't you go to the park just across the street, and after my class I will come and join you?"

2

Billy walked to the park and sat down on a bench shaded by a large oak tree. It was a delightful spot with spring flowers all about.

He had made up his mind. This was the day that he would propose to Dolores. Almost nine years had passed since that fall day in 1852 when he had first set eyes upon Dolores de Castilla in Cuba. He had never seen such a beautiful girl, never experienced such emotion, such excitement and such desire. He saw that image of her as he took the little jewelry box out of his pocket. He opened it, revealing the diamond engagement ring that he had purchased in Charleston. It sparkled as he moved it, catching the rays of sunlight in a dazzling display of luminescence. Gently lifting it out of the box, he slipped it on his little finger. It fit snuggly. He had described Dolores to the sales clerk, who told him that it should fit her ring finger.

He went over in his mind what he would say and how he would say it. *But what if she says no? What if she has met someone here in Washington? Surely, she knows that you have been planning to ask for her hand. Your letters have been intimating that for quite some time, and there was nothing in her letters to suggest that she would not accept.*

He took his watch from his vest pocket and checked the time. She would be here soon.

Sangre de negro, sangre de negro, does it matter? Does it matter that she has sangre de negro? But It's not noticeable. No one in Washington is aware of it. But you know it! And your father and mother know it! What if it were noticeable? Would you still love her? Would you still want to marry her? It was a last minute internal debate, and he sought to silence it. *I am going to propose to Dolores today no matter what, and with the grace of God, she will accept my proposal.*

He looked up now and there she was, and he stood up and embraced her.

"Sit down with me, Dolores. There's something important I want to say to you."

She looked lovely. Her long dark hair glistened in the sunlight. She had placed one of the pink camellias in her hair, and her smile would have lit up the darkest of rooms and warmed the coldest of hearts. Billy smiled and drank in her loveliness, but he could feel his throat drying up and his palms beginning to sweat. He took a deep breath, gathered up the courage, and looked deeply and longingly into her eyes.

"Dolores, I've never really told you before, at least not in person. I love you. I love you with all my heart. I have loved you from the very first day I saw you years ago in the courtyard of *La Dulce Gardenia*. I want you to be my wife. I want to spend the rest of my life with you. Will you marry me?"

Dolores blushed as she reached for his hand.

"Oh, Billy, yes I will. I love you dearly, and I have been waiting for this day. I have always known that it was our destiny to be man and wife."

Billy removed the ring from the jewelry box and placed it on her finger.

"Oh, Billy, it's just beautiful and it's a perfect fit."

Dolores's smile was radiant as she held up her hand, admiring the ring.

"I love you with all my heart, Dolores," Billy said, tears of happiness welling up in his eyes.

"And I love you too, Billy. I've loved you since that very first day, and I'll always love you."

They kissed, long and passionately.

"I adore the ring, Billy. It's so beautiful!"

"Like the beautiful woman whose finger it adorns. I want to give you the world, *mi amor*." I truly feel that I am the luckiest man in the world, Dolores."

"And I am the luckiest woman, Billy."

She took his hand and kissed it tenderly.

"I want to marry soon, Billy. We need to set a date that I can tell my family, so they can plan their travel to Washington for the wedding."

"The sooner the better," Billy said. "What about the first Saturday in June?"

"That doesn't leave much time, *mi amor*. April is almost gone."

"Then how about the last Saturday in June?"

"Well, that's a little more reasonable. It will be a hectic time but a joyous one," she said.

"We are now officially engaged, *mi amor*, oh, but wait before I forget. I have to return to the school to get my lesson book for tomorrow's class. What time is it?"

"It's half past four, my love."

"Come with me, *mi amor* We'll go together and get my lesson book, and then I will take you home and show you my flat."

They walked together arm in arm, the sweet scent of spring flowers and the sensual sound of songbirds bearing witness to the love that fully blossomed this beautiful spring day in the Nation's Capital.

As they exited the park, they heard martial music and caught sight of a column of troops a block away on Pennsylvania Avenue.

"Have you seen signs of the war here in Washington, my love?" Billy asked. "When I left Charleston, the whole city was preparing for war."

"Yes, I have, Billy. There seems to be more troops in the city every day. I hope that's not a sign of what's to come."

"Let's hope not, Dolores, but the struggle over slavery is so contentious that it's divided the nation and divided my own family as well."

He thought of telling her about his father's hostile reaction when he told him that he was going north, but decided not to.

They entered the school and walked past the administrative offices. Miss Winslow was seated in the receptionist's chair going through some papers. She looked up and smiled artificially as Dolores and Billy walked by.

3

On Saturday 29 June 1861, Father Jacob Walter at Saint Patrick's Roman Catholic Church joined William C. McHugh and Dolores de Castilla together in holy matrimony. It was a rainy day and there were few guests in attendance, attributable neither to the weather nor to the popularity and character of the bride and the groom; rather because both had only recently moved to the city and were still relatively unknown.

Don Fernando and Sofia attended. Sofia served as Dolores's Maid of Honor. Constancia, Felipe, and Arturo sent congratulations via telegraph. Brad Mitchum, a young lawyer from Billy's law firm, served as Best Man. Though there were few guests on the groom's side of the aisle, the presence of the esteemed South Carolina lawyer and statesman, James Petigru, lent an air of added dignity to the occasion. All eyes were turned toward him as he was acknowledged by Father Jacob.

Petigru had recently made his way to Washington under very difficult circumstances, to conduct what turned out to be a last ditch attempt to maintain open communication with the Confederate States. Weeks before, he had written a highly complimentary letter of recommendation for Billy, who was hired by the esteemed law firm of Henry Phipps & Partners.

Billy tried to notify his family of the wedding, but the letter he wrote to his mother was returned, because mail service to the South had been suspended. He had also sent several telegraphs, none of which were acknowledged.

The wedding reception was held at the Willard Hotel, all expenses paid by don Fernando. He also supplied the couple with the funds to lease and furnish a good-sized flat in a nice area of the city. Don Fernando wanted to bring them to Havana for their honeymoon, but they declined his generous offer, because of the commitments to their new jobs. They decided instead to honeymoon in New York City and Niagara Falls. It was a good decision, particularly the Niagara Falls part. Early July was the ideal time to visit Niagara, when the rush of water from the spring melt was at its peak.

They stayed at a charming hotel overlooking the falls, where the view was awe-inspiring. As newlyweds, they felt as though the sight was theirs alone, a wedding gift from God. During the day, they took river cruises, picnicked in secluded places in the surrounding hills, and hiked to other promenades from which to view the falls. They rode horseback, picked flowers, cooed, and kissed, and doted upon each other as only young newlyweds do.

They took their meals in the hotel's picturesque dining room, chatting joyously with other couples. In the evening, there was an orchestra, and they danced to the latest European waltzes. It was the first time that they had spent any significant time together, a time in which their romantic fantasies faced their first test. Reality proved to be every bit as sweet, proving that their instincts and feelings had been sound from the very first time they had met.

Although there were many other newlyweds at the hotel, none stood out like Dolores and Billy. Their love shone forth like halos for all to see. The desk clerks, the dining room waiters and the other hotel attendants all delighted in serving them. The hotel manager even asked if they would pose for a photograph of "The Happy Newlyweds" for a brochure, and they agreed.

During the trip back to Washington, signs of a military buildup were everywhere. The railroad stations were filled with young men in blue uniforms carrying duffle bags, cartridge boxes, canteens, and muskets with bayonets attached. At their sides were dewy-cheeked young sweethearts and other loved ones, offering words of encouragement and sweet, departing kisses. Trumpets blared and cymbals resounded as the young warriors boarded trains for yet unspecified destinations and destinies. The trains were full, and it seemed that more than half the passengers were newly requisitioned troops from the northern states. There were smiles, laughs, pats on the back and much hooting, hollering, and boasting: "We'll show them rebels a thing or two. This whole thing will be over in a matter of weeks." There was glory, honor, and fame to be had, and by golly, they were going to get their share of it.

The B&O Railroad Station in Washington was packed with troops. Negro newsboys sold newspapers whose headlines read **Union Troops Mass for Defense of Capital.** In the hectic comings and goings, a young, fair-skinned man in a corporal's uniform bumped into Billy, knocking the valise out of his hand.

"I'm very sorry, mister," he said, as he bent down, picked it up, and gave it back to him.

"Where are all you boys going?" Billy asked, while Dolores tried to get out of the way of a baggage wagon that was racing down the platform.

"Well, sir, we heard there's supposed to be some real fighting' near a stream in Virginia called Bull Run, and that's where I think we're going. Course, in all this chaos we won't know till we get there, the way I see it."

"Well, you take good care," Billy said, "and good luck to you."

The corporal smiled, and said good-bye as he followed a stout sergeant, who was doing his best to create some order and herd the troops down the platform to the street. Dolores took on a worried look as she rushed to keep up with Billy.

"Billy, is this something to be concerned about? I don't know exactly where the borders are, but I know that we are very close to Virginia. When I first got here, I read in the newspaper that the land they used for the Capital used to be a part of Virginia."

Billy reached for her hand. "Don't you fret, my love. They are not going to allow Confederate forces to enter the Capital. I'm sure they have the strategy and the forces to prevent it. So, don't you worry. Wait here and watch the luggage. I'll see if I can flag down a carriage."

As Dolores stood just outside the station, a handsome, young, light-skinned mulatto walked up.

"You be needing transportation, Miss?"

"Yes, my husband is out there right now trying to get us a carriage."

"Well, why don't you go tell him that you've got one here right now? You can trust me. Your luggage will be safe with me."

Dolores noticed the man's fine English and accent, so different from what she'd been hearing from the negro maintenance employees in the Congressional School. She also noticed that he was looking at her intensely.

"You from these parts, Miss?" he asked. "You remind me of someone, but I can't quite fix it in my mind."

Dolores hesitated, questioning whether the man was being impertinent and whether she should answer him.

"*Uh, now I know, my cousin Rebecca in Richmond.*"

"Oh, there he is! Billy, this man says he has a carriage for us."

"Well, now that's a stroke of luck. I was the last one in line out there and would have had a long wait."

Billy asked about the fare, and though it seemed high, he was not about to say no. The coachman picked up their luggage and led them to his carriage on the side of the station. He helped Dolores in, and when Billy stepped in, he asked the coachman if he knew anything about a battle looming in a place called Bull Run.

"Well, sir, from what I've heard and read in the newspapers, this General Beauregard and General Johnston have amassed a large Confederate force in the town of Manassas, Virginia, and they are just hankering for a fight."

As the coachman spoke, Billy, too, focused on his English, judging the grammar and vocabulary to be practically indistinguishable from his own. He wondered about the man's background and education, but decided not to question him.

"Do you happen to know the size of the Union forces assembled to defend the Capital?" Billy asked.

"Well, as you could see back there at the station, troops have been pouring into the city, and I've heard numbers as high as one hundred thousand."

The coachman turned onto Seventh Street, one of the few partially paved roads in the city, and pulled up to their building. Billy paid the fare and gave the coachman a generous tip, after which the coachman bowed and tipped his hat, all the while continuing to sneak admiring glances at Dolores.

4

The honeymoon was now a thing of the past, but the marital bliss it engendered did not diminish when Billy and Dolores returned to Washington. Indeed, it continued to blossom. They leased a flat on 7th Street that overlooked a park, and they settled in, furnishing and decorating it with joy and enthusiasm. Both were progressing nicely in their positions at work. During Billy's initial interview with Henry Phipps & Partners, he related how at the age of sixteen he had sailed to Africa as a cabin boy on his father's ship, continuing on to Cuba. He did not hide the fact that it was a slave ship, but explained that he had come to abhor the institution of slavery. He told the two senior partners how he had traveled to California aboard a steamer that stopped in Brazil and then sailed around Cape Horn, stopping in Cartagena, Colombia. He emphasized his long time interest in Spanish America and his growing fluency in Spanish. He went on to describe how he had crossed the Isthmus of Panama on the new railroad when returning east. Finally, he told them how he had come to be a passenger on the ill-fated *Central America* that had gone to the bottom off Cape Hatteras with over four hundred souls and tons of gold. Both Phipps and Bartlett were familiar with the *Central America*, having represented several clients on insurance claims. Billy related all that, and gave a detailed account of his legal work with James Petigru & Partners in Charleston. The partners were surprised and impressed with his exploits, given that he was only in his mid-twenties; he had accumulated a portfolio of international travel and experience greater than most men twice his age. On a personal note, Billy mentioned that he had married a Cuban girl, whom he had met on that first voyage aboard his father's vessel. When the interview ended, the partners were unanimous in their decision to offer Billy the position of associate attorney in the firm. Billy was pleased, and even more so when he was assigned to Mister Joseph Bartlett, the senior partner who specialized in international trade and commerce. Bartlett represented some large international shipping companies and was co-counsel in Washington for the Union Pacific Railroad. Early in his career, Bartlett had served as a clerk at the State Department and had come to acquire some knowledge of the diplomatic function. Over the years, he had made connections that went all the way up to the Secretary of State himself, William Seward.

For the first six months, Billy served an apprenticeship. He had already served one with James Petigru in Charleston, but Joseph Bartlett was not quite ready to permit Billy to work directly with his more important clients. In time Bartlett came to see, just as James Petigru had seen before him, that though he was young, Billy was more than capable of taking on responsibility and solving difficult problems; he was, in fact, already a first rate lawyer, thorough and resourceful with sound judgment. Before long, Bartlett came to rely on him just as James Petigru had.

The war brought additional legal work to Henry Phipps & Partners. The first great battle of Bull Run that summer resulted in a hurricane of litigation over damaged and requisitioned property. And Joseph Bartlett's shipping company clients found themselves embroiled in maritime litigation as their vessels were being increasingly "plastered" with claims, resulting from suspected blockade running. Billy soon found himself immersed in the erudite intricacies of maritime law, adding another area of the law to his growing portfolio.

As for Dolores, she began teaching much sooner than she or Mister Meadows had planned. Within a few months, she had successfully filled the position in a way that surprised and pleased the administration, the faculty and her students as well.

The couple's social life had also begun to take root. On weekends, they entertained guests in their flat or were themselves invited to the homes of others. At first, it was mostly with the lawyers and their spouses from Billy's firm or the teachers and their spouses from Dolores's school. But it gradually spread. Billy and Dolores were an attractive and interesting couple, and as they came to be known as such, they solidified their place in society and gradually expanded their social web. Henry Phipps and Joseph Bartlett, who were well known and highly respected among Washington's social and political elite, were instrumental in furthering Billy's emergence as an up-and-coming young lawyer. The firm had made substantial contributions to Abraham Lincoln's presidential campaign and was known to be firmly in the Republican camp. Phipps and Bartlett attended all the important social gatherings, including those at the White House; and they often brought one or two young associates with them. Increasingly, Billy was one of those chosen.

The war, which everyone had thought would be over in a matter of weeks, stretched on. Casualties mounted on both sides, but the South had gotten in the best licks. It was indeed beginning to look like the rebels' boast, that one Confederate soldier was worth ten Yankees, was not mere hyperbole.

5

By Christmas 1861, Billy and Dolores McHugh were comfortably established in Washington. Although Confederate forces were still close to the Capital, it seemed that the Army of the Potomac, led by General George McClellan, had things under control.

Billy and Dolores celebrated at their flat, and when Billy asked

Julius to help with the preparations, he learned that Becky had fled Charleston and was now in Washington. Julius described Becky's long and difficult journey north, assisted by numerous abolitionist organizations along the Underground Railroad. Billy knew that his parents, and particularly his mother, would be at a great loss without Becky, who did most of the McHugh's' household chores. But he also knew that Julius and Becky were a loving and devoted couple, and that they had been suffering from a lengthy and painful separation. Billy had to admit that in spite of his parents' loss, he was glad that Becky had come north to be with Julius. Julius told Billy that they were also devising plans to get their two boys to come north as well, either by escape or by purchasing their freedom from the Pringles.

Billy and Dolores had a Christmas party and invited Henry Phipps, Joseph Bartlett and several young associate lawyers, including Brad Mitchum. The party was a resounding success with lots of good food, good wine, and holiday cheer. Phipps and Bartlett noticed the young couple's poise and confidence in their roles as host and hostess and complimented them on it. When the party ended and the guests had departed, Dolores took Billy by the hand and walked him over to the fireplace, where they sat down together on the sofa next to the Christmas tree. It was a proud and happy moment, and Dolores smiled, pointing to a large box wrapped in red paper and tied with a green ribbon.

"That one is for you, my sweet." With a wide smile, Billy reached for the box.

"My, but it's really heavy. I can't for the life of me guess what's inside." Dolores leaned over and kissed him warmly.

"Well, there's only one way to find out, my love. So, go ahead and open it."

He opened it, and much to his delight found a beautiful globe, which he slowly lifted out of the box.

"It's incredibly beautiful, Dolores!"

The oceans were crafted of stunning lapis. Each country was fashioned of semi-precious stones, and the latitude and longitude lines were of gold. Set within a highly polished tripod mahogany frame, it was unquestionably stunning. He had never seen anything like it and marveled as he spun it slowly within its orbit.

"The craftsmanship is remarkable. Where in the world did you ever find it?"

"Papá sent me a catalogue from a shop he knew in Madrid, and when he visited Spain recently, I asked him to get it for me. I paid for it with my own money from my salary."

"It's just exquisite. And look, sweetheart, it even has little tables showing distances to and from some key countries."

Billy was just beaming as he leaned over and kissed his young wife, love and affection flowing from his every pore. He reached under the tree now and picked up a little package wrapped in gold paper. "This is for you, *mi vida*." Dolores's eyes lit up and she smiled with delight. "Open it, my sweet," Billy said.

"Hmm, good things come in little boxes."

"And sometimes in big boxes," Billy said, giving his globe another gentle spin.

Oh, Billy pearls! How precious!"

It was a pearl ring with matching earrings in yellow gold. They glistened in the light from the fire, the black and white pearl set diagonally to each other on both the ring and the earrings. She took the ring out of the box and placed it on the ring finger of her right hand.

"Oh, my love, look how beautiful! It's a perfect fit. You have such good taste!"

"It's what led me to marry you, my love. Try on the earrings."

She got up, walked over to the large parlor mirror, and fastened them on her ears.

"Look how lovely, Billy! I will always treasure them!"

She came back to the fireplace and kissed him tenderly. "Sit down, Billy. I have some very special news for you. She reached for his hand.

"You're going to be a father." Billy practically leaped off the sofa. "That's wonderful, but are you sure?"

"Yes, my love, I'm sure. I found out last month but wanted to wait until now to tell you. I wanted it to be a special Christmas present."

"This is the most precious Christmas gift I've ever gotten. We must toast this moment!" He walked to the kitchen, returning shortly with a bottle of wine and two crystal glasses. He filled the glasses.

"To us, my love, and to our beautiful child soon to be!"

"To us and to our beautiful child and children soon to be!" Dolores said, looking lovingly at her handsome young husband.

"When is the baby due, my love?"

"Sometime in late July or early August. We have a while yet to wait."

Billy got up and walked to the Christmas tree, inhaling the fresh scent of its wintry greenness

"We must start thinking of names. Will it be a boy or a girl?"

"We'll just have to wait and see," said Dolores.

Billy walked back to the fireplace, sat down on the sofa and filled their glasses with wine.

"Now, my love, give me another kiss, because I have some very good news for you too. It is nowhere near as good as the news you just gave me, but still it is very good. We have been invited to accompany Henry Phipps and Joseph Bartlett and their wives to the White House for the President's New Year's Reception. Mr. and Mrs. Lincoln and the entire cabinet will be there. Now, what do you think of that and your up-and-coming young lawyer husband?"

"Oh, Billy, that's wonderful! How did you ever manage to get invited to the White House?"

"Well, to be perfectly honest I didn't manage anything of the sort. It was the work of Mister Bartlett and Mister Phipps. The doors of the White House will be open to the public on New Years Day, but those with invitations, that means us, will get in first and attend a private reception in the East Room."

"Oh, but New Year's is only a week away, and that doesn't leave much time. I'll have to find a dress and have my hair fixed."

Dolores felt a twinge of anxiety, remembering that grand ball years before, when she had innocently caused a stir and a duel, in which don Eduardo de Cadiz was shot and almost died.

"You'll be the loveliest woman, the loveliest expectant woman at the White House or anywhere else you go for that matter. Of that I'm certain, my love."

"Will Brad Mitchum's wife, Julie, be there?"

"Yes, the Mitchums will be there as well." Dolores breathed a sigh of relief.

"That's good. I'll have someone to talk to."

"You'll have no difficulty finding people to talk to, my love. I'm certain of that.

CHAPTER IX

The White House

It was New Year's Day, 1862, and unusually warm in the nation's capital. As Dolores and Billy mounted the carriage that would take them to the White House. The driver remarked that it was the warmest New Year's he could ever recall. Billy removed his coat and loosened his cravat, while Dolores, accustomed to years in tropical Cuba, did not seem to notice the temperature. The mild weather contrasted sharply with the bare wintry look of the trees and shrubs that they rode past. As the carriage approached Pennsylvania Avenue, they spotted some Union troops. One was a blond-haired lad hobbling along between two burly soldiers, his arms strung around their shoulders as though he had been injured. But as the carriage got closer, it became clear that the three of them had likely been celebrating.

"I can see now why the rebels whipped us so darn good at Manassas," said the driver.

"Aah'm told that Ole Jeff Davis don't allow no drinkin."

Billy hadn't heard that, but if true, he wondered how in the world Davis could enforce it.

As they neared the White House, they saw a long line of citizens that snaked its way around the grounds from the street. Billy reached into his vest pocket and took out his official invitation.

He told the driver to drop them off at the North Gate, where he had been instructed to meet Joseph Bartlett. As they walked up the gravel path, they spotted Brad and his wife, Julie, standing behind Bartlett and Phipps and their spouses.

"Oh, here they are, Henry," said Bartlett.

Dolores smiled and curtsied. Bartlett smiled and shook her hand. He then introduced his wife, Bess, and turned to his partner.

"Henry, you remember Mrs. McHugh from their Christmas party."

"Yes, of course," said Phipps as he shook Dolores's hand.

He introduced his wife, Mary, a pretty woman much younger than he, who spoke with a distinctly southern drawl.

Brad and Julie Mitchum greeted Billy and Dolores, wishing them a happy new year, as did the Phipps and Bartletts.

As they entered the presidential mansion, a black attendant directed them to put their coats in the cloakroom off to the side. Bartlett had attended many receptions at the White House and led all of them along to the East Room.

Despite the fact that under the Buchanan administration, twenty thousand dollars had been appropriated to decorate the White House for the new president, Lincoln's wife, Mary Todd, had undertaken to redecorate to her own taste, expressing dislike for what President Buchanan's niece, Miss Hanes, had done. There had been several articles written about Mary Todd's elaborate redecorating, including one in the *Washington Star*, which was widely read; and all the ladies in attendance this New Year's Day were anxious to see what the new First Lady had accomplished.

The East Room was the largest room in the White House, running the entire length of the mansion from north to south. It was the President's grand parlor, and the First Lady spared no effort or expense to assure that the guests were impressed with the good taste of the White House's new occupants. She had chosen a luxurious pale green carpet adorned with roses. Some said that it gave the impression of roses rising from the depths of a brilliant green lake. The First Lady adored mirrors, and she had purchased several elaborately crafted gilded models and had them placed strategically throughout the room. Two enormous crystal chandeliers hung from the ceiling, their gleaming light reflected throughout the spacious room. Mary and Abe were fond of black walnut furniture, and the room was filled with it. Mary, always curious and meticulous, had also discovered some dusty portraits of past Presidents and Secretaries of State locked away in storage; she retrieved them and had them cleaned and hung on the walls. Finally, Mary had found two large grandfather clocks and had them refinished and strategically placed in the East Room. Overall, the ladies of Washington were favorably impressed with Mary's efforts.

There were already quite a few distinguished guests in attendance when the representatives of Henry Phipps & Partners entered. Billy and Brad were advised that in addition to the President and the First Lady, they could expect to see many prominent cabinet members, including William Seward, Secretary of State, and Salmon Chase, Secretary of the Treasury.

They had no difficulty recognizing President Lincoln, who stood out no matter where he was in the room. Another prominent and easy to recognize guest was General Winfield Scott. Though in his seventies, he struck an impressive pose at six feet four, resplendent in his full dress uniform.

There was a large crowd around President Lincoln, so Billy decided to save him for later. For now, he walked toward the group surrounding General Scott, noticing that Bartlett had already engaged William Seward, whom Billy recognized from newspaper photographs. Meanwhile, Dolores and Julie Mitchum had gathered together with a group of ladies, all of whom were dressed in elegant, colorful gowns.

Billy managed to squeeze into the group surrounding General Scott and listened, waiting for an opportunity to join the conversation.

"…But what do you attribute the loss to, General Scott? We had superior forces."

"Yes, sir, we had the advantage in numbers, but they were all green troops, ninety-day troops. Bull Run was the first engagement, and the first battle of any war is always unpredictable and inconclusive. I'm sure you'll see an entirely different result once General McClellan gets himself organized and deploys that massive army he's building."

The General finished speaking and there was a slight pause, enabling Billy to join the conversation.

"I'm Billy McHugh, General Scott. It's a real pleasure to meet you, sir. I've read so much about you."

"Most of it good, I would hope," said the General as he shook Billy's hand with a firm grip before placing it back on the handle of his gleaming sword.

"It certainly was, sir, more than just good. I took a history course at The College of Charleston and we studied the Mexican War."

"So, young man, you attended The College of Charleston?"

"Yes, sir, Charleston was my home up until April of this year." Billy paused for a second, not sure what General Scott's reaction would be. The General looked pleased.

"I spent quite some time in Columbia, South Carolina early in my legal career before it occurred to me that I was better suited for fighting than talking and writing. So, I put on the uniform of my country and have been wearing it ever since."

"I'm a lawyer too, sir. I clerked and read law in Charleston under James Petigru."

"Well, you're indeed fortunate. James Petigru is a fine gentleman and a distinguished lawyer, much better than I ever could have been. Were you in Charleston when General Beauregard fired on Fort Sumter?" asked General Scott.

"Yes, sir, I was."

"May I ask you, young man, why you decided to leave the south?" Everyone in the group turned their eyes upon Billy, awaiting his response.

"Well, sir, I was against breaking this nation apart, and I guess you could also say that I'm an abolitionist of sorts."

"As are all fair-minded people," said General Scott. "Slavery's been a dark and evil stain on the conscience of this country for centuries, and it's time to close the book on it." Mostly everyone in the group nodded their heads in agreement.

A short man in a faded black waistcoat and trousers moved closer now to the General. The contrast was one of a giant looming over a dwarf.

"General Scott, do you suppose that the United States will eventually acquire the rest of Mexico and parts of Spanish America and incorporate them into our national territory?"

"Well, I don't see Manifest Destiny stretching that far to the South, sir, though it wouldn't hurt to sprinkle that land with some good old-fashioned stock of hard-working North Americans. They'd likely bring about more stability and progress."

"Sir, what about Cuba?" Billy asked."

"The island of Cuba is an altogether different matter," said General Scott. "It's very close to the continental United States and occupies a strategic position in the Gulf of Mexico. Cuba is essential for the security of this country and we cannot allow it to remain in foreign hands."

It was at this point that Billy caught a glimpse of Bartlett talking with the Secretary of State, and decided to try to join them.

William H. Seward was a tall, wiry man of sixty with a hook-nose, bushy eyebrows, and rumpled hair in need of a good combing. His dress bordered on the disheveled, and he stood with a slight stoop from years of leaning over a desk. The crowd around the Secretary was somewhat smaller than that for General Scott, and Billy had no difficulty moving into position.

"Oh, there you are, Billy. Mister Secretary, this is one of our newest young lawyers, Billy McHugh."

Billy stepped around several other onlookers, moved up and shook Secretary Seward's hand.

"Billy's from Charleston, and he read law under James Petigru. He speaks Spanish and has spent time in Cuba and Central America. He's also been to Africa."

"Well, that's quite a portfolio of experience for such a young man," said the Secretary.

Billy smiled, grateful for the accolades that Joseph Bartlett was bestowing upon him but aware that Bartlett was reminding the Secretary of the firm's expanding capabilities in the international practice.

"What about French?" Seward asked.

"No, sir, I don't speak French, but I think I could learn it pretty easily, because just like Spanish it's derived from Latin."

"Speaking of *Latin*, Mister Secretary, it appears that that self-styled-emperor, Napoleon III of France, has his eye on Mexico," interjected Joseph Bartlett. "I read an article in *Harpers* stating that in spite of our *Monroe Doctrine*, Napoleon envisions expanding his empire over all that vast territory colonized by the Spanish and the Portuguese. According to *Harpers,* he argues that the French people's heritage and historical roots somehow give them that right."

"We're well aware of that, Joseph," said Secretary Seward, exhaling a cloud of pungent gray smoke from a long black cigar. "We know exactly what that arrogant little Frenchman has in mind, but he's not going to get away with it. He knows we have our hands full with this burgeoning civil war. But don't worry, we'll attend to him in due time."

The Secretary turned again to Billy.

"What were you doing in Cuba, young man?"

Billy was reluctant to tell the Secretary that he had sailed aboard his father's slave ship, aware that Secretary Seward was known to be an ardent abolitionist.

"Well, sir, back in 1852, I sailed aboard my father's ship, and we made port in Havana. There was a lot of talk at the time that the United States wanted to acquire Cuba. And I was in Havana again briefly in 1857 aboard the steamer *Central America*, when I was returning home from California."

Secretary Seward continued puffing on his cigar.

"The *Central America?* That vessel that sank off of Cape Hatteras with all that gold?"

"Yes, sir. That's the one. I was very fortunate to have survived. Four hundred and fifty souls were not so fortunate"

"He's just twenty-six, Mister Secretary, but he's had more experience than men twice his age," interjected Joseph Bartlett.

"I can see that," Said Seward.

Just then, the two large grandfather clocks in the East Room signaled the arrival of the noon hour with twelve loud bongs.

"It's twelve o'clock," said Joseph Bartlett, "the public will be coming in now."

"Yes, did you see the First Lady hand the President those white gloves? He will be shaking hands for the next two hours, and his right hand gets so sore and swollen from all that hand shaking that a simple thing like signing a bill into law is painful for him.

But he continues to want to meet the public," said Seward. "If you want to meet the President, young man, you better get over there right away."

"Here, come with me," said Bartlett. "I'll introduce you."

Billy followed Joseph Bartlett over to where President Lincoln was holding court. The President was dressed in a slightly wrinkled black broadcloth suit, and Billy quickly noticed what he had heard and read about President Lincoln. He did indeed have deep set, piercing eyes but a kindly looking face, a face that expressed both wisdom and gentleness. And he certainly was tall and lean as reported and kept bending down as he greeted and spoke with those of more average stature. He appeared fatigued, but he smiled warmly, greeting the populace with patience and equanimity.

As Bartlett and Billy were approaching, Lincoln spotted Bartlett and called out to him. Bartlett smiled and shook the President's hand then introduced Billy McHugh, describing him as a new lawyer in the firm and adding that he was from Charleston and read law under James Petigru. The President smiled and extended his white-gloved hand.

"Well, young man, with the exception of James Petigru, I can't say that I've welcomed anyone from Charleston lately. What brought you to Washington, may I ask? Is it McHugh? Did I get it right?"

"Yes, sir, 'McHugh.' Well, my fiancé was here in Washington sir, and I am also deeply opposed to secession and believe that slavery is immoral. So, there was no good reason for me to stay in Charleston and every reason to come to Washington."

Billy now caught a glimpse of the President's Secretary, who was looking very impatient to introduce the members of the public. They had entered the East Room and were standing in line, waiting to shake the President's hand. The President, however, did not seem to be in a hurry and continued talking to Billy.

"Well, you're very fortunate to have clerked under James Petigru. That certainly surpasses this old lawyer's initiation to the Bar. James Petigru is a statesman and one of the finest lawyers I know. I understand why he had to remain in Charleston, and no one can hold that against him. But as for you, lad, I think you made the right decision to leave."

Billy smiled with appreciation. As it turned out, he was the last one to meet President Lincoln before he devoted himself exclusively to meeting the public.

Billy thanked the President graciously and stepped back with Joseph Bartlett, watching as the public stepped forward. The President's personal secretary, John Hay, took his position and began introducing people one by one. The line stretched all the way back to the street at the north entrance to the Presidential Mansion, and it looked like President Lincoln would have another sore right hand.

2

Billy and Dolores said good-bye to the Phipps and the Bartletts and left the White House with Brad and Julie Mitchum. He hailed a carriage, said good-bye to the Mitchums and wished them a happy new year. As chance would have it, the carriage driver was the same mulatto man whom they had ridden home with that summer when returning from their honeymoon. He was smartly dressed in a red waistcoat with black trousers and top hat. When Billy told him the address, he replied that he remembered them from that summer. He was quite talkative and volunteered his name as Francis. He also asked how they had enjoyed the reception with President Lincoln. Dolores noticed again the driver's flawless English and guessed that he was an educated man. She surmised that he was driving a carriage because there was little other choice because of his mixed race.

"Oh, so, you did get to meet the President, my love? I lost track of you when I was talking to General Scott and Secretary of State, Seward."

"Yes, I got to meet him," said Dolores, "but just for a brief moment. I had a longer conversation with the First Lady. She is really quite charming. She told me about her decorating project for the White House."

Dolores noticed that the driver was turning around and glancing at her from time to time. Billy noticed it also and leaned over to Dolores, lowering his voice.

"I think this driver's a little too intrusive. Is he bothering you as much as he's bothering me?"

"No, my love. I'm sure he means no harm."

"I don't like the way he keeps looking at you. He should just stick to driving the carriage."

Dolores whispered for him to pay it no mind and changed the subject.

"Julie asked if we could visit them next week. It's her husband's birthday, and she is planning a little party for him. They have a flat close to the Capitol, and I'd like to see it."

Billy nodded his agreement.

The carriage pulled up to their building. The driver stepped down and quickly went back and extended his hand to Dolores, helping her down from the carriage and avoiding a mud puddle in her path. When he extended his hand to Billy, Billy waved him off and paid the fare, giving him a less than generous tip.

"Hope to see you both again. You might want to know that I can be messaged at the Willard, and will provide transportation anywhere in the city or beyond. I'll come right to your building, pick you up and provide you with a safe and comfortable ride."

"Yes, thank you and good day," Billy said curtly. The driver turned to Dolores, smiling.

"Good day, ma'am."

Billy nudged Dolores up the walkway to the entrance of their building. The driver stood there watching until they entered the building. Once inside their flat, they shed their formal dress, changing into more comfortable clothes.

"*Quieres tomar un tecito, mi amor?*" (Would you like some tea, my love?) Dolores asked.

"*Sí, por favor,*" (Yes, please) Billy responded. They were accustomed to speaking Spanish at home, mainly because it provided a means of maintaining and improving Billy's fluency in the language. Dolores was now completely bilingual.

"What did you think of Secretary of State Seward, my love?" Dolores asked, as she poured the tea, filling two exquisite cups from the fine English China given to them as a wedding gift.

"He's a knowledgeable man. Not much of a dresser and a bit gruff in manner, but you can tell that he is highly intelligent and sly. Funny, he asked me if I spoke French. Of course, I had to say no. We were talking about Napoleon III of France and his grand design to annex Mexico. You know, *mi amor*, it would be good if I could learn some French. It is the language of international diplomacy and commerce. There's only one other lawyer in the firm who speaks French, and he's about to retire, so it would help my career."

Dolores sipped her tea and smiled at her young husband, aware of his ever-expanding ambition.

"I studied French in Cuba with Sofia," said Dolores, "but I never learned to speak it very well. Sofia speaks it very well."

"How is Sofia doing?" Billy asked. "Do you write to her?"

"Yes, of course, my love. She is in her final year in the Faculty of Law and is very active in political affairs. Papá is concerned.

I told you what happened with one of her early boyfriends, Carlos Santiago, and the attempted assassination of the Captain General. But as for French, maybe you could take a course here in Washington. I'm sure you could find one."

"I'll ask Joseph Bartlett. He should know."

"What about your family, Billy? Have you heard from them?

"No, my love, not a word, unfortunately. There's no mail and no telegraph to the south."

He considered again telling her about the bitter estrangement from his father but decided that this was not the time for it.

"Becky and Julius said they were able to make contact with their sons in Charleston by way of some servants of a businessman here in Washington. I need to get some more details from them because I'm very concerned about my mother. She's all alone there since Julius and Becky left."

"I'm sure there's a better way to contact them, Billy. Does your father still go to Cuba? Because I could tell papá to have him give his letters to papá or Sofía and they can forward them to me when they write."

Billy frowned. "I'd rather not do that."

"Why not? It would be a lot easier than going through people whom you don't even know."

"I'd rather not. I have my reasons. Look, my sweet, come over here. We've had a busy day, and I suggest we take a little siesta."

Clearly knowing what he had in mind, she got up from the table, went over, and kissed him. He put his arm around her shoulder; she put her arm around his waist, and they walked off together to the bedroom. Several hours later found Billy looking lovingly at his beautiful, sweet wife as she dozed peacefully beside him. A warm and gentle smile blossomed on his lips. He leaned over and kissed her tenderly on the cheek. She stirred slightly but did not awaken.

3

Francis the coachman sat in his carriage near the entrance to the Congressional School, reading a newspaper.

The Washington Star, April 9 1862
Shiloh—The Bloodiest Battle to Date

The recent two-day battle of Shiloh in eastern Tennessee accounted for an estimated 13,050 Union and 10,600 Confederate casualties, making it the bloodiest battle to date in this nascent civil war. Shiloh's 23,000 casualties exceeds the total number of American casualties suffered in the Revolutionary War, the War of 1812, and the Mexican War, combined.

"Hello Francis, are you waiting for someone?" asked Dolores

"No, Miss McHugh, I'm free. Are you going home?"

"Yes, Francis." The coachman smiled broadly, stepped down and helped her into the cab.

"Do you work at the Congressional School, Miss McHugh?"

"It's *Mrs.* McHugh Francis."

"Yes, ma'am. I'll try to remember that," he said, smiling.

He brought down the switch, and the horse galloped off. Francis opened the little window that separated coachman from passenger and continued some small talk. Now, as they were rounding a wide curve, a big, black dog suddenly ran out, chasing the carriage wheels and barking ferociously.

"WHOA MICKY! WHOA BOY! HOLD ON MISS MCHUGH!"

Francis pulled back hard on the reins to avoid the dog and brought the carriage to a sudden stop, thrusting Dolores forward in the cab. She put both hands on the wall, bracing herself, and her left wrist buckled from the impact. She screamed and grimaced in pain.

"Are you all right, Miss McHugh?" Francis yelled, forgetting again the *Mrs* as he jumped down and swung open the door.

"I'm not sure," said Dolores. "I hit my hand against the wall here!"

"Let me see," Francis said, as he grasped her hand and began rubbing it.

"Ow! That hurts!" Dolores cried. He let go of her hand.

"Maybe we should have a doctor take a look just to make sure there's nothing broken."

"No, Francis. I don't want to see a doctor. Just take me home. My husband will be waiting for me."

"I've passed that dog many times in this neighborhood and was always wary of the danger," Francis said. "He just runs wild and chases carriages."

Dolores stopped listening and continued to rub her wrist. As they neared her flat, Francis asked again:

"How's your wrist, Mrs. McHugh? Does it feel any better?"

"I'm not sure," Dolores said, feeling some pain when she moved it.

They pulled up to the building, and Francis helped her out of the carriage.

Billy heard the carriage out on the street, and when he looked out the window, he saw the mulatto carriage driver rubbing Dolores's hand. He rushed down the stairs and ran to the street.

Dolores opened her purse and was about to pay the fare.

"There's no charge, ma'am," said Francis. "I can't take your money after what happened."

"What's the problem here?" Billy asked, glancing coldly at the mulatto coachman.

"There's no problem, Billy," Dolores said as she insisted on paying the fare, but Francis would not accept it. With that, Francis the coachman bid them good day and drove off.

Back in their flat, Dolores told Billy how she had hurt her hand when they tried to avoid the dog and the carriage came to a sudden stop.

"Oh, so that's why he was rubbing your hand?"

"Of course, my love. Why else would he be rubbing it?" Billy reached for Dolores's hand and began examining it closely, too closely.

"Ow! That hurts," Dolores cried.

"I'm so sorry, my love, but we better get you to a doctor."

"No, I don't need a doctor, Billy. I'm all right."

"I was afraid that coachman was bothering you, Dolores. I told you before I don't like him. Are you sure there wasn't something else that upset you?"

"No, I told you Billy that the dog ran out, the carriage came to a sudden stop and I hit my hand against the carriage wall. That was all there was to it. Then, when I tried to pay him, he refused to take the money, saying that he was responsible."

"I told you, Dolores. I don't like the way he looks at you."

"Please, Billy, you're not jealous, are you? That would be silly. He's just a man driving a carriage, trying to make a living."

"But why do you keep riding with him? Aren't there any other carriages you can take?"

"I'm not trying to ride with him. It's just that he keeps showing up when I need a carriage. It's simply a coincidence, nothing more."

"All right, let's forget about it," Billy said, sounding irritable. He was quiet for a moment. Then "Mr. Bartlett received a telegraph yesterday saying that his son, Martin, was killed. He was a lieutenant in the Ohio Fourth Brigade. Bartlett and his family are terribly distraught. The whole office is in mourning, and work has come to a complete standstill."

"Oh, that's awful, Billy. Poor Mrs. Bartlett. We should send some flowers with our condolences."

"All the lawyers sent flowers, and we've formed a committee to assist Mister and Mrs. Bartlett during their period of mourning."

"I thank God that you don't have to fight in this terrible war! I'd be worried sick."

All of a sudden, Dolores felt the baby kick, and she felt nauseous. She walked over to the sofa and sat down. Billy followed her, saying again that they should get a doctor to look at her wrist.

"It's not my wrist, Billy. It's the 'morning sickness.' I thought it only happened in the morning, but I get it in the afternoon and at other times as well."

"How about if I make you some tea, my love? Sit here, please and don't move. Just try to relax. I'll fix it for you."

"That would be sweet of you, Billy."

He smiled and walked off toward the kitchen. When he returned with the tea, she looked even worse.

"What's wrong, my love? Is there something else bothering you?" Billy asked.

She knew that he was still wondering about the carriage driver.

"No, my love, it's just the morning sickness."

CHAPTER X

Sangre de Negro

It was late July, and Dolores lay in bed perspiring profusely. It had not been an easy time for her. She had continually suffered from morning sickness and had gained too much weight and much too rapidly. To make matters worse, Washington was in the midst of a heat wave. Dolores was no stranger to heat and humidity, but the summers at *La Dulce Gardenia* in Cuba were breezy and comfortable compared to the stiflingly humid climes and stagnant air of Washington. Yet in spite of her discomfort, she remained cheerful and optimistic, for that was her nature.

Becky was downstairs in the kitchen preparing lemonade and medicinal victuals for Dolores recommended by Doctor Frederick Barnes. The good doctor had said the baby was due during the first week of August, which was now just a few days away. When Dolores wrote to her family in Cuba, informing them that she was "*embarazada,*" (pregnant) don Fernando was delighted, but urged her to return to *La Dulce Gardenia* to give birth. He stressed that Carmen, the upstairs housemaid, whom Dolores had always been so fond of, was an experienced midwife. Carmen had assisted Soledad and Daisy in the birth of their children. And Dolores would be assured that family members could provide all the care and attention she could possibly need. But Billy was opposed to it and insisted that she stay in Washington. He said he had more trust in American doctors, and Doctor Barnes had been highly recommended by the wife of senior partner, Henry Phipps. In addition, Billy had arranged for Becky to care for Dolores, and today she was accompanied by her niece, Clara, a nineteen-year-old free negro, who herself had given birth the year before.

"Sho is steamy hot today, Mizz Dolores," Becky said as she entered the bedroom. "Aah brung ya some lemonade."

In spite of the heat, Dolores had managed to doze off. She looked up now and smiled at Becky, whom she had found to be every bit as sweet and kind as Billy had promised.

"Thank you, Becky. Your lemonade reminds me of my home in Cuba. It seems better in fact."

"Oh, ya don't need ta go complimentin me, Mizz Dolores. It jest plain ole lemonade, da kind we make in Charleston. Oh, my! Let me see ya arm."

Becky reached for Dolores's arm and examined the welts. "Look like dem moskeetaas been bitin at ya again. Aah thought Julius done fixed da windows, but look like dey still gettin in. Aah seen 'em down in da kitchen too, big uns dey was, bigga den da ones in Charleston. Do dey hurt ya, Mizz Dolores?"

"No, but they sure do itch," Dolores said, as she reached for the lemonade. Suddenly, Dolores grimaced, nearly spilling the lemonade. Becky took the glass and put it back on the table.

"Look and sound like you startin yo labor, Mizz Dolores. Aah better go fetch Doctor Barnes and tell Massa Billy."

"Not yet, Becky," Dolores said, still grimacing from the contraction. "Doctor Barnes said to summon him only after the cramps started coming regularly. I don't want to disturb Billy needlessly. He's been terribly busy with another big project."

Dolores turned on her side now and stretched out her legs,

trying to relieve the severe cramps in her stomach and back. Becky reached for Dolores's hand.

"Squeeze ma hand, Mizz Dolores. Squeeze it hard as ya can. Aah remembers all too well jests how it was. Wid ma fust boy, Thomas, dey started in da early mornin and went all day long. Labor pains sho ain't pleasant, Mizz Dolores, but Aah got tru dem and you can too. It all jest part o bein a woman. Men, now, dey don't undastand. Ma Julius at da time done run plum outta da house. Course, Massa Billy, he different, Miss Dolores. He a fine young gennelman. Sho did help ma Julius claim his freedom and get outta Charleston."

The morning passed, and by late afternoon, Dolores was well into her labor. They decided to alert Doctor Barnes, and Becky sent Clara outside to hail a carriage. It seemed the strangest of coincidences, but once again there was Francis, the handsome mulatto coachman; the one whom Dolores and Billy had ridden with so often; the one whom Billy had come to distrust and dislike. When Billy saw him, he refused to get in the carriage, insisting that they hail another. Doctor Barnes and Becky, however, had already seated themselves, and they had told the driver to hurry, saying they needed to get back and aid a woman about to give birth. In the end, Billy was forced to acquiesce, and he got in the carriage and shouted at Francis the coachman to make haste.

By the time the carriage pulled up to the McHughs' flat, Dolores was entering the final stages of her labor. Billy rushed to her side, but Doctor Barnes said it would be best for him to wait outside the bedroom while he and the two women assisted in the delivery. Some two hours later as he sat in a chair just outside the bedroom, rising occasionally to pace nervously about, he heard the faint cry of a baby and rushed to the bedroom door. Finding it locked, he knocked, but no one opened it. He knocked louder now and more insistently, and finally Becky opened the door. Billy entered and rushed to Dolores's bedside. Her eyes were closed, and she appeared to be asleep. Billy reached for her hand, bent down, and kissed her tenderly on the forehead.

"Is it a boy or a girl?" he asked, turning to Doctor Barnes.

"It's a boy, Mister McHugh. The delivery went smoothly, but your wife needs plenty of rest now. So I gave her a mild sedative and she's dozed off."

"But where's the baby?" Billy asked. Doctor Barnes nodded toward Becky, who was seated back against the wall in the large bedroom.

"Aah hav 'im, Massa Billy," Becky said shyly.

She held the newborn infant bundled in a little white blanket, and rocked him slowly back and forth. Doctor Barnes glanced at Becky, then walked over to the water basin and began washing his hands, which were covered with blood. Becky's niece, Clara, began picking up the bloodstained cotton clothes that were scattered on the floor around the bed. When Billy started walking toward Becky to see his newborn son, Dolores began to stir, moaning as though in some pain. Billy stopped in his tracks, turned again and reached for her hand.

"*Soy yo, mi amor. Estoy aquí* (It's me, my love. I'm here). Dolores slowly opened her eyes.

"Billy, *eres tú. Pero donde está nuestro bebe?*" (It's you Billy, but where is our baby? she said in a weak and shaky voice. Becky looked over at Doctor Barnes.

"It's all right for her to hold him now," said Doctor Barnes as he finished drying his hands.

Becky got up and brought the baby to Dolores, carefully placing him in her arms. It was the first time Dolores had held the baby, and at first she didn't seem to notice. But Billy noticed. He noticed immediately. His face flushed, his eyes narrowed and his teeth suddenly clenched. He was dumbstruck! The baby had brown skin. Billy glared at Dolores, and if looks could kill, she would have been slain that very instant.

Francis, the mulatto coachman!

Billy didn't say a word but turned and rushed out of the room, motioning for Doctor Barnes to follow him. Doctor Barnes hesitated at first then followed reluctantly.

"Why is that baby so dark-skinned?"

"I don't know, Mister McHugh." Billy moved up to within inches of Doctor Barnes' face, looking angry enough to strike him.

"Do I look like a negro? I'm Irish, Doctor Barnes. My father and mother are Irish!"

Doctor Barnes turned away and began walking back into the bedroom. Billy grabbed him by the arm. "I'm asking you!" Doctor Barnes stopped.

"What about Mrs. McHugh?"

"My wife is white! Can't you see that? We both..." He stopped in mid-sentence as the image of Dolores's mother, Beatriz, flashed before his mind.

"I can see that, Mister McHugh, but I can't answer your question, and I'm not sure anyone else can. But you will have to excuse me now. I must be going. The baby is healthy, and your wife is doing fine. I will stop by tomorrow afternoon and check on them again. Good day, Mister McHugh."

Billy was in shock and sat down on the straight-back chair in the hallway. The bedroom door was closed, and he could hear Becky and her niece talking, but he could not make out their words. Suddenly, he heard the baby crying and stood up quickly, the image of its dark-skinned face firmly etched in his mind. Anger and humiliation swept over him.

The mulatto carriage driver.

It had never occurred to him that there was any risk in marrying Dolores. Her mixed blood was not an issue for him. He was fond of and tolerant of negroes and people of mixed race. Dolores was beautiful. She was sweet and shy, kind and loving, and he had fallen deeply in love with her. He had never even thought about having children before he learned that Dolores was expecting. If he had thought about it, it never would have occurred to him that their children would be other than white. Dolores had always passed for white.

The bedroom door suddenly opened, and he looked up and saw Becky standing there.

"Come on in, Massa Billy. Aah knows what's troublin ya, but tain't nothin no one can do bout it. You and me's always bin mo den jest massa and slave. We bin friends. And Aah needs ta tell ya somethin. Aah could tell from da day Aah fust set eyes on Mizz Dolores dat she had some black blood. Aah knows what Aah'm talkin bout, cause Aah'v been livin all ma life clothed in dis black skin. Aah seen otha cases jest like dissin. So, don't ya go doubtin fo a minute dat dat lil baby boy in der is yos. Iffin ya does, ya gonna hurt him, gonna hurt him awful bad. He gonna need ya mo den most sons need der papa. He gonna need da love and protection of you and Mizz Dolores every wakin day of his life. So, Billy, go on in der right now and pick 'im up. Hold 'im in yer arms and let 'im know dat ya love 'im and dat ya gonna take good care of 'im."

Billy looked at Becky, her words having moved him some. He got up now, entered the bedroom and went to Dolores's bedside. She was awake and lay with the baby nestled in her arms. She looked up at her husband, and the tears began to flow. Billy remained silent and made no effort to console her.

"Go head, Billy, pick 'im up," Becky whispered.

"May I hold him?" he asked, expressionless. Dolores nodded. He leaned over and picked him up, and the baby immediately began to cry, which triggered his own tears. He quickly placed him back in Dolores's arms and turned away, not wanting Dolores to see his tears. Dolores made no effort to conceal her own.

2

Sebastián was a healthy baby boy with big brown eyes and mounds of dark brown curly hair. Dolores chose the name Sebastián, to which Billy did not object. He looked like a child of the tropics, and though it was still too early to tell, he appeared to resemble his mother. If he had been born in Cuba, he would have been described as "*acanelado*," that is, cinnamon-colored. His facial features, however, were noticeably caucasian, and he bore no sign of the wider, flatter nose, the thicker lips, or the nappy hair of a negro. Except for the *acanelado* complexion, he would have easily passed for white just like his mother.

Sebastián was an unusually happy baby, manifesting that trait from the day he was born. He would coo and gurgle and look up at his mother with an adorable baby smile that was simply irresistible. Dolores nursed Sebastián and he rapidly gained weight, avoiding the colic and other common infant ailments. His little face had an angelic glow about it, and he was unusually easy to care for and please. Becky, who had remained with the McHughs as a nanny and housemaid, remarked that she had never seen nor heard of a baby who had so easily adopted his parents' schedule and routine. Billy too found himself falling under the spell of Sebastián's infectious baby charm. His initial reaction at seeing the newborn baby, had been one of shock and anger. Had he been cuckolded by the handsome mulatto carriage driver? Could his sweet Dolores have betrayed him? The mere thought of it sickened and enraged him. But Becky, who had been practically a second mother to

Billy since his childhood, did everything possible to disavow him of that notion.

Billy McHugh was a child of the south. He had lived with negroes, mulattos and People of mixed blood, and he knew the various terms to describe them. There were the pure, jet-black "negroes" or "niggers." There were the "mulattos," half-black and half-white, the "quadroons," one-quarter black, "octoroons," one-eighth black and so on. Billy knew of course that in South Carolina and the south in general, any portion of negro blood, no matter how small, was sufficient to qualify, or better said, to stigmatize, a person as a "nigger." When Billy came north, he discovered the same notion applied right here in Washington, though not legally sanctioned as in the South. The city of Washington was the Nation's Capital and the heart of the Union, presided over by President Abraham Lincoln and other powerful abolitionists. But negroes were still considered inferior and were treated as such. Billy knew, though he often forgot, that Dolores was the product of an amalgamation between Beatriz, a mulatto slave, and don Fernando de Castilla, a white Spaniard. To him the question got down to a matter of logic. He recalled the Latin maxim—*a fortiori*—"with even stronger reason," which he had learned while studying law and clerking for James Petigru. Dolores was one-quarter black but had light skin and easily passed for white. As for him, he was wholly white. Therefore, if he were the father, Sebastián would be seven-eighths white and only one-eighth black. So, *a fortiori*, Sebastián should have lighter skin than his mother, Dolores. But Sebastián had darker skin. Was there another fountain from which the black blood flowed? His analysis seemed to leave a lingering doubt.

Billy believed Becky when she told him about similar cases of darker-skinned babies born to lighter-skinned women of mixed blood, who had always passed for white and were married to a white man.

"Ya not da only one, Billy. Dat's fo sho," Becky had said.

Though his heart urged him to move closer to Sebastián, his judgment urged him to stay away, cautioning him of the danger. A little brown baby with seemingly white parents stood out in Washington society, a society that was still very much racist at heart. Within the privacy of their flat, Billy could enjoy the pleasures of fatherhood as he watched Sebastián grow and mature, his learning to crawl, his first tooth and his first word. Billy's natural paternal instinct came to the fore, engendering genuine feelings of love and affection for his son. However, he was loathe to be seen with him outside the home, for how could he explain Sebastián's darker skin color? He saw only two obvious conclusions that people would draw, the one only slightly less painful and humiliating than the other; but both potentially damaging to him and his career; that Dolores had been unfaithful to him, had consorted with a negro and had given birth to a "nigger" baby. Or, alternatively, that one of them, and likely Dolores, had black blood, which meant that he had married a "nigger." Billy was particularly worried that senior partners Bartlett and Phipps would learn about Sebastián, and that it would seriously jeopardize his chances of rising in the firm. There was no easy answer to Billy's dilemma, and it was inevitable that the word would get out.

It happened first under the most normal of circumstances for mother and child. Dolores asked Julius to make a carriage for Sebastián, so she could take him for walks in the fresh air and sunshine. Using bicycle wheels, rattan and other available materials, Julius constructed a sturdy miniature carriage, and Dolores began taking Sebastián out for an afternoon stroll. On one such occasion, a Mister Richard Peabody, one of Dolores's colleagues at the Congressional School, who lived in the flat on the third floor above the McHughs', happened to have returned home early one afternoon. As he was walking up the path to the entrance of their building, he saw Dolores pushing the little carriage out to the walkway and greeted her warmly. Commenting on the cleverly built little carriage, Mister Peabody then bent over to see the baby. Dolores tried to cover Sebastián, but it was too late. Meanwhile, Sebastián was turning and smiling and cooing, delighting in the sunshine and fresh air.

"Oh, so here's the new addition to the McHugh household. Ah, yes, a lively baby boy."

Peabody's face bore a look of surprise. Undoubtedly, he had noticed. Dolores thought of trying to explain, but her better judgment took hold and she kept quiet. Mister Peabody was a polite and considerate individual, and he graciously changed the subject.

"Tell me, Dolores, are you planning to return to the Congressional School and assume your teaching career?" He backed away now from the carriage.

"Oh yes, Mister Peabody! I certainly want to, if they still have a position for me. I do miss my work and my students."

"And I'm sure your students miss you too, Dolores. Well, I must be going now. I have some papers to correct. Enjoy your walk."

Later that evening she recounted the incident to Billy, who expressed alarm. He of course had no way of knowing Mister Peabody's thoughts and reaction. What he did know, however, was that Mister Peabody had been a client of Henry Phipps in an insurance-related matter. Billy had seen him in the office and knew that Brad Mitchum had done some research on the matter.

"What if he happens to mention it to Henry Phipps?" Billy asked. "It would be all over the office in a matter of minutes. And not only that, he might mention it in the Congressional School, and that could be the end of your teaching career. I don't want you walking Sebastián around here any more! Do you understand,

Dolores? Get Becky to walk him, or better yet, don't take him out at all."

"We can't keep him penned up. He needs to get out in the fresh air and sunshine, just like any other child."

But Billy was not listening. He heard only his inner voice, cautioning him to avoid a disastrous scandal and protect his blossoming career. Billy's harsh words hurt Dolores, but she sought to conceal it, wishing to avoid a painful confrontation. What Billy said next, however, was just too hurtful.

"I've been thinking we should have Becky and Julius take him for the time being and keep him out of sight."

"What did you say? How could you even think of it? He's our son, Billy, our own flesh and blood! No, I won't have it! Never, Billy, never! I could not bear to be without him!"

"Well, then maybe you could take him back to Cuba with you." She collapsed on the bed and began sobbing uncontrollably. He stared at her, unsure of what to say and not quite aware of the pain his words had caused. She looked up now and cried out.

"Is that what you want? Is that really what you want?"

He did not respond and looked away, unwilling to meet her sad, yet angry eyes. It occurred to him that it was the first time in their decade-long relationship that they had ever quarreled. As he realized the terrible import of his words, it was like being struck by a lightning bolt. His eyes welled up with tears, and his heart ached with guilt and remorse. He sat down on the bed and put his arms around her.

"I'm so sorry, my love. Please forgive me. I could never bear to be without you, never."

He kissed her tenderly on the cheek. Her crying eased, but his harsh and painful words lingered, and she would not easily forget them. She had seen a different Billy this day, different from the kind and dear boy she had met in Cuba years before; different from the courageous young man she was reunited with aboard the ill-fated *Central America*; and different from the man she had married just two years before.

PART IV

Spring 1861–Spring 1863

CHAPTER XI

The Confederate Cavalry

The shrill sound of reveille resounded throughout the rebel camp, awakening the men of Company E 1st South Carolina Cavalry. Charlie Flynn pulled the blankets up over his head and otherwise did not move. His hut mate, Second Lieutenant Norm Christianson, had already sprung from his cot and stood shivering in the cold damp air of northern Virginia.

"You best get yourself up, Charlie, lest you'll be late again," Norm said in a voice loud enough for Charlie to hear from under his blankets. But Charlie did not move.

"All right, don't say I didn't warn ya." Minutes later a bugle sounded Assembly, and the men filed out and took their positions in the field for roll call. Charlie didn't make it. However, when the third bugle call of the day sounded Stable Call, Charlie rose from his cot. He heard a horse whinnying, and there was no mistaking that whinny.

"Damn you, Compass! When you gonna learn to ignore that bugler?"

Unlike the Yankee troopers who were provided with horses from the Union herd, Confederate Cavalry had to provide their own. Charlie brought Compass with him when he joined the cavalry shortly after war broke out. Like all his fellow troopers, he complained about how much better the Yankees had it, but he would not have settled for any other horse. For true to his name, the big red roan had an uncanny sense of direction, at times even contrary to the signals that Charlie sent through the reins. Charlie put on his trousers, his shirt and his worn-out shoes and headed for the stable as Compass continued to whinny nervously.

"All right, Compass! I'm comin! I'm comin!"

Swirling snow flurries descended on the camp, obscuring the pale orange of a feeble sunrise. One side of the stable was open to the elements, and was even colder than outside. The horses stood shivering, streaks of whitish-gray mist shooting from their nostrils. Eli, the young negro stable boy, had already arrived and was feeding the horses.

"Mornin, Massa Charlie! Ole Compass, here won't eat till he see ya. He a strange one, all right but a goodin."

"I wouldn't trade him for anything, Eli. But I want you to check his left back shoe, you hear? He seemed to be steppin' kinda funny yesterday, and I'm afraid that his shoe might of loosened up."

Eli placed the bucket of oats under Compass' mouth and the horse began to eat.

"Yessuh, Aah'l look at it, an iffen he need a new shoe, Aah'l take 'im on ova to da blacksmith," Eli said, flashing a mouth full of strong white teeth.

The men of the First Cavalry Company E were unaccustomed to the cold Virginia winters, and the Confederacy lacked the resources to supply warm clothing. Many troopers got their warmest clothing from the bodies of dead Yankees, of which there were plenty, thanks to the many raids and skirmishes that fall.

Charlie had returned to Charleston from the California gold fields in the spring of 1861, broke but excited about the prospect of fighting for the new Confederate States of America. His parents, well-off members of Charleston's merchant class, did their best to persuade him to go to work in his father's clothing store.

"This is not your fight," his mother said, "and it's just not worth getting killed over or losing an arm or a leg."

But Charlie could no more think of himself as a storekeeper than a plantation owner could think of himself as a slave. He was a proud and happy-go-lucky son of the South, and could hardly wait to don the uniform of the CSA. The choice between the infantry or the cavalry was an easy one. Having had some training in cavalry strategy and tactics during his two years at The Citadel, he breezed through the weeks of drill and training. After showing his daring and prowess in some initial skirmishes on the coast of South Carolina, the troopers in Company E elected Charlie to be an officer, and he assumed the rank of second lieutenant. Unlike the Union forces, the southern elected its officers.

In the fall of 1862, the First Cavalry was ordered to join the Army of Northern Virginia under the flamboyant leadership of Major General J.E.B. Stuart. Charlie and his fellow troopers felt privileged to be a part of Stuart's forces, knowing that they would be fighting under an audacious leader, whose aggressive and unorthodox tactics would keep them in the thick of the action and bring pride and fame to them and their unit. Company E was led by Colonel John Logan Black, a West Point alumnus and a highly regarded senior officer. Charlie was no model of military discipline and bearing, but he was a fine horseman and an expert shot, and his superiors were willing to overlook his obvious shortcomings. Charlie's hut mate, Norm Christianson, also from Charleston, was a close friend. Norm would often cover for Charlie, even answering for him at Assembly roll call when Charlie failed to appear after his late night escapades in neighboring towns in search of wine, women, and sin.

The bugler sounded the Breakfast Call, and Charlie entered

the mess tent and sat down with his fellow junior officers for a breakfast of bacon, corn bread, coffee, and grits, all of it prepared and served by the negro cooks assigned to Company E.

"Well, lookee who's here. Glad to see you could make it today," said Barney Muldoon, a second lieutenant from Abbeville. Charlie sat down, smiled and reached for the coffee.

"I heard they had some eggs, but I'll be damned if I see any," Charlie said.

"You heard right," said Phil Forrester, a first lieutenant from Allendale, "but your partner, Norm, here got the last of them." Norm looked at Charlie and grinned.

"I called you, but you just rolled over."

"Colonel Black and his staff ate most of them," said Muldoon. Ole Bull Foley rustled them up from a neighboring farm during a recon ride yesterday. Said they saw a skinny lil gal on that farm with udders bigger than a Guernsey cow. Real good lookin' too, he said." The table erupted with laughter.

"I'm surprised you didn't know 'bout her, Charlie," Forrester said. "You must be slippin."

Charlie looked at Forrester and grinned sheepishly.

"Who told ya 'bout this little farm gal, Phil?"

"A corporal in Foley's unit." Forrester smiled. "Well now, gentlemen, sounds like Ole Charlie here's suddenly interested, don't it?"

"Take Danny Doyle 'long with ya, Charlie," said Lieutenant Forrester. "He ain't been with a woman in a coon's age."

Doyle didn't know whether to feel offended, and started to answer when the piercing sound of the bugle resonated throughout the camp, signaling Stable Call, and directing the men to prepare their mounts for drill. They cursed and left the mess tent. Charlie gulped down his coffee then got up and followed them.

When Charlie entered the stable, he found Eli grooming Compass.

"Compass don't need no shoe, Massa Charlie. Aah found a thorn stickin in his left foot, and Aah jest pulled it out. He be fine now."

Charlie placed the horse blanket on Compass' back, then threw the saddle up and carefully strapped it on. Next came the bridle and then the bit. Finally, he strapped on his backpack, mounted his big roan, and rode him out to the drill field, where the eighty-five troopers of Company E were assembling. The war would resume when the weather warmed, but for now it was drill, drill, drill, and more drill.

2

Her name was Maggie Burke, and Charlie just had to see her for himself. So, he devised a scheme and convinced his immediate superior, Captain Harvey Fields, that they should ride down and inform Mister Burke that the First Cavalry, Company E, might be required to utilize the farm as a staging area for defending a possible attack from Yankee infantry encamped across the river.

One early afternoon in late December he rode to the farm and spoke with Mister Burke. Burke assembled his wife, his son and his daughter Maggie in the parlor, and Charlie briefed them all. Maggie was pretty much as Lieutenant Forrester had described, although "slender" would have been a better word than "skinny." As for her bosom, his description was dead-on accurate, at least judging from the way her chest stuck out. Maggie was indeed a "lil gal," standing just under five feet tall with an elegant hour-glass waist and golden blond hair. As things turned out, Mister Burke relieved Charlie of the need to concoct additional artifices to get to see Maggie again. He had previously planned a New Year's Eve party and asked Charlie to convey to Colonel Black and a delegation of officers, an invitation to attend the festivities. Charlie had noticed that Maggie had been casting admiring glances in his direction, as he stood before the family, tall, proud and handsome in his neatly-ironed CSA Cavalry uniform complete with shiny saber.

It was a cold, clear New Year's Eve when the delegation from Company E rode to the Burke farmhouse. The Burkes were well off, owning one of the largest tobacco farms in Northern Virginia. When Charlie and his three companions arrived, the party was in full swing, with two fiddlers entertaining the guests. When they entered the parlor, more musicians appeared with trumpets, French horns, and tubas, and struck up a lively rendition of "Dixie." All eyes turned to Charlie and his comrades, resplendent in their uniforms, and they all sang along. When the music stopped, a loud round of applause broke out, and Mister Burke stepped forward to address his guests.

"My dear friends and neighbors, I want to take the time to salute our special guests from Company E First Cavalry of the great state of South Carolina."

A loud round of applause broke out, complete with whistlin' whoopin' and hollerin'.

"In just a few short hours we'll be welcoming in the New Year, 1863. And Aah feel confident in predicting that this will be the year in which our southern forces achieve a full and final victory over the tyranny and oppression of the North. But now it's time to enjoy ourselves and welcome in the New Year. And may God bless all our brave southern boys, all of you here tonight and the glorious Confederate States of America!"

Shouts and cheers rang out, and the band once again struck up a rousing version of "Dixie," followed by "The Bonny Blue Flag."

Guests stepped forward and shook hands with Charlie and his

fellow officers. Charlie spotted Maggie by the punch bowl, and he excused himself and walked over. Maggie wore a low-cut yellow dress, and her lovely bosom was bulging out to the delight of a bevy of eager and admiring men young and old. Her mother, Mrs. Milly Burke, was behind a richly decorated table, serving punch.

"Good evening, Lieutenant Flynn," said Mrs. Burke. "May I serve you?" She was not well-endowed like her daughter Maggie, but was still an attractive woman, elegantly attired in a lavender dress, her blond hair coiffed high on her head. She smiled and ladled punch as Charlie moved closer to the table, all the while keeping Maggie in his line of vision.

"Good evening, Mrs. Burke. Don't mind if I do. Aah have to say, ma'am, you certainly look lovely tonight. Hope Mister Burke won't mind my sayin' so."

"Well, thank you, Lieutenant, but I just bet you say that to all the ladies, now don't you?" Charlie smiled and threw her another bouquet of flowery compliments. All the while Maggie had been listening, and she excused herself and moved closer to the table.

"Well, good evening, Lieutenant Flynn. We're so pleased that you could attend." Just then the band, which kept expanding as more musicians arrived, took up a slow waltz.

"Do you dance, Lieutenant?" Maggie asked.

"I've been known to waltz a little, Miss Burke."

"Would you care to demonstrate?"

"Why, Aah'd be delighted!"

Maggie joined hands with Charlie, and they walked through the throng of guests toward the parlor.

"I promise to try to keep off yer feet."

They reached the parlor, and Charlie took Maggie in his arms and began waltzing her around the room.

"I must say that you are quite light on your feet, Lieutenant Flynn."

"Well, thank you, my dear. I hope we can do it again," Charlie said as the music stopped.

"Would you like some more punch, Lieutenant?" Maggie asked, squeezing Charlie's hand affectionately and smiling coquettishly.

"Indeed, I would, Miss Burke. It is after all New Year's Eve."

As he walked with her over to the punch bowl, he used his great advantage in height to peer down at her lovely bosom, wondering just *how in the world such a lil gal could be so doggone big?*

"Are you two enjoying yourselves?" asked Mrs. Burke.

"I sure am, ma'am," said Charlie.

"Yes, Mama. Lieutenant Flynn is quite a good dancer."

"Y'all mustn't forget now to put your names in the baskets in the parlor for our couples' drawing," said Mrs. Burke.

"We won't forget, Mama."

Maggie explained to Charlie that it was a tradition at the Burke's annual New Year's Eve party for the ladies and gentlemen to couple up by means of a raffle, and that if the inclination was present and mutual, to share a first kiss for the New Year beneath the mistletoe, which was strategically placed around the farmhouse.

They danced every waltz together, and with each dance he held her a little closer and tighter, enjoying the delightful touch of her breasts pressing against his chest. At times his hand would unintentionally slip off her shoulder and touch them, encountering no noticeable objection.

Charlie told her about his life in Charleston. He recounted his adventures in California, embellishing the tale with talk of gold strikes that never actually happened. When it came time, for them to put their names in the couples' baskets, Maggie said she would attend to it and walked off, leaving Charlie by the punch bowl. The drawing commenced at fifteen minutes before midnight, and lo and behold Maggie and Charlie were coupled together. Maggie had seen to it. At the stroke of twelve the musicians played *Auld Lang Syne*, and Charlie embraced a very willing Maggie under the mistletoe, kissing her passionately. Mister and Mrs. Burke, who didn't participate in the drawing, shared a modest marital kiss and watched as Maggie was embraced by the dashing young Lieutenant Flynn in his strikingly handsome CSA cavalry uniform. After their kiss Charlie wasted little time.

"Where could we go to be alone, Maggie, my dear?"

"Well, the only possible place would be the barn. Can you keep me warm, Lieutenant?"

Charlie smiled and kissed her again, this time just a little peck on the cheek.

"Why, Maggie, ma dear, I'm a warm-blooded suthern man from the great state of South Carolina. There's not a chance in hell you'll be cold with me."

Once again, the musicians struck up "Dixie," and it was Charlie's patriotic duty to join his fellow officers and sing along. Maggie said she'd meet him in the kitchen when the music ended. And that's where he found her. She had an arm full of wool blankets.

"Just in case, Lieutenant," she said, smiling coquettishly as she tugged him along by his jacket sleeve.

They walked out the door and into the cold night air. Entering the barn, Maggie picked up a small lantern. Charlie reached in the inside pocket of his uniform, found a match and lit the lantern. Maggie grabbed his jacket sleeve again and pulled him along like an unruly child to a far corner of the barn where the horses were stabled. One of the stalls was vacant. She spread out a blanket, placed the lantern on a board in back, then lay down, beckoning Charlie to join her. Charlie grabbed another blanket, then covered Maggie and lay down. At first they were both shivering from the cold, but it didn't take long for Charlie's kisses and caresses to warm things up. Maggie then said something that truly surprised but delighted Charlie.

"Don't you want to kiss my breasts, Lieutenant? You were staring at them all evening."

"So, you noticed, did you?" Charlie said, smiling devilishly. He needn't have waited for her permission, but now that he had it he wasted no time, slipping his hand down into her bosom and groping for the top hooks on her corset.

"Are you having difficulty, Lieutenant?" Maggie asked with a grin. "I thought you were experienced. Here, let me help you." She quickly and easily unfastened the hooks and pulled down the top of her dress and corset, releasing her magnificent breasts. Charlie watched spellbound as they flopped out big and bouncy. He'd never seen anything like it, and he reached for them, touching them, at first gently and tentatively, but then more firmly. They were big and soft and warm and perfectly formed. To call them "bigger than a Guernsey Cow" seemed gross and crude, for they were truly beautiful works of art from the glorious hand of mother nature.

"My God, they're beautiful!" he exclaimed.

Maggie remained silent, a slight smile on her face, as though she were questioning how a man could be so totally absorbed with a woman's breasts. Meanwhile, Charlie continued fondling them with both hands.

"So, you like them, Lieutenant."

"Yes, ma'am, I sure do." She lay down again on the blanket, and he bent down and began kissing them, his lips and tongue alighting on her pinkish erect nipples. He could feel his manhood pulsing, and now he wanted it all. He reached his hand up her dress but met resistance both from the hooks on her corset and from Maggie herself.

"No, no, Lieutenant, not now," she said, brusquely removing

his hand. "That's enough for tonight. We'll save the rest for a later date, that is, of course, if you're still interested."

She stood up now, quickly pulled the corset up over her breasts, fastened the hooks, and adjusted her dress. Charlie was taken aback, his passion having abruptly waned. He was disappointed, but he was still interested. How could he not be? This was one extraordinary "lil gal." And he'd play by her rules, at least for the time being.

3

The night sky was extraordinarily clear, so clear that it did in fact look like you could reach up and touch the stars. The cold spell that began at the close of 1862 continued into the New Year, and the temperature inside the huts and tents was every bit as cold as the temperature outside. The only way the men could keep warm was to build large fires. Charlie, Norm Christiansen, and a small group of Company E enlisted men were seated around a campfire roasting three good-sized chickens. The chickens were provided by one Corporal Travis Carmichael of Columbia, a handsome young man of twenty and an expert horseman. He'd gotten them in an exchange for a Yankee flag that he'd captured in a raid in the coastal areas of Charleston before Company E had come north to Virginia.

"Damn, you done right this time, Carmichael," said Private Paul Stanley, a tall, skinny trooper from Greeneville. "Best damn chicken Aah'v had since leavin' home." Stanley sat there looking longingly at the second bird which appeared to be just about done. When he reached for it however, Charlie spoke up.

"Keep yo hands offa that bird, Private. Me and Norm's sharing it with Carmichael!"

"Yes, sir!" said the young private, moving back, while licking his fingers and smiling sheepishly.

All of a sudden, they heard an uproar from somewhere out in the drill field.

"What' d'ya spose that's all about?" asked Lieutenant Christiansen, turning to Corporal Carmichael.

"Go see what all the hollerin's about, Travis. Don't worry. We'll take good care of your chickens."

Carmichael walked off in the direction of the drill field. Ten minutes later he returned with Bobby Joe Lane, who had just returned from a scouting mission where he'd picked up a recent copy of the *Richmond Examiner*. Charlie reached out for the paper and moved closer to the fire. Lieutenant Christiansen and the contingent of enlisted men moved closer to join them.

"Listen to this," Charlie said.

The Richmond Examiner January 3 1863
Lincoln Signs Emancipation Proclamation

On Sunday, January 1st, President Abraham Lincoln signed a document purporting to give legal effect to the terms of his earlier decree of September 1862, which stated that if any state in rebellion against the United States failed to end such rebellion by January 1, 1863, all slaves in such states thenceforward shall be forever free.

"Why, that's the silliest shit Aah've heard in all my days," said Private Johnny Andrews, who hailed from Tatum, South Carolina. "Aah'm no lawyer, but he ain't got no jurisdiction over people and property in the CSA. His decrees don't mean a damn thing in my opinion. Charlie continued to read aloud:

The most startling political crime, the most stupid political blunder yet known in American political history, aimed at servile insurrection with the result that southern people have now only to choose between victory and death.

The families of Lieutenants Flynn and Christiansen owned slaves back in South Carolina. Charlie's father had two who worked in his warehouse, and Christiansen's family had many, laboring on their rice farm. It was not yet clear what this decree would mean for southern slave holders, but it surely would not be favorable.

"Aah agree with Johnny. That monkey Lincoln has no jurisdiction over what happens in the CSA. The problem is them niggers don't understand that and couldn't care less. That's the bad part, cause once they get wind of this here decree, they'll consider themselves free and all hell will break loose."

"What' d'ya mean once they get wind of it? Them niggers ain't as dumb as y'all might think, and you can bet they been followin' it all very closely. I damn sure would if I was a nigger!"

The chickens were coated with lard, and as it dripped down on the fire, the flames flared way up and smoke billowed from the spit.

"Hey, you're gonna burn them birds." Take 'em off, ya hear?" Christiansen shouted.

Private Carmichael jumped to it, but not before the flames had burned the skin black.

Charlie and Norm finished reading the article and were about to throw the newspaper in the fire, when a young private spoke up:

"If y'all wouldn't mind, suh, Aah'd like to stuff that newspaper in ma boots. These holes been gettin bigger and bigger by the day." Charlie looked at him sympathetically, knowing just how hard it was to get a pair of new boots; most of them taken from the bodies of dead or captured Yankees.

"Be my guest, Private," Charlie said, watching as the young man took off his worn out boots and stuffed them with the newspaper.

"You know the reason Lincoln ain't mentionin' niggers in his own Union states is cause he's not really a nigger lover as most people believe," said Norm Christianson. "Don't ya'll deny Ole Uncle Abe! He's one clever son-of-a-bitch. Freein' the slaves in our southern states, or purportin to do so anyway, is sure as hell gonna help his war effort. Might even create a slave revolt when the owners refuse to let their niggers go. Lincoln ain't no nigger lover any more than we are. He's been advocatin' all along that they ship 'em all back to Africa or find a place for 'em somewhere in Central America."

"Listen, y'all need not worry now 'bout no Uncle Abe decrees or free slaves or anything else for that matter," offered Charlie, as he cut off and discarded some badly burned chicken skin with his razor-sharp hunting knife.

"Once Ole Jeb Stuart and our First Cavalry meet their sorry ass Yankee forces on the field of battle, this whole damn struggle will be over, and we can all go home and live our lives as we please in a free and independent Confederate States of America."

Just then one of Colonel Black's orderlies approached the campfire.

"Y'all got a Lieutenant Flynn here amongst ya?" He asked. Charlie looked up from his plate of chicken.

"Yeah, I'm Lieutenant Flynn."

Norm Christiansen smiled, wondering whether Colonel Black might have gotten wind of Charlie's visit to the Burke's farmhouse the day before, the details of which Charlie had already related to Norm.

"Colonel Black wants to see you at HQ."

Charlie got up and reluctantly followed the orderly, noticing that Norm was chuckling to himself.

"What's this all about?" Charlie asked.

"Aah don't know, Lieutenant. He just told me to go and fetch ya. That's all Aah know."

Charlie walked into Colonel Black's tent and saluted sharply, displaying the proper military bearing and respect. Colonel Black returned the salute.

"Have a seat, Lieutenant." Charlie sat down and looked around. In addition to the Colonel's desk there were three rickety chairs and a wood-burning stove vented via a stove pipe to the outside. Unlike Charlie's hut, the tent was warm but somewhat smoky. Behind the Colonel's desk stood a slightly soiled Stars and Bars, on the top of which the Colonel had hung his saber.

"Do you know why I called you here, Lieutenant?"

Charlie shook his head, thinking it best not to volunteer the likely reason.

"No, sir, Aah don't rightly know."

"Well, Lieutenant, I had a visit this afternoon from the owner of that tobacco farm east of here, a Mister Burke. He claims that you took his daughter, Maggie, down to his leaf dryin' barn, and that when he followed you and entered the barn, he saw you on top of her, screwin' like a stallion stud. Says he didn't know whether you were imitating the horse or the horse was imitating you, because your horse was right next to you screwin his wife's prize horse." Charlie tried his best to adopt the appropriate expression of guilt and contrition, but he had all he could do to suppress the gut-busting laugh that was threatening to erupt from the way in which Colonel Black was describing things. "Now, I'm asking you, Lieutenant Flynn, is it true what Mister Burke has accused you of?"

"Well, sir, I wouldn't have described it like that. It was more..."

Colonel Black stood up, pointing his finger at Charlie.

"Do you know how influential this Burke family is, Lieutenant?"

Charlie struggled to adopt a humble look, shaking his head in the negative.

"He's a personal friend of President Jefferson Davis and visits him in Richmond. And the Davises have stayed at the Burke's farm on several occasions."

The dressing down that Colonel Black gave Lieutenant Charlie Flynn continued for a good five minutes, and that was in spite of the fact that an orderly rode up with an urgent scouting report from Jeb Stuart. Colonel Black said he had a good mind to bust Charlie to Private and throw him in the stockade for the next six months. And he said he would do just that, if it weren't for the fact that he needed every last officer to confront the large Union cavalry force camped just ten miles away, which was growing in strength by the day. In the end, Colonel Black docked Charlie two months' pay and restricted him to camp until "further notice." When Charlie ventured to ask when he could expect to receive "further notice," the Colonel exploded.

"You get the hell outta here, Lieutenant, before I change my mind and give you what you truly deserve!"

4

It was springtime. The brutally cold winter had finally ended, and the cavalries of the Army of Virginia and the Army of the Potomac were still encamped on opposite sides of the Rappahannock River in northern Virginia. The battle of Chancellorsville was now history, and although the rebel forces had gotten the better of it, it was a costly victory. They'd lost General "Stonewall" Jackson, who was accidentally shot by his own men, losing his arm and succumbing then to pneumonia. The mission of the men of the South Carolina First Cavalry continued to be restricted to scouting, reconnaissance, and raiding Union supply depots and railroad lines. Rumors continued that the Cavalry's mission was about to be expanded, and that they were going to play a greater role in the actual fighting. In the meantime they continued to drill, to drill, and to drill some more. They grumbled and complained bitterly, for they were, generally speaking, an unruly and individualistic breed, unaccustomed to taking orders and bowing to authority. In their spare time the troopers played poker, chuck-a-luck and every other imaginable form of gambling game. On Sundays it was baseball, which they gambled on as well.

Charlie Flynn was still restricted to camp. He did, however, manage to sneak out under the cover of darkness on occasion, straggling back just before reveille and entering camp unchallenged by his loyal enlisted men on guard duty. On days when he was unable to get to Maggie's side, he played poker, acquiring a reputation as one of the best players in camp. This evening found Charlie fully engaged in a lively game.

"Can you beat three kings?" asked Lieutenant Phil Forrester as he turned over his cards.

"Aah believe a straight does beat it, at least the last time Aah checked," Charlie said, turning over his jack high straight.

It was a large pot, consisting of silver coins, Confederate currency, and another good sized share of Yankee greenbacks. Lieutenant Forrester shook his head in dismay.

"Damn, look at all those Yankee dollars he's winnin'. He's got enough there to buy that 'lil gal' of his the finest clothes in Richmond."

"Hell, from what Aah done heard, she don't need no fine clothes," joked Lieutenant Christiansen. "She likes nothin' better than bein' wrapped in tobacco leaves. Am Aah right, Charlie?" Everyone around the table laughed themselves silly.

"Hey, Eli!" Charlie yelled. "Where the hell's that boy, anyway?"

Eli peeked out of the hut. "Fetch us another bottle o' that Scotch whiskey, will ya! This one's about empty."

The young black boy smiled, went into the hut again, and returned with another bottle.

"Fill their glasses, boy, and all the way up, ya hear!"

Eli complied, but in doing so spilled some whiskey on the makeshift poker table.

"God damnit, boy, don't spill it! Aah'm spendin' good Yankee dollars to get it."

Charlie won on most days, but the losers always got to share in Charlie's stash of fine whiskey.

As the poker game continued, the corporal who distributed the mail appeared and began calling out the names.

"Lieutenant Muldoon?" Barney Muldoon looked up and raised his hand, and the corporal flipped the letter to him. "Lieutenant Forrester? A package sir."

"Lieutenant Flynn?"

"Right here," Charlie said. The corporal flipped the letter to him.

The men moved off by themselves to get a little piece of home. Charlie went into his hut and lay down on the cot. He lit the oil lamp and saw that the letter was from his mother. He'd misread the return address on the envelope, thinking the letter was from Martha Brown, the pretty young girl he'd been seeing before going off to war.

Charleston 30 April 1863

Your father and I miss you, and pray that God will bless you and keep you under his protective wing for the duration of this terrible war.

Have you had any word on your possible fur-lough? We saw Martha Brown in church last Sunday, and she asked us when you'd be coming home. We commiserated about how hard it is on us womenfolk to be without our sons, sweethearts and husbands. Your father of course is still here with me and didn't have to fight, but he suffers from this war nonetheless. His business is dying because the Yankee embargo has had a devastating effect on the availability of goods.

I saw Bonnie McHugh, Billy's mother, in church. You know of course that when the war started, he went north. She said she hasn't had a letter from him in more than a year, and that he'd married a Cuban girl. Apparently...

Charlie put the letter down. He remembered the last time he'd seen Billy in Charleston Station with a contraband nigger slave belonging to his father, waiting for a train to take him to Fayetteville and on to Washington. Charlie winced and clenched his teeth, recalling his shock and dismay when Billy told him he was not going to volunteer and fight for the South. He'd accepted that Billy had good reason for abandoning him in California, but to abandon his country in its time of greatest need was unforgivable.

...Apparently, the Cuban girl and Billy had gotten positions in Washington. I tried to be polite and listen to Mrs. McHugh, but all the while I was thinking about our boys who were dying in the war, and I just couldn't help but to feel disgust for her Billy.

"Hey, Charlie, you gonna give us a chance to win back some of what we've lost?" asked Lieutenant Muldoon as he poked his head in the hut.

"You got any more of that Scotch whiskey?" he added.

Charlie sat up and put the letter back on the table.

"Look in my knapsack over there." Barney went over and found the bottle.

"How much you ahead, if I may ask."

"Aah don't know, fifty, maybe sixty. What does it matter? You know, Barney. Aah was just thinkin' about this former friend of mine from Charleston."

Barney brought the bottle of scotch and sat down with Charlie on the cot. He reached over and grabbed two glasses on the little table, filling them to the brim.

"To our beloved southland."

"To our southland!" They clinked glasses.

"Anyway, me and this high school friend of mine prospected together for a spell out in California. Well, it wasn't exactly an easy time, and one day he just up and left and went back to Charleston. Decided he wanted to be a lawyer. I give him credit. He was able to get a position with the Petigru law firm, the very best one in the city. And he was admitted to the Bar. From our high school days he was always talkin' 'bout this Cuban gal whom he'd met in Havana when he was just sixteen years old. My mom told me in her letter here that he married her finally."

Barney wondered where he was going with his story.

"Aah always liked this ole boy, Barney. We were good friends, that is, until Aah found out where his loyalties lay. The last time Aah saw him he was waitin' for a train in Charleston Station to take him north to the Yankee Capital. Said he was not about to fight for the South or the North."

"Aah know what you're sayin' Charlie. Aah knew two boys

like him from Saint Louis who joined the Yankee Army. Makes me sick every time Aah think about them. There's nothin' Aah'd like better than to find them on the field of battle. Aah'd run my sword right through their turncoat Yankee bellies quicker than you could say Bobby Lee!"

Barney drained his glass, looked quickly at Charlie to make sure he didn't mind, and poured himself another. "Aah reckon you'd do the same, wouldn't ya now, Charlie?"

"You put your finger on it, Barney. That's the very point Aah was gettin' at. Aah was wonderin just what Aah'd do in that situation. Lieutenant Forrester stuck his head in the hut.

"Say, Charlie, you gonna join us?"

"In a minute," Charlie said, a pensive expression on his handsome face.

5

It was a late afternoon in early June, and Charlie was shaving in preparation for a hoped-for midnight tryst with Maggie Burke. Norm Christiansen suddenly appeared alongside the hut looking somewhat excited.

"We're movin' out, Charlie. We're takin' us a train ride!"

"What?" Charlie looked up then flipped a wet blob of soap on the ground from his straight razor.

"Aah was comin back from waterin ma horse and walked past Colonel Black's tent. General Hampdon's in camp, and Aah heard him say somethin' bout Culpepper. Said there's a big build-up of forces in the area, both infantry and cavalry.

"Damn! Did they say when? I will need some time. Me and Maggie planned on…"

"Could be as soon as tomorrow, but Aah couldn't hear everything."

Charlie wiped the soap from his face and hands and went inside the hut, returning with a tattered map that looked like it had been folded too many times.

"Culpepper, huh? Here it is," he said, pointing his index finger on the map. "There's a railroad depot close by—Brandy Station. I'm gonna have to sneak out tonight, Norm..."

Charlie stopped in mid-sentence. It was unclear whether he'd lost his train of thought or whether he'd thought it best not to disclose it to his hut mate.

"You're flirtin' with fire, Charlie. They'll be postin' extra pickets and sentries now that we're mobilizin'. And they won't all be Company E boys. You could get yoself shot."

A corporal walked up, saluting smartly.

"Lieutenant, suh, Colonel Black wants to see all officers in his tent right away, suh."

Charlie wiped his face, put on his jacket and followed Norm Christiansen to Colonel Black's tent.

"...Y'all stand at ease, men. Aah called y'all here to tell ya that we're movin' out tomorrow. General Lee's got the bulk of our infantry assembled now at Culpepper, and our Cavalry's assemblin' at Brandy Station not too far from there. General Stuart wants to present a full-dress parade at Brandy Station for General Lee this week. Our latest reconnaissance estimates show that the Yankees have assembled more than a hundred thousand infantry and a cavalry force of eleven thousand five hundred all under the command of General Alfred Pleasonton..."

The briefing ended, and the men walked back to their huts and tents, grumbling and second-guessing as subordinates are wont to do.

"That egotistical dandy Jeb Stuart just wants ta show off in front of General Lee. Wants ta add another fancy red plume to that ridiculous hat and uniform of his," said Lieutenant Barney Muldoon.

"Yeah, Bobby Lee don't want and don't need no pomp and ceremony. It's a big waste of ammunition," said Lieutenant Forrester. "All it ever does is tire out the horses and the men."

The next morning at dawn the men of Company E boarded railroad cars of the Orange & Alexandria line and set off with their horses, supplies, and equipment for Brandy Station, Virginia. And on the 5th and 8th of June the combined forces of some ninety-five hundred Confederate Cavalry participated in a full field review, complete with cavalry charges and artillery barrages. The troopers of First Cavalry were dressed in neatly pressed uniforms, highly polished boots, and gleaming sabers. All for the benefit and delight of General Stuart, who pranced about on his prize mount, urging on his men, leading the charges to the rousing sound of martial music and the waving of the Stars and Bars. As for General Lee, he was not in camp on June 5th for the main part of the review, appearing only briefly on the 8th.

Company E bivouacked with the bulk of the First Cavalry in the area known as Fleetwood Hill, an elevated patch of land that rose up from the flat grassy plain of Brandy Station. Early on the morning of June 9th, General Pleasonton's Union Cavalry managed to slip into the area, launching a surprise attack, which caught General Stuart's forces completely off guard. The bullets flew and the sabers flashed as the Union forces bore down on the Confederates who were at rest. The entire exchange lasted a few short minutes, but as intelligence later reported, this fight was about to become the largest cavalry battle in the war to date, the Union fielding some eleven thousand five hundred blue-shirted troopers and the Confederates some nine thousand five hundred "butternuts." Such a massive military engagement of men on horseback had never been seen before; not in any war, not here, not anywhere else in the world. It was hard to imagine the violence, the death and destruction that could result from it.

The rumors had been well founded. The Confederate Cavalry was indeed undertaking a new mission. This was it, and for the first time in their military careers, Lieutenants Charlie Flynn, Norm Christiansen and thousands of other CSA Cavalry officers and enlisted men were to engage the enemy in a direct combat role.

It was moments after the Union's surprise attack that the men of the First Cavalry regrouped and saddled up. They lined up in formation as they'd done so many times during those many months of drill and training. Generals Jeb Stuart and Wade Hampdon were in front of the pack. Colonel Black was at the head of Company E. Lieutenants Flynn and Christiansen took their positions side by side, their enlisted men behind them, waiting for the signal. The drums rolled, the bugle sounded, and the men raised their sabers and their Colt revolvers:

Charge!

Immediately, there rose a shrill and frightening sound, the "Rebel Yell." Born in the gut, it traveled up and through the windpipe, exiting the mouth as a terrifying, devilish din. *EEE-YOO-EEE-YOO-WEE-YOO-Wee* No one knows when or where the Rebel Yell was first heard or where it originated, but one thing was certain, the Yankees dreaded and feared it. Prisoners reported that it made their blood run cold and their knees tremble; they knew that within seconds the rebels would be upon them. On this June 9th, 1863, doubtless the Rebel Yell was louder and more frightening still as the First Cavalry's massive mounted force of thousands raced up the grassy field to engage the enemy and retake Fleetwood Hill.

The Yankee Cavalry under General Pleasanton prepared to

meet them, and the two massive forces raced hell bent toward each other, meeting head on, clashing with a deafening boom that for a second or two even overpowered the Rebel Yell. Men and horses fell, littering the field with bloody, mangled bodies. Heavy clouds of smoke and dust blanketed the field, obscuring one's vision and making it difficult to distinguish between friend and foe. Sabers stabbed and slashed, severing arms and legs from torsos. As the bodies and body parts piled up, they created obstacles, tripping up the continually charging waves of mounted men that followed. It was truly a horrid scene, an ungodly baptism under fire for those who had wished for a new combat role for the South Carolina First Cavalry.

Charlie witnessed the death of Norm Christiansen, who was shot in the head by Yankee Sergeant with a Spencer Repeating Rifle. Charlie's emotions got the better of him, and seemingly oblivious to the slashing swords and whistling bullets all around him, he took off after the Yankee Sergeant and killed him with a bullet to the heart from his 45 Colt revolver. But when he bent down from his horse to pick up the dead Yankee's rifle, he felt a violent impact and a red-hot pain from a 45 caliber bullet that entered the right side of his buttocks. The shock and pain was intense and more than enough to bring him back to his senses. He immediately began defending himself once again, avoiding a saber thrust from a Union Lieutenant, who'd seen him strip the sergeant of the state-of-the-art weapon. Fortunately, Charlie had also seen him, and before the Yankee officer could raise his saber anew, Charlie shot him in the face. By then his backside was bleeding profusely. Blood soaked his trousers and accumulated on his saddle, running down his leg and collecting in his boot. He needed medical attention, and he needed it now. Grabbing hold of the reins, he spurred Compass hard, and the big red roan burst through the chaotic clog of opposing forces and ran toward the perimeter of the grassy field, barely evading numerous Yankee saber thrusts along the way.

When Charlie awoke the next day, he was lying on a badly soiled cot in a hastily constructed field hospital. He'd lost a lot of blood and was as weak as a newborn lamb. When he was able to focus his eyes, he saw Lieutenant Barney Muldoon entering the tent.

"How ya feelin', Trooper?" Muldoon sat on the side of the cot, whereupon Charlie grimaced in pain, pointing to his backside. Muldoon immediately stood as Charlie struggled to speak.

"Well, it's a damn good thing Aah've been constipated," he said in a voice just stronger than a whisper. "I'll tell ya that, Barney, cause that Yankee son-of-a-bitch shot me right in the ass."

Muldoon tried to suppress his laugh but failed. Charlie continued with his humor, which Barney interpreted as a good sign.

"I prefer the original hole in ma backside. It don't hurt as much as this new one I got."

Barney laughed openly this time, then turned serious and went on to describe the battle, most of which Charlie had missed.

"Aah don't know how many cavalry charges there were, Charlie, but it musta' been more than ten as best Aah can recall. But when it was all over, we was back on Fleetwood Hill, and there weren't no more blue shirts in sight. Our people are sayin', and Aah think rightly so, that we licked 'em. Course ole Jeb Stuart is comin' under some heated criticism. Newspapers said the fox shoulda known where the foxhunters were before the chase began; and that Stuart hadn't the faintest idea where them Yankees was hidin'. The papers are sayin' that his errors and poor judgment cost us some good men, and that would include our own Norm Christiansen."

Charlie pursed his lips and a sad expression bloomed on his pain-ridden face.

"Aah spoke with Doc Walker just now, and he says that you're lucky ta be alive, cause you lost a bucket of blood." Barney smiled now. "We're all hopin' you'll come back real soon, Charlie, cause that ole Compass o' yours jest keeps on makin a ruckus. He kept us awake last night with all his constant whinnyin'. Eli can't get him ta eat a thing." Charlie chuckled, but once again the pain was there

"We're all torn up bout Norm. We're gonna miss him. He was a good friend and a damn fine trooper." It looked like Charlie was about to say something, but he let it pass. "Well, Aah better be gettin' back, Charlie. You take care of yourself, and I'll try to come and see ya again tomorrow."

CHAPTER XII

French Invade Mexico

A month had passed since the epic battle of Gettysburg, and stories about the terrible slaughter in the farmland of central Pennsylvania still dominated the front pages of the newspapers.

The Washington Evening Star August 4 1863
Battle of Gettysburg: A Union Victory?

Did Union forces achieve a victory at Gettysburg? Some observers have said so, citing Confederate casualties of some 28,000 and Union of "only" 23,050, "only" 23,050. The plain truth of the matter is that it was a slaughter, a devastating loss for both the Confederacy and the Union. How else can one characterize such human carnage? While the generals can disagree over which side got the best of it, the soldiers themselves know. They know very well, and the ever-rising number of desertions on both sides tells the story. These poor wretches are hunted down, captured and brought back to their units. They tell their superiors that they were so traumatized by the senseless slaughter that they are no longer able to fight. They need no defense other than their appearance, which speaks for itself, usually

*manifesting symptoms of insanity. Nonetheless, they
are charged with desertion, court-martialed and when
convicted, many are executed...*

The carriage passed the White House, and Billy McHugh turned the page of the newspaper he had borrowed from the coachman.

French Consolidate Power in Mexico

*On June 14th thousands of French troops under the
command of General Francois Bazaine joined those of
General Forey and triumphantly entered Mexico City.
A conservative government was installed and will rule
until Archduke Ferdinand Maximilian is placed on
the throne as Emperor of Mexico early next year.*

Billy was keenly aware of the other civil war being fought south of the border in the United Mexican States. It had begun long before the Civil War presently raging in the United States, and pitted conservative landowners, mostly white and of Spanish blood, against Indian and Mestizo peasant farmers. The Conservatives achieved power, and their government was temporarily recognized by every major power except the United States. But alas, in January of 1861, the Liberal forces finally prevailed, entering Mexico City under the leadership of Benito Juárez, a Zapotec Indian and former Governor of the State of Oaxaca. The Conservatives fled, many going to Europe in search of money and arms to continue their struggle.

The Juárez Government assumed power, and found itself burdened with large debts and little money to repay them. Juárez announced a two-year moratorium on debt repayment. France found that unacceptable, and in December of 1861 sent troops to Mexico to aid in their debt collection efforts. It soon became evident that the French Monarch, Napoleon III, had designs on an expanded empire in the Americas. The army fielded by the Juárez Government was no match for the French, and in June of 1863, a month before the Battle of Gettysburg, the French captured Mexico City and installed another conservative government. The United States continued to support the Juárez government in exile. Secretary of State Seward was in favor of taking strong action against the French, but gradually came to agree with the President that dealing with the French in Mexico would have to wait. "*One war at a time, William,*" Lincoln had wisely said.

The carriage pulled up now to Henry Phipps & Partners. Billy returned the newspaper and paid the fare, tipping the coachman generously.

"Good monin, Massa McHugh," said the doorman, as Billy entered the firm's offices. "Look like it gonna be anotha hot one tiday."

"Good morning, Percy. Yes, it's plenty hot already."

Billy walked to his desk, looked up and saw Brad Mitchum coming through the door.

"Well, I see you're here early as usual, McHugh. Be sure to let me know when you've made partner, you hear? So I know when to bow!"

"You'll be the first to know, Mitchum."

"Bartlett was looking for you last night, McHugh. I had to tell him that you'd left for the day." Brad smiled, adding, "I was here last night until eight thirty."

"Did he say what he wanted?"

Brad just shook his head.

Billy looked over toward Joseph Bartlett's office, wondering whether he should go see for himself. Just then, Bartlett opened his door and signaled for him to come in.

"Good morning, Billy. Have a seat."

"Good morning, sir." He sat in one of the elegant wing chairs in front of Bartlett's enormous mahogany desk, a desk that always seemed to be amazingly neat and uncluttered.

"Can I get you a cup of tea?"

"Yes, sir, thank you, sir." Bartlett pulled the servant's cord behind his desk. An attractive young negress entered.

"Millie, Bring us some tea, please, with…" He turned to Billy. Do you take it with lemon?"

"Yes, sir, lemon and sugar."

"Bring some milk too, Millie, and some of those chocolate brownies." Millie smiled shyly and walked out.

"Do you happen to know her story?" Bartlett asked. "It's really quite remarkable."

"Well, I know that her brother's an aide to Frederick Douglass, and I heard that she actually fought with the Union army at Shiloh."

Billy suddenly wished he hadn't mentioned Shiloh, remembering that Bartlett's son, had been killed there. Bartlett didn't seem to react.

"Yes, that's right. She disguised herself as a man and fought with the troops. She was wounded, but continued to fight, killing several rebels who had sneaked in behind Union lines. She's quite the young lady. It was only when they were pinning the medals on her that they discovered she was a female. We plan to start her clerking right here in this office."

Bartlett went on some more about Frederick Douglass and how Henry Phipps & Partners had raised money for one of his whirlwind speaking tours.

Millie returned carrying a silver tray with the tea and brownies.

She was about to serve the tea, but Bartlett waved her off and began serving it himself.

"Will you have a brownie, Billy? They're quite good."

"Yes, please." Bartlett held the tray for him, and Billy took one, then put some sugar in his tea.

"Tell me, are you still studying French?"

It was an unexpected question, and Billy wondered if it was simply small talk or whether it had something to do with why Bartlett wanted to see him.

"Yes, sir, I am. I have a tutor who comes to my flat in the morning, and we practice for an hour before I leave for the office."

"So, you've achieved a decent level of fluency, have you?"

Before Billy could respond, Bartlett added, "I know your Spanish is fluent."

"Well, sir, the French is coming along pretty well, but I can't honestly say that it's as good as my Spanish, not yet at least."

Bartlett took a sip of his tea then leaned up in his chair.

"Billy, I had dinner last night with Secretary of State Seward and a young Mexican diplomat by the name of Matías Romero. I wanted you to join us, but unfortunately you had already left for the day."

Billy felt a sinking feeling in his stomach, realizing what a golden opportunity he had missed.

"I'm terribly sorry, Mister Bartlett. My wife had some trouble yesterday and I had to leave early."

"Well, there'll be other opportunities, maybe sooner than you might think. You must have made a very good impression on Secretary Seward because he remembered you from New Year's Day at the White House."

"Well, that's certainly good to know. Thank you for telling me, sir."

Bartlett turned serious.

"Knowing your keen interest in Spanish America, Billy, I'm sure you've followed events in Mexico and know that Napoleon III is about to create a Mexican Monarchy and place Archduke Maxmilian of the Austrian Hapsburgs on the throne. Of course he has only gotten away with it so far because the United States has its hands full with this ongoing Civil War."

Billy wondered if Bartlett had read the same newspaper that he had read on his way to work. Bartlett leaned back now in his chair, nestling his cup of tea on his lap.

"Do you know anything about this Matías Romero, the Mexican diplomat I mentioned?"

"I've seen his name in the newspapers, sir. That's about all."

"Well, he's now the ranking member of the Juárez Government's Diplomatic Mission to the United States. He's here to shape American foreign policy and persuade public opinion that the United States is duty bound to drive the French from Mexico. He's been wining and dining members of Congress on a daily basis, promising investment deals for their constituents, writing articles and doing everything possible to focus attention on this issue."

Billy looked at Bartlett.

Why is he telling me all this? What's this have to do with me and my French?

"By the way," Bartlett continued, "did you know that the Confederacy is actively seeking diplomatic recognition from the French puppet regime in Mexico?"

"Well, that would make sense from their point of view, sir."

Bartlett put his teacup back on his desk, leaned up in his chair and looked at Billy, a sly grin on his face. "Now I'm sure you've been asking yourself just what all this has to do with you, Billy McHugh. Am I right?"

"Yes, sir, you certainly are."

"Well, I won't beat around the bush with you. We want to

send you to Mexico, and when I say *we,* I mean Secretary of State Seward and Henry Phipps & Partners."

Billy leaned up in his chair, almost spilling his tea.

"You want *me* to go to Mexico? Why?"

"Secretary Seward needs someone to snoop around, someone who's multilingual, clever and can determine just what the French and the Confederates are up to."

"I'm truly flattered that you and Secretary Seward have such confidence in me, but I really don't understand. Why doesn't he send someone from the State Department or someone from our embassy? Surely, he has people there who speak Spanish and French as well?"

Bartlett sipped his tea before responding.

"Well, the simple answer is that Seward believes that the Confederates and the French would readily detect a State Department official. He thinks that a young lawyer like you, a private individual, would have a much better chance of going undetected. Of course, I've also told the Secretary just how much we at Henry Phipps & Partners value your abilities. And as I said, he remembers you." There was a slight pause.

"You said Henry Phipps & Partners wants me to go..." He didn't finish the sentence.

"Yes, that's right. The firm wants you to go. We're confident that there are some good possibilities in Mexico to develop our international practice, especially in the mining and railroad sectors. I remember that you had an introduction to Mexican mining law during your gold mining sojourn in California."

"Yes, sir, but that's all it was, just a brief introduction."

"But you liked it, didn't you, and you said it was one of the reasons why you decided to study law as I recall during your interview."

Billy smiled.

"You have a good memory, Mister Bartlett."

"A good lawyer needs a good memory, Billy. Anyway, Matías Romero has confirmed that there are lots of opportunities and there will be even more once the French have gone."

"This all comes as a complete surprise to me, Mister Bartlett, and to be perfectly frank, it's a bit overwhelming. I don't know what to say. I'm going to need some time to let it all sink in."

"We understand. It has indeed come together suddenly, but we want to be responsive to Secretary Seward. The more the State Department is aware of our capabilities, the more business will be coming our way in the future. And this is the time to plant the firm's flag in Mexico. It will certainly be a good opportunity for you. I can say without any hesitation that I would have loved to have had such an opportunity when I was your age."

"When would you want me to go, Mister Bartlett, and how long will I be expected to stay?"

"As soon as possible, and I think you can count on at least six months, probably a year."

"What about my wife?"

"I'm afraid she's not included in the plans, at least not at this time."

Bartlett left no time for Billy to respond.

"Now, you're to meet tomorrow morning at ten o'clock with a Mister Jonathan Ambrose at the State Department. I'm sure Secretary Seward will want to talk to you as well. I must tell you that those Pinkerton people will be asking you some questions about your background and professional experience. Henry and I have already spoken to one of their investigators, and we've both vouched for your excellent character and complete trustworthiness. And I've arranged another dinner with Matías Romero for tomorrow night. I'm sure he'll have some important contacts and insights for you."

2

The following day, Bartlett and Phipps briefed Billy further on the assignment, after which he walked to the State Department for his meeting with Jonathan Ambrose.

"Ah, yes, Billy McHugh. Have a seat and make yourself comfortable. I'll be with you in a minute."

Billy sat down in an easy chair just outside of Ambrose's office. The door was open, and he watched Ambrose remove a pile of files from his desk, and put them in a safe in back. There was a young woman with him, and when she walked out, he signaled for Billy to come in.

"Good morning, Mister McHugh, I'm Jonathan Ambrose." He extended his hand and Billy shook it. "I'm informed that we need to brief you for a mission in Mexico, a country which holds a warm spot in my heart."

Jonathan Ambrose was a short, stout man in his forties. He was clean-shaven, but like his boss, William Seward, slovenly dressed with an unkempt look about him.

"I had a three-year tour there in the late fifties during the Juárez Government and its Reforma. You, young man, are going to have it much easier than I did. While we despise what the French have done in Mexico and will do everything we can to thwart their objectives and eventually oust them, they have instituted a much more civilized and comfortable life style."

Ambrose signaled now for the young woman to reenter.

"Charlotte, bring me some tea, please. And, Mister McHugh, what would you like?"

"Tea would be fine, sir, thank you."

"How do you take it?" Ambrose had a unique and distinct

way of enunciating his words, as though he was teaching a listener non-too-familiar with the language, the proper pronunciation.

"With lemon and sugar, thank you." The young woman left the room.

"Santa Anna knew how to live, but the Juaristas for the most part were illiterate Indians…"

Ambrose went on for a good five minutes, telling little anecdotes of his time in Mexico.

"Well, so much for my history. Now, let's get down to business. I'm informed that you're expected to be in Mexico for up to a year, and that you'll be staying in Mexico City, but may also be expected to make trips to the northern provinces. Is that correct?"

"Yes, sir, that's what I was told."

The young woman came with a silver teapot, exquisite teacups bearing the State Department logo and some sweet biscuits.

"Thank you, Charlotte. Oh, and close the door on your way out. Help yourself, Mister McHugh."

Billy waited while Ambrose poured himself some tea and placed several biscuits on his saucer. Once he'd finished chewing the biscuits, he adopted a most serious expression and stared intently at Billy.

"Mister McHugh." Billy had thought of asking him to call him Billy, or even William, but decided that Ambrose was just too formal a person for such informality. "I cannot emphasize enough the need to keep your mission absolutely secret. Tell me, are you married?"

"Yes, sir, I am."

"Well, we cannot even allow you to tell your wife what you'll be doing in the country. Do you understand?"

"I understand, Mister Ambrose."

"You'll hear more about this need for absolute secrecy when you visit with the Pinkerton people after I'm through with you."

Ambrose smiled slightly, then opened one of his desk drawers and took out a large stack of files. "We need you to go through these documents today here in the building. I can give you some idea of what you'll find in them, but I'd first like to know how much you already know about the Confederacy's activities in Mexico, especially their efforts to create a monarchy with Maximilian on the throne. And what's most important, their efforts to achieve diplomatic recognition from France, England and other key nations."

"Well, sir, I know that British and French recognition is critical for the Confederate States of America, if it is to be accepted as an independent nation."

"Yes, of course, and it was in all the newspapers, wasn't it?" Ambrose sipped his tea and continued to munch on the sweet biscuits.

"Yes, sir, I read it in the press, and I also thought that recognition of the CSA might facilitate their acquiring additional territory in North America."

"You're absolutely right, Mister McHugh. That's very important. Would you mind if I called you Billy? My briefing papers refer to you as Billy McHugh."

"No, sir, please do." Ambrose smiled, then brushed some biscuit crumbs off his shirt.

"Tell me, Billy, are you aware of efforts by the Confederacy to obtain recognition from France?"

"Well, of course, I've no personal knowledge of that sir, but when the War between the States first broke out..." Ambrose, smiling slightly interrupted Billy.

"Pardon my interruption, but I find it curious that you people from the South, and regardless of your sympathies, all seem to refer to our ongoing war as the War between the States.

"I believe it has something to do with the States Rights

movement and in particular the struggles over John C. Calhoun's Nullification Doctrine."

"I can tell that you know your history, young man"

"Well, as to your question whether I have any knowledge of the Confederacy's efforts to obtain France's recognition, nothing more than what I've read, sir. But I can understand why the French would want to side with the South. They don't want the United States to acquire more territory via Manifest Destiny. They themselves want to acquire more territory in this hemisphere."

"You're so right about that, Billy. Napoleon's so-called '*Grande Pensee*' includes all of Latin America. His megalomania knows no bounds." There was a knock on the door.

"Come in," said Ambrose. It was his assistant, Charlotte.

"Excuse me, Mister Ambrose. Secretary Seward told me to give you this telegraph."

"Thank you, Charlotte."

Billy watched as Ambrose read it.

"You'll have to excuse me, Billy, but I must see the Secretary. I would suggest that you begin your briefing by reading that file tied with the ribbon." Ambrose rushed out of the room.

"THE CSA'S DIPLOMATIC AND ESPIONAGE ACTIVITIES IN MEXICO

The CSA seeks more than just recognition in Mexico. Their grand design envisions the incorporation of Mexico into the greater Confederacy. The establishment of the Mexican Monarchy with Maximilian on the throne will provide further opportunities.

The northern Mexican provinces of Chihuahua, Sonora and Nuevo León have rich deposits of silver, gold and other valuable minerals. The Confederacy seeks these resources to pay for the war and to fund the new government. They seek the Pacific port of Guaymas, which will enable them to export their cotton to Europe. Our present blockade of the CSA's southern ports both in the Atlantic and the Gulf of Mexico has severely limited their exports.

The northern provinces of Mexico are basically free of control from Mexico City. Their Governments are headed by strong, independent *caudillos*, who rule these provinces as virtual fiefdoms. The Confederacy is now dealing directly with these leaders with a view towards annexing them to the greater Confederacy. The CSA is prepared to achieve these objectives through negotiation or, if need be, by military conquest. Negotiations are progressing at present.

Early in the Civil War, the CSA seized lands in the territories of Arizona and New Mexico, and the Confederate Congress enacted legislation proclaiming them *Confederate Territories*. These lands were part of the same territories ceded by Mexico to the United States by the *Treaty of Guadalupe Hidalgo* and the *Gadsden Purchase...*"

Ambrose walked back into the room, and Billy looked up.

"I'm sorry, Billy, but something urgent has come up, and I will not be able to spend as much time with you as I'd originally planned."

Ambrose opened the safe behind his desk and began extracting files. He then called for Charlotte to come and carry some of them.

"I'm afraid you'll have to go though those files without my comments..."

"Excuse me for interrupting Mister Ambrose, but before you go, my boss, Joseph Bartlett, told me that I'm to snoop around and see what the Confederates and the French are up to in Mexico. But I was hoping to get more clarification and guidance from you this morning."

"I'm sorry, but I'm not able to tell you much more than what Joseph told you, and that is that we want you to snoop around and gather information."

And how am I to get the information back to the State Department? No one has given me any instructions. Do I go to the Embassy?"

"There is no embassy, Billy. It shut down when Juárez was chased into exile. The best I can do now is to say that you will be informed in due time. Now, I really must be going.

I wish you good luck."

CHAPTER XIII

Dolores in Cuba

Dolores stood at the rail holding baby Sebastián as the steamer *Wide Horizon* approached El Morro Castle. Don Fernando selected the vessel. His New York contacts assured him that it would not be carrying contraband goods and could be trusted to transport his daughter and grandson safely back to Cuba. As the vessel passed El Morro, it sounded its horn, startling Dolores but not little Sebastián, who giggled and looked at his mother as though wanting her to do it again. Dolores laughed, feeling a deep sense of joy to be the mother of this delightful baby boy.

"Oh, so you like that horn, do you?" There was an elderly couple standing at the rail next to Dolores, and the woman looked at Sebastián, smiled broadly then turned to her husband:

"*Ay, Felipe, mira qué monito este nene!*" (Hey, Felipe look at this cute little baby.) The man looked, then asked Dolores:

"*De quá edad es el nene, señora?*" (How old is your baby, ma'am?)

"*Acaba de cumplir un año, señor.*" He just turned one-year-old, sir."

The voyage was uneventful, and Dolores breathed a sigh of relief. Ever since the sinking of the *Central America*, she had been apprehensive about boarding another ocean-going vessel. As the *Wide Horizon* slowly inched into its berth and docked.

Dolores kissed Sebastián, then looked up at the azure colored sky garnished with puffy white cumulous clouds. It was a beautiful day in Havana, a beautiful day to be home. She walked up to the bow and scanned the quay below, looking for Sofia and don Fernando. Little Sebastián had fallen asleep, and as Dolores stood gently rocking him back and forth, she felt the joyful anticipation of seeing her family again and introducing them all to Sebastián Roberto McHugh.

There was a flurry of activity down on the quay as carriages came and went, discharging passengers and offloading freight. Dolores thought she saw the elegant black carriage off in the distance and guessed that it was don Fernando's. Meanwhile, the crew set down the gangplank, and the signal was given for passengers to disembark. Dolores had two large trunks, and she'd arranged for a steward to carry them ashore. A handsome young ship's officer stood at the top of the gangplank, bidding passengers good-bye and wishing them a pleasant stay in Havana. As she started walking down the gangplank with Sebastián, she heard a familiar voice.

"Doloresita! Doloresita!"

It was Sofia, and Dolores stepped more lively now, and when she reached the bottom, Sofia rushed over and greeted her sister with a wide smile and a kiss on the lips.

"*Bienvenida, querida hermana! Ay, mira mi nuevo sobrinito! Que precioso! Que monito! Y su cabello bonito como el de su madre!* (Welcome, dear sister! Ah, look at my new nephew! How precious! How cute! And his hair, beautiful just like his mother's!).

"May I hold him?" Sofía asked, beaming with anticipation. Just then, Sebastián opened his eyes and quickly closed them against the bright sunshine.

"*Ay, pobresito, le molesta el sol,*" (Ah, the poor thing, the sun is bothering him) Sofia said, removing her large, floppy hat and shading him with it. Sebastián continued his cute little wake up routine, yawning and stretching his little arms and legs.

"Where's papá, Sofía?" Dolores asked, looking around but seeing no sign of him.

"He's waiting in the carriage, Dolores. I'm afraid he's getting old, and he suffers from rheumatism."

The sisters had not seen each other since Dolores's wedding some two years earlier, and had much to talk about. Sofía was smitten with little Sebastián and peppered Dolores with questions, wanting to know everything about him from the very day of his birth to the present.

Now that he was awake, she played with his little hands and feet. She'd brought a baby rattle with her and shook it for him, imitating his cute little gurgles and baby talk. At one point Sofía referred to him as "the most beautiful baby in the world", which brought back a long forgotten memory of a scene in the garden of *La Dulce Gardenia*, years before when Sofía had referred to Billy McHugh as "the most beautiful boy in the world."

The two sisters continued to talk, delighting in each other's company. Dolores was struck by how good it felt to be home and to be speaking Spanish exclusively. She'd missed the comfort and simple pleasure of conversing in her native tongue, the language of the immortal Miguel de Cervantes. It was just one more reason why she was happy to be back in her native Cuba.

As they approached the carriage, they saw don Fernando peering out the window. Dolores now handed Sebastián over to a smiling Sofía and rushed to her father.

"Papá! papá!"

Don Fernando, assisted by the coachman, stepped down from the carriage, and embraced his daughter.

"Doloresita! Welcome home. I can't tell you how happy you

make your old papá just to see your face. But where is my new grandson?"

"I have him, papá," said Sofía. "and he's so adorable that I just might keep him all for myself. Look, papá. Look how beautiful! Have you ever seen a cuter baby in all your life?"

Don Fernando turned and looked at his new grandson for the first time.

"Ah, yes, little Sebastián. He's certainly a cute little lad, isn't he?" Though don Fernando smiled warmly, he didn't seem to have the same enthusiasm for Sebastián as did Sofía.

Dolores wondered whether it was because of Sebastián's *acanelado* skin color. She let it pass without mention.

"Papá, are you all right? Sofía tells me you have some rheumatism."

"Yes, I'm all right, but I'm getting old, and I must accept what comes with age."

Dolores noticed then that don Fernando stood leaning on a cane, a fancy black one with a large silver nob at the top, but a cane nonetheless.

"As you can see, I now walk with a cane."

Once Dolores's trunks had been loaded aboard the carriage, don Fernando signaled to the coachman to depart. The carriage set off in the direction of the railroad depot, but don Fernando then shouted to the coachman to take them to the Hotel Telégrafo, having decided that Dolores and Sebastián had had a long journey and that it would be best for them to rest and travel to *La Dulce Gardenia* the following day. He then sat back and lit a long, black cigar, puffing on it contentedly.

"And tell me, Dolores, you said your husband Billy has gone to Mexico?"

"Yes, papá, He went to Mexico for his law firm."

"How long will he be there?" Sofía asked.

"He said it will be at least six months, possibly a year."

"That's a long time," said Sofía, who was holding Sebastián. "Won't you miss him terribly?"

Sebastián began to cry now, and Dolores wondered whether it was don Fernando's cigar smoke or whether he simply wanted to be with his mother. She signaled for Sofia to pass him back, and Dolores took him, kissed him, and began gently rocking him until he stopped crying.

"Yes, it is a long time, Sofia, and I will miss him terribly, but I have Sebastián now, and I'm back home in Cuba with you and papá. So, I'm sure the time will pass quickly."

Don Fernando exhaled a bluish-white cloud of smoke which, quickly dispersed out the window.

"You will be with us then until he returns? Don Fernando asked.

"Of course she will, papá. Won't you, dear sister?"

Dolores turned to don Fernando.

"Well, I'm not yet sure, papá. I want to leave the door open to regain my teaching position at the Congressional School in Washington, and that might require my going back for the winter semester."

"The only way we'll permit you to go is if you leave little Sebastián here with us," Sofia said, smiling.

Don Fernando glanced at Sebastián again.

"What exactly will Billy be doing in Mexico?" he asked, exhaling another puff of cigar smoke that lingered in the coach this time.

"Well, as I understand it, papá, Henry Phipps & Partners, his law firm…"

"That's an excellent firm," interrupted don Fernando, "though I must say I disagree with their politics."

"…wants him to lay the groundwork for establishing a presence, an office, in Mexico. They foresee good opportunities for future business in Mexico, especially in the mining and railroad sectors."

Sofia listened intently now as Dolores spoke, noticing how articulate, how poised and confident she was. It was quite the contrast with that shy young girl whom Sofia had grown up with. Dolores had matured. She was a college-educated married woman now with a child and seemingly capable of holding her own with her half-brothers, Arturo and Felipe de Castilla, who were now the principal managers of don Fernando's sugar plantations and related businesses.

The carriage pulled up to the hotel, and they were greeted by two doormen, who called for the baggage clerks.

"Be here tomorrow at eight o'clock sharp," don Fernando said to the coachman. "And for now, go pick up Victorio Arquídez at the warehouse and take him to the docks."

Dolores cringed when she heard mention of the cruel Chief Overseer, who years before had beaten, raped and terrorized her ailing mother.

2

There was a knock on the door, which awakened Dolores.

"It's half past six, señoras."

Dolores got out of bed and immediately went over to check on Sebastián. He was awake but quiet, lying in the crib undoubtedly hungry. She picked him up, carried him over to the bed and lay down. Then she unbuttoned her nightshirt and offered her breast, which he eagerly began suckling.

Sofia was also awake but remained in bed, watching with great interest as Dolores breast fed Sebastián. She felt a tinge of envy at Dolores's status as a wife and mother. Sofia had devoted most of her youthful energy to the pursuit of radical politics, and in particular, independence from Spain, but she too had hoped to be a wife and a mother by this stage of her life. Her first relationship ended in the tragic assassination attempt on the life of the Captain General by her law student *novio*, Carlos Santiago. She'd had other relationships, one in particular with a law school professor that she'd felt certain would result in marriage, but it didn't. Now with only a few short years before her thirtieth birthday, she found herself in grave danger of living the life of a spinster. She tried to suppress these unpleasant thoughts before getting out of bed and dressing, all the while aware of her sister Dolores, who continued to perform her motherly functions.

Down in the garden breakfast salon, don Fernando sat smoking his first cigar of the day, awaiting his daughters.

"Good morning, papá," said Dolores. "What a delightful spot for breakfast." Don Fernando rose and kissed them both.

"Did you sleep well?" He looked at Sebastián, nestled in Dolores's arms, and tugged his little hands.

"And how is Sebastiánito doing this morning?" Dolores was pleased with her father's attention to his grandson, recalling his less than warm reception the day before.

A waiter appeared with a crib for Sebastián.

"Let me see now, who does he look like his mama or his papá?" Don Fernando asked leaning over the crib.

"I thought he looked like both," said Sofia. "His eyes and his hair are definitely Dolores's, but there's something about his facial features that remind me of his father. Don't you agree, Dolores?"

"Yes, Sofia, I think you're right. What do you think, papá?" Dolores asked, looking at her father more seriously and wondering whether he would say something about Sebastián's *acanelado* skin.

"I think it's too early to tell, but I do think he's inherited something from his grandmother on his mother's side." There it was, her papá's reference to Beatriz and his acknowledgment of Sebastián's *sangre de negro*. It could have been worse, Dolores thought, letting it pass without further ado.

"Have the fruit salad to start," said don Fernando. "It's delicious."

The waiter smiled and nodded in agreement.

"That's exactly what I had in mind, papá. We don't get this kind of fresh fruit in Washington."

"So, you've come back home to Cuba for its fruit, have you?".

"That's one more little reason, papá." She smiled, reached over, and affectionately touched his hand. "I've come back for you, papá, for you and for Sofia."

Dolores leaned back in the comfortable chair and looked up at the early morning sun peeking through the thick cluster of tall palms overhead. She heard the soothing sound of the fountain in the center of the garden and caught sight of the colorful birds that flew to its sparkling waters to drink and bathe. It was a truly delightful setting, one that nourished her senses. She felt completely relaxed, and happy, happy to be back home in her native Cuba.

"And how do you like Cuba, Sebastiánito?" She reached in the crib and patted him lovingly on his curly top head.

As his two daughters ate their breakfast, don Fernando brought up the subject of the Civil War in the United States.

"Is Washington still vulnerable to attack, Dolores? I read that after the South's defeat at Gettysburg they pulled back to Virginia and made camp again very close to the Capital."

"That's true papá, but there's a very large Union force protecting the Capital, and it's not expected that the rebels will attack it, especially not after their large losses at Gettysburg."

"Gettysburg must have been simply horrible," said Sofia. "I read that the casualties were more than fifty thousand. Can you imagine all those poor young men?"

"Do you have any feel for which side will win this war, Dolores? You live there and I'm sure you have a sense of it."

"I have to confess, papá, that I try not to think about the war. I'm just thankful that Billy doesn't have to fight. It's all so sad and depressing; all those poor young men being slaughtered, all the terrible injuries and amputations. It's too horrible for words. Billy says it's still pretty much a draw."

"Even after Gettysburg?"

"Yes, papá. He describes it as a 'stalemate.' I didn't know the meaning of the word, and he explained that a stalemate means that neither side is winning. But he did say that the South has better generals. Everyone talks about General Lee and General Johnston and this cavalry General Jeb Stewart. Apparently, President Lincoln has not been able to find anyone comparable."

The waiter came over and refilled their cups with thick black Cuban coffee.

"I remember when Billy's father, Patrick, said something similar to that, Do you remember, papá," Asked Sofia, "He said the South really didn't need to win the war, that they only needed not to lose it." Dolores looked surprised."

"Patrick McHugh is still coming to Cuba!"

"Yes, your father-in-law still comes to Cuba. He'd been absent for a while, but we found that he was more reliable than the *criollos*. He's expanded his operations and acquired a small steamship, and he's doing a thriving business running the Yankee blockade. But that's another matter altogether and strictly his business. What's important for us is that he's able to bring us African slaves for our sugar plantations. You know, I don't fathom why these high-handed abolitionists in the United States don't understand that we here in Cuba have no choice. We have no choice. It's not so much that we fancy the institution of slavery. We simply need their labor, and I'm sure that it's the same in the Confederate States of America. It's a matter of necessity and survival, and that's all there is to it."

Dolores could tell that her papá was passionate on the issue.

"You know, papá, Billy hasn't had any news from his family since the war began. There's no mail and no telegraph service to the South, and he's terribly worried about his mother."

"Well, you'll be glad to know that Patrick McHugh is due to arrive here any day now, so you'll be able to get some news for your husband."

Dolores was surprised and felt anxiety at the thought of meeting her father-in-law, whom she hadn't seen since she was a girl.

The waiter came with the check, and seconds later Victorio Arquídez entered the garden salon and walked to their table.

"Good morning, don Fernando and uuh, ladies." He removed his wide-brimmed hat. "Lalo is here with the carriage, sir, so whenever you're ready."

"I'll settle this check and we can depart." Don Fernando looked up at Victorio. "You remember my daughter, Dolores, don't you Victorio?"

"Yes, of course. How are you, señorita?" Victorio caught himself glancing at Sebastián.

"Uuh, pardon me. I mean señora." The close presence of the Chief Overseer sent a cold chill down Dolores's spine.

"She has come to Cuba with her new baby, my latest grandson," continued don Fernando.

Victorio's forced smile bordered on a sneer, undoubtedly the product of his many years of mistreating his fellow human beings, rendering him irrevocably incapable of graciousness.

The carriage ride to the railroad depot was uneventful, but when they arrived, there was a ruckus in progress between two rival Chiefs of the Lucumi and Kongo tribes. Victorio Arquídez immediately jumped down from the carriage and rushed over to the railroad cars, shouting threateningly in the African dialect that he'd acquired over the years. Sofia reached for the door handle.

"No, stay in the carriage," don Fernando said.

They watched as the Chief Overseer cracked his thick leather whip over the backs and bodies of the two offending slaves, drawing blood after several lashes. But the two slave Chiefs, strong warrior types, continued to battle. Victorio then drew his pistol and looked like he was about to fire. Don Fernando leaned out the window and shouted, "Shoot in the air, Victorio!" But it was too late. The Chief Overseer fired two shots, hitting one of them in the hip and the other in the leg. The two slaves fell to the ground, grimacing and moaning in pain. The gunshots frightened Sebastián who started crying.

"It's all right, Sebastiánito, mamá's here," Dolores said, slowly rocking him. She herself felt the onslaught of tears, which Sofia noticed.

"Try not to be alarmed, Dolores. You have been living in the United States for quite some time and may have become unaccustomed to our ways."

The incident left Dolores with a sense of foreboding.

Before they boarded the train, don Fernando reprimanded Victorio Arquídez for disobeying his order to fire his pistol in the air. The Chief Overseer defended his action by denying that he had heard the order. He also argued that both don Fernando and his son, Arturo, had instructed him and all the other overseers that inter-tribal fighting amongst their slaves would not be tolerated under any circumstances.

"We have to set an example. You yourself told me so, don Fernando."

3

By the time the carriage turned up the road to the Main House, Dolores's spirits were calmed. She was struck anew with the majesty of the stately royal palms and the fiery red bougainvillea that adorned them at the base. Colorful tropical birds flew about, alighting on the bushes, filling the air with their delightful calls. As the carriage proceeded up to the Main House, the field slaves tending the grounds rose from their toil, smiled and waved as the carriage passed. There was a welcoming party to greet them. Smiling broadly and waving happily were her sister, Constancia, her sisters-in-law, Soledad and Daisy, and a bevy of house slaves, including Carmen, Dolores's favorite, and Mario Luis, the dean of the house slaves, and last but not least the two cooks, Panchito and Panchita.

When Dolores stepped down from the carriage, Carmen rushed over and embraced her.

"Bienvenida doña Dolores! Ay, mira que bonito su bebe. Como se llama el nene?"

(Welcome Dolores! Ah, look how beautiful your baby. What's his name?)

"His name is Sebastián."

"Oh, that's a beautiful name!" Constancia said. "Maybe he'll be an athlete like Saint Sebastián."

Soledad and Daisy rushed over to view the new addition to the de Castilla family. All the talk and excitement awakened Sebastián, and Dolores noticed he was soaking wet with perspiration.

"Oh, *pobresito!* (Oh, the poor thing) He's not accustomed to the tropical climate," said Sofia.

Don Fernando suggested that Dolores retire to her living quarters to attend to Sebastián and to rest after their long journey.

"Come with me, doña Dolores. We are so pleased to have you back home again," said Mario Luis as he picked up Dolores's luggage and escorted her inside. The sweet scent of gardenias reminded her once again that she was home. She followed Mario Luis up the spiral staircase. Halfway up, she stopped beneath the magnificent crystal chandelier, where the family's portraits were hung on the wall. She stared at the young girl depicted there, trying hard to remember her as she was back then, but the image and the memories that emerged were muddled and indistinct. She mused, *so much has changed.*

"Whenever I walk past here, señora, I think of you," said Mario Luis. "But from now on I shall think of you and your beautiful little boy. Perhaps in time his portrait will be hanging there with yours."

"You hear that, Sebastián? Mario Luis says that one day your portrait will be hanging there too."

Mario Luis led them up to the living quarters.

The dinner party that evening was a gala affair. The dining salon was beautifully decorated, and Panchito and Panchita prepared a feast fit for a king. Arturo and Felipe were in attendance as was Dolores's brother-in-law, Ricardo. Before dinner was served they gathered together, sharing some conversation and some fine Cuban rum.

"Doloresita, how nice it is to see you!" said Arturo, as he kissed her on the cheek.

"Where is my new nephew, whom I've heard so much about?" He asked.

"He's upstairs asleep, Arturo." Carmen is taking good care of him. There will be time tomorrow for you to see him. How are you and your family doing?"

"Daisy is here and she's fine, as are the children, but tell me, how is Billy? I understand he has gone to Mexico for his law firm…"

Arturo soon launched into a long description of how sugarcane production had plummeted because of a shortage of African slaves.

"Fortunately, however, we are expecting *The Wandering Maiden* any day now. Your father-in-law will be delivering a cargo of Kongo slaves, which we desperately need. Oh, but before I forget, Dolores, we need you to sign some documents before the *Notario*. We will arrange it in the next few days, that is if you are going to be available."

"Yes, of course, Arturo."

Felipe now approached, reached for Dolores's hand and kissed her on the cheek.

"How are you, dear sister? It's so nice to see you after all this time…"

They all took their seats at the dinner table, and the waiters entered carrying bottles of champagne, after which don Fernando rose and turned to Dolores.

"Welcome home, Dolores. To your health and happiness, and to Sebastián's as the newest member of the de Castilla family!" They all smiled and drank the toast. Don Fernando remained standing.

"And to the memory of my loving wife, doña Teresa, the mother of my children! May we always remember and honor her."

Dolores caught the words "the mother of my children," realizing that the words of his toast did not include her mother, Beatriz. She bowed her head slightly and said a little prayer for her.

A sumptuous dinner of red snapper, lechón, and shrimp was served along with choice wines and more French champagne. When the cooks brought in the pastry dessert, the conversation turned to Billy McHugh.

"I hope you will bring him with you next time, Dolores," said

Constancia. "I wasn't able to attend your wedding, so unlike Sofia and papá here, I'm not sure I would recognize him after all these years. How long has it been now? What year was it, 1852, Is that possible? I have lost track of time since it passes so rapidly. Do you have any photographs of Billy, Dolores?"

"As a matter of fact I do, Constancia. Before Billy departed for Mexico, we went down to the photographer's studio, the same one used by President Lincoln, and had a family portrait taken. I brought it with me. I promise I'll show it to you tomorrow."

"How long will Billy be in Mexico?" asked Soledad, who had been silent until then.

"It's expected to be at least a six-month assignment, but it could be as long as a year."

"How fortunate! Felipe said, interrupting the women. "He will get to see that stooge Archduke Maximiliano, crowned as the Emperor of Mexico. Napoleon ought to be hanged for his treachery."

Arturo had a different point of view.

"How do you know what's right for the Mexican people, Felipe? For all we know a benevolent monarch might be beneficial for them."

"I should have known that you would be supporting a Mexican Monarchy, just as you continue to support the tyrannical monarchy that Spain forces Cubans to live under."

Dolores looked at her father, expecting him to silence his two argumentative sons as he had always done in the past. Don Fernando, however, just sat there, puffing on his cigar. Dolores was struck with how frail and old-looking he had become. Finally, the peacemaker role fell to Sofia.

"Arturo and Felipe, please, that's enough. Let's just try to enjoy each other's company, shall we?"

Felipe and Arturo glared at each other but remained silent,

at least for the time being, bringing about a slight pause in the conversation. Constancia ended the silence.

"How is your life in Washington, Dolores? Were you safe in spite of that terrible war?"

"Yes, of course, Constancia. The city itself was never in serious danger of attack."

"She will be a lot safer now with us," said don Fernando, "and I would venture to say a lot happier as well."

"I'm happy in both places, papá," Dolores said. "I enjoy teaching and now that I have Sebastián, I can carry my happiness with me. Of course, I do miss Billy. I miss him terribly, but I understand that he must pursue his career. It's very important to him."

"You're blessed to have such a healthy and handsome baby boy," Sofia said. "He's gotten the best of both worlds from you and Billy. I could see it yesterday the moment I set eyes upon him. He has the Cuban and the American people in him, and I predict that he is going to grow up to be a very special person."

"Of that I have no doubt," said don Fernando, raising his glass. "To Sebastián!"

"To Sebastián!" they all repeated in unison.

4

Dolores awoke early. She quickly dressed, picked up Sebastián and quietly made her way down the staircase, through the kitchen and out the back door to the garden path. The morning air was heavy and wet, but the temperature had not yet risen. She inhaled the sweet scent of gardenias along the path and heard the familiar call of the *tregón* in the tall palms overhead. The sun was still a giant orange ball rising in the east, casting intricate shadows on the beautiful grounds of *La Dulce Gardenia*.

She reached the garden patio, and two shapely young female slaves immediately emerged from the hut.

"Buenos días, señora. Please you?" Their Spanish was primitive, and Dolores guessed that they had gotten this choice assignment in exchange for satisfaction of an overseer's carnal desires.

"Good morning. What do they call you?" They smiled shyly, not fully understanding. Dolores asked them for orange juice, papaya, bread, and a pot of coffee, which they did understand. When they brought the food, Dolores asked if they had a basket or other container that she could put Sebastián in while she ate. They looked puzzled and didn't understand, but Dolores eventually got through to them and they brought out a sturdy little fruit basket. Dolores put him in the basket, placed him on the chair next to her and ate her breakfast.

She had promised herself that one of the first things she would do when returning home was to visit her mother's gravesite. The slave graveyard was behind the slave quarters, both of which were isolated from the rest of the plantation grounds. Carmencita told her that there was a little-known path behind the garden patio that led to the slave quarters. There she would find the "Guardian of the Graves," who would have to unlock the iron gate entrance to the graveyard. Carmen strongly advised Dolores not to bring Sebastián to the slave quarters. It was the season of the cholera in Cuba, and the slave quarters were thought to harbor a miasma associated with the disease. Dolores decided that she had to bring him. He was Beatriz' only grandchild, and she would have wanted him to come. Dolores finished her breakfast, bid the two slave women good day, and set out for the slave quarters, carrying Sebastián in the fruit basket.

The slave quarters were a large, dilapidated and unpainted wooden structure, suffering greatly from dry rot and years of termite infestation. When she opened the door, she was struck by the stench. She'd been to the slave quarters hundreds of times to visit her mother, but never fully appreciated how horrid were the conditions under which these African slaves were forced to live. She stood at the entrance, allowing her eyes to adjust to the darkness. She stepped inside, noticing how strangely quiet it was until she realized the slaves were out in the cane fields and had been since before sunrise. Sebastián began whimpering and stretching his little body.

"There now, Sebastiánito." She kissed him and rocked him gently. Then she called out

"Hello, anybody here?"

"*Doloresita? Ave Maria Purisima! Eres tú!*" (Doloresita, it's you, Blessed be the Purest Virgin Mother) Dolores scanned the dark recesses of the slave quarters until the forgotten image and the voice coalesced and she knew who it was.

"Angelina! Angelina!" she cried. The frail old slave woman struggled to rise from her bed of rags, but got only half-way up before toppling back down.

"Wait, Angelina! I'll come over to you."

Angelina had been every slave child's surrogate grandmother. She herself had given birth to more than fifteen children, fathered by countless Lucumi and Kongo slaves. Not surprisingly, she was highly prized at *La Dulce Gardenia* because of her prolific fertility. Angelina and Beatriz had been inseparable, particularly after Angelina had come to Beatriz's aid, freeing her from the grip of Victorio Arquidez. The Chief Overseer dealt out punishment so severe that she almost died. Beatriz and Angelina were also devotees and faithful practitioners of santería, the ancient African religion of the Yoruba peoples.

"Don't try to get up, Angelina."

"I can still walk, Doloresita," Angelina said.

Once again, however, she fell back down when she attempted

to rise. Dolores walked over to her bedside and reached for her hand.

"What is that you have in the basket, Doloresita? Ay, it's a baby! A baby boy! Come closer! My eyes are still good. Let me see him!"

She leaned up now as best she could and looked at Sebastián.

"*Ay, que hermoso, acanelado nene!* (Well, what a beautiful cinnamon-colored baby). He has Beatriz's blood! Lucumi blood! I can see it in his face, Doloresita. Your mother Beatriz would be very proud. What is his name?"

"His name is Sebastián"

Sebastián started crying now, and Dolores knew she had to take him outside for some fresh air.

"I want to visit my mother's grave, Angelina. Carmen told me that I must find the Guardian of the Graves."

"Oh, but you must visit with the *Santero* before you go to the grave, Doloresita. You do not want to offend *O*batala, your mother's sacred *Orisha*." But Dolores was undeterred and promised that she would do so before her next visit to the gravesite.

"You must not forget, Doloresita. But for now you will find the Guardian of the Graves in back. His name is Rodrigo, and he is the only one who can allow entrance to the graveyard."

Dolores bid good-bye to Angelina, promising to return.

The Guardian of the Graves was a thin, wiry and coal-black man with sunken cheeks and deep-set eyes. When Dolores told him she wanted to enter the graveyard, he looked at her suspiciously, asking what her purpose was. Clearly, he didn't recognize her, wondering perhaps why a white woman would want to visit the slave graveyard. Dolores then thought it best to identify herself.

"I'm the daughter of señor don Fernando de Castilla." Rodrigo's entire face became tense and he humbly bowed his head.

"I beg you forgive me, señora de Castilla. This is the first time that I have the honor of seeing you." She noticed his obvious discomfort and sought to put him at ease.

"I understand, Rodrigo. It's the first time I've seen you as well. I'm here to visit the grave of my mother, Beatriz. Carmen told me I would find it at the foot of a giant mango tree."

Rodrigo nodded his head, recalling the history of don Fernando de Castilla's affair with the Lucumi slave woman, Beatriz; the affair that spawned the birth of Felicidad, the light-skinned baby girl—now the woman standing there before him.

Rodrigo led Dolores to the massive iron gate, which he then unlocked. When he swung it open, it groaned ominously as though it did not wish to be opened.

"Follow me, please, señora. I will help you find your mother's grave."

"Thank you, Rodrigo, but I should like to find it myself."

"As you wish, señora, but please be careful, there are..." He never finished the sentence.

When Rodrigo put the keys back in his pocket, she could see that his hand was shaking, fearing perhaps some retribution from don Fernando or Victorio Arquídez for questioning her right to enter the graveyard. Slaves were severely punished for far less serious infractions.

The graveyard was eerily quiet and still. The melodic calls of tropical songbirds and the rhythmic drone of the cicadas, ubiquitous throughout the grounds of La Dulce Gardenia, were nowhere to be heard. The only sound to be heard were her own footfalls. It was as though nature knew that here was a sacred and venerated place, a place deserving of absolute silence, tranquility and peace. For here at last was a resting place, a sanctuary for those ill-fated Africans who had been kidnapped and taken to a strange and hostile land to toil, suffer and die after a short and meaningless life as the white man's slave.

Though it was early morning, it was stiflingly hot and humid, and the stagnant air hung over the graveyard like a massive shroud. Dolores noticed that Sebastián's little white cotton suit was soaked with perspiration. And she too was perspiring profusely. She spotted the giant mango tree and saw a flat gravestone at the base of the trunk. She put the basket down, bent down and brushed away the dirt and leaves from the stone. She read the simple epitaph out loud: "Beatriz a Lucumi slave." That was all it took to release the river of tears that had been dammed up in her heart for years. She looked at her darling little boy asleep in the basket and cried even harder, wanting to tell him about his grandmother. How sad it was that Beatriz would never see him or hold him in her arms! She leaned back on the trunk of the mango tree, closed her eyes and tried to conjure up her mother's spirit.

"I am here, mamá, and I've brought you a gift. It's your grandson, Sebastián. Look how adorable, mamá!" All of a sudden, Thump.

A large ripe mango fell to the ground at the outer edge of the tree's overhanging branches.

"I'll get it for you, mamá." She got up and went over to retrieve it. Her back turned, she did not see the large boa constrictor that had slowly slithered down from the upper branches of the tree. It hovered there just above the basket, poised to strike, its rapid tongue movements having confirmed the presence of prey. Dolores picked up the mango and then turned.

"Sebastián!" She screamed, as she tried to run to him. But her legs would not respond, and she stood there paralyzed with fear. By the Grace of God, the Guardian of the Graves sprang from behind the clump of bushes, and with one mighty swing of his razor-sharp machete, cut the serpent in two. Crying hysterically, Dolores ran over and picked up Sebastián, smothering him with hugs and kisses, awakening him from his peaceful and innocent sleep. Seconds later she saw the snake's deadly thick coils unwind from the tree branch and drop into the basket.

Rodrigo's disobedience had saved Sebastián's life, for had he obeyed her command not to accompany her, the large boa would have dropped down upon Sebastián and sunk its razor-sharp teeth into his little body, immobilizing him before winding its powerful coils around him and squeezing him to death.

5

It was early afternoon, and Dolores and Carmen were bathing Sebastián.

"You see these little red spots?" asked Dolores.

"Yes, I see them," said Carmen. "It's a heat rash and nothing serious, but you should probably keep him inside for the next week and certainly don't take him out in the sun. How lucky you are, Doloresita, that his only ailment is a heat rash. Every time I think of that snake in the mango tree I shudder. Thank God for Rodrigo! He certainly is the Guardian of the Graves and now the guardian of those who visit the graves as well."

Dolores leaned over and kissed Sebastián as he playfully swung his little arms down and splashed water out of the bassinette. Just then Sofia walked into the room.

"Patrick McHugh has arrived. He's resting now, but he will be joining us for dinner. And how is my darling little nephew?"

She leaned over and nuzzled him.

"He will be all nice and clean when he meets his grandfather. Dolores, there's something I'd like to discuss with you. Why don't you let Carmen finish bathing him, and we can walk back to the garden patio where it's cooler?"

They had not yet sat down when the two young Lucumi slave

girls rushed over to serve them. They asked for a pot of coffee and some pastries.

"They are certainly enthusiastic, aren't they?" Dolores said. "They were new to me. I came here that terrible day I visited the slave graveyard."

"Victorio Arquídez gave them the positions last year, putting them ahead of two older women, who had been waiting for those jobs for years. He of course exacts his price."

"I remember what his price was, Sofia. He made this plantation a living hell for my poor mother."

The slave women brought the coffee and pastries, and Sofia filled their cups. Sofia took on a more serious expression.

"There is something in papá's last will and testament that I must tell you about, Dolores."

Sofia was now a duly licensed lawyer, an extraordinary achievement for a Cuban woman in a man's profession. She had graduated from the Faculty of Law at the University of Havana at the top of her class. But she had chosen not to practice law, at least not at first, electing to teach at the law school. It was a way for her to stay in close contact with her radical compatriots, who were fighting for Cuban independence from Spain. One of the courses Sofia taught was the Civil Code, sections of which govern the law of wills, estates and inheritances.

"Mamá and papá had a joint will," explained Sofia. "They executed the will before papá had recognized you as his rightful daughter, and as a result there are no bequests to you under its terms. Now, I am ashamed to tell you this, my dear sister"—she reached out for Dolores's hand—"but our brothers are insisting that the terms of the joint will be implemented as written, which would deny you any part of papá's estate."

Dolores was about to say something, but before she could Sofia continued.

"There is a section of the Spanish Civil Code that may be applicable to your situation. It may provide you with a proportionate share of the estate, irrespective of the fact that the will itself makes no provision for you."

"I don't understand, Sofia. If the will is so out of date, why doesn't papá just make another will? Wouldn't that take care of this problem?"

"Yes, it certainly would, and Constancia and I have suggested that. But Arturo and Felipe will not agree. Furthermore, they want you to sign an *instrumento público* before the local *Notario* containing a *finiquito* (waiver) by which you would relinquish your rights under the Civil Code."

"So, that's the document that Arturo mentioned the other night at dinner that he wanted me to sign?"

"Yes, Dolores, I am sure that is the one." Dolores looked surprised and confused.

"Constancia and I have always believed that no distinction should be made between us. The three of us are sisters, and Arturo and Felipe are our brothers. We should all be treated the same."

"Does papá wish to exclude me from his estate, Sofia?"

"No, I am sure he wants to include you, but as his health has deteriorated, he's fallen completely under the influence of Arturo and Felipe, especially Arturo. They told him not to create another will, arguing that mamá would not have wanted him to. Your best course of action, and my legal advice to you, is do not sign any document that Arturo and Felipe present to you. Their only recourse then would be to hope that the courts will uphold the validity of the joint will as written."

"Isn't all this legal talk really premature, Sofia? I mean it isn't as though papá is on his death bed, or at least I hope he isn't."

"You are probably not aware of it, Dolores, but papá is suffering from more than just rheumatism. He has a serious heart condition, and his doctors have strongly advised him to avoid strenuous physical activity. Yet in spite of that, everyone knows that he's sleeping with his young secretary. That in itself could certainly cause his death, yet no one has the courage to tell him to stop it, not even his doctors."

Dolores was troubled by everything Sofia had said, especially the bad news about her father. But as for her inheritance, she had never thought much about it. It was not as though she was impecunious; she had a career, and a husband. But in spite of that she also wanted what was rightly hers and was hurt to learn that her two half-brothers were conspiring to deprive her of it.

"I also advise you, Dolores, to confer with Billy on this matter. He's a lawyer, and from what I've heard an excellent one. He may be able to add something to my analysis, for example the fact that you're now a United States citizen. That could have a bearing on this.

By the way, Dolores, how is Billy, and how is he adjusting to his fatherhood? You haven't spoken much of him."

Dolores was not surprised by Sofia's question. Indeed, she had been expecting it, even dreading it, wondering why it had not come up earlier.

"Billy, Billy is…" Tears welled up in her eyes. Sofia reached for her hand. "Billy is…" She struggled to control her emotions, but she could not get it out. Finally, "Billy is mortified that little Sebastián is, well, you must have noticed though you didn't say anything."

"Now, now, Dolores. Sebastián is a sweet and beautiful child!"

"He has *sangre de negro*, Sofia, from my mother and maybe from me. Papá noticed it, and even Angelina noticed it in the darkness of the slave quarters. Billy was shocked, Sofia, and he hasn't gotten over it. He's afraid his law firm will learn of it, afraid it will hurt his career. You noticed, Sofia, didn't you? You noticed it immediately. Tell me the truth!"

"He's a healthy and happy baby boy, and that's the only thing that really matters," said Sofia.

"Billy told me to keep him out of sight and not to take him outside!"

Dolores cried hard now and began to tremble, suddenly knocking a cup off the table that shattered on the ground. Dolores leaned over, laid her head on Sofia's breast and cried her eyes out.

"You don't know Billy, Sofia. You only know the sweet and kind Billy, the Billy of our adolescence."

"Now, now Dolores. Billy will come to love and accept Sebastián, anyone would."

"When Billy first saw him minutes after his birth, he glared at me with hate in his eyes. I know what he thought. He thought that I had been unfaithful and betrayed him with a mulatto coachman. He fell into a fit of rage and rushed out of the room. I could hear him out in the hallway, screaming at the doctor, asking why the baby had such dark skin. It's much worse in the United States, Sofia. It's not just *sangre de negro* or *acanelado*. Sebastián is a *nigger* in the United States, a nigger, and the color of his skin is a badge of inferiority that he will be forced to wear for the rest of his life. I would stay in Cuba with him, Sofía, but I cannot leave Billy. I love him, Sofia. I love him dearly! Oh, dear God. What am I going to do?"

Dolores sobbed and trembled, and though Sofia tried her best, she was unable to console and comfort her.

6

Patrick McHugh looked in the mirror, noticing a trace of blood where he had cut his face shaving. There was a knock on the door.

"Come in, the door's open," He turned and saw Mario Luis standing there.

"I have your trousers, señor McHugh."

"Put them over there on the chair."

"Si, señor. Is there anything else I can get for you?"

"No, that will be all. Thank you."

"I have something for that cut that will stop the bleeding, señor."

Patrick turned and said rather sternly:

"I said that will be all."

"As you wish, señor."

The old slave turned and walked toward the door, casting one last glance at the irritable North American.

Patrick McHugh had been supplying African slaves for don Fernando and *La Dulce Gardenia* for more than a decade. It was a mutually beneficial and profitable business for both sides. And in spite of the worldwide efforts to end the slave trade, he had always managed to elude capture and seizure of his vessel and its cargoes. Even though Spain, *la madre patria,* had outlawed the slave trade, it was well known that the Spanish looked the other way. *The Wandering Maiden* and a few other daring and fearless slavers, continued to supply the labor that fueled the agricultural economy of Cuba.

Patrick was now in his fifties and had accumulated a small fortune. While he had longed to retire from a life at sea and return to Bonny in Charleston, he chose to undertake a few more voyages that could provide the additional resources with which to buy that plantation up country, the one he had promised Bonny; the one he had been thinking of for all those many years.

But like Captain Sturgis, who had sold him *The Wandering Maiden*, Patrick had by now had enough of Africa. He had had more than enough of the long and difficult voyages, the torrid temperatures, the deadly diseases and the slave trade itself. He would leave all that behind him now, never again to set foot on the Dark Continent. He had a better and easier way to enrich himself, at least so he thought.

A year after the War broke out, Patrick purchased a small steamer, *The City of Mobile*. It needed repairs and was mortgaged to the hilt, but during his time ashore he restored it and made it sea worthy. He knew that a man could get rich, and very quickly, if he had the intestinal fortitude, the wherewithal and a little luck to elude the Union naval patrols and successfully run the Yankee Blockade. Patrick knew that steam power was here to stay, and the heyday of the swift sailing Baltimore Clippers was rapidly disappearing. He was in Cuba now, having delivered his final cargo of Kongo slaves. And because he did not want to leave don Fernando in the lurch, he had brought with him his colleague and mate, Daniel Morrison. Patrick sold *The Wandering Maiden* to Morrison, who was willing and able to continue supplying *La Dulce Gardenia* with African slaves.

There was another knock on the door.

"Come in!" It was Mario Luis again.

"Dinner is served, señor McHugh."

"Thank you, uh. Thank you."

I'll be damned if I can ever remember the names of these niggers, especially not in Spanish. They make such a fuss over this one. God knows why! He strikes me as an old fool nigger who belongs in the slave quarters.

As he started down the elegant staircase, Patrick paused for a second under the crystal chandelier and glanced at the portraits on the wall.

That must be her. Yes, looks almost white.

"Oh, Mister McHugh! How nice to see you again!" It was Constancia, the oldest of the three sisters. "Do you know which one is Dolores's? I know you haven't seen her since you came to Cuba years ago. And you've never seen your grandson, Sebastián, have you? He's such a delightful and darling little boy."

Patrick looked at her, avoiding a direct response to her remarks.

"Oh, hello there. It's Constancia, if I remember correctly."

"Yes, Constancia, I'm Sofia's older sister. Well, really not that much older." She chuckled. "And this is my husband, Ricardo."

Patrick turned and saw a middle-aged, distinctly Latin-looking man with a thin mustache. He reached for Patrick's hand and shook it heartily.

"How are you, Mister McHugh? It's been a while since we've seen you in Cuba."

"Yes, it has, Ricardo, the War and all, but please call me Patrick. 'Mister McHugh' makes me sound old."

"Well, shall we go down to dinner?" said Constancia. "I'm sure Mister McHugh, I mean Patrick, wants to see his daughter-in-law in the flesh and of course meet his grandson."

The truth of the matter was that Patrick had no desire to see them. He hadn't forgiven his son Billy, and still considered him a turncoat and a traitor, who had abandoned his family, his homeland and his country. Patrick considered Billy to be thief, a thief who had stolen his slave, Julius and taken him north in violation of the law; showing the way for Becky, who ran away just weeks later. No, he never wanted to see his son Billy again, not ever. So, why then would he want to see his nigger wife and baby?

When Patrick entered the dining room with Constancia and Ricardo, Dolores recognized him immediately. She was nervous but stood up and smiled warmly, assuming he would walk over and greet her. But he didn't, and there followed an awkward moment. Sofia saw Dolores's predicament and walked over to Patrick. Tugging him gently, she led him over to Dolores.

"Allow me, Mister McHugh, to introduce you to your daughter-in-law, Dolores McHugh and your darling little grandson, Sebastián McHugh. He just now woke up, and you can see what a handsome child he is. I know that Dolores was an adolescent when you last saw her, but did you recognize her just now when you entered the room?"

Patrick did his best to force a weak smile, but did not respond.

"It's so nice to see you, Mister McHugh, after all these years," said Dolores, having somehow found the courage to be the first to speak. She then moved ever so slightly toward him, but Patrick ignored her, and Dolores felt the cold rush of embarrassment and hurt.

At that moment, Panchita entered the room with a tray of champagne and rum drinks. Patrick reached for a glass of Cuban rum and drank it down. He noticed then the astonished expressions on the faces of all the family members, realizing then that he had better acknowledge his daughter-in-law and avoid the ugly scene that was unfolding in front of don Fernando and the entire de Castilla family. So, he took a few steps toward her and reached out for Dolores's hand, and everyone breathed a sign of relief.

"Yes, I remember her, Sofia, he said. "I have a good memory, and eleven years is not that long when you get to be my age."

Don Fernando was well aware of Patrick's estrangement from his son, Billy. Patrick had made a trip to Cuba over the previous two years, and the subject, though awkward, had come up. Given the choice, don Fernando would not have chosen to bring Patrick and Dolores together at *La Dulce Gardenia* and subject them to this awkward meeting. The fact that they were here at the same time was a mere coincidence.

Sofia too had learned of Patrick and Billy's breach of relations, but had been reluctant to talk about it with Dolores. She thought that once Patrick saw his cute little grandson, any resentment which he might have had for Dolores as Billy's wife, would likely melt away or at least be softened. As it turned out, Sofia was right.

It happened after the dessert was served. The men were sipping their brandy and puffing on their cigars, and the conversation had gotten serious, centering on the War Between the States. During the course of the conversation, Patrick sought to spit out a piece of tobacco that was caught in his teeth. Part of it came out with a sputtering sound. Sebastián was awake, and it made him giggle. Patrick hadn't expelled all of it and followed with two more spitting sputters. That brought forth more and louder giggles from little Sebastián, who was by then smiling up at his grandfather. By now, everyone in the room was laughing hard, urging Patrick to continue doing it.

"Your grandfather makes funny noises, doesn't he?" said don Fernando, laughing hard between puffs of his cigar.

"You're so lucky, Dolores, to have such a happy baby," said Constancia. "He's such a joy to us all."

For the first time that evening, Patrick looked directly at Dolores and smiled. Then he leaned over the crib, reached in and tugged on Sebastián's little hands, receiving in return a cute little toothless baby smile. Dolores was so relieved she could have hugged and kissed Patrick right then and there. At that point, Carmen entered the room to take Sebastián back upstairs. She picked up the crib and began walking out, whereupon a chorus of sputters broke out from all the men. To the delight of everyone, Sebastián giggled louder and louder.

CHAPTER XIV

Billy in Mexico

When Billy arrived in Mexico City, he contacted Roberto Montero, a local attorney whom Macías Romero had recommended. Montero was the senior partner in a highly regarded law firm that specialized in Mining and Business law. He had four partners, several associates and a full staff of clerks, secretaries and messengers. Montero was not aware of Billy's true mission in Mexico, and for reasons of security was not to be made aware. A secretary in Montero's firm found Billy a furnished flat in a prime area not far from Chapultepec Castle. It was large and quite comfortable, and within two days the housekeeper from the previous tenant approached Billy and offered her services. Her name was Margarita, and Billy hired her.

"Margarita, compró el periódico?" ("Margarita, did you buy the newspaper?").

"*Sí, señor. Aquí lo tengo.* (Yes, sir, I have it right here). She handed him the paper and he read the headline.

**People Approve Maximilian
As Emperor of Mexico**

The Mexican people voted nearly unanimously to approve Archduke Ferdinand Maximilian as Emperor

> *of Mexico. The vote in favor was an overwhelming 99%...*

Billy knew that the plebiscite was a fraud. The French invaded Mexico in 1861 and overthrew the Benito Juárez regime. France's Napoleon III proclaimed Archduke Ferdinand Maximilian the Emperor of Mexico, but Maximilian was reluctant to assume the position until he was assured that the Mexican people truly wanted him. The French authorities and their conservative Mexican collaborators staged a plebiscite and fraudulently manipulated the vote count. Maximilian and his lovely young wife, Carlota, were informed of the results and agreed then to come to Mexico and assume their duties as Emperor and Empress of Mexico.

Billy's flat was within walking distance of the magnificent *Zócalo*, a plaza so enormous that it made all those he'd seen before in Havana, Charleston, and Washington seem miniscule by comparison. He spent the next few months familiarizing himself with the sites, the people and the culture of Mexico City.

As a student of languages, Billy came to notice the distinctly different accents and vocabularies of Mexican and Cuban speakers of Spanish. It was, in fact, how he came to meet Henri Pavillons, an important member of the Montero firm, who paved the way to an invaluable contact. One Friday afternoon in mid-December Pavillons overheard Billy discussing some linguistic points. He went over, joined the conversation and ended up inviting him to lunch.

"...But I understood that you were from South Carolina, William. That's a Confederate State, the original one in fact, wasn't it? So, how did you happen to wind up in Washington?"

Billy had come to use his proper name, William, when meeting people of Pavillons' status, believing it sounded more mature and gained him a greater measure of respect.

"That's correct, Henri. I was born and raised in Charleston and read law under James Petigru, the South Carolinian statesman; but about the time the War broke out, I left to accept a position with Henry Phipps & Partners in Washington."

"I see," said Pavillons, nodding his head and then signaling to the waiter. "Oh, Francois, bring us a bottle of that excellent white burgundy."

"Right away, monsieur Pavillons."

"But as for the War, please understand, Henri, I don't take sides."

That was of course disingenuous on Billy's part.

"But isn't your family still in Charleston? How do you…"

Billy didn't like the direction the conversation was taking, and he sought to redirect it. As luck would have it, the waiter arrived with the wine, providing a diversion. Billy then reluctantly but cautiously returned to Pavillons' questions.

"You were asking about my move to Washington, Henri. I must say that it wasn't easy to leave my family and James Petigru, especially during a time of war. But my fiancé got a position in Washington teaching, and of course I wanted to be with her."

"And what exactly brought you to Mexico, William?"

"Well, Henri, I've been interested in all things Spanish American for many years now. I speak Spanish, I've studied the history, and I like the culture and the people. Henry Phipps & Partners wants to expand their international practice, and so they sent me down here to get things started."

"Does your firm's interests include Central America?"

"Yes, indeed, and I have some experience in Central America. Back in 1857 I rode the new Panama Railroad across the Isthmus, then sailed to Cuba aboard the steamer *Central America*."

"That side-wheeler steamer that went down with all the gold?"

"That's the one. By coincidence my fiancé was also a

passenger. We were amongst the fortunate who survived. There were four-hundred-and twenty-five unfortunate souls who went down with her." Just then the waiter arrived with the food.

"It looks like you made a good choice, William. That pheasant looks delicious."

"Indeed it does," Billy said as he started cutting it.

"Our firm sees Panama as a bright spot for future legal work," Henri said. "It so happens that my family is friends with Ferdinand de Lesseps, the French industrialist, who's currently working on that canal in Suez, Egypt."

It was obvious where Pavillons was going with that comment.

"I'm told that the work in Egypt won't be finished for several years, but de Lesseps has already expressed interest in a canal across the Isthmus of Panama. Part of our job would be to nego-tiate a concession agreement with the Government of Colombia."

"Very interesting, Henri, very interesting indeed. Do you hap-pen to know what the financing would be?"

"No, but I'm sure they will have to issue stock. It's much too early to address that question, but perhaps your firm could raise some interest and some capital if and when the project becomes feasible?"

"I'm sure we could," said Billy. "There's bound to be great interest in the United States. There certainly was for the Panama Railroad, that saves having to go all the way around Cape Horn. I did just that back in 1855 on my way to the California gold fields."

"So, you've also dug for gold, have you? I must say, William, that for a young man you've certainly had more than your share of experiences and adventure. But tell me, did you find any gold?"

"Not enough to make it worth while," Billy said, smiling. "But it sure was an interesting time."

"I suppose that if you had had any luck, you wouldn't be here right now in Mexico, would you?"

Henri smiled and drained the wine in his glass, whereupon the waiter came over and replenished it.

The luncheon turned out to be a two-hour affair, and just about the time that the waiter presented the check, there came a propitious opportunity.

"William, we're having a gala Christmas Celebration next Tuesday at the French Legation. Would you be interested in attending?" Billy's face lit up.

"I would be delighted, Henri."

"Good, I think you'll enjoy it. The Welcoming Committee for the Emperor and Empress are sponsoring the event. You may even get to meet the head of the Regency Government and his entourage. The Committee Members are of course the most wealthy and prominent people in Mexico City and the country at large. And, there will be a bevy of lovely French and Spanish ladies." Pavillons looked at Billy with an expression that bordered on a grin. "Are you a single man, William?"

"No, Henri, not any more. I've been married two years."

"Oh, that's right. You mentioned earlier that your fiancé had gotten a position in Washington and that's why you moved there."

"Yes, that's right. We were married in Washington. Dolores is Cuban, and we've known each other since we were adolescents."

"A Cuban girl. How interesting! There are quite a few Cubans here in Mexico City."

By the time Billy returned to his flat, it was already late afternoon. Margarita had left for the day, but she had been to the post office, because there on his desk was a letter from Dolores. When he opened it, he found a letter from his mother enclosed. He was struck with emotion, for he had not seen nor heard from her since that day back in April of 1861, when he'd rushed out of the house with Julius and fled in the carriage, bombarded by a torrent of threats and curses from his father Patrick.

20 November 1863

My Dear son, Billy,

Your father returned from Cuba last month and I know now that you are in Mexico. I have Dolores to thank for finding a way to reach you with my letters. Though Dolores and I have never met, I know now that she's a sweet and caring woman. And I understand why you love her so much. I'm so sorry for having doubted your good judgment and your deep love for her, Billy. It was unkind of me, and I beg your forgiveness.

I cried for joy when I learned that you are the father of a baby boy named Sebastián, and I'm so happy for the two of you. Dolores said he's a healthy child with a sunny disposition, and that he looks like the two of you. I only wish I could see him and hold him in my arms. As I write this letter, there are tears in my eyes, for it is so sad that we have not been able to see each other or even write in more than two years, all because of this dreadful war. I pray to God that it will soon end. I don't care whether the South is victorious, just so it ends.

Dolores said you were worried about me because Patrick is frequently away on long trips, our former slaves are gone, and I'm all alone. It is true that I'm often alone, but I am well, thank God. And I have the Church and its kind parishioners, and they have been a blessing to me. There are of course terrible shortages and hardships here in Charleston. Food is becoming more and more scarce. But we are still better off than most because your father is able to earn Yankee dollars and gold.

Billy, I hope and pray that you and your father will put aside your hard feelings and reconcile with each other. He did after all give me the letter from Dolores. In spite of all his faults, your father is a good man. He's been a good husband and a good provider, and I think it's safe to say that he was a good father to you until this awful war tore us all apart. I hope and pray that you will consider that and reconcile with him. We will all be better off for it.

Please write, Billy, and may God bless and keep you.

Your loving Mother

2

A slow but steady rain fell as Billy mounted the steps of the stately French Legation, awaiting the arrival of Henri Pavillons. It was the official residence of the Marquis de Montholon, Napoleon's Minister to Mexico. French soldiers stood guard at the portal checking the invitations as a continuous flow of Mexico's elite made their entrance.

"Good evening, William. I trust you haven't been waiting too long."

"No, your timing is fine, Henri. I just now arrived."

Henri smiled and handed Billy the invitation, which was exquisitely crafted of gold and green silk paper, bearing the likeness of Napoleon III, Maximilian and Carlota. It was a handsome keepsake.

"*Allons-y*, William?"

"*Allons-y*, Henri!" He motioned for Billy to enter and he followed behind. Two soldiers stood guard at the entrance. One of
them carefully examined Billy's invitation, and then waved him
through. The soldier apparently recognized Henri and waved him
through without further ado. The Hall was crowded with exquisitely dressed guests, and a string quartet played violin concertos,
adding to the atmosphere and elegance. A waiter happened by
carrying a tray of champagne. Henri took a glass.

"Have one, William. It's a vintage 1836 *Moet et Chandon*."
Billy reached for a glass as an attractive blond-haired woman in a
low-cut lavender gown greeted Henri.

"*Henri, mon amour, comment ça va?*" (Henri, my love, how
are you?). She smiled coquettishly, extending her hand, which he
kissed in a manner that conveyed that there was more than just
familiarity. They spoke for a moment in French, but Henri then
switched to English, apologizing to Billy.

"No, please, Henri, there's no need to speak English for my
account. I understand French." But Henri continued in English.

"Allow me to introduce Mister William McHugh, Suzette.
William, this is Mademoiselle Suzette de la Croix, one of the most
enchanting women in all of Mexico."

"How do you do, Mister McHugh?" She smiled and extended
her hand.

"*Je suis enchanté de faire votre connaissance.*" (I am delighted to
make your acquaintance) It was correct and proper French, but
in spite of that, Suzette responded in English, perfect, mellifluous
English.

"Your accent is quite good, Mister McHugh. Where did you
learn your French?"

The waiter passed by again, and Henri reached for another
glass of champagne, which he handed to Suzette.

"I don't yet claim French as one of my languages, but I

continue to study it. It's the language of international commerce and diplomacy."

This apparently pleased Suzette, which she showed by smiling and moving a bit closer, thinking perhaps that here was a different kind of American than the usual parochial type she had come to expect.

"William is a member of Henry Phipps & Partners, Suzette, one of the best law firms in the United States."

Billy had not yet been made partner, but he did not want to contradict Henri so he let it pass.

"I'm curious, Mister McHugh—"

"Oh, please, mademoiselle, call me William."

"As you wish, William. I'm curious, how do you view the establishment of a monarchy here in Mexico? Your government, of course, supports the Juárez Regime and has refused to recognize the Regency Government and the Monarchy."

Her question was quite provocative, and he paused for a second before responding. Mademoiselle de la Croix smiled and sipped her champagne while she waited for his response.

"Well, mademoiselle..." A well-dressed man in a swallowtail suit suddenly walked up to Henri Pavillons.

"You'll excuse me, William. I need to talk with my colleague. I'll leave you in the capable and charming hands of Mademoiselle de la Croix." Pavillons kissed Suzette on the cheek and walked off with the man.

"...I make it a point not to get involved in politics. I'm a lawyer, and I try to stick to legal matters and represent my clients to the best of my ability. Now, from what I understand, the Mexican people approved the monarchy and Maximilian. That's good enough for me, whether or not it's good enough for my government."

It was disingenuous of Billy but effective, because Suzette

smiled approvingly and suggested that he accompany her to the buffet table, where the French Legation had spared no expense in providing a sumptuous and regal feast for its distinguished guests. They got in line, and Billy followed Mademoiselle de la Croix, choosing from the tempting selection of delicacies, including caviar. All of a sudden, he heard something drop behind him and felt something wet down around his ankle.

"Ooh, how clumsy of me!"

Billy looked down at his feet and saw broken glass. When he turned, he saw a petite, dark-haired woman in a blue gown.

"I'm so sorry. I do hope it didn't cut you."

Billy felt nothing other than a wet stocking, but when he looked down again, he saw that the glass had shattered into many jagged pieces. Nonetheless, he downplayed the seriousness of the incident.

"No, it's just a wet stocking," he said.

But just to be sure, he thought he had better check it more closely. So, he got out of line, found an unoccupied chair, and sat down. Then, as discretely as possible, he pulled up his pant leg, rolled down his stocking and examined his ankle. Fortunately, there was no cut.

"I'm so sorry for ruining your dinner." When he looked up, he saw the young woman who had dropped the glass.

"Why don't you sit right there, and I'll go and get you another plate? Tell me what you would like."

"No, that won't be necessary," Billy said. "It's nothing more than a wet stocking."

"I'm María de Quesada, and I'm very sorry to have met you under these circumstances."

"Billy McHugh," he said, extending his hand. "Let's get back in line, María."

She smiled and followed behind him as he chose from the delectable selection of seafood.

"I see you like shrimp and lobster," María said.

"Yes, very much so. I should be careful, though, because Mexico City is not that close to the sea."

"I'm sure you would like the shrimp in my country. They are large and quite delicious. We call them 'langostinos'."

"Oh, that sounds delicious, and where are you from?"

"From Cuba."

"I thought I recognized your accent." Billy said, excitedly.

"You've been to Cuba, have you?"

"Yes, when I was a boy," Billy said.

"How interesting, and where are you from?" She asked.

"I'm an American." He caught himself. "Or I should say, a North American, from the United States. Let's try to find a place to sit down and eat our dinner?"

"I would enjoy that," she said.

He found a quiet table and they sat down together.

"So, you've been to Cuba?"

"Yes, when I was sixteen. I was a cabin boy on my father's ship. We stayed at a large *ingenio* called *La Dulce Gardenia,* which was about fifteen miles west of Havana."

"And what, may I ask, are you doing here in Mexico?"

A waiter passed by carrying bottles of wine, and Billy signaled for him. Maria asked for the red and Billy chose the white.

"I promise not to drop this glass on you," she said, and they both laughed.

"To your health, María! It's a real pleasure to meet you!"

"And to yours, Billy!"

"I'm here in Mexico on behalf of my law firm. We're building our international practice and see some good opportunities here. What about you, María?"

He caught her with her mouth full and had to wait until she'd swallowed her food.

"I came here two years ago..."

Suddenly, an intense-looking man with a beard and a mustache rushed up to the table.

"Get up, María and now! We need to talk!"

He grabbed her by the arm and tried to pull her up. She resisted.

"For God's sake, José, leave me alone! I'm eating my dinner!"

The man glanced at Billy.

"I'm sorry, señor, but this is a personal matter."

María struggled and managed to free her arm from his grip, but he persisted and grabbed it again. Billy was prepared to come to her aid, but as it turned out, he didn't have to, because the man suddenly let go of her arm and rushed off without another word. The entire incident was over in just seconds.

"I'm so sorry for all this trouble. First, I drop a glass of champagne on you and then my crazy ex-husband comes and spoils your dinner. He won't leave me..."

"Oh, there you are, William. We were looking for you." It was Henri Pavillon with Mademoiselle de la Croix. "The Marquis de Montholon is about to give a little talk, and there are some French and Mexican officials whom I'm sure you would like to meet," said Henri, glancing at Maria.

"Yes, Henri, I'll be right with you. Do you know María de Quesada?"

"Yes, we have met."

"Will you excuse me, María?" I do want to continue our conversation. Let's try to meet again later."

"I'm not planning on leaving just yet," Maria said.

"Good, then I'll look for you."

Billy walked with Henri and Mademoiselle de la Croix to the

front of the large Reception Hall where the guests were gathered to hear the words of the Marquis de Montholon, France's Official Representative to Mexico.

The Marquis was a rotund little man, effete and foppish-looking. He was the former French Consular General in New York, and being the nephew of Napoleon, was later rewarded with the position of Minister to Mexico.

After the Marquis' remarks, Billy looked for María de Quesada but was unable to find her. It was only when they were both departing for the evening and descending the steps of the Legation that he was able to say good night. When he extended an invitation to dinner for the following week, she accepted it enthusiasticly.

3

Billy put on his new suit and checked himself in the mirror. It was very expensive, but he deemed it worth the price.

"Wait, señor," said Margarita. "There are threads on the back. Stay right there. I'll get the brush." She returned shortly and brushed them off. "It's nothing, señor, just some threads from the tailor's shop."

"Thank you, Margarita. You're very helpful. I'm so glad I found you, or was it that you found me?"

Margarita smiled warmly. It was clear that she liked her American employer, and it showed in the way she fussed over him.

"Will you be home for dinner, señor?"

"No, Margarita, not tonight, so please feel free to leave for the day."

"You're very kind, señor, but I have some more cleaning to do."

"As you wish."

As he headed toward the door to leave, he walked past his desk and noticed Dolores's letter. When he picked it up, a photograph fell out. It had somehow escaped his notice. Baby Sebastián stood between Dolores and Sofia as they held his little hands, all three smiling brightly.

He read the letter again.

12 December 1863

My dear husband Billy,

I haven't had a letter from you in weeks and I pray that you are well. Though I'm with my family, I am terribly lonely without you. I reach out for you in bed at night and awaken sad and lonely. Billy, couldn't you come to Cuba for a short stay? There are steamers from Mexico arriving in Havana every day. Or I could visit you in Mexico. Sofia has volunteered to take care of Sebastián.

There is also a legal matter involving papá's will, which Sofia strongly advised me to bring to your attention. She said it must be resolved, and soon...

My dear husband, my dear husband, the words echoed through his conscience as he walked out the door and hurried down the steps to the street. He was a married man with a child, and yet here he was hurrying off to meet another woman, hoping to quiet the persistent call of lust he'd been living with these past months. He was embarrassed by the stained sheets, not wanting Margarita to see them. He had even tried to clean them himself. Margarita had surely noticed.

When he reached the restaurant, he glanced through the window and saw Maria standing there. She wore a bright red dress, and her shiny black hair looked recently coifed. She was not a beautiful woman, certainly no match for Dolores, but the sight of her excited him.

"*Buenas tardes,* María. It's so nice to see you again!"

"Buenas tardes, Billy."

"I hope I haven't kept you waiting."

"Not at all, I just arrived."

Billy requested a quiet table, and the maître d' led them to one in back. They sat down and smiled at each other.

"Some wine perhaps, señor?" asked the maître d'.

"Would you like some wine, María?"

"That would be nice. Have you tried the reds from the Monterrey district? They're quite good, the whites much less so."

"Your wife has excellent taste, señor," said the maître d'.

They smiled, but didn't correct him.

"No, I haven't," Billy said.

"I have one that I know will please you, señor." said the maître d' who smiled, returning quickly with a bottle, which he uncorked and poured a little for Billy to sample.

"You're right, María. It is excellent."

"I'll send a waiter to take your order, sir."

"Do I smell gardenias?" Billy asked.

"It's my perfume. Do you like it?"

"Yes, very much so. It reminds me of Cuba. As I mentioned the other night, I stayed at an *ingenio* where they cultivated gardenias and decorated the Main House with them. In fact, the name of the *ingenio* was *La Dulce Gardenia.*"

"How interesting that you've been to Cuba!"

He observed her closely as she spoke. He liked her lips and her shiny dark hair, but there was something else about her, *a je ne sais pas quoi,* (I can't quite put my finger on it) that he found attractive.

Was it simply the fact that I have not been with a woman in months?

331

"Anyway, I had started to tell you the other night. I came to Mexico with José two years ago. We lived for a year in Vera Cruz and everything was fine, but when we came to Mexico City, our marriage went to pieces. I'm an artist and I joined a group of artists here in the capital, and that's when the trouble began. José is a brilliant man but insanely jealous."

She paused now, looked intently at Billy, then took another sip of her wine before continuing.

"He got it into his mind that I was unfaithful to him and insisted that I not attend the artists' group. When I refused, he beat me."

She paused again, and this time her expression turned sour and sad.

"I was frightened and turned to one of my artist friends, who recommended that I move out. He found me a flat, and one day when José was away on business, I did just that. But when I returned to remove my things, he beat me again. He broke my nose, destroyed my paintings and threatened to kill me."

She was close to tears.

"I consulted a lawyer, and he prepared a petition for annulment. He told me it would be a slow process, as it would have to go to Rome for approval."

Billy refilled her glass, and the waiter appeared and asked if they were ready to order. Billy waved him off.

"It sounds like you have had a very difficult time of it, María. I'm so sorry for you, but what exactly is señor de Quesada's business here in Mexico?"

"His name is not de Quesada. It's Quintero, José Agustín Quintero. De Quesada is my family name. My lawyer said I could use it now because we are separated. As for José, he was sent to Mexico on behalf of the Confederate States of America."

Billy coughed, trying hard to suppress his astonishment. He then reached for his wine, coming close to spilling it.

"But just what is his function here?"

"He's a Confederate spy. Well, his official title is 'confidential agent.' He's not the only one in Mexico. There are several here in the Capital and more in Vera Cruz and the northern provinces. I have met some of them. You being from Washington and all and presumably on the other side, I imagine…"

"I'm on neither side, María," Billy interrupted. "I was born and raised in the south. But I'm against this war, and all wars, for that matter."

He used the same disingenuousness with Henri Pavillons. In both cases, it was out of character for Billy McHugh. However, under the circumstances, it was quite necessary in both instances. Thoughts raced through his mind, and he became concerned that she might notice his extreme interest. He sought a diversion now and signaled for the waiter.

"We'd like to order now."

"Sí, señor, what can I serve you?" The waiter reached for the wine to refill their glasses but found it empty.

"Would you like some more wine, señor?"

"María?"

"I can drink some more if you can." He ordered another bottle of the Monterrey red, and they both ordered the roast beef.

"What is your husband's background, María?"

"Please don't refer to him as my husband. I'm trying to break the habit myself."

"I understand."

"José is a man for all seasons, as they say. He's a lawyer, a writer, a journalist, even a poet. We met in Havana and worked together for Cuban independence. We were so perfectly suited and so happy together."

She choked up with emotion. Billy reached over and placed his hand on hers until she regained her composure.

"His inflammatory writing landed him in El Morro, and he was sentenced to death. But he managed to escape and flee to Texas. José is resourceful, very resourceful."

Billy noticed that she was drinking much faster than he was.

"Have you ever heard of the Quitman Rifles?" She asked.

"Yes, we had a unit in Charleston."

"José fought with them in Texas and later in Virginia. Somewhere along the way, he managed to meet Jefferson Davis himself, and they became friends. José has an impressive list of friends..."

They ate their dinner, and María went on telling her story until the second bottle of wine was about empty. By then most of the other patrons had departed for the evening, and the waiter was circling around their table looking like he too wished to go home. Billy signaled for the check and told the waiter to hail them a carriage. When they rose to leave, María latched onto Billy's arm and drew close. As he led her out of the restaurant, she staggered slightly. When he was helping her into the carriage, she took on a silly little smile.

"You don't even know where I live," she said, slurring her words. The coachman must have heard it and looked back for his instructions.

"Tell me where you live, María?" Billy asked.

"It's just past the *Correo* on the new road," she whispered. Billy told the coachman and he drove off.

There was a light rain and patches of fog as the carriage made its way over the cobblestone streets. María leaned back and rested her head on Billy's shoulder. In spite of the bulkiness of her dress, he could feel her legs against his, and within seconds he felt himself becoming aroused, so much so that he feared she would notice.

But she was about to doze off, and by the time they reached her building she was sound asleep. He nudged her gently, calling her name until she lifted her head and looked out the window, realizing that she was home. As he helped her out of the carriage, she latched onto his arm. His passion had waned, chased into remission by his good judgment and by her condition. He understood that this was neither the right time nor the right circumstances, and the nascent relationship was too important to risk jeopardizing. He walked her to the door, then stepped back slightly, reaching for her hand. She smiled, offered her cheek and he kissed her softly and said good night.

4

Following that first dinner engagement, Billy devoted substantial time and effort to building a relationship with María de Quesada. José Quintero was now out of the way, having returned to Vera Cruz. Billy took advantage of the situation, offering praise and encouragement for her painting and assisting at several exhibitions of her work. They were seen together at the opera, the theatre and concerts. They traveled to Acapulco and toured the Pacific Coast.

María provided Billy with important information, which he wanted to relay to Washington. However, he still had not been instructed how to send it back to Washington. The next week, however, a letter arrived, and the return address indicated that it was from James Petigru. He knew, of course, that Petigru had passed away the previous year, and he thought perhaps the letter had gone astray and only now had shown up. When he opened the letter, however, he discovered it was from Jonathan Ambrose, Secretary of State Seward's Assistant. The letter instructed Billy to return to Washington the next month and included instructions on how he was to relay the information he had already obtained to the State Department. It was a complicated and convoluted procedure involving sending reports via vessels sailing from Vera Cruz to Havana on the first and last Tuesdays of the month. He was told to address his "letters" to Mister James Petigru at his Charleston, South Carolina address.

Some of the last information that Billy obtained from Maria de Quesada detailed an ongoing *Juarista* plot to assassinate Maximiliano. During the early months of 1864, the newspapers were full of reports about Maximilian and Carlota; how they had set sail aboard the vessel *Novara* bound for Mexico; how the Mexican people anxiously awaited their arrival in Vera Cruz and in Mexico City. The great moment arrived at eleven o'clock on June 12 1864 as Maximilian and Carlota made their long-awaited and triumphal entry to Mexico City.

Standing amongst the multitudes were Billy McHugh and Maria de Quesada, watching as the Royal Couple approached. When their carriage was passing directly in front of them, a man in a black cape pointed a long-barreled pistol at the Royal Couple. But when he pulled the trigger, it yielded nothing more than a "click." He pulled it again in rapid succession, but there was no report. Men and women screamed, and the man in the black cape quickly turned and fled, disappearing into the crowd. Hearing the screams, soldiers ran to the scene. Several onlookers reported what they had seen, but Billy and Maria wisely chose to leave the area.

The following week Billy received a telegraph from Joseph Bartlett, who advised him to wrap up his work in Mexico and return to Washington. Billy was jubilant. He would go to Havana to be with Dolores, and together they would return to Washington. He spent the next week making preparations. He wrote a lengthy memorandum, summarizing his espionage activities in Mexico, and as instructed, placed it in an envelope addressed to James

Petigru. He wrote a letter to Dolores, informing her of his arrival on the first of July aboard the *Caribbean Waters*.

Later that afternoon Billy walked through the many stalls of the *Zócalo* to purchase some gifts for Dolores, and by the time he headed back to his flat, it was already late afternoon. Nevertheless, when he walked past the Cathedral, he felt a strong urge to enter. Climbing the stairs, he had to step around a throng of beggars with bloodshot eyes and outstretched hands. He reached for his leather purse and found some coins, which he tried to distribute equitably amongst them. Then he opened the massive wooden door and stepped inside. He paused at the holy water font, dipped his fingers in and touched his forehead, making the sign of the cross, as he had been taught to do as a child. He walked slowly down the nave toward the altar, stopping to genuflect before entering a pew on the left. He knelt down, closed his eyes and prayed to the God whom he had ignored the entire time he had been in Mexico. When he opened his eyes, he saw a short line of supplicants waiting to make their confession. He got in line and waited. He entered the confessional and kneeled. The flickering light of a candle shone through the partially opaque screen that separated priest from penitent.

"Forgive me, Father, for I have sinned. It's been many years since my last confession." He waited for the priest's customary greeting, but it never came. Deathly silence took hold, increasing his anxiety. Finally:

"I am listening."

"Father, I'm, uh… I'm a married man, and I was with, with another woman."

"You had illicit relations with her?"

"Yes, Father."

"You committed adultery?"

"Yes, Father."

"Do you know that adultery is a mortal sin, a sin which could condemn you to spend all Eternity in hell after death?" The priest's words cut into him like a stiletto.

"There were extenuating circumstances, Father. I…"

"Extenuating circumstances? There are no circumstances that would sanction or mitigate adultery. Adultery is a grave and serious sin, señor, a mortal sin."

Billy could just make out the shadowy figure of the priest, moving forward toward the screen, seemingly attempting to add greater force to his words. Silence prevailed, exacerbating Billy's anxiety.

"Are you estranged from your wife?"

"No, Father. I love her deeply. I came to Mexico on business and she remained at home. I'm a North American and am here on behalf of my Government. I met this woman who had important information, information which I was sent to obtain for my Government."

No sooner had the words left his lips when he felt shocked that he'd actually spoken them.

"I must tell you again and warn you that there are no circumstances, none whatsoever that would permit or excuse adultery. What was it that led you to believe that there were?"

Billy said nothing.

"Are you aware that to have a valid confession, you must reveal everything in your heart and in your mind?"

"Yes, Father."

"Well, then, tell me about those circumstances. Otherwise, I cannot grant you absolution, and you will continue to live with the stain of mortal sin and reap its dire consequences."

"I was sent to Mexico by my Government to obtain information on the activities of the Confederate States of America in Mexico."

There it was. He said it.

"Your government being the United States of America?"

"Yes, Father, but I was also here to explore opportunities for expanding my firm's legal practice."

"You are a lawyer?"

"Yes, Father. The woman was the wife of a Confederate spy, and I developed a relationship with her to gain information for my Government."

"An adulterous relationship?"

"Yes, an adulterous relationship but under the circumstances, which I just explained."

"How many times did you commit adultery with this woman?"

"Many times. I can't give you an exact number, but we spent months together."

"The number of times is important, because each and every time you had an illicit sexual union with her constitutes the sin of adultery, and they all must be confessed. Did you tell her that you were a married man?"

The lawyer in Billy responded.

"No, I didn't, but why does it matter? I admit that I committed adultery. Isn't that enough?"

"No, it's not!" said the priest loudly and emphatically. "And I told you why. Was the woman married?"

"She was separated and seeking an annulment."

"So, she was Catholic?"

"I must presume so."

Billy could see the figure of the priest leaning back now away from the screen.

"This woman is also an adulteress and must confess her sins, failing which she will risk the same condemnation and punishment as you, to suffer an afterlife in the flames of hell."

Billy was now seriously considering bolting out of the confessional, for it appeared now that this was not a confession but rather an inquisition. He knew not why, but he decided to stay and let it run its course.

"I ask you again, how many times did you commit adultery?"

"I told you. I cannot be certain, but many times and over a period of several months."

Billy heard some whispering and heard the sound of a door opening. What came next was surprising.

"In the name of the Father, the Son, and the Holy Ghost, I absolve you of your sins. As your penance, say three Our Fathers and three Hail Marys."

Out of habit, Billy responded:

"Thanks be to God." He then exited the confessional, walked back to a pew, knelt down and quickly prayed his penance feeling little if any contrition.

5

The *Caribbean Waters* lay at dockside in Vera Cruz, a plume of black smoke rising from its tall stack. Overhead, puffy white cumulous clouds shepherded the last of the storm clouds, and a southwesterly wind blew them out to sea. Thunder rumbled in the distance as the remnants of the tropical downpour surrendered to a blazing late-morning sun.

Billy stepped out of the carriage and waited as the coachman went back to unload his trunk. He paid the driver, adding a generous tip. He was in a fine mood, buoyant and upbeat. He was headed home after almost a year in Mexico, a year in which he had often questioned why he was there, and whether he was doing any good. That was all behind him now, and the anticipated bliss of the reunion with Dolores dominated his thoughts.

"I'll tote your trunk," said a negro porter with a rickety-looking wagon.

"All right," Billy said, awakened from his amorous fantasy by the porter's words. Billy was carrying a handsome leather document pouch in which he had placed his State Department reports as well as all the information and contact items he had collected for Henry Phipps & Partners while in Mexico.

"Would you like me to carry that pouch, sir?"

"No, just the trunk."

He boarded the vessel and went directly to his assigned stateroom, placing his leather pouch on a table anchored to the floor. It had been a long and tiring carriage and train ride from Mexico City, and he thought he would take a nice little nap. When he lay down on the bed, however, he realized that he was just too excited to sleep. So, he decided to go up on deck and watch their departure. The trunk arrived, and as he headed for the door, he glanced at his document pouch lying there on the table, remembering that he needed to get his final State Department report into the ship's mail pouch. He'd already addressed the envelope to James Petigru as previously instructed, but had not sealed it. It also occurred to him that he should read the report through again and add something more about the attempted assassination of Maximilian. *I'll do it tomorrow.* He wanted to relax and bask in the joy of knowing that he was on his way to be reunited with Dolores. Just then, there was a knock on the stateroom door. It was a ship's steward.

"We're preparing to depart, sir, and I'm taking a headcount. You are Mister William McHugh, are you?"

"Yes, that's right."

"And you are going to Havana?"

"Yes, Havana."

The steward wrote something on his pad, smiled, and left. Billy put the key to the stateroom in his pocket and followed behind the steward, forgetting to lock the door behind him. "Oh, steward, what is the quickest way to get back up on deck? I haven't yet gotten my bearings."

"Follow me, sir." He led him down a corridor and up a stairs, where Billy heard a piano playing and some singing. "This is the First-Class Bar, sir. That next stair on your right will take you topside."

Billy entered, where he found a long, highly polished mahogany bar lined with patrons. It was still early in the day, and he had not planned to drink; but the bartender called out to him.

"Good afternoon, suh. What can Aah serve ya?" He was a big, burly, red-haired man with a deep southern drawl, an Irishman from Dixie if ever there was one.

"Do you have any red wine?"

"You're in luck, suh. Aah jest opened a bottle fo our new piano playaa, Miss LeBlanc." He reached underneath, produced a bottle and placed it on the bar. Billy immediately recognized the label. It was the same Monterrey red that he had drunk with María de Quesada. The bartender filled the glass, and Billy paid him with a Mexican five-peso gold piece, receiving his change in Mexican silver coins.

Wine in hand, Billy walked over to the easy chairs. He saw a Havana newspaper and underneath it a New Orleans *Times-Picayune* that was only three days old. He picked it up along with the *Diario de la Habana* and sat down. The headline in the Cuban paper caught his attention: **Slave Revolt Foiled**. The article reported that a slave revolt had been put down in Cienfuegos, which was on the other side of the island and would not have affected the de Castilla family. He turned the page.

Union Gunboat Battles Blockade Runners

The Union gunboat, Freedom of Boston, captured one blockade runner and sank another last Friday just after midnight about a mile offshore of Havana. One of the vessels, The City of Mobile, attempted to outrun the Union warship. When that failed, it chose to open fire. The Union warship's firepower proved superior and quickly sent the vessel to the bottom...

Just then the ship's horn sounded, startling everyone, including the piano player, who stopped playing. Billy got up and followed the crowd topside. The horn sounded again, and the cry rang out "All ashore that's going ashore." Billy went over to the rail and propped up his foot to watch their departure, but within seconds he was struck with a wave of fatigue and decided he would take that nap after all. When he arrived back at his stateroom, he reached for his key with one hand and turned the knob with the other. The door opened, and he realized then that he had forgotten to lock the door.

The soft bed and the faint rhythmic rumble of the vessel's engines had a hypnotic effect, and he fell into a deep, dream-laden sleep.

He was back on The Wandering Maiden, en route to Cuba with a hold full of African slaves. They were in full flight from the Royal Navy Frigate, and its cannons boomed...

Suddenly, he sat up in bed, slowly realizing that what he had heard was real and wasn't his dream. He looked out the porthole, noticing that there was much less sunlight than when he had lain down for the nap. He got out of bed and checked his watch, seeing that it was almost five o'clock. That is when he noticed there were no vibrations from the ship's engines. Something was amiss. He went topside and discovered that the ship was dead in the water. On their port side lay a sinister-looking black ironside flying the Stars and Bars high up on its masthead. A crew of armed personnel shouted threats and commands as they herded passengers up against the rail. Billy heard someone say they were CSA marines. He immediately tried to duck back into the stairway. But it was too late.

"Git ova there at the rail with the rest o' them," shouted one of the marines, Colt revolver at the ready.

A Confederate Naval Officer in an immaculately tailored gray uniform now took center stage before the frightened passengers.

"Please give me y'alls' attention. Aah assure y'all there's nuthin' ta fear as long as y'all do as ya told." He turned then to one of his subordinates.

"Bobby, go on down ta First Mate Mackenzie's cabin and git me the passenger list on the double. Carl, Pedro and the rest of you mates, search the ship, and take these stewards with ya. Y'all be sho ta check all the staterooms and git everyone up here on the double!"

"Aye aye, sir."

Some of the women passengers began to cry.

"Why are they treating us like prisoners?" one of the women asked. "We're just passengers on a ship. Why don't they attack the Yankee vessels?"

"Yeah, Aah'm sure as hell not military, and Aah damn sho ain't no Yankee!" said one man.

"They are not jest CSA marines. They're raiders," a man whispered to Billy.

"The marines started going down the line of passengers, relieving them of their valuables. Just then, Miss LeBlanc, the piano player, appeared on deck, and a rebel non-commissioned officer called out to her:

"Do ya stuff, mademoiselle."

With that, Miss LeBlanc began making her way from one

woman to the next, seizing their purses and their jewelry. Many passengers, both men and women, protested loudly and firmly, declaring that they were southerners, but to no avail. The men were forced to turn over their billfolds, their leather pouches of gold and silver coins, their watches, their rings and everything else of any potential value. In the few instances when a passenger resisted, the marines drew their revolvers and the goods were quickly surrendered.

In addition to his billfold, Billy was forced to turn over the handsome gold watch that Dolores had given him on their second wedding anniversary. As more passengers were flushed from their staterooms and herded up to the main deck, they were ordered to stand at the rail and were frisked and fleeced in the same manner. This continued until the Confederate Captain was satisfied that most of the ship's passengers had been accounted for.

"Now, ladies and gentlemen, y'all can return to ya staterooms, and Aah'm gonna turn command of this vessel back ova to Captain Pierce. He will take y'all safely on ta Havana. So, fo' now, y'all are dismissed."

The Confederate Captain and his marines watched as the passengers rushed to go below. Billy started to walk away, but did not get far before two husky marines grabbed hold of him.

"Yo name William McHugh?" Billy nodded. The marine drew his revolver.

"Stay right where you are! We got 'im, Captain Murphy."

The Confederate Captain walked over, carrying Billy's leather pouch. Billy's heart sank.

"We picked this up in yo stateroom, Mista McHugh. Found some very incriminatin' documents inside. You're under arrest."

"Those are not mine, Captain," is all Billy could think of saying.

"Take 'im onboard and shackle 'im"

6

When the Confederate raider made port in Mobile Bay, the Captain turned Billy over to the Provost Marshall. Billy was imprisoned in the stockade at Spanish Fort and held pending further instructions from Richmond. Two weeks later a telegraph arrived with instructions to transport the prisoner to Camp Sumter, a Confederate prisoner of war facility in Andersonville, Georgia, to await further instructions.

Billy spent the first two weeks at Andersonville in a cell within the administrative building. The commandant was an officious martinet of Swiss descent named Henry Wirtz. Wirtz interrogated Billy for days, depriving him of sleep, water, and food, and demanding he reveal even more than what he had written in his reports to the State Department. When it became clear that Billy knew nothing more, Wirtz became angry and frustrated and threw him into the prison grounds, awaiting further instructions from Richmond.

Billy quickly discovered that Andersonville was a living hell. Made to hold some ten thousand prisoners, there were already more than twenty-five thousand, and hundreds more arriving every day. Food was scarce, and when available, meager and rancid. Drinking water was supplied by a creek that ran through the prison grounds. It also served as a latrine. The prisoners coped as best they could. They built crude, makeshift huts made of tree branches, blankets, and anything else they could scrounge together. Though the huts provided only a bare minimum of shelter, the communities of prisoners within them afforded protection from prison raiders, who preyed upon the sick, the weak and the new arrivals. Word quickly spread that Billy McHugh was a Union spy and a lawyer, and one group after another urged him to join them. Billy joined one of the more sturdy-looking huts, the members of which appeared to be in better health.

Two long months passed. Billy developed leg ulcers, lost a lot of weight and was infected with lice. He was barely recognizable, his face obscured behind a thick beard, his hair overgrown and matted down. He had not washed and had taken on an uncharacteristic taciturnity, unable to accept the painful reality that he was now a prisoner charged with espionage, a charge that carried the death sentence. His hutmates tried their best to draw him out, but he remained in a state of shock, suffering silently, withdrawn and depressed.

One blisteringly hot late August morning the men were standing outside awaiting distribution of their meager rations, when suddenly the sharp retort of a rifle cut through the thick damp air, echoing throughout the entire prison grounds. It startled Billy, and he grimaced. The others barely looked up. They were long-term veterans of this God-forsaken rebel prison, and another visit from the Grim Reaper was nothing new.

"Who was it?" asked Jim McClendon, a twenty-two-year-old corporal of the 10th New York.

"Paddy O'Brien," said Jack Delaney, a twenty-eight-year-old sergeant of the 83rd Pennsylvania. "Seems he was tryin to get to a cleaner part of the stream and take a drink."

"That was a costly drink of water now, wasn't it?" said Rob Meadows, a tall sergeant of the 24th Illinois Cavalry.

"At least he got to see them raiders get hung."

Everyone looked up and stared out toward the center of the prison grounds, where the lifeless bodies of the five raiders slowly turned, twisting on the ropes that hung from the gallows. They'd been hanged two days before, witnessed by all. These were the heartless bullies of Andersonville, who had been unmercifully preying on their fellow prisoners, beating, stealing, plundering them of their meager rations, their clothing, their shoes and all their personal effects. After months of ruthless predation, they'd been rounded up by order of the Commandant and turned over to the Prisoners' Committee to be judged and sentenced.

"Sure looks ta me that hangin's a cruel way ta die, but they got what they deserved," said Bobby Kaiser, a corporal from the 25th Indiana. Bobby was unaware of the effect his words had on Billy McHugh, whose eyes were inevitably drawn to the gallows, to those five raiders swinging on the ropes, turning and twisting grotesquely. Billy began to weep.

Weeks later, a rebel sergeant with a clean gray uniform showed up at the hut, a clear sign that he had come from the Administrative Building. "Y'all got a Billy McHugh in here with ya?"

"Yes, we do," said Jack Delaney, patting Billy on the shoulder.

"The Commandant wants to see ya, McHugh."

"Kick that no good German's ass for us, will ya, Billy boy" said Delaney. The rebel sergeant smiled.

"Just so y'all know. He's not German, he's Swiss."

"Same difference," said Delaney.

The rebel sergeant marched Billy over to the Administrative Building.

"We're sending you to Richmond to be hanged, McHugh," said Commandant Wirtz. I wanted to do it right here in Andersonville, but I was overruled."

The next day, Billy was loaded on a wagon and driven to the railroad depot.

"Come on, Yank. You smell worse than a polecat, and we ain't gonna punish the other passengers with yo foul smell."

The guards dragged Billy over to a horse watering trough, ducked him down and scrubbed him real good with lye soap and stiff brushes. Then, still soaking wet, they hauled him aboard the rickety old train.

CHAPTER XV

Train to Richmond

Charlie Flynn spent his convalescence in a CSA hospital in northern Virginia. The lead ball that entered his backside during the Battle of Brandy Station was more serious than either Charlie or the surgeons had thought. It went through and struck his hipbone, shearing off a large piece of it, and the surgeons decided that the leg would have to be amputated. Charlie would have none of it, and he rose up on his cot and shouted that he would shoot the first man who attempted to amputate his leg. The next morning, Charlie awoke *sans* his Colt revolver and Spencer repeating rifle. He'd made such a fuss, however, that a young doctor hailing from New Orleans and educated in Paris, said he knew of a controversial procedure from medical school to extract the lead ball and avoid amputation. He was persuasive, and the surgeons agreed to try it. It was successful, and Charlie kept his leg, though he was left with a noticeable limp.

Charlie's 'lil' gal, Maggie Burke, visited him frequently during his convalescence, offering encouragement, and when the doctors weren't looking, amorous caresses. She brought him home-cooked food, fed him and nursed him back to health. In a moment of weakness, Charlie proposed to her, such was the effect that the 'lil' bosomy gal had on him. Maggie accepted, and the Catholic

Chaplain married them in the hospital. Lieutenant Barney Muldoon served as Charlie's best man and was heard to whisper:

"Aah never would a believed that Charlie'd be a marryin, cause if ever there was a ramblin man, it was Charlie Flynn."

When Charlie finished his convalescence, he got a fifteen-day furlough. It was autumn, and the newlyweds returned to the Burke farmhouse for an abbreviated honeymoon. Few would have believed it, but it looked as though Charlie was already on the road to domestication. When the furlough ended, he was reluctant to leave his new bride and the comforts of the Burke estate.

The South's disastrous defeat at Gettysburg had resulted in a wave of pessimism, and Confederate morale was sinking. A consensus was forming amongst soldiers and civilians alike that the War was lost. Why then, Charlie asked, should he put his life at risk? And for the first time ever, he considered deserting and going west. Maggie reminded him, however, that desertion was punishable by death, adding that it was "unbecoming of a southern gentleman to betray his honor and desert his country in its time of need." She talked him out of it, and by the fall of 1863, Charlie had rejoined his regiment at Chambersburg, Virginia, where General Lee had ordered Jeb Stuart and all the cavalry forces to regroup after the Gettysburg debacle.

In March of 1864 Colonel Black was ordered to leave the Army of Northern Virginia and return to Charleston to defend his native state under the new Command of the Department of South Carolina, Georgia and Florida. The troopers of 1st Cavalry were pleased, for they'd be going home and could see their families, at least for a time.

Three years had passed since that momentous day of April 12th, 1861, when General P.G.T. Beauregard ordered the bombardment of Fort Sumter in Charleston Harbor, initiating the War Between the States. It was now April 1864, and a sad and somber springtime in Charleston. The city itself was under daily bombardment. Not even the churches were spared. Come hell or high water the Yankees were determined to take Charleston, for as General Sherman was reported to have said:

"Here is where treason began and by God here is where it shall end."

The faces of the citizens of Charleston told the story. The smiles and the cocky countenances were gone. Their heads hung down, their shoulders slumped. Gone was the twinkle in their eyes and the confidence in their step. That was what stood out even more than the constant shelling, the piles of rubble and the constant fires. That was what those three years of War had wrought on the once proud city of Charleston.

The shelves of the general stores were bare. The haberdasheries were without clothing, and even the taverns were at times without beer and spirits. Food was scarce, and increasingly expensive. Money was available, but it was Confederate money and depreciating rapidly. What was once ten Confederate dollars to the Yankee Greenback was now fifteen then twenty then fifty. And it was anyone's guess what it would be tomorrow. Such was the Charleston that Charlie Flynn returned to in the spring of 1864, a sad and forlorn Charleston, a Charleston that smelled of defeat.

2

The Most Reverend Patrick N. Lynch, Bishop of Charleston, rose and stood before the congregation of Saint Mary's Roman Catholic Church to deliver the homily. He'd been invited to serve mass this Sunday in April by Father William Bailey on the occasion of the three-year anniversary of the Confederate States of America's War of Independence. Father Bailey also asked Bishop Lynch to say a few words about his up-coming mission to the Vatican, on behalf of President Jefferson Davis and the Confederate States of America, to seek the Vatican's recognition.

When the mass ended, Bonny McHugh spotted the Flynns as they were leaving the church and hurried over to speak to them. She got behind them, waiting for an opportune time, because Mr. Flynn was engaged in an animated conversation with Charlie.

"...Yes, now that you mention it, we were disappointed that you didn't bring her along. Your mother would have liked her to accompany us to mass, even though we understand that Maggie is a Baptist."

"I wanted to bring her, Dad, but Mr. and Mrs. Burke were against it. I don't need to tell you that Charleston's gettin' more dangerous by the day. In fact I think it's time for you and Mom ta start headin upcountry to Columbia."

"I wish it were that easy, son, but I've got a business to run, and I can't just abandon it."

"Good morning, Mary!" said Bonny McHugh. "Good morning Mister Flynn. And welcome home, Charlie. My, you look so handsome in your uniform!"

"Thank you, ma'am, nice to see you." Charlie said, smiling politely.

"And good morning to you, Bonny!" said Mary Flynn. "You remember Bonny McHugh, don't you, Michael?"

"Yes, of course. Good morning, ma'am! How are you?"

"About as good as could be expected under the circumstances. I was finally able to make contact with Billy. He's in Mexico, but I haven't heard from my husband Patrick in quite some time and that worries me..."

Charlie started looking around for a reason to excuse himself, and as luck would have it, he spotted Martha Brown, one of his ex-girlfriends, standing near the portico.

"Y'all excuse me a minute! There's someone I want to say hello to." And off he went.

"What is Billy doing in Mexico?" asked Mary Flynn.

"As far as I can gather he's trying to drum up business for his law firm. I don't have much more information than that, and what I get comes by way of Cuba. Oh, I guess you didn't know it, but Billy married a Cuban girl from Havana, and they have a one-year old son. I've not yet met his wife or the baby. Billy went to Mexico, and his wife went back to Cuba to visit her family. She's a teacher, a beautiful young woman, at least from her photographs."

"How interesting!" said Mary Flynn. "You know, Charlie also got married. He married a young woman in Virginia, the daughter of a prominent landholder and tobacco farmer. No children as yet, but it does look like Charlie's finally settled down."

Michael Flynn smiled as if to say it may be too early to draw that conclusion.

"Maybe I'll also get to be a grandmother one of these days. At least I hope so!" Mary said.

When Charlie walked back over to his parents, Bonny noticed that he was limping.

"Is your leg bothering you, son?" asked Mary Flynn.

Charlie shook his head.

"He darn near lost his leg at the Battle of Brandy Station in Virginia," said Michael Flynn. Stopped a Yankee musket ball with his hip and it's left him with a limp."

"It was the buttocks, Dad, and ya don't need to pump it up so."

"Well, I must be going," Bonny said. "I need to go down to the wharf and see if anyone's seen or heard from Patrick."

"Seems that y'all are still on friendly terms with Billy McHugh's family," Charlie said.

"And why shouldn't we be?" asked his mother, Mary, whose views had mellowed after three long years of war. "It's not their fault that Billy went north. I'm sure they didn't want him to. I know that his father practically disowned him because of it."

"I don't have any quarrel with the McHugh's or with Billy himself," added Michael Flynn. "First of all he's not fightin' for the Yankees. He's a lawyer, and if I were him, I'da probably gone and joined that Washington law firm too. Let's face it, Charlie! The North's gonna win this War, and Billy was just lookin' out for himself, something you should be thinking more about."

Charlie looked at his father, whose words had for once hung true.

He's right. This war's a lost cause for the South, a lost cause for me. Why and hell should I risk my limbs and my life for a lost cause? It's just not worth it.

3

The next day Charlie boarded a Charleston & Savannah Railroad train headed south. The South Carolina 1st Cavalry was now part of the CSA's Department of South Carolina, Georgia and Florida, and was given the mission of defending the railroads.

Charlie's decision had come suddenly, as though it had been waiting to invade his conscious mind. His father's words were the catalyst, but as Charlie looked out the window, he asked himself whether he was doing the right thing. Soon the train came to a stop, and he watched as his fellow troopers got up and began exiting the car. Charlie's long time friend, Barney Muldoon, got up now with the rest of them.

"How 'bout we go see what that confectionary store has to offer?" said Barney.

"Wait a minute. Sit down, Barney. I need to talk to you."

"We only got ten minutes, Charlie. We can talk outside."

"Sit down, Barney. This is important." Barney sat down. Charlie waited until all the other troopers had left the car.

"I'm goin' today, Barney."

"You're goin' where?"

"I'm goin' west. I'm gettin' off this train, and I'm not gettin' back on."

Barney looked at his old friend, knowing what he meant. But just to be certain, he used *the* word, stressing it.

"You're gonna *desert*!"

"Call it what ya want, but I'm done fightin'. It's a lost cause, Barney, and I'm not willin' to die for a lost cause. I was hopin' maybe you'd come with me."

"I can't go with ya, Charlie. My mom, my dad and sweetheart would never forgive me. I want to go home when this war's over. I want to go home real bad, and I want to go home and stay. Ya understand?"

A few troopers came back in the car now and sat down, where-upon Charlie got up and headed for the exit. Barney followed behind him, and they headed for the confectionary store. A group of negroes were seated on the wooden steps talking about what they were going to do when the War ended.

"Aah'm gonna git me a 'lil' piece o land and farm it fo' maself."

"Yeah, won't be long now fo' Ole Gennel Sherman take Atlanta."

They showed little mind or respect for the two Confederate officers, barely moving aside to make room for them to climb the stairs.

The moment Charlie and Barney entered the store the train whistle blew, and the conductor called out in a loud voice:

"We leave in five minutes, boys."

Other than some dried-out-looking apples and molasses candy, there was very little to buy. But Charlie spotted a bottle way up on the top shelf behind some old newspapers.

"What's that bottle up there?" he asked.

"Corn liquor, but we ain't got no glasses," said the storekeeper.

"That don't matter. Pull it on down here." The old man reached way up, brought it down and set it on the counter. Charlie reached into his pocket, took out a wrinkled $100 Confederate note and slapped it down on the counter. The storekeeper nodded, and Charlie picked up the bottle and took a long swallow.

"Won't ya reconsider, Barney? You and me's been through a whole helluva lot together."

"You're really gonna do it, aren't ya?" Barney said, picking up the bottle. "And what the hell am I supposed to tell Colonel Black when he asks me what happened to ya? Ya know damn well he's gonna ask me."

Barney took a swig of the corn liquor as the train whistle blew again.

"ALL ABOARD!" The call rang out. Charlie reached for the bottle and took another big swallow.

"That'll be another hundred," said the storekeeper. Charlie put another $100 Confederate note down on the counter.

"I want ya to take my horse, Barney. I know you'll take good care of him. I'm gonna miss ole Compass almost as much as I'll miss you, partner. But at least I know he'll be in good hands."

"ALL ABOARD!"

"Have another swallow fo' the road, Barney!"

But it was too late. The locomotive had already started huffing, puffing, and pulling out of the station. Charlie hugged his longtime friend and colleague and watched as he rushed out the door and jumped aboard the train before it picked up speed. A look of deep sadness formed on Charlie's face, which he sought to wash away with another hearty swallow of the corn liquor. He turned then and rushed out the back door of the confectionary store, nearly knocking down the old storekeeper who had come out from behind the counter, demanding more money.

Charlie's plan was to head for Mobile, Alabama, which he'd read was the last Confederate port still open. He'd take a steamer to Mexico, or better yet Panama, where he'd cross the Isthmus on the Panama Railroad and board another steamer for San Francisco.

He had ample funds in gold and Yankee dollars, owing to his skill and luck at poker, which he'd played every day for a week before the 1st Cavalry boarded that train. Though Mobile was hundreds of miles away, his first thought was to buy a good horse and ride night and day to get there. And as he walked into the little town just outside of Savannah trying his best to look inconspicuous, he spotted the **Savannah Livery Stable & Blacksmith Shop** and went inside.

"Say, ya got any decent mounts for sale? Mine was shot out from under me a few days ago."

"Very few, lieutenant. Most o' thems been taken fo' the War, but ya welcome ta go back and look fo' yoself." Charlie went back to the stables and saw "for sale" signs on two of the stalls, but the horses were old and sickly looking.

"I'm afraid those won't do," he said to the proprietor.

"Suit yoself, lieutenant."

As he headed for the door, he noticed a young woman standing at the counter staring at him. He paid it little mind, accustomed as he was to attracting the attention of women. This one, however, went a step further and called out to him.

"Wait a minute, lieutenant!" She said and walked over. "Aah apologize for starin' at ya, but ya look so much like ma husband that Aah just couldn't help myself. He was a Fust Lieutenant Cavalry Officer just like you. Ma name's Rosemary Cooper."

She extended her hand, and Charlie smiled and shook it, but he didn't give his name.

"Would ya mind terribly if Aah walked with ya a spell?"

"Not at all, ma'am," Charlie replied.

Rosemary told Charlie that her husband Carl had been killed six months earlier.

"There's a little park up ahead, lieutenant. Could ya maybe sit and talk fo' a spell?"

"Yes, ma'am but just fo' a minute o' two. I really need to get movin' on."

They sat down on a bench, and she showed Charlie a photograph of her husband. But when she asked Charlie about his unit, he began to feel very uncomfortable and was about to bid her good-bye. That's when she looked him in the eye and gave him some advice.

"Ya better get outta that uniform, lieutenant. It's a dead give-away." Charlie played dumb.

"What ya gettin' at ma'am?"

"You've *taken a walk* haven't ya?"

"And what makes ya think that?" he asked, rather unconvincingly.

"Ya wearin' a cavalry officer's uniform, and there ain't no cavalry forces in this area."

"What if Aah'm home on furlough?"

"If ya was, Aah'd know 'bout it. Please understand, lieutenant, Aah don't blame ya one bit, but let me say again that ya best get outta that uniform."

It hadn't occurred to Charlie that being in uniform would actually attract more attention and suspicion than if he'd been in civilian clothes.

"Listen, why don't ya come on home with me, and Aah'l give ya some of ma husband's clothes."

By now Charlie concluded that Rosemary was not a threat. On the contrary, she seemed genuinely sympathetic and sincere. Once they reached her little house, she showed him her husband's clothes and told him he could take whatever he liked. Charlie felt certain that had he wanted to, he could have shared her bed that night, but he really wasn't in the mood and, more importantly, he didn't want to be unfaithful to his 'lil' gal, Maggie.

The next morning after breakfast Charlie selected a pair of trousers, a casual shirt, and a leather jacket from her deceased husband's wardrobe. In return Charlie gave her his Cavalry Officer's sword, which he knew she could sell or barter for food or other necessities.

Charlie spent the next week riding the poorly maintained railroads of the South, traveling hundreds of miles to reach his final destination in Mobile, Alabama. While en route he took on the identity of a horse trader, which fit him perfectly since he'd always been a fine horseman and an excellent judge of horseflesh. In the many conversations he had with soldiers and civilians alike, his story was that he was on his way to Mexico to purchase horses for the Confederacy.

When he finally arrived in Mobile, he found the city under siege, but still holding out. The port was under frequent attack from the Union naval forces of Vice-Admiral David Farragut, but Gulf steamers were still operating and able to slip in and out of the harbor. Charlie checked into a hotel, took a bath, and had a decent meal. And for the first time in more than ten days he began to relax. When he went to purchase a ticket for passage to Vera Cruz that afternoon, he was arrested by two husky Confederate Provost guards. They took him to a stockade where he spent the night. The next day they took him to Spanish Fort, charged him with desertion and locked him up.

4

The Yankees were doing a good job of destroying the South's railroad system, and Billy's guards had loaded him aboard one broken down train after another over a period of several weeks, before finding one that looked like it could make it all the way to Richmond.

He was sitting in the window seat in dire need of relieving himself. Fortunately, the train began to slow and gradually came to stop. The rebel sergeant stretched his long legs in the aisle and Billy started to get up.

"Hold your horses, Billy Boy," said the sergeant, who was sitting across from Billy. He yawned, put down the copy of the *Atlanta Intelligencer* and stood up.

"All right, let's go," he said, taking hold of Billy's arm. They followed the rebel soldier passengers, who were dressed in a rag-tag mixture of worn out Confederate uniforms and worn out civilian clothes, most of them without shoes. They exited the car and headed for the woods in back of the station to relieve themselves. As they started walking back to the train, one young rebel turned to Billy and asked him:

"You been followin' the election up nawth, Yank?" Billy didn't respond.

"Hell, he ain't no Yankee!" said the sergeant. "He's a suthen boy from Charleston, ain't ya, Billy Boy? They caught him spyin fo' the Yankees, and that makes him a turncoat and a coward, don't it, Billy?"

Some of the rebel soldiers overheard the sergeant, and one of them looked over at Billy.

"So, he's a turncoat, is he? Where y'all takin' 'im?"

"He's goin to Richmond. Got an appointment with the hang-man, don't ya Billy?"

The sergeant marched Billy back to the train, and as the rebel soldiers reentered the car, they stopped, stared, and jeered at the prisoner. An injured private with a large bandage wrapped around his head, glared at him. The only visible part of his face was red with rage:

"You sorry son-of-a-Yankee-bitch! Aah'd like ta—"

"Aah'm sho ya would, son, but we're savin him fo the hang-man, so just take yo seat and be calm. We'll take care of him all right."

The train rolled on all day through the Carolinas. Long about dusk it came to a stop, and the conductor came through and announced that they could go no farther because there was a different gauge of track ahead. So, they had to get out and hike a quarter-mile to the Piedmont Line to continue on to Richmond. If ever there was a time and a place to attempt an escape, this was it. But Billy wore shackles, and the rebel sergeant had warned him when they departed Andersonville, that if he tried to escape, they would not hesitate to shoot him.

The next morning two rebel guards brought a Confederate prisoner on board. He was pencil thin. His hair was long, dirty and matted down, and his clothes, except for a leather jacket, were tattered and filthy. The three sat down in an open row of seats in front of Billy but on the other side of the aisle.

"Take that window seat," said one of the guards.

"Aren't y'all afraid I might jest jump out the window?" said the prisoner.

"That's yo choice, lieutenant, suh, but ya'd jest be tradin' a rope fo' a bullet," the guard said with a wry little smile.

It was the voice that identified him, because the way he looked even his mother would have had difficulty recognizing him. But the voice, the voice had not changed.

"Why, I think I know that man," Billy said softly, as though talking to himself. The Confederate prisoner continued to talk, and Billy kept staring and listening.

"Charlie, Charlie Flynn?" Billy called out. Charlie turned and looked directly at him.

"Why, Aah'l be damned if it ain't ma old partner, Billy McHugh! What and the hell are you doin' on this train?"

"I've been asking myself that same question over and over again," Billy said. "The only answer I get is that I've been a fool."

"Birds of the feather, huh, Bobby?" said the rebel sergeant to another rebel guard.

"Where y'all takin' yo prisoner, corporal?"

"Richmond, how 'bout y'all?"

"This one's also goin' ta Richmond."

"Maybe not as foolish as me," Charlie said. "I took myself a walk, and they're fixin' ta hang me fo' it. But meetin you on this train has got to be one of the strangest coincidences of all time. How and the hell'd a lawyer like you livin up nawth end up a prisoner like me here in the South?"

"Why don't ya tell yo friend how you was spyin' fo' the Yankees in Mexico," said Billy's guard.

In spite of the heavy growth of beard on Charlie Flynn's face, no one could have missed his look of astonishment.

"Who would'a eva guessed that ma old friend, Billy McHugh, would'a gotten himself in such a mess! You and me shoulda stayed in California, partner. We'da both been millionaires by now."

"Sounds like ya got yoself a special prisoner there, sergeant," said Billy's guard. "This one's special too, ain't ya, lieutenant? We got a telegraph here sayin he's gonna be the one hundredth CSA deserter to be hanged. That makes him special too, don't ya think? Maybe President Jeff Davis ought to see that they be hung together. It would make a damn good story for the *Richmond Examiner*, don't ya think? Two old friends from Charleston, one of them winds up spyin' fo' the nawth, and the otha deserts and winds up with the title of 100th rebel deserter to be hung. A damn fine story! Don't y'all agree?..."

In spite of their long estrangement, Charlie seemed ready and willing to reach out to his old friend. Billy, however, was too despondent to reciprocate. When at last the train neared Richmond, they stopped for their final rest break. With his guards' consent, Charlie made his way over to Billy, and the two former friends began to talk.

"Ma mom told me you'd gotten hitched. Was it that Cuban gal? Uh, what was her name, Dolores?"

Billy nodded, his eyes misty, his expression sad and forlorn.

"I've been married for two years, Charlie, and I have a son who's a year old. He's in Cuba with Dolores. Funny, but I never thought I'd miss him."

The guards stood back, carefully watching the two prisoners, their colt revolvers at the ready. Just then, the train blew its whistle.

"Y'all keep it short, McHugh. We only got a few minutes," said the CSA sergeant.

"Aah got married too, Billy, would ya believe it? A damn fine woman, if Aah do say so maself. Good family, Virginia tobacco growers. Maggie's ma whole world now."

Until then there had been no sign of Charlie becoming emotional, but suddenly, his eyes filled with tears and he lowered his head.

"She don't know where I am, and don't know I am gonna be hung."

It had been more than three years since that day back in April of 1861 at the Charleston train depot, when Billy told Charlie he was going to Washington. Charlie considered Billy a traitor and a coward, but three years of war and their common tragic fate seemed now to melt the anger and resentment. And as the guards looked on, Charlie put his arm around Billy's shoulder and the two old friends embraced and talked animatedly.

"All right, y'all, let's get onboard," yelled the sergeant.

The guards bowed to their prisoners' request and allowed them to sit on the aisle seats adjacent to each other so they could continue to talk.

5

Joseph Bartlett looked down at the letter on his desk, his expression uncharacteristically grim. Just then, there was a knock on the door. Millie peeked in.

"Your tea's ready, Mr. Bartlett.

"I hope it's good and strong," he said.

"It's good and strong all right," said Millie. "Aah know how you like it, suh."

She placed the tray down on his desk.

"Oh, and Aah almost fogot. Mista Mitchum is waitin' ta see ya, suh." Bartlett nodded.

"Is there anything else Aah can get ya, suh?"

"No, that's all, Millie. Thank you." Bartlett put sugar in his tea, then picked up the letter and began reading it once more.

Dear Mister Bartlett:

My name is Bonnie McHugh. I'm the mother of Billy McHugh, and I'm in desperate need of your help. Billy was a passenger on the Caribbean Waters en route to Havana from Vera Cruz on June 28th. The vessel was stopped by a Confederate raider and he was taken prisoner and charged with being a spy for the North. I learned of Billy's fate from his wife, Dolores, who was in Havana and questioned the Captain of the vessel when Billy failed to appear. There's been a terrible mistake here, Mister Bartlett, and it could have deadly serious consequences. The CSA has been known to execute people on very little evidence. Billy's no spy, Mister Bartlett. He's a lawyer, and as you well know he was sent to Mexico on behalf of Henry Phipps & Partners. I recently lost my husband, Patrick, and God knows it's terribly difficult being all alone in Charleston, but I simply could not survive if anything were to happen to Billy...

Bonny McHugh had learned that Patrick's blockade runner, *The City of Mobile*, had been sunk by Admiral Farrugut's ironside offshore Cuba. There were no survivors.

Henry Phipps suddenly walked into Bartlett's office holding a letter.

"I have a letter here from Billy McHugh's wife, Dolores. It arrived last evening from Havana, but you had left for the day, Joseph, and I wasn't able to show it to you till now."

"I got one from Billy's mother in Charleston," said Bartlett, holding it up. "This is serious, Henry."

"It was Secretary Seward who gave him that espionage mission, not us. We sent him as a lawyer," said Phipps.

"That's a neat distinction, Henry, but you know as well as I do that we were trying to curry favor with the Secretary. Look, I have already contacted Secretary Seward and hope to get in to see him tomorrow. We need to act quickly. Billy's mother apparently hired a lawyer and they made inquiries and learned that the CSA are holding him in that infamous prison in Andersonville, Georgia. It is a dreadful place from what I have heard. According to Mrs. McHugh's letter, they will soon send him to Richmond, where he will be tried, likely convicted and hanged. His blood will be on my hands, Henry, because I offered him up to the Secretary."

Bartlett looked rattled, so much so that he spilled the tea on his handsome cravat.

"Calm down, Joseph, I'm sure Seward would be willing to consider a prisoner exchange. The rebels too will likely go along with it, depending of course on who we offer in exchange."

"You're right, Henry. I'm sure you are. They will work it out."

"Here's the letter from Billy's wife, Henry. Let me see the one you got from his mother." They exchanged letters and Phipps started to walk out, but stopped, turned and asked:

"Would you like me to accompany you to the State Department, Joseph?"

"No, I think not. I got us into this mess, and I'm obliged to get us out."

When Joseph Bartlett entered the Willard Hotel that afternoon, his first thought was that Secretary Seward's decision to meet there for lunch was a bad idea, because it was Friday, and the place was crowded for its weekly oyster fest.

"Good afternoon, Mister Bartlett! I haven't seen you in a while," said the maître d'. "How have you been?"

"Just fine Martin, thank you. I am meeting the Secretary of State for lunch this afternoon. Would it be possible to get one of your private rooms?"

The maître d' smiled.

"Why, of course, Mister Bartlett! How could we possibly deny such distinguished patrons? I will have our waiters prepare our best room for you right away, sir."

"Thank you, Martin."

Just then a loud round of applause broke out somewhere back in the dining hall.

"What's all the commotion, Martin?"

"It's General Grant and his son, Mr. Bartlett. I had the pleasure of taking his order a few minutes ago and found him to be quite approachable."

"Yes, he is that. I had the pleasure of meeting him once myself. Oh, here comes Secretary Seward now. Good afternoon, William."

"Good afternoon, Joseph." Seward looked into the dining room. "Oh, it's quite crowded, isn't it?"

"That's General Grant back there with his son. I'm glad he's here because he'll attract all the attention..."

"Your room is ready, Mister Bartlett," said the maître d'. "Follow me, gentlemen."

As they walked through a narrow hallway to the private dining rooms, Bartlett engaged in small talk with the Secretary, noticing his usual wrinkled suit, uncombed hair and overall unkempt appearance, something that had come to be the Secretary's calling card. No one, however, could deny his perspicacity and brilliance at formulating and directing the Nation's foreign policy during an extraordinarily difficult wartime setting.

The maître d' led them to a richly appointed dining room set for a table of six.

"Would you like some wine, perhaps, gentlemen?"

"Yes, Martin, some chilled white burgundy," said Bartlett, "and a dozen oysters to start."

"Make that two dozen!" said Secretary Seward.

"Right away, gentlemen. Enjoy your lunch." No sooner had the maître d' left than Bartlett cast a serious look at his friend.

"I'm sure you know that Billy McHugh was taken prisoner

by the Confederates on his way to Havana and was charged with espionage."

"Yes, of course, we're well aware of that, Joseph. My assistant, Jonathan Ambrose, is working on it this very moment."

The door opened and a waiter walked in with fresh-looking oysters and a bottle of white wine. Bartlett stared at Seward with a worried look on his face. Seward stared at the oysters.

"Don't they look delicious?" said the Secretary. "I hope you have more because I'm sure I could finish all of these myself, assuming Mister Bartlett here would let me."

"We have plenty more where those came from, sir," said the waiter, who filled their glasses with the white burgundy.

"Now for lunch, we have some fresh trout on the menu, gentlemen, and I highly recommend it."

"Ah, yes, the trout was excellent last time. I'll try it again."

"I'll have the same," said Bartlett.

"Bring us some more oysters also," said Seward."

"Right away, sir."

Seward continued to devour the oysters, looking up after swallowing two more.

"Henry and I both got letters, William, the one from Billy's mother in Charleston and the other from his wife in Cuba. I am deeply pained by Billy McHugh's predicament, William, and I feel directly responsible. Henry Phipps and I believe that a prisoner exchange would be a good way to handle this. You, of course would have to get Lincoln's approval. I know some time ago General Grant stopped the exchanges, saying it just gave the rebels more men to continue the war, but I believe that this should be an exception."

Seward stopped eating and looked directly at Bartlett.

"Well, Joseph, it would not be a general prisoner exchange. It's more like a swap, one prisoner for another. It just so happens that we have a good Confederate candidate; someone the South's wanted to get back for quite some time—Lucy May Thornton."

"That woman who was sleeping with the generals on both sides?"

"That's the one, Joseph. She is one of their preeminent spies, responsible for the deaths of thousands of our Union soldiers."

Seward paused, his expression turned pensive for a moment.

"Stanton, of course, will have to sign off on this, and that could be an obstacle. He would boil her in oil if he could, but I think the President will bring him around if need be."

"What about the Confederates? Are you sure they'll go for a prisoner swap?"

"They'd do a lot more than that, Joseph, to get Lucy May back."

The door opened, and a parade of waiters walked in with the trout, fresh vegetables, and another bottle of white burgundy. Secretary Seward smiled, then popped the last of the oysters into his mouth and washed them down with the white wine.

"You'll keep me informed, William?"

"Of course, but for the moment how about if we just enjoy our lunch?"

6

It was mid-morning and the Confederate Secretary of State, Judah Benjamin, a Jew, walked briskly down K Street in Richmond. The man the northern press called "the brains of the Confederacy," approached the Executive Mansion. He walked under a low-lying oak tree that brushed against his top hat. Pausing, he straightened it before climbing the stairs to the stately structure. He was greeted by the negro doorman and a lone soldier standing guard.

"Good monin' Mista Benjamin, suh."

"Good morning, Clarence," said the Secretary, removing his hat and handing it to the doorman.

As he climbed the stairs to the second-floor office, he wondered about the President's health. He knocked on the door.

"Come in," said the President in a louder than usual voice, which caused him to wheeze slightly.

Benjamin entered, smiled and sat down in a wing chair in front of the President's desk.

"How are you feeling today, Jefferson?"

"I would feel a whole lot better if I could shake this malaria, Judah."

Secretary Benjamin looked at the President, well aware of just how much he had aged under the crushing weight of his Office.

"The President picked up a file on his desk.

"I presume you've seen this Evacuation Plan Secretary Sodden put together." Benjamin leaned forward in his chair.

"Yes, Mister President, I've seen it, and I must say that the Secretary would have done well to consult with the Mayor of Richmond before laying out all the details, details of which he obviously has very little actual knowledge."

"Are conditions really so dire that we need to plan now for the evacuation of our Capital?" asked the President. "It seems to me that if the public were to get hold of this, it could incite a state of panic. It's all terribly premature and unwarranted by my way of thinking."

"That's my sentiment as well," said Secretary Benjamin. "I would suggest that we get together with Secretary Sodden and the mayor and review the matter.

There's also this proposed prisoner swap that we need to decide," said Benjamin, holding up the letter he had received from Ethan Hitchcock, the Union's representative for prisoner exchanges.

"Let me say at the outset, Jefferson, that I am against the swap. This man McHugh is a turncoat and a spy. He was born and raised in Charleston, but when the War broke out, he came north. He's a practicing lawyer, Jefferson, but for some reason the Yankees sent him to Mexico to spy on our activities. He was there almost a year and had an affair with the wife of our confidential agent, José Quintero. Apparently, she was his main source of information. By my way of thinking this man should be hanged."

The President looked intensely at his Secretary of State, nodding as though in agreement.

"But I understand, Judah, that Robert Ould, our prisoner exchange man, is working on a plan with the Union's Hitchcock to swap him for our Lucy May Thornton. So, it seems to me that if we back out now and hang McHugh, they will hang Lucy May."

"They have never executed a woman, Jefferson. I don't think Lincoln would let them."

"Nonetheless, Judah, if we have the chance to get Miss Lucy May released, don't you think we should? Don't you believe that we owe it to her."

The President got up, walked to the window and looked down on the Street.

"The folks down there need some uplifting, Judah, and if we can bring Lucy May home, they will get it. Trust me, Judah, we need to do this swap."

There was a knock on the door, and a negro servant brought in their lunch. As the two most powerful leaders of the Confederate States of America ate their lunch, the President opened his desk drawer and took out a letter.

"I got a letter here, Judah, from my old friend, Francis Burke. His daughter, Maggie, is the wife of this South Carolina Cavalry

Lieutenant, Charlie Flynn, who deserted. They sent him here to be hanged, and I am between a rock and a hard place on this one, Judah. You and I both know that General Lee is insisting that we do something to stem the flow of these desertions. Though I strongly condemn what this lieutenant did, deserting his comrades and his country in their time of need, Burke is counting on me to grant his son-in-law a pardon. There is a big hubbub over this case, Judah. Somebody determined that cavalry lieutenant Charlie Flynn would be the 100th deserter to be hanged, and the *Richmond Examiner* and even some Yankee newspapers, are playing it up real big. I am stymied, Judah, and don't know which way to turn."

"The way I see it, Jefferson, you've got no choice. You have to go ahead and execute this deserter," said Secretary Benjamin. "General Lee has been very merciful. As you well know, he has asked you to grant many pardons. But all that has changed, and mercy must give way now to discipline and expediency. General Lee has reached his limit on pardons, and the country has as well."

The President nodded, seemingly in agreement with his Secretary of State, but he remained silent, keeping his decision to himself.

7

The Richmond Examiner October 14, 1864
The One Hundreth CSA Deserter and a Yankee Spy to Share the Gallows.

First Lieutenant Charlie Flynn of the 1st South Carolina Cavalry Company E will have the honor of being the 100th Confederate deserter to be hanged. His partner on the gallows will be Billy McHugh,

*a Yankee spy. The two condemned men hail from
Charleston, South Carolina and were good friends
before the War. The commandant of Castle Thunder
prison, Lieutenant Dennis Callahan, stated that a
small public audience will be admitted to the prison
grounds to witness the executions...*

It was October 15 1864 and Charlie's pardon had not mate-
rialized. As for Billy, he had not received the final word on the
prisoner swap.

As the two old friends walked about in the exercise yard under
the watchful eyes of rebel sharpshooters, they talked of nothing
but their hoped-for releases.

"If ma pardon don't come through, Billy, I'm gonna bust outta
this Castle Thunder prison."

"That won't be easy, Charlie. Those guards up there are
trigger-happy, and they take great pleasure in shooting escapees,
especially when they're deserters and spies. You saw what happened to that Yankee Ohio corporal. They shot him full of holes
before he had a chance to climb that wall. Besides, you are in no
condition to break out of here. You're half-starved and skinny as
a rail, just like the rest of us. You're too weak to make it over that
wall, Charlie."

"So, you are advisin' me not to attempt it? Come on partner,
that's easy for you to say. Your government's gonna spring you, but
there's not been a word bout ma presidential pardon. So, I don't
have a choice. I've got to think about escapin'. It comes down to
this, Billy. Wouldn't you too choose a bullet over a hangin'? It's a
helluva lot quicker and less painful."

"I'm sorry, Charlie, I didn't mean to—"

"At least it's a chance, a slim chance, but a chance nonetheless.
What chance would I have after they walk me up to the gallows

and put that rope round ma neck? Ya get ma point? Of course, I still got two weeks, and ole President Davis still might come through for me. Ma father-in-law, Francis Burke, is a good friend of Jefferson Davis', and he's doin' all he can to get him to issue me a pardon..."

It was two o'clock in the morning of October 31 1864--Halloween. Billy's prisoner exchange was finalized just days before, subject only to last minute details on the release date for Lucy May Thornton. There was no word on Charlie Flynn's Presidential pardon, and it was clear now that there would be none.

Most prisoners were asleep in their dream world, having escaped for a while from the horror of their waking hours. Charlie Flynn and Billy McHugh, however, were wide awake. They whispered back and forth in their lice-infested bunks.

"I met a rebel sergeant in the latrine, Billy, and he said they're gonna replace yo spot on the gallows with that Yank who spit in Callahan's face. I'm jealous of ya, partner, and Aah'd be lyin' if I said I wasn't. But I gotta do what I gotta do, and it's time for me to make ma move."

They got up from their bunks and walked quietly to the back of the barracks. In spite of the darkness, Billy could see the fear on Charlie's face.

"You want me to come to the latrine with you? You might need some help to get through that window."

"That's mighty kind and brave of ya, Billy, but ya don't wanna be seen with me, not now, whether or not I make it outta here. You'd be charged with aidin' ma escape, and they'd string you up after all. You wanna help me, Billy? Pray for me. You've always been good at prayin', partner."

"I'll pray for you, Charlie, I'll pray real hard," Billy said, his eyes now misty.

"I wrote letters to ma wife, Maggie, and ma mom, and I'd be much obliged if you'd post them for me." Charlie handed them to Billy, who was struck with pangs of guilt, for he would be returning to his beloved Dolores, while Charlie almost certainly would never see his loved ones again.

"I really wish ya coulda met Maggie, Billy. She's one fine woman, the light of my life. I really didn't deserve her, didn't deserve all the love she gave me. We were plannin' on havin a family. Maggie wanted that real bad, and I did too. It shoulda been..." Charlie's words trailed off now, as he lowered his head and weeped.

"There's still hope, Charlie, and with God's help you can make it out of here."

"Aah want ya ta know, Billy, that it don't matter a whit ta me that ya went nawth. You're still ma best friend, partner, and Aah love ya like a brother."

The words moved Billy to tears.

"You don't know how much that means to me, Charlie. You've always been like a brother to me." The two old friends embraced one last time.

"It's time to go. Wish me luck, partner and start prayin'."

"Good luck, partner, and God willing I will see you in Charleston." Billy watched as Charlie started walking slowly along the rows of bunks to the guard station. The guard was half-asleep and slumped over, but he sprang up as Charlie approached.

"Aah need ta relieve myself, suh." The guard stood up.

"Make it quick, ya hear?" he said as he unlocked the door.

Billy looked out the window, watching as Charlie walked toward the latrine. He stayed glued to that window and prayed. He saw Charlie enter the latrine. Several minutes passed and Billy thought maybe, just maybe his prayers had been answered.

Pop, Pop, Pop, Pop Pop.

William C. McHugh was released from Castle Thunder Prison on December 24 1864. The Provost Marshall issued a Letter of Marque, authorizing Billy to pass through Confederate territory to the Union lines. As he walked out the gate a free man, Charlie's face flashed before him, followed by the macabre image of that Confederate guard pushing the wheelbarrow that bore Charlie's body to the pit, where he dumped it like so much trash.

PART V

Winter 1864–Fall 1867

CHAPTER XVI

❦

Can't Hide Him

The B&O Station was crowded with soldiers and holiday travelers. Dolores shivered, as she stood on the platform with Sebastián asleep in her arms. Mother and child had been back in Washington only recently and had not yet acclimated to the cold.

"Wake up, Sebastián. Your papá is coming." Sebastián yawned and rubbed his eyes.

"Your papá's train will be here shortly." No sooner had the words left her lips, than she heard a whistle blow.

"Twain, twain!" said Sebastián.

"Yes, train, your papá's train. Here it comes," Dolores said, as the train blew its whistle and drew near.

"Papá's twain," Sebastián said, his voice loud and full of excitement, his little face beaming.

The train pulled into the station. A conductor standing in the doorway of the middle car called out:

"B and O Station, Washington, last stop," after which a flood of blue-uniformed soldiers rushed out of the cars, whooping and hollering as they went.

Little Sebastián stood mesmerized at the sight of the locomotive, and Dolores had to tug him along as she moved closer to the passenger cars.

"Twain, twain", Sebastián said, again and again.

"Hurry, Sebastián. Let's find your papá." Billy, however, was nowhere in sight. Finally, when the only ones left on the platform were railroad people, she spotted a lone figure exiting from the very last car, walking slowly toward them with a noticeable limp.

"Billy, Billy!" Dolores shouted, waving excitedly. "There's your papá, Sebastián!"

Her heart raced, and she picked up Sebastián and ran to meet her long-lost husband.

"Doloresita," cried Billy, as he threw his arms around her and smothered them both with hugs and kisses.

"I was so worried, Billy, but you are finally here." She kissed him and cried for joy.

"Where's papá?" asked Sebastián.

"This is your papá, Sebastián. Oh, he does not remember you, Billy. He was just a baby when you left."

"Where's papá?" Sebastián repeated as Dolores put him down.

"He was used to calling his grandfather 'papa', mi amor," Billy paid it no mind, while Dolores noticed just how thin and gaunt Billy was.

"I'm cold, mamá!" said Sebastián, shivering. Dolores picked him up again and held him at eye level with Billy. Billy reached out and rubbed Sebastián's curly-top head of thick brown hair. And as he looked at him again, he was struck with the stark realization of Sebastián's *sangre de negro*.

He looks even darker than before.

Billy hadn't thought about the problem once he had left Washington, and he tried now to put it out of his mind.

Dolores put Sebastián down again, and the three of them started walking out of the station.

"Billy, I was able to lease a nice flat in the same building. Julius and Becky have been helping us, and they are so anxious to see you, *mi amor*. That's all they've been talking about..."

Billy was barely listening and glanced again at Sebastián.

You must not blame him. He is just an innocent child. He didn't choose his skin color. It's not his fault.

"And I spoke with Mister Meadows at the Congressional School, Billy, and he said there might still be an opening for me."

Billy did not respond.

"I'm cold, mamá."

"We'll be home soon, Sebastián. We must start talking to him in English, Billy, because he only speaks Spanish now, and we must prepare him for school."

As they walked down the platform, Dolores became more aware of Billy's weakened condition. He walked with some difficulty and seemed to be in pain. When she asked him about it, he told her that he was suffering from leg ulcers.

"You must see a doctor, Billy, tomorrow at the latest. Come on, Sebastián, Let's take your papá home and cook him a nice meal.

As they reached the exit, they noticed a days' old copy of the *Washington Star* sitting atop a baggage wagon:

Sherman Takes Savannah Next Stop the Carolinas

"The newspapers say the war will be over by spring," said Dolores. "I just hope and pray that your mother will be safe in Charleston. I have not heard from her since I left Cuba. Billy. We were so saddened to learn of your father's death."

Billy stopped short in his tracks, and looked at Dolores.

"What did you say?"

"Oh, Billy, you didn't know, did you? Of course, not, how

could you? You were in the Confederate prison. I'm so sorry to be the one to tell you."

"What happened to him?" Billy asked, his tone sounding angry, as though Dolores, the bearer of the bad news, was somehow responsible for it.

"A Union gunboat sank his vessel. We read it in the Havana newspapers. It said he was running the blockade."

Billy's face turned even paler than it had been, and for a second he looked like he would burst into tears. However, he regained control, and they started walking again, as Billy's tangled, conflicting feelings for his father played out silently within him. It was just a few short weeks since his dear friend, Charlie Flynn, was shot and killed, and now his father.

"We were all so terribly upset and saddened, Billy. Patrick came to Cuba just before you were due to arrive, and we had such a wonderful visit. He was very happy to see his grandson for the first time."

Billy's thoughts now turned to his mother. She was all alone in Charleston; and if Sherman were to do to Charleston what he had done to Atlanta, there would be great death and destruction.

A cold and blustery wind greeted them out on the street, and mindful of Billy's weakened condition, Dolores took it upon herself to hail a carriage.

"You wait here with Sebastián, Billy, and I'll see if I can find a carriage."

Sebastián tried to follow his mother, and Billy had to hold him back. Billy's thoughts turned to the happy times he had had with his father: when Patrick had taken him fishing; when he had sailed with him on *The Wandering Maiden*; when he taught him to ride a horse and helped him with his lessons. He recalled his mother's letter, urging him to reconcile with his father. But it was too late now. Billy looked up and saw Dolores signaling that she had found a carriage.

"Ride with Mickey, ride with Mickey," Sebastián cried. He tried to run, pulling Billy's hand to get him to walk faster. "That's a different horsie. That's not Mickey. Where's Mickey?"

"Mickey's not here today, Sebastián. But this is a very nice horsie."

The coachman took hold of Sebastián, lifted him up and placed him in Dolores's arms, turning then to Billy, who waved him off and stepped up himself, grimacing as he did so.

"Mickey's a horse that Sebastián has befriended. He feeds him apples, don't you Sebastián?"

"Mickey tickles my hand," said Sebastián.

"My horse's name is Comet," said the coachman. "You can give him a lump of sugar when we get you home." Dolores told Sebastián in Spanish, and he got very excited, smiling with delight.

"Tell the coachman 'thank you,'" Sebastián, said Dolores, pronouncing the words slowly and phonetically for him.

"Tank you," repeated Sebastián in English.

"We're teaching him English," added Dolores. "He's been living in Cuba, where they speak Spanish."

"Oh, it's nice and warm there year round, isn't it? How nice. Now, where can I take you, ma'am?"

Dolores gave him the directions, and they rode off. Billy remained somber throughout this exchange and all during the ride home.

2

Three weeks passed since Billy's return. His leg ulcers were healing, and he had gained some weight. All in all his convalescence was proceeding satisfactorily.

Dolores had gone out for a walk with Sebastián. Billy was

sitting in an easy chair with a blanket around him, when there came a knock on the door.

"Jest sit still, Massa Billy. Aah'l git da door," Becky said.

"Well, there he is home safe and sound," said Joseph Bartlett, standing there with Henry Phipps. The appearance of the two senior partners was unexpected, and Billy immediately felt uncomfortable.

"Come right in, Mister Phipps, Mister Bartlett, it's so good to see you," Billy said.

Becky smiled, stepped out of the way, and the two senior partners shook Billy's hand.

"Don't get up, Billy. We know you need your rest," said Bartlett, smiling broadly

"Please sit down, gentlemen. Oh, we need another chair, and Becky, maybe you could make us some tea."

"Sho 'nuf, Massa Billy."

"I've been trying to break Becky of her habit of calling me 'Master' but she keeps right on doing it," Billy said.

Phipps and Bartlett both smiled. Phipps took a seat in the other easy chair. Becky returned with a straight back chair for Mister Bartlett.

"The sofa hasn't arrived yet. This is a new flat for us," said Billy, "and we're still getting it set up."

"We understand," said Henry Phipps, "and that's not important. What is important is that you're home and you're safe and we all thank God for that."

"Amen!" said Joseph Bartlett, who smiled, put his hand on Billy's shoulder and continued. "I must tell you, Billy, that I very much regret having agreed to lend you to the State Department. If I had known what was in store for you…"

"Oh, you need not regret anything, Mister Bartlett," interrupted

Billy. "I went willingly. It was in fact a great honor. You couldn't have known what the future held."

"It was Secretary of State Seward who'd brought up the idea, and I didn't want to disappoint him. On balance I thought it would be good for you and good for the firm as well."

Becky came in with a pot of tea and some sweet biscuits and put them down on the table.

"Thank you, Becky," said Billy, smiling and taking her by the hand. "I don't know what I'd do without this woman. She's been with me since I was a child and takes such good care of me."

Becky beamed with appreciation.

"Oh, but, Massa Billy, it's yo sweet wife who look afta ya so good. Aah jest looks afta lil Sebastián and do da chores. He sho is a sweet child, lil Sebastián is."

"May I pour you some tea, gentlemen?" Billy asked as he leaned up slightly in his chair.

"You just relax, young man. We'll pour it," Bartlett said.

Henry Phipps picked up the teapot and filled the three cups. Then he reached for one of Becky's sweet biscuits.

"You've certainly returned at an interesting time, Billy. The firm has been expanding at a very rapid rate. Our clientele has more than doubled in the past year. We've had to hire more law-yers to handle all the work, and..."

"Tell him about the Central American project, Henry," inter-jected Bartlett.

"I'm going to let you tell him about that, Joseph," said Phipps, continuing: "and we've had to lease another floor in our building. If things continue like that, we will need more space next year at this time. I don't think you knew about this before you left, Billy, but we are now sole legal advisors for the Union Pacific. We are involved in every aspect of their business from land acquisition and rights of way to trial work in the courts. We advise on their financing and help them raise capital as well…"

Billy heard the key turning in the lock, and a second later the door opened, and in walked Dolores with little Sebastián. Phipps and Bartlett both stood up.

"Mrs. McHugh! How good to see you," said Henry Phipps. "Oh, and this is your little boy."

"Hello, Mister Phipps. What a pleasant surprise," said Dolores. "Yes, this is Sebastián. Say hello, Sebastián."

Sebastián smiled shyly and struggled to pronounce the English word.

"You've been in Cuba, haven't you, Mrs. McHugh? We got your letters and they were very helpful," said Joseph Bartlett.

Becky heard Dolores's voice and came back into the room, whereupon Sebastián quickly ran over to her.

"Yes, we were in Cuba while Billy was in Mexico, so Sebastián only speaks Spanish, but Billy and I are teaching him English. Or perhaps I should say Billy more than I. He's much more of a linguist, aren't you, my love?" Dolores said, reaching out for Billy's hand, which had instantly turned clammy.

Billy forced a weak smile, but it immediately turned sour. Then he gestured to Becky, who got the message, and took Sebastián back to the kitchen.

"But don't let me interrupt your conversation," said Dolores. "Sebastián and I were just out for a walk."

"Oh, please, it's no interruption. Won't you sit and chat a while?"

"I'd love to, but you'll have to excuse me for now. Sebastián is hungry; it's his lunchtime," said Dolores, smiling as she walked back to the kitchen.

"All right, Joseph, now tell him about the Central American project."

Bartlett smiled and then looked at Billy very seriously.

"You're going to like this Billy, I promise you. We are now representing Mister Minor C. Keith, the railroad, lumber, and shipping tycoon. He wants to build a railroad across Costa Rica, acquire land and cultivate bananas for shipment to New Orleans. He would market them throughout the United States and possibly even in Europe, aboard his fleet of steamers. You are to be his lead counsel and will be involved in every phase of this project right from the very beginning, including the financing and negotiation of the principal contracts with the Costa Rican Government. We'll set up a meeting with Minor Keith the week you return to work, so that should be an incentive for you to make a rapid recovery."

All of a sudden, little Sebastián ran into the room, smiling, giggling, and holding a large wooden spoon, his face covered with what looked like chocolate. Billy's face immediately flushed. Phipps and Bartlett chuckled. Becky then walked in, and Sebastián ducked down behind Billy's armchair, giggling all the while.

"Y'all escuse me, genelmen. A lil boy bin lickin da chocolate icin pot and done took ma bakin' spoon," said Becky, giggling some herself, "and Aah needs it ta finish ma cake".

Dolores then came in looking for Sebastián, who then ske-daddled behind Mister Phipps' armchair. Dolores went over and began speaking to him in Spanish, trying to coax him out from behind the chair. But he continued to giggle and duck out of her reach. It was only when she promised him a big piece of chocolate cake that he surrendered the spoon and came out from behind the chair. The whole scene was quite comical, cute, and amusing to everyone, and they all laughed, everyone, that is, except Billy. He directed a cold hard look at Dolores, leaving no doubt that he wanted Sebastián out of the room and out of sight. Dolores took him by the hand now, smiled and walked him into the kitchen.

The talk continued, and Phipps and Bartlett briefed Billy on all the happenings at the firm, including the sad news of the sons of personnel who had been killed in the war.

"Well, Billy, we know that you still need your rest, so we best be getting along," said Bartlett. "I know you'll start thinking about the Costa Rican venture. It's a wonderful opportunity for you and the firm." Billy started to get up.

"No, don't bother yourself," said Mister Phipps. We can see ourselves out."

"All right, Billy, take good care and we'll see you soon," said Phipps.

In spite of Phipps' having told him not to, Billy got up and showed the two senior partners to the door, all the while wondering what they thought, having discovered that he was the father of a mulatto child.

Out on the street, a fancy black and white carriage stood waiting for the two prominent lawyers, a light-skinned mulatto coachman at the reins. The coachman jumped down, opened the door for them and they climbed inside.

"Where to, Mister Phipps?" asked the coachman.

"Back to the office, Francis."

"Giddy up, Mickey," said the coachman, snapping the reins.

"What do you make of that mulatto child, Joseph?" Bartlett did not respond at first. He was looking out the window where a group of negroes, supervised by two white overseers, were busy digging up the street.

"I don't know what to make of it, Henry. Perhaps they adopted him."

"You don't suppose his wife had a child in Cuba before she married Billy, do you? Of course that would be putting a more favorable face on it than other interpretations I can think of."

Bartlett turned and faced his partner.

"And just what would those *other interpretations* be, pray tell?"

"Well, Billy McHugh wouldn't be the first man to be cuck-olded, and..."

"Oh, that's absurd, Henry," interrupted Bartlett. "Billy McHugh is not the kind of man to sprout horns, and besides, his wife is a sweet and lovely woman, and we have no right or reason to think otherwise."

"Calm down, Joseph. I am not accusing either one of them. I'm just saying that it's peculiar that they have a mulatto child."

Phipps had a querulous expression on his face. "You don't suppose his wife has black blood, do you?"

"His wife's as white as you, Henry. And even if she weren't, what of it? Our firm has been proud of its progressive politics."

"That's all well and good, Joseph, but what about Minor Keith? He did not support Lincoln. He's a conservative, and so are many of our other clients."

"You're making the proverbial mountain out of the mole hill, Henry. Billy McHugh is the lawyer not his wife and child."

No sooner had Phipps and Bartlett left the flat, when Billy shouted for Dolores to come into the living room. Dolores came in from the kitchen, and he motioned for her to sit down in the armchair next to him as he struggled to modulate his anger.

"How many times have I told you to keep Sebastián out of sight and especially out of sight of my bosses!"

"I'm truly sorry, my love. I had no idea they were here. How could I have known? But it will be all right. Sebastián was so cute, and you saw how they reacted and laughed. I'm sure they won't hold it against you, Billy."

"You better hope for my sake and for yours as well that they don't."

Dolores was about to respond but reconsidered, afraid she would only make things worse.

"I want to make partner, Dolores. Do you hear me? partner

in what is considered to be one of the premier law firms in this country. Do you know what a partnership in Henry Phipps & Partners means to me?"

"I know what it means to you, but..."

"Do you know what it means for you?" Billy interrupted. "It means a big, beautiful house in the nicest section of Washington. It means admittance into the highest echelons of society. It means wealth, trips to Europe, social status, and a life of comfort and prestige. It means..."

"And what does it mean for our son!" Dolores said, raising her voice and interrupting her husband, something quite out of character for her. "What does it mean for Sebastián ? Will we continue to have to hide him, hide him from your partners, hide him from your clients, hide him from our own friends, disrupting his development and depriving him of a normal childhood?"

"You're the origin of that problem, you and your family," shouted Billy angrily.

Dolores's face flushed. He had touched a raw nerve, and her emotions rapidly ran the gamut from pain to anger to sadness.

"You knew all about me and my family, Billy, and you never complained. You said you loved me. You said you wanted to spend the rest of your life with me!"

"I do love you, Dolores."

"What about Sebastián? What about your son? Do you love him, Billy?"

She burst out crying, unable to hold back the pent up pain and sadness she had been forced to endure. "If you don't love Sebastián, you don't love me."

She cried hard now, sobbing, laying her head on the arm of the chair, hoping that he'd come and comfort her, hoping that he'd tell her that everything would be all right.

He got up and walked out of the room.

3

Billy made a full and rapid recovery, and returned to his law practice at Henry Phipps & Partners. Bartlett arranged a luncheon with Minor C. Keith, and it all went very well. Keith was duly impressed with Billy's astuteness, drive, and fluency in Spanish. The following week, Keith sent two of his key subordinates to the law firm, and they began planning the first stage of the Costa Rican venture—a series of meetings with the Costa Rican Minister of Finance and the Minister of Transportation and Commerce, both of whom were in Washington.

Dolores, meanwhile, had accepted a substitute teaching assignment at the Congressional School.

With the approach of spring, all eyes focused on the long and bloody siege of Petersburg, Virginia. It was common knowledge that when it fell, the Confederate Capital of Richmond would soon follow, ending the long and bloody Civil War.

As for Sebastián, he seemed to be growing taller and cuter by the day. His bubbly, mischievous personality served to ingratiate everyone with whom he came in contact. Billy, however, remained adamant that they should keep him out of sight and turn him over to Becky and Julius when necessary. He became even more insistent after it appeared that as Sebastián grew older, he seemed to be taking on a darker hue. Dolores suffered terribly because of these constraints, but as a loyal wife, she tried her best to obey her husband, endeavoring nonetheless to provide her son with a semblance of normalcy. Becky usually took Sebastián for walks and completed necessary chores for him at home. Dolores did not, however, yield her maternal and parental rights and responsibilities, nor was she willing to do so.

One bright and sunny day in spring, Dolores decided to take

Sebastián with her to visit Julie Mitchum, who had a flat near the Capitol. Julie had a son about the same age as Sebastián. Dolores had mentioned the proposed visit to Billy and he had not objected. As Dolores walked out of their flat and approached the street, a carriage drove slowly by as though waiting for a fare. Sebastián immediately spotted his favorite horse.

"Mickey, mamá, Mickey." he cried, jumping up and down excitedly. The carriage came to a halt. "Mickey, Mickey, mamá!" he said, tugging her hand.

"Good afternoon, Mrs. McHugh," said Francis, as he jumped down from the carriage. "By any chance does your husband work for Henry Phipps & Partners?"

Sebastián broke away now and ran up to Mickey. The horse whinnied and licked his little hand.

"Come here, Sebastián," Dolores called out, responding then to Francis. "Yes, he does."

Francis helped Dolores into the cab.

"I thought so. I drove Mister Phipps and Mister Bartlett here some time back." Dolores called out again to Sebastián. "Don't worry, Mrs. McHugh. I'll bring him." Francis walked up now to the horse, picked him up and brought him back to Dolores.

"Mickey horsie wants apple," Sebastián said in his broken English.

"Well, now, young man, it just so happens that I have an apple. And you can give it to him when we get you to where you're going."

Francis reached into his pocket and pulled out a nice red apple, which he gave to Sebastián, who continued to chatter about Mickey in Spanish and English.

"This is not the same carriage that we've ridden in before, is it?" Dolores asked. Francis drove off, sliding open the little window to the cab so he could talk as he drove.

"No, you're right. This is a different carriage, ma'am. I have several carriages, several drivers as well, all of it thanks to President Lincoln. Two years ago, he got the Congress to repeal the City's Black Code that had been in force since the 1840s. Under those laws, negroes who came to Washington had to register and post a bond just to be here. They were prohibited from engaging in any remunerative activities other than carriage drivers. That's when I started my own business, ma'am."

"You are to be commended, Francis."

"Thank you, Mrs. McHugh. But I can tell you that even without the Black Code it's still not easy for black folk here in Washington."

"Mickey wants apple."

"Hold your horses, Sebastián. We're almost there," Dolores said. But he continued to fuss.

The carriage pulled up to the Mitchums' flat, and by this time, Sebastián was beside himself with excitement. He began opening the carriage door and was poised to jump out, when Francis came to the rescue, picked him up and carried him up to Mickey.

"Look, Mickey!" said Sebastián, wearing a devilish little grin and holding out the apple only to quickly draw it back.

"Don't tease him, Sebastián. That's not nice," said Dolores.

This time he held out the apple and Mickey started chewing. Sebastián laughed with delight.

"He tickles, mama."

Dolores paid the fare, adding a generous tip. Francis thanked her, and as was his usual practice, he stood by the carriage and watched as they walked up the path, departing only when they entered the building.

Julie Mitchum was a plain looking woman, and Dolores was surprised the first time she had seen her son, Jackie, who was as cute as a button. It was clear that Jackie inherited his good looks from his dad, Brad Mitchum. Henry Phipps & Partners hired Brad about the same time they hired Billy. The Mitchums were from Saint Louis, Missouri. Brad was Billy's closest friend in the firm, and the two couples saw each other frequently, attending the firm's social and cultural events throughout the city. This, however, would be the first time that their two little boys would play together.

"It's so good to see you, Dolores. Oh, and this is Sebastián. He's taller now since the last time I saw him. What a cute little fellow."

"This is Mrs. Mitchum, Sebastián. Say hello, Mrs. Mitchum." Sebastián struggled to repeat the words.

"Oh, and it sounds like his English is improving also. Jackie, Sebastián is here. Come on out and say hello," Julie said.

Seconds later Jackie appeared, carrying a little blanket and sucking his thumb. Sebastián went over, sat on the floor, and began playing with the toy soldiers. That got Jackie's attention, and he dropped his blanket, stopped sucking his thumb and rushed over to assert his ownership.

"We've tried everything to get him to stop the thumb sucking, but he persists." Julie said.

"I'm sure it will pass. He is still very young, Julie. Give him time."

"I hope you're right, Dolores. Let's go into the kitchen, and I'll make some tea."

They both looked over at the two little boys, who began playing together peacefully.

The two women sat and talked about everything, from their husbands' heavy workloads to their in-laws. Just then, Jackie and Sebastián ran into the kitchen, asking for some sweets. Julie went to the cupboard and returned with a jar of jellied candies. When she gave Sebastián his candy, Jackie suddenly reached out and grasped Sebastián's hand.

"Look, mama, Sebastián has funny hands. This side is white and the other side is brown." Sebastián paid it no mind whatsoever and ate his candy, asking then for another. Julie smiled but remained silent. Dolores did not. She looked directly at Jackie and surprised even herself by saying:

"Sebastián has Cuban blood, Jackie, proud Cuban blood."

4

The Rebel fortifications and supply depot at Petersburg, Virginia, was under Union siege for almost a year. On April 3 1865, it finally fell. Later that day, Richmond fell, and within a week, Lee surrendered to Grant at Appomattox Station. The long and bloody War was finally over, and the Nation breathed a sigh of relief. Celebrations erupted throughout the Capital and the country. Black folk were jubilant and hopeful. Mostly everyone was, but there were still many die-hard Rebel supporters in the city. And just five days after Lee's surrender, one of them, actor John Wilkes Booth, played the real life role of assassin, shooting and killing President Lincoln while he was attending a play at Washington's Ford Theatre. The Nation was stunned and went into shock. Negroes felt an indescribable loss. The cowardly Booth had suddenly and tragically assassinated their Savier. What would now be their fate? Would they be cast again into slavery?

Before Lincoln's death, rumors had been circulating in Washington that former slaves would be allocated "forty acres of land and a mule." As a result, many began planning to return to the South to start a new life as freemen farmers.

One Saturday morning in early summer, Billy was home alone

going over some draft contracts. It was Becky's day off, and Dolores had taken Sebastián to the park. There was a knock on the door. It was Julius, and he was carrying a night table, which he had made for their bedroom. It was a model of fine craftsmanship, and Billy was pleased and grateful as always.

"It's beautiful, Julius. Come into the kitchen with me. I want to pay you right now."

"No need ta pay me now, Billy. Next week gonna be fine, when Aah finish dem chairs." Billy insisted that he pay him now, and did so.

"Thank ya, Billy. Dat's mo den genrous of ya, but iffen ya got a minute, ders somethin Aah'd like ta talk ta ya bout."

"Of course, Julius, Have a seat. What's on your mind?"

Julius sat down, reached into his breast pocket and took out a wrinkled page from the *Charleston Courier,* which he handed to Billy.

"Ma boy, Clarence, send me dis newspapa bout free land fo forma slaves in Charleston. We was hopin ya can help us unda-stand dis Special Orda from Genral Sherman."

Billy started reading it silently, but Julius asked him to read it out loud.

> "Major General William T. Sherman Special Field Orders, No. 15, January 16, 1865, providing for land to be allocated to former black slaves: the islands from Charleston, south, the abandoned rice fields along the rivers for thirty miles back from the sea, and the country bordering the St. Johns River, Florida…"

Julius spoke up immediately. "Aah sho does like da sound o dat, Billy. Ma boys want me and Becky ta come back on home ta

Charleston and git us a piece o dat land. Dey also say dat da Army gonna give us mules fo plowin."

Other than having heard that President Lincoln had advocated allocating land for former slaves, Billy knew nothing about Sherman's Order. He immediately thought of his parents' house and land holdings. Upon the death of his father, the house would legally belong to his mother. However, he remembered his surprise when he found a negro family residing in the house during his last visit to Charleston.

"Anyways, Billy, befo me and Becky consida packin up and goin back ta Charleston, we needs ta know iffen we really gonna git dat land and dat it's legal and all."

Billy put the Order down on the table and looked directly at Julius.

"Well, if Lincoln were alive, you'd have much less to worry about, Julius. But it's still too early to know what President Johnson will do."

Julius' expression turned sad, and he shook his head slowly and then bowed it, bringing both hands up to cover his face as though he wanted to hide from the world. When he uncovered his face, there were tears in his eyes.

"God, how po Presdent Lincoln done suffad durin da War, and now when it finely ova, he don't git to see da peace. How could dey do dat to da Presdent of da United States of America? What kinda people are dey, Billy?"

"Bad people, Julius. The War caused a lot of anger, a lot of hate. And it is going to be hard to put it all behind us, reconcile with our former enemies and heal the Nation's wounds. And as for that land referred to in Sherman's Order, it seems to me that the present owners will certainly have something to say about the Government trying to take it away, no matter how good and right a cause it may be."

Julius wiped his eyes. "So yo sayin dat we shoulden count on gitten dat land?"

"That's right, Julius, not just yet anyway. You need to wait and see what develops."

Julius thanked Billy and got up to leave.

"Oh, and befo Aah fogets, Billy, der's somethin else dat Aah been meanin to say to ya." Julius' expression turned very serious.

"Aah know dat it's none o ma business, and Aah begs ya ta fogive me, Billy. Becky has been wit da McHughs fo decades and Aah been wid ya a long time too. Y'all been family ta us, and yo and me's been mo den jest friends. Ya been ma true, ma true, what's da word, Billy? Ma true benefactor. Ya brung me wid ya when ya come nawth. Ya give me ma freedom. Do ya know what Aah'm tryin ta say, Billy?"

"No, I don't," said Billy, "but I hope you're not trying to tell me that you've found other employment."

"No need ta worry bout dat, Billy. But we been worried bout yo family, Billy, worried bout Mizz McHugh and worried bout lil Sebastián. We worried dat he causin problems in ya marriage cause o his negro blood."

Billy was taken aback, but let Julius continue.

Maybe he's going to suggest that Sebastián come to live with him and Becky.

"Sebastián a fine lil boy, Billy, but he got black blood. Dat's a problem here in Washington. Should not be but it sho is. Becky told me dat Mistaa Phipps and Mistaa Bartlett visited ya some time back and done seen lil Sebastián. So now dey know bout it. Ya can't hide him Billy; ya can't hide him. God knows tain't easy fo black folk here in Washington. It's not da free and open place Aah thought it was when Aah fust come nawth wid ya. Aah knows now tain't much different den Charleston. Der's lots o white folk here who makes it hard fo black folk. Da

Black Code been outlawed but nothin done changed. Racism's all round us, Billy."

Suddenly, the door opened, and in walked Dolores and Sebastián. Billy stared hard at Sebastián, Julius' words still resonating within him.

"Go in and take off those dirty britches, Sebastián, I'm going to give you a bath." Julius immediately stood up. Billy remained seated.

"Good morning, Julius." Said Dolores. "Becky told me you would be stopping by today."

"Good mornin, ma'am. Aah done finish yawl bedroom table but Aah still wuken on dose chairs. But Aah best be goin home now."

Dolores went in to bathe Sebastián. Billy sat there thinking, hearing again Julius' somber words.

Ya can't hide him. Ya can't hide him.

5

The Henry Phipps & Partners' annual 4th of July picnic was approaching. The firm's clients would be there, including Minor Keith. Billy had already decided that Sebastián would not be going with them, but he had not yet informed Dolores. He had planned to sit her down and have a frank talk about his career, about Sebastián, about their marriage; and what they might do to ease the conflicts that had arisen. He had wanted to have that talk weeks before, when Phipps and Bartlett showed up unexpectedly to their flat.

"I gave Sebastián a bath and took one myself. He's taking a nap now," said Dolores as she sat down on the arm of Billy's chair. "Did you finish reviewing your contracts, mi amor?"

Billy did not respond, for her sensuous feminine scent and the touch of her silky smooth skin immediately enveloped him in a wave of intense desire. His intent to have that serious talk simply vanished, and he put his arms around her and kissed her long and hard. She kissed him back, and he picked her up and carried her into the guest room and put her down on the bed.

It was only during the past few months that his strong desire had returned. It was as though he was obliged to make up for all those dreadful months he had endured in Confederate prisons. His passion was at a fever pitch, and he tore off his clothes and helped her take off hers. He smothered her with kisses and caresses. She too had been waiting for this and responded, matching his passion. He wondered whether she was aware of just how much power she had over him at such moments, whether she realized that he would do anything for her, grant her every wish, give her the world so long as she would give herself to him, so long as he could have her body.

He finished in a rush and lay there beside her, his passion sated for the moment. Neither of them spoke. He wanted to apologize for how he had acted the day Phipps and Bartlett showed up at the flat. He wanted to tell her how very much he wanted to find a compromise. However, before he could do so, Dolores snuggled up to him, and once again his passion rose. No sooner had their coupling commenced anew, when little Sebastián ran into the room.

"Mamá, I want some sweets."

6

The 4th of July picnic went off without a hitch. Dolores acquiesced to Billy's wishes and Sebastián spent the day with Julius and Becky. Billy circulated amongst the firm's lawyers and clients and made a point of spending as much time as possible with Minor C. Keith. Phipps and Bartlett were relieved that Billy had not brought his mulatto little boy to the picnic.

The Costa Rican venture was going well, and Minor Keith had met with Phipps and Bartlett on several occasions and told them how very pleased he was with Billy McHugh's representation. Everyone involved in the venture was duly impressed with the young lawyer's skill and depth of knowledge in the Spanish language and his grasp of Spanish-American law.

Dolores began her duties as a substitute teacher at the Congressional School and was optimistic that the School would be offering her a permanent teaching position in the near future. On days she was not teaching, she would take Sebastián to a park that Francis the carriage driver had recommended. The park was farther away than those she had been visiting, but this one afforded the benefit of greater privacy, which Billy always urged. During her first trip to the park, she met Francis' wife, Blanche, an educated black woman. She had two children, a four-year-old boy named Luther with dark skin and a three-year-old girl named Harriet with light skin like her father. Dolores frequented the park all that summer and became quite friendly with Blanche.

One day in late August, Dolores and Blanche were on their favorite bench, chatting. The children were playing, hopping back and forth across a brook that ran through the park. Suddenly, little Harriet slipped and fell, bloodying her nose and cutting her lip. She cried out, and both women rushed to her aid.

"I told her to be careful, mommy," Luther said.

Blanche at first tried to stem the flow of blood with her hand.

"Oh, here, Blanche, take my handkerchief." Blanche placed it over Harriet's nose and lip and applied some pressure. ".

"It hurts, mommy," cried Harriet.

"I think it would be wise to take her home and wash out those cuts," Dolores said.

"We live pretty far away, Dolores. Francis always drives us here."

"We can take her to my flat, Blanche. But have her hold her head back. It will help stop the bleeding," said Dolores.

"She's not holding her head back. You better carry her Blanche," said Dolores.

Blanche picked up her little girl and they set off for the McHugh's flat. They took turns carrying Harriet, and when they arrived at the building, they put her down on the lawn for a moment and continued to apply pressure to her nose and lips. It was late afternoon, and the building residents began arriving home from work. Some simply stared, walked by and entered the building. Others complained in muffled voices about "those negroes on our lawn."

"We better take her inside," said Dolores. Blanche picked up Harriet, and they entered the building. As they walked up the stairs to the McHugh flat, other tenants followed behind. Dolores stopped at her door, and a middle-aged couple who had been walking behind them walked past and continued up the stairs.

"You don't suppose all those negroes live here, do you, Jonathan?" whispered the woman. "I've seen the attractive young woman who lives there with a little brown-skinned mulatto boy."

The man slowed, glanced down at her and whispered back.

"No, they don't live here. They don't allow negroes in this building. Don't you remember what the owner told us when we moved here?"

Dolores and Blanche entered Dolores's flat with the children. They were able to stop the bleeding in Harriet's nose. They cleaned her up, and she calmed down and stopped crying. Dolores made some tea, and she sat with Blanche and they chatted a while. Soon it was time to leave. Blanche said good-bye, went outside and hailed a carriage, which as it turned out, was one of her husband's.

Dolores's trips to the park continued into the fall. White folk also frequented the park, and though Sebastián and Luther always played together, they also played with the white children. One day when they were playing together down by the brook, two white children came down and joined them, and the four youngsters began jumping from stone to stone across the brook. It was slippery, and one of the white children slipped, fell in and got soaking wet. The boy's mother rushed down to the brook, yelling:

"I told you, Robert, that I don't want you playing with those negroes."

Dolores was upset by the incident, but Blanche remained calm and told Dolores that it was a common occurrence that Luther was falsely blamed for such unfortunate incidents. She described it as "the blatant racism that exists in the Capitol of the United States of America".

Billy was away now for weeks at a time, traveling to San José, Costa Rica. He was largely unaware of the day-to-day life of Dolores and Sebastián. His work and career always took precedence over his family life, and when he heard that he was being considered for partner, his quest to achieve that goal became an obsession. With the exception of his physical needs, he had little time for his wife, and even less time for his mulatto son. One day when he returned from a lengthy trip, he was surprised and shocked to find a threatening letter from their landlord.

"Come in here right now, Dolores," he shouted. "I want to talk to you."

Dolores came in the living room and saw Billy standing there with the letter in his hand.

"Listen to this."

Dear Mister McHugh:

In the last few months, I have received numerous complaints from other residents that there are negroes living in your flat. This is a violation of the terms of your lease, and I am hereby informing you that if this practice continues, I will have you evicted from the premises.

"Do you know anything about this, Dolores?" Billy asked, his eyes radiating anger, so much so that Dolores backed away from him.

"I can't imagine what he's talking about, Billy. There is no one else living here, just you and I and Sebastián."

"Well, what in God's name, then, are these *complaints* he's referring to! This is serious Dolores, and I want to get to the bottom of it."

Billy turned and started nervously pacing back and forth, squeezing and crumpling the letter in his hand and throwing it against the wall.

"You don't suppose they mean Becky and Julius, do you? But they have been with us all along, and surely people know they are just servants and do not live with us."

"No, that couldn' be. I told the owner about them when I signed the lease!" Shouted Billy, his face contorted with anger.

"Have any other negroes besides Julius and Becky been here in our flat? Tell me the truth, Goddamit!"

Dolores was a devout Catholic and had never before heard Billy take the Lord's name in vain, and it shocked and saddened her.

"No one, Billy. I told you." Dolores began to shake and looked away, sensing that she had better tell him.

"Well, sometimes I go to the park with a friend and her children. Francis takes us."

"What? Francis? That mulatto carriage driver has been in our flat?!! How could you Dolores? You know how I feel about him."

"No, Billy, he hasn't been in our flat, but he drives me to the park with his wife, Blanche, and their two children."

"And they are black; they are negroes!"

"Yes."

"Well, they are damn well not coming here any more, Dolores! Do you understand? They are not to set foot in our flat ever again! And for the last time, I don't want you riding with that nigger, Francis!"

Billy was furious, so much so that it appeared he was about to strike her. He grabbed her by the shoulders and began shaking her, shaking her really hard.

"You are not to see them again! Do you understand? Do you understand me?"

Dolores struggled to free herself, but he was too strong. Finally, he pushed her away and with such force that she stumbled and almost fell. She stood there for a moment, stunned, staring at him in disbelief before busting into tears and running into the bedroom. Billy turned and rushed out of the flat, slamming the door behind him. When he returned, he had liquor on his breath and rage in his words.

"...Your little mulatto child is putting my chances of a partnership at risk."

"Oh, so he's *my* mulatto child, is he? You're his father Billy, and he's your son. You are father and son, and you always will be, whether you like it or not."

"He's been nothing but trouble for me from the day he was born, and I wish to God he had never been born. He would have been better off born of your nigger friend, Francis, the mulatto carriage driver whom you're so fond of..."

Their fighting went on for days, and after every round, Dolores would burst into tears and uncontrollable sobs. A long and painful period of estrangement ensued before they finally made up. Billy apologized, and an uneasy peace took hold, aided no doubt by the fact that he set off on another trip to San José, Costa Rica. Within days of his departure, Dolores received a telegraph from Sofia.

My dear sister Dolores,

It pains me terribly to have to tell you that our papá passed away on Saturday. Stop
By the grace of God he was not in pain and died in his sleep. Stop
The funeral will be held next Sunday. Stop

Your loving sister, Sofía

Though it had been expected, it still came as a shock and Dolores was saddened and deeply aggrieved. She hurried about making travel arrangements to assure that she would arrive in time for the funeral. She considered leaving Sebastián with Becky and Julius, but decided she could not. She didn't know how long she would be in Cuba, and knew that she would miss him terribly. With a sad heart and little three-year-old Sebastián in tow, she departed Washington for New York, where she would board a steamer bound for Havana.

CHAPTER XVII

Embarasada (Pregnant)

Mother and child arrived in Havana without incident. There to meet them were Dolores's sisters, Sofia and Constancia. They boarded the last train of the day for *La Dulce Gardenia* and cried and commiserated with each other most of the way. At one point, however, Sofia mentioned that in spite of the protestations of Arturo and Felipe, don Fernando executed a new will just days before he died, naming Dolores an equal heir together with her half-sisters and brothers. By the terms of don Fernando's new will. Dolores was entitled to a one-fifth share of don Fernando's estate, estimated to be some forty million United States Dollars. Dolores, however, showed little interest in her good fortune; the painful loss of her beloved papá was devastating, overshadowing the news of her inheritance.

They arrived at *La Dulce Gardenia* well after dark, and the heavy humid air and smell of gardenias hung over the mansion like the funereal hand of death. Mario Luis and the other house slaves were dressed in black and offered Dolores their sincere condolences. Noticeably absent were her half-brothers, Arturo and Felipe.

Dolores was exhausted, having slept little during the long voyage, and she immediately put on her nightclothes and got ready for bed. She checked on Sebastián and was just about to get in bed, when there was a knock on the door. It was Sofia and Constancia.

"We know you are very tired, Dolores," said Sofia, but we wanted to say goodnight and tell you how happy we are to see you in spite of the sad occasion."

"Good night, Dolores" said her two sisters.

They embraced, and Sofia and Constancia peeked in at Sebastián and then left the room. Dolores then climbed into her soft secure bed, the one she had slept in when she lived there with the family. It was only then that she began to think about her inheritance, about Billy, and about her marriage.

We can buy a big beautiful house in the nicest section of Washington, a house that Billy can be proud of, a house in which he can entertain clients, a house that will convince Henry Phipps & Partners that he is ready to join the partnership. We can have servants and send Sebastián to the best schools. We can have it all. He will no longer have to worry about hiding Sebastián and about hiding my sangre de negro. I am a wealthy woman, and everything will be different now.

2

Clusters of carriages stood beside the majestic royal palms that bordered the roadway leading to the Main House. Hundreds of black African slaves stood on the surrounding lawns, chanting for the departed spirit of the Massa, don Fernando de Castilla. Mourners packed the entranceway to the Main House, waiting to enter the library where the body lay in a gold-encrusted casket atop the massive mahogany table, the same table where the cholera-ridden body of doña Teresa had lain almost a decade earlier.

The five offspring of don Fernando stood solemn-faced at the front of the multitude beside the coffin. Father Ignacio offered prayers for the soul of the deceased, eulogizing him, and at one point, in a feeble and quivering voice, uttering:

"And yes, he was a sinner like all of us, a man of flesh and bone. He strayed, transgressing the laws of God, engendering an illicit but innocent child. Unlike others, however, he reconciled with his conscience and his Lord..."

Dolores's face flushed. Sofia gasped and Constancia was shocked. Arturo and Felipe, however, showed no reaction, standing there stone-faced.

When the service ended, Dolores rushed out of the library. The Mayor of Havana's son, Don Eduardo de Cadiz, rushed up to greet her. He had been promoted since Dolores had seen him last and was wearing the uniform of a colonel in the Spanish Army.

"My dear Dolores, I was so saddened to learn of the death of your esteemed father. He was such a fine man. Is there anything that I can do for you during this darkest hour, anything at all?" he asked, most effusively, bowing his head and reaching for her hand.

"Thank you don Eduardo, you're very kind. I shall keep that in mind, but you must excuse me now. I have to attend to my son."

"Oh, I heard that you were now a mother. I am certain that he is a handsome little lad."

"Please excuse me, don Eduardo," said Dolores, amidst the din of the multitude departing the Main House en route to the cemetery.

As Dolores climbed the stairs, she concluded that she had done right to rush off from the handsome aristocrat, who had so fervently courted her years before. She did not wish to be reminded of that tragic night years before at the Military Ball, that triggered a duel in which don Eduardo was shot by the Count of Calais.

The moment Dolores entered her living quarters, Sebastián cried out.

"Where's papá?"

Dolores immediately burst into tears. Carmen ran to her side and tried to comfort her.

"I've been a good boy, mamá. Don't cry," said Sebastián.

But cry she did, and by the time she stopped, her handkerchief was soaked with tears.

The carriages were lined up on the plaza, preparing to carry the mourners to the cemetery. Though there was ample room in the carriage for Arturo and Felipe, they chose not to join their sisters and rode in a separate carriage along with the Chief Overseer, Victorio Arquídez. Hundreds had gathered at the gravesite. A young priest joined Father Ignacio and conducted the Catholic Rite of Committal and the Final Prayers. They interred don Fernando in the enormous crypt of marble and alabaster beside doña Teresa. Dolores watched teary-eyed as her father was laid to rest. He had recognized her before the world as his rightful daughter, which dramatically changed her life forever. She had a new identity; she was doña Dolores, a member of the wealthy and highly respected de Castilla family. He provided her with a fine education in the United States of America. She would miss her dear papá, she would miss him terribly.

3

Weeks passed, and although they were still in mourning, tensions between the de Castilla brothers and sisters intensified. Arturo threatened to challenge in court the validity of don Fernando's new will. Then he capitulated unexpectedly, acknowledging Dolores's right as a beneficiary and reopening communication with his three sisters. Felipe played a passive role, seemingly willing to accept whatever agreement the others would reach. Arturo adopted new tactics to achieve his goals, reinstituting the family dinners at *La Dulce Gardenia* so much enjoyed by the family during the life of don Fernando. He tried to assume the role of leader and father, but he lacked don Fernando's tact and charm, and his domineering and patronizing attitude further alienated his siblings. He pushed Felipe aside, assuming for himself the management decisions formerly made by don Fernando, and his arrogance and acquisitiveness alienated Sofia, who was not fooled by his newfound willingness to cooperate.

Arturo called for a settlement meeting to be held in the offices of don Francisco Alguilera, the esteemed *Notario* and lawyer, who had faithfully served don Fernando de Castilla for so many years.

The five siblings sat in the reception area, waiting to see the *Notario.*

"Don Francisco is ready to receive you, señor de Castilla. Go right in," said the receptionist.

It was a large office, exquisitely decorated with flowering tropical plants, a marble floor, and elegant, richly upholstered wing chairs. Don Francisco's desk was piled high with documents, tied with red ribbons, bearing the several stamps of the Colonial Spanish Transaction taxes.

"Good morning, señoras and señores. Please be seated," said don Francisco, smiling broadly and revealing a strong-looking set of very white teeth. "To what do I owe the pleasure of a visit from the entire de Castilla family?"

"Don Francisco, we are here to try to settle some questions that have arisen under don Fernando de Castilla's last will and testament," said Arturo.

Sofia and Constancia reacted with surprise. They had believed that Arturo had recently agreed to accept the validity of the new will.

"I have formulated a plan which I firmly believe is the best way to proceed to implement the terms of the will. My lawyers have prepared the necessary documents. I'm proposing that we enter into an

Instrumento Público that will give legal effect to the plan." Arturo opened his leather pouch and took out a stack of documents.

Sofia leaned up in her chair.

What the devil is he talking about? I know of no such plan. The estate has to be split into five equal parts. That is what we need to do.

"We will form a new corporation to be called *Las Dulces Gardenias*." He smiled, though artificially. We have 'pluralized' grandfather's original name for his enterprises. All the vast holdings and assets of *La Dulce Gardenia* shall be transferred to *Las Dulces Gardenias,* and we, the five beneficiaries under the will, shall be the sole shareholders and hold an equal number of shares."

"Hold it right there, Arturo," said Sofia, forcefully. "How will the assets be divided and distributed? And I'll certainly need to examine those documents."

"I want to examine them also," said Constancia. Dolores and Felipe remained silent.

"Allow me to explain, Sofia," said Arturo. "Under my plan, our inheritances will be distributed as periodic dividends of the corporation. This will eliminate the need to break up the operations and assets." At this point Arturo looked at the Notario as though expecting to get his support for the plan.

"It's a rather clever device, don Arturo, and in principle I think it has merit," said don Francisco.

Sofia and her two sisters listened, but their demeanor revealed their skepticism.

"There's a shareholders agreement," continued Arturo, "which defines the relationship between the shareholders and governs the management and operations of the corporation."

"Let me see it," interrupted Sofia.

"As you wish," said Arturo, handing her the document.

Sofia immediately began thumbing through it, stopping at the section concerning the corporation's board of directors.

"You and Felipe are the sole directors? That's completely unacceptable."

"No, you're mistaken, Sofia. Read on and you will see that don Francisco is also a director. We presumed that you and your sisters would not wish to be involved in the everyday affairs of the corporation and would pursue your own individual interests."

"Before I could even consider what you're proposing, Arturo," interrupted Sofia, "I will have to review those documents".

"We all need to review them," said Constancia.

Dolores nodded in agreement. Felipe remained silent, apparently familiar with the documents.

"Can you have your scribe prepare copies for us, don Francisco?" Sofia asked.

"Yes, of course, doña Sofia, but it will take a while since by the looks of them they are quite lengthy."

The meeting broke up without further ado. Arturo and Felipe lingered, talking with don Francisco. Sofia, Constancia and Dolores left the office and walked to their carriage.

"I know what he's trying to do," said Sofia. "He does not want to divide the assets and give us our rightful share. He is creating a corporation over which he has complete control. From a fast glance at the section on directors and dividend policy, he and Felipe would decide when and if the corporation would declare a dividend. As for don Francisco, he would be nothing more than a passive, powerless director."

"That is unacceptable," said Constancia. "I want my share and I want it now. Papá would want me to have it now. He knew that Ricardo and I wanted our own house and wanted to live our own lives."

Dolores looked at Constancia but remained strangely silent. She knew nothing of corporations or shareholders agreements. She was still trying to get used to the idea of being a wealthy woman, wondering how, if at all, it would change her and change her husband Billy.

"Don't worry, Constancia," said Sofia. "We're not going to sign anything that Arturo proposes without giving it very careful thought and review. I don't trust him. I know it's a terrible thing to say about your own brother, but I just don't trust him."

When Dolores returned from the *Notario's* office, Mario Luis followed her to her quarters and delivered a telegraph from Joseph Bartlett in the United States. Bartlett said that he had informed Billy that his wife was in Havana attending her father's funeral. He further stated that the firm expected Billy would remain in Costa Rica for at least another month. Dolores put the telegraph down on the table and walked over to Sebastián.

"Mamá, I fed the horsies," he said, in mixed English and Spanish, "There's a black and white one. He tickled like Mickey."

"He's only been here a few short weeks, and his Spanish is already coming back," said Carmen. "Oh, and I gave him a bath, doña Dolores, so he's all nice and clean. You should have seen him when he came back from the stables."

Carmen then went about her business of refilling the water basins. Dolores suddenly felt tired and went over and lay down on the bed.

"Are you feeling all right, doña Dolores?" Carmen asked. "Can I bring you some tea?"

"Not now, Carmen, thank you. I am just very tired all of a sudden, and my stomach is upset. It must have been all that legal talk at the Notario's office."

It was the heart of the cholera season in Cuba, but Carmen would say nothing for fear it might bring bad luck.

4

It was a beautiful morning as Dolores walked along the garden path towards the secluded patio bar at the edge of the Main House grounds. The sweet scent of gardenias wafted through the heavy, humid air. Large rain drops, remnants of the overnight shower, fell rhythmically to the ground from the tall palms and mango trees. All about the lush, verdant landscape, multicolored tropical birds welcomed the morning with their exotic serenades. Though she was still mourning the death of her beloved father, Dolores could not help but notice the beauty all around her, the beauty of *La Dulce Gardenia,* the beauty of which she was now an owner.

She sat down on one of the iron chairs but then immediately got up, finding it wet from the rain. One of the female slaves, who was apparently only half-awake and surprised by the unusually early visitor, rushed out of the servants' hut and greeted her.

"Buenos días, Mizza. Aah fix coffee."

"Buenos días," said Dolores, smiling. "Could you wipe this chair for me? What is your name?"

"Call me Clara, Mizza."

"And Clara, please bring me some bread, fresh fruit juice, and the coffee when it's ready."

"Right away, Mizza."

Clara prepared the food very quicky, and she carried it out and placed it on the table smiling broadly. Dolores buttered a piece of bread and began eating it. However, after the first few bites, she felt suddenly nauseous and called out to Clara to bring her some water. A moment later, she was struck with painful stomach cramps, and she rushed over, leaned on the mango tree and threw up. Clara rushed over.

"Mizza sick. Aah get help."

"No, I am all right," Dolores struggled to say. "Don't call anyone," she said as she vomited a second time.

Clara handed her a napkin, and Dolores wiped her face, then turned and hurried back to the Main House. She climbed the stairs, thinking she would lie down and rest. Sofia and Constancia were just coming down the stairs to breakfast.

"You look pale, Dolores, are you ill?" Sofia asked.

"I have an upset stomach," said Dolores. "I'm going to lie down for a while."

The sisters were concerned, and headed back up the stairs with her. Dolores went into her room and lay down on the bed. Sofia placed her hand on Dolores's forehead.

"You feel a little warm, Dolores, but then you were outside, weren't you?"

"Yes, I went back to the patio bar, and when I started eating my breakfast, I felt nauseous and had stomach cramps." She did not tell them that she had thrown up.

"How do you feel now?" Sofia asked, as she began affectionately smoothing Dolores's beautiful long dark hair.

"I feel a little better," said Dolores, "but I better check on Sebastián. Where did you take him, Carmen?" Dolores asked as she got up from the bed.

"He's at Soledad's, playing with her little boy. I'll go get him," said Carmen.

"Are you sure you're all right, Dolores? This is after all the cholera season, and we normally call Doctor Morales at the first sign of any symptoms. Have you had loose bowels and a terrible thirst?" Sofia asked

"No, no," said Dolores. "I'm all right. There's no need to call Doctor Morales."

"Just to be safe I'm going to ask Panchita to fix you some lemon and guava drink, "Sofia said.

Constancia nodded her head in agreement.

"You can't be too careful at this time of the year, Dolores. In addition, do not forget that cholera is highly contagious. So you must think of Sebastián also."

Just then, Carmen entered with Sebastián.

"Mamá, look what I got from Auntie Soledad, a stuffed horse. Can I go to the stables to see the real horsies? Will you take me, mamá?"

"Not now, Sebastián. It's time for your nap," Dolores said curtly.

Sofia noticed Dolores's irritable tone of voice, something out of character for her normally sweet sister. Sebastián may have noticed as well, because he began to cry.

"Take him in the back room for his nap, Carmen."

"Come along, Sebastiánito."

"I want to go see the horsies," cried Sebastián.

The following week news spread quickly throughout *La Dulce Gardenia* that several slaves had died of cholera, and no one would go near the slave quarters. The stables, however, were a separate structure and removed from the slave quarters. And on several occasions Constancia had taken Sebastián to see the horses. One afternoon during the siesta hour, he awoke early from his nap, snuck out of the room and went down the staircase and out the entrance to the Main House, entering the stables completely undetected. Some time later Mario Luis went to the stables and told the stable hands to saddle two horses for don Felipe and his wife. He saw little Sebastián laughing and playing there with several slave children. When he returned, he told Carmen, who then rushed down to the stables and brought Sebastián back to the Main House. He was covered with dirt, and his hands and face were filthy. Dolores and Carmen were alarmed and immediately gave him a bath, after which they looked him over carefully but saw nothing. They knew, however, that it often takes several days after exposure for cholera symptoms to appear. Sofia then, sent word to Doctor Morales to come to *La Dulce Gardenia* as soon as possible.

Doctor Mario Morales was a silver-haired, highly respected physician in his sixties. He had been the de Castilla's family doctor for many years and had in fact delivered both Sofia and Constancia. He had not delivered Dolores, that task having fallen to a midwife in the slave quarters.

"Doctor Morales, thank you so much for coming. Do you remember my sister, Dolores?"

"Yes, indeed I do," he said as he stepped down from the carriage, "but she was just a young girl the last time I saw her."

Dolores smiled and shook Doctor Morales' hand, as did both Sofia and Constancia. They entered the Main House, walked to the courtyard and sat under the shade of some large palms. Panchita came immediately and served them lemonade. Sofia explained that Dolores's little boy may have been exposed to the cholera, and they wanted the good doctor to examine him, since the disease was so virulent that summer.

"How old is the boy?" asked Doctor Morales as he sipped his lemonade.

"He was three in July, Doctor, and thank God he's always been a healthy child," said Dolores.

"And what was the nature of his exposure?" Doctor Morales asked.

"Earlier in the week we found him playing with several slave children in the stables and became concerned."

"Has he had any symptoms, by that I mean watery, gray-colored stool, a constant thirst, stomach pain?" The sisters glanced at each other, after which Sofia responded:

"Not that we've noticed, Doctor. Of course, it has only been a few days since he was exposed. But our housemaid, who attends to the boy on a daily basis, said that he looked a little pale all of a sudden."

"These slave children he was playing with, do you know if they were sick with the cholera?"

"That's what I wanted to know," interjected Dolores. "If they weren't, then there's no reason to be concerned, is there, Doctor?"

Constancia now spoke up.

"Dolores, those little black children live in the slave quarters where just last week two adult slaves died of cholera. Therefore, we must assume that the slave children were exposed. And since Sebastián was playing with them, he too was exposed." Dolores did not take issue with that, nor did Doctor Morales.

"Well, let me see the boy," said the doctor. They all got up.

"Come with us," said Sofia, leading the way back through the parlor and up the staircase to the living quarters.

Mario Luis stood at the head of the stairs and moved to the side. They entered Dolores's suite, where they found Sebastián with Carmen.

"Mamá, Carmen is teaching me words. She says I'm smart."

"You are smart, Sebastiánito, very smart, and we want to make sure that you're also very healthy." Sebastián looked up at the un-known man carrying a little black satchel and frowned slightly.

"This is Doctor Morales, Sebastián. He's a very nice man and a very smart doctor, and he's going to examine you and ask you some questions."

"Take him over and put him on the bed, please," said the doctor. "Guess what I have in my bag, Sebastián? It's something I always give to good little boys and girls."

Doctor Morales opened his bag, took out a piece of red-colored hard candy and gave it to him. Sebastián smiled but looked a little scared as Dolores picked him up and placed him on the bed. Doctor Morales raised Sebastián's shirt and pressed slightly on his belly from side to side.

"Tell me if this hurts."

Doctor Morales listened to his heart and lungs, turned him over on his back, and tapped here and there. He examined his hands and his feet; looked in his throat, announcing finally to the great joy of everyone.

"I don't believe he has cholera, but of course you should still watch him, and if anything changes, if symptoms appear, get word to me immediately."

Sebastián climbed down from the bed and ate his candy. Sofia quickly followed the doctor and asked if he could also examine Dolores, since she too had been looking pale and had had some stomach problems. Doctor Morales agreed, and Sofia and Constancia took Dolores aside and told her that they were just as concerned about her as they were about Sebastián, and since Doctor Morales was here, it would be prudent to have the doctor examine her as well. Dolores said it was not necessary and resisted, but her sisters insisted, and Dolores eventually acquiesced. Doctor Morales asked Sofia and Constancia to leave the room.

"Tell me about these stomach problems, señora. I am going to raise your blouse and tap your tummy. Don't be alarmed."

"I've had an upset stomach, doctor, but my sisters are really overly concerned without reason."

"You've felt nauseous, have you?" Dolores flinched slightly, when he pressed rather hard on her stomach.

"Yes, it came on suddenly."

"And you vomited?"

"Yes, Doctor, but it was nothing serious."

"I see. In addition, can you recall any situation in which you may have been exposed to someone with the cholera? I mean someone other than your child who had been playing with the slave children?" Dolores shook her head.

"No, Doctor Morales, I can't think of anyone."

Doctor Morales opened his black bag and took out his stethoscope. He discreetly placed it on Dolores's chest and listened to her heart and lungs, then put it back in the bag.

"When was your last menstrual period, señora? And by any chance are you having it now?" Dolores shook her head and blushed. The question embarrassed her, in spite of the fact that he was a doctor.

When was it? I missed one recently, but that doesn't mean I'm... they always come back...

"I don't remember, Doctor. My periods have always been irregular..."

Doctor Morales nodded his head then opened his satchel and searched amongst its contents, taking out a small wooden instrument and a thermometer.

"I'd like to examine you more closely, señora. You'll need to remove your undergarments." Dolores closed her eyes and gritted her teeth, wishing it were over before it had begun. Moments later, Doctor Morales finished his examination and went over to the water basin to wash his hands.

"You can get dressed now, señora." When he dried his hands, he came over to the bed and took her by the hand.

"You don't have the cholera, señora, but I do believe you are pregnant."

Dolores turned pale, and burst into tears, unaware that she was squeezing Doctor Morales' hand quite tightly

5

In the days that followed, Dolores continued to suffer from stomach distress, especially in the morning, and became even more frantic. Finally, she decided to consult another doctor. The De Wolfs, who lived on the neighboring plantation, had used a Doctor Enrique Bocafría. Dolores approached Mario Luis and told him to make an appointment for her to see him in Havana. She instructed Mario Luis not to tell anyone.

The next week, Dolores took the train to Havana, telling her sisters that she had not brought enough summer clothing, and since it looked as though she would be staying in Cuba longer than planned to sort out the issues of don Fernando's estate, she needed to go to Havana and buy some clothes.

When Dolores arrived at Doctor Bocafría's office, she was jittery, anticipating another intrusive and embarrassing examination. Doctor Bocafría examined her carefully from head to toe, including her private parts, asking much the same questions asked by Doctor Morales. When he had finished, he told her she could get dressed, then went over and washed his hands.

"I believe I can safely say that you don't have the cholera, señora, but I do believe that you are pregnant."

Dolores covered her face with her hands and began to cry. She cried hard. Doctor Bocafra tried his best to comfort her, but the crowd of patients waiting to see him left him little time to do so. Dolores walked into the waiting room teary-eyed, the subject of everyone's stares. She left the office and walked down the stairs to the street below, drying her eyes with a handkerchief and struggling to regain control.

The train ride to *La Dulce Gardenia* seemed never ending, and by the time she arrived, she was exhausted and her eyes were red from crying. As she entered the Main House and climbed the stairs to her quarters, she managed to avoid everyone except Mario Luis, who was at the top of the stairs. He smiled and greeted her, certainly noticing her sad countenance and red eyes. She entered her quarters and found Sebastián and Carmen seated at a table playing a game. Carmen looked at Dolores and knew immediately there was something terribly wrong.

"Mamá, look what I have," said Sebastián.

"You can go now, Carmen," said Dolores devoid of her customary smile.

"Did you find some pretty clothes in Havana, doña Dolores?" Carmen asked. Dolores did not respond.

"Look what Auntie Constancia gave me, mamá." Sebastián held up a toy soldier. Dolores tried her best to maintain her composure, but the moment she hugged her dear little boy with the *acanelado* skin, she burst into tears, wondering if the child in her womb would be the same.

"Don't cry, mamá. I've been a good boy."

"I know you have, Sebastián. You are always a good boy. Your mamá is just very tired."

There was a knock on the door, and Sofia walked in.

"What's wrong, Dolores? It's not Arturo, is it? Tell me. I'll take Sebastián over to Carmen, so we can talk. Come with me, Sebastián."

"I'm hungry, mamá" he said

"Carmen will fix your dinner," said Sofia. "Come along now."

Sofia returned a moment later, and no sooner had she entered the room, when Dolores rushed to her side, threw her arms around her and burst into tears.

"Now, now, my dear sister, what is it? It cannot be all that bad. Come sit with me and we'll talk about it."

"I'm pregnant, Sofia. I'm pregnant!" Dolores blurted out.

Sofia looked surprised, but almost immediately, a little smile appeared on her face.

"So that's what's troubling you. Here I thought it was something terrible."

"I can't bring another mulatto child into this world. It would mean the end of my marriage. Billy will leave me."

Dolores wiped her eyes and blew her nose, but could not stop crying.

"He still has not accepted Sebastián. He is ashamed of him, afraid of what people might think, especially the senior partners in his law firm. If he finds out that I'm pregnant again, he'll leave me, he'll leave me, Sofia."

"My dear sister, Dolores, please try to calm down. I should not say this, but I must be honest with you. If Billy rejects this child and rejects you too because of it, then you will know what kind of man he is. And in that case, you should leave him and come home to live here in Cuba. You are going to be a wealthy woman, Dolores, and this is your homeland. Leave Billy to his career and to his own kind in Washington."

"What are you saying, Sofia? I could never leave Billy! He is my husband, and will remain my husband until the day I die. I cannot let this unborn child destroy our marriage, Sofia."

"If you are contemplating what I think you are, Dolores, then I am ashamed of you."

"My mother did it, Sofia. Would you have wanted her to bear a child from that monster, Victorio Arquídez? She survived and was none the worse for it."

"It is the most evil of all mortal sins, Dolores. You could be excommunicated."

"And would that be any worse than losing my Billy? Don't you see, Sofia? I have no choice. Oh, please, you must help me. There's no one else I can turn to."

Sofia suddenly thought of a solution to Dolores's painful dilemma, but she was not yet prepared to reveal it.

𝔟

Several months passed, and Dolores was now in her second trimester and it was beginning to show. She felt the first signs of the nascent life developing within her, and it was then that she realized she could not destroy the innocent child. She was now faced with the difficult and painful task of informing Billy that she was pregnant. She struggled over the question of writing him or waiting to tell him in person. She had written to him in Costa Rica and in Washington C/O Henry Phipps & Partners, but had not yet received a response. Sofia was the only one who knew that Dolores was pregnant, and they both agreed that it was time to tell the other family members.

It was Sunday morning and Dolores was in her room dressing for mass when there was a knock on the door. It was Mario Luis.

"This letter arrived yesterday, doña Dolores. I looked for you, but you were nowhere to be found." Dolores jumped up excitedly and rushed over to him.

"Finally!" she exclaimed excitedly. "Thank you, Mario Luis!"

She went over now and sat down at her dressing table.

10 october 1865

My dearest Dolores,

I got your letters and wrote back, but it sounds like you never received mine. Mail service from here to Cuba and the United States is terribly unreliable, but I shall keep writing whenever I have the chance. You will probably get all my letters at the same time.

I was deeply saddened to learn of the death of your father. He was a wise and wonderful man, and I know you will miss him as will I and everyone who ever had the pleasure of knowing him. People say that even the most tragic of events produces some good, and the fact that you will now inherit one-fifth of your father's estate testifies to that. You were his rightful daughter, and you are certainly entitled to it.

You are now a wealthy woman, Dolores, and it could not have come at a better time. I recently learned that there was a partnership vote last month for a certain William C. McHugh. The vote was locked at four. The four negative votes were based upon the view that a little more seasoning was required. It is not unusual that it takes several rounds of voting before a lawyer is made a partner. And I know that once this Costa Rican project is completed, I will have had more than sufficient seasoning. The icing on the cake will come when they learn that I am now the husband of a very wealthy woman.

We are expecting a ten-day recess in our negotiations, while the Costa Rican Government's team attends to a non-related issue in Panama. There is a good chance that I will be able to visit you in Cuba. I shall write and give you the details. I hope that you will get the letter. I miss you terribly, Doloresita.

Your loving husband

She read it a second time, greatly relieved to have heard from him but disappointed that there was not one word about Sebastián.

After mass, Dolores decided that she would make an announcement at the weekly family dinner. Dolores's older brother Arturo was having little success in convincing his siblings to adopt his corporate plan for dividing and distributing the assets of don Fernando's large estate; but he had succeeded in reinstituting the weekly family dinners so much enjoyed when don Fernando was alive.

No sooner had they all been seated, than Dolores looked to Sofia to bolster her confidence. Sofia reached for Dolores's hand.

"I have an announcement to make; I'm going to have my second child."

"Oh, Doloresita, how wonderful!" exclaimed Constancia. "Little Sebastián will have a brother or maybe a little sister to play with."

"Congratulations, Doloresita!" exclaimed her sisters-in-law. Arturo and Felipe smiled and congratulated her.

"I'm so happy for you, Dolores," said her brother-in-law, Ricardo. "When can we expect the blessed event?"

"It will be winter, Ricardo, December to be exact," Dolores said, feeling more confident now with her decision to have the child.

"Well, now, this calls for a toast," said Arturo, as he called out loudly to Panchito to open the champagne. "Tell me, *Doloresita,* are you hoping for a girl this time?"

Dolores hesitated before responding, surprised and grated by Arturo's use of the affectionate diminutive, *Doloresita,* which rang hollow and artificial.

"I'll be happy with either, so long as it's healthy," said Dolores. Panchito brought the champagne and filled their glasses.

"To Dolores's future child," said Arturo, lifting his glass. "Although we don't yet know its gender or its name, we toast it all the same!"

They drank to it, the women happily clinking glasses with Dolores.

"Now, dear brothers and sisters, I too have an announcement to make," said Arturo.

They all waited for the words of the self-proclaimed successor to don Fernando, not knowing what to expect.

"I have decided to drop my proposal to form a new corporation for the distribution of papá's estate. I believe that if we all make a good faith effort, we can value and divide the assets in a fair and equitable manner. However, as for the management of the enterprise, I think I can safely say that none of you wishes to assume that responsibility; and since I have worked directly with papá for these many years, I have the experience and am ready and able to assume that responsibility."

"Let me make something clear, Arturo," said Felipe. "I am going to share some of that management responsibility. I too worked for years under the guidance of our papá, and he would want me to continue to learn the business."

"There's no reason, Felipe, to subject the others to our personal discussions," interrupted Arturo. "We will settle that between ourselves."

"Yes, we will, Arturo, but I want to remind you that I too have some management capability and will not be pushed aside."

When the dinner broke up, Arturo and Felipe lingered over their cognac and cigars. The three sisters left the dining room and walked up the staircase. Constancia paused beside the family portraits.

"We will be adding a few more portraits, won't we, Dolores?

One for Sebastián and one for your child to be. Oh, and you haven't said, Dolores, what is Billy hoping for, a boy or a girl?"

"I haven't told Billy, Constancia. He's been in Costa Rica working on an important project, but he will be coming to Cuba in the near future."

CHAPTER XVIII

Shocked and Dismayed

When Billy stepped down from the train, he found the station deserted except for several slaves lounging about under the shade of the water tower. He wondered how he was going to get to the Main House. Not knowing what else to do at that point, he picked up his luggage, walked over and sat down on a bench. It was not long before he saw a carriage approaching. The slaves also spotted it and scurried off, climbing aboard an empty railroad car on the sidetrack.

The carriage pulled up close to the water tower, and two slaves jumped out. A moment later, the driver jumped down. Though it had been many years, Billy felt sure he recognized him and stood up.

"Good afternoon. I'm Billy McHugh, Dolores de Castilla's husband. I was here many years ago with my father, Patrick McHugh. He was the owner of the vessel *The Wandering Maiden*, and we delivered hundreds of Lucumi and Kongo slaves to don Fernando de Castilla. Perhaps you remember us," Billy said in Spanish.

The Chief Overseer looked at him suspiciously.

"I remember," he said, his mouth forming a sneer that had become a habit. He looked even meaner, and Billy recognized him as Victorio Arquídez, the Chief Overseer of *La Dulce Gardenia*.

"Can you give me a ride to the Main House," Billy asked.

"You'll have to wait, señor. I must attend to these water towers," said Victorio Arquidez.

Billy watched as two slaves off-loaded the heavy barrels of water and carried them over to the water tower.

The ride to the Main House was uneventful. Billy tried to engage the Chief Overseer with small talk but got little response.

It was dusk when Billy entered the Main House. Mario Luis was just leaving the kitchen and looked surprised at the sight of the American.

"You might not remember me. I'm Billy McHugh, Dolores's husband."

"Yes, of course, señor McHugh, it's been many years but I do remember you. We were very pleased to learn that you and doña Dolores had married. Come with me, please. I will tell her that you are here. I know she'll be very happy to see you."

"No, please don't tell her. I want to surprise her. And what is your name again?"

"I'm Mario Luis, señor. Please follow me."

The aged dean of the house slaves began slowly walking up the spiral staircase. Billy followed behind, noticing the portraits hanging on the wall and especially Dolores's. Mario Luis led him up to the door of Dolores's quarters.

"I believe that doña Sofia is in there with her," whispered Mario Luis.

"Thank you," said Billy. He knocked and heard Dolores's voice. "Come in, Carmen."

Billy opened the door and walked in.

"It's not Carmen, Dolores it's me."

"Billy, oh Billy! I didn't expect you!"

She frowned for an instant and then smiled.

"What a wonderful surprise," she managed to say as she backed away and smoothed out the folds of the shawl that she wore to conceal her condition.

"Oh how I've missed you, my love" Billy said, as he moved closer, about to throw his arms around her and kiss her with abandon. Dolores could see and feel his fervent desire, and she backed away. Sofia's presence in the room made Dolores's chilly response to Billy's advances seem more appropriate.

"Billy, Billy McHugh," said Sofia. "What a wonderful surprise! I haven't seen you since the wedding."

"How nice to see you, Sofia," Billy managed to say as he kissed her on the cheek.

"Well, I must leave you two alone now," said Sofia. "I'm sure you have a lot to tell each other." Dolores wondered whether Sofia was signaling that this might be the right time to tell him.

"Sofia, please tell Carmen to send Sebastián over to see his papá."

No sooner had Sofia left the room, than Billy once again rushed to Dolores's side and tried to throw his arms around her. But Dolores was able to spin away, stumbling as she did so.

"What's wrong, Dolores? What's wrong? I wrote you that I was coming! Didn't you get my letter?" Billy asked, obviously disappointed and disturbed by Dolores's rather cold reception.

Sebastián suddenly burst into the room.

"Mamá, I know how to write," he said excitedly as he ran to her side.

"Say hello to your papá Sebastián. He's come a long way to see you," said Dolores.

"My, my, he has grown, hasn't he?" Billy said, seeking to conceal his extreme disappointment at the cool reception.

"Where's my other papá" asked Sebastián, looking to his mamá for comfort.

"This is your only papá, Sebastián. Your grandpapá is in heaven now with God."

"How about if I take you riding tomorrow, little man? I know how you love horses,"

"Yes, please papá, I want to ride the black and white horse!"

"He's too young to ride a horse, Billy. He rides in the *volantes*."

"Please take me, papá!"

"I will, Sebastián. I promise you."

Carmen came back in the room.

"Should I give Sebastián his dinner now, doña Dolores?"

"Yes, Carmen, this is his dinner time."

No sooner had Carmen left the room with Sebastián, than Billy rushed to Dolores's side and attempted to ease her over to the bed. Dolores's first impulse was to tell him right then and there, but she immediately had second thoughts. She'd given the matter a great deal of thought and had discussed it thoroughly with Sofia, resolving to wait for just the right moment. She decided that this was not the right moment, so she steadied herself as best she could and moved quickly away from the bed.

2

Billy slept in a separate bed that night, unaware of the real reason why. Dolores said nothing other than she was not feeling well. He assumed that she was having her menstrual period, but was worried that there was something else troubling her.

The next morning they took their breakfast together with Sebastián at the patio bar, and Billy went out of his way to pay attention to Sebastián. After breakfast, he took him to the stables to see the horses. Later, they went for a ride in a *volante*, pulled by

Sebastián's favorite black and white horse. And in those few short hours together, Sebastián began to warm to his "new papá."

When they returned to the stables, a young gentleman dressed in riding britches approached them.

"Oh, it's Sebastiánito," he said, "and this must be your papá. Welcome to *La Dulce Gardenia*! I'm Felipe de Castilla, in case you don't remember me." He extended his hand.

"Billy McHugh, Felipe, thank you," said Billy, shaking his hand. "Yes, I do remember you Felipe, though it has been many years."

"Yes, it has," said Felipe, "but I think I would have recognized you even without little Sebastián here."

"I was very sorry to learn of your father's death, Felipe."

"Thank you, Billy. It was a shock to all of us, though we knew he had a bad heart.".

Sebastián tugged on Billy's hand.

"I'm hungry, papá."

"All right, little man, we're going now."

"Oh, and Billy, we were all so pleased to learn that Dolores is expecting your second child." Billy's face flushed, and he looked at Felipe with shock and disbelief.

"Oh, so you didn't know? I'm terribly sorry for having said anything."

Billy rushed off without another word, tugging Sebastián along at a faster pace than his little legs could carry him. When they reached the stairs in the Main House, he picked him up and carried him upstairs. then stormed into Dolores's quarters. Dolores was just stepping out of the bathtub, Carmen stood there holding a towel.

"Billy!" Dolores gasped. "You mustn't barge in like that!" She reached frantically for the towel, but it was too late. He'd already seen her distended belly, and he stood now glaring at her.

"You're pregnant!" he shouted.

"Carmen, take Sebastián in the other room." Dolores said, trying to stay calm.

"You're pregnant, and I had to hear it from your brother!"

"I'm sorry, Billy. I was going to tell you. I swear I wasn't trying to hide it from you." She wrapped the towel around her more tightly and walked over to her dressing table.

"You're not going to have this baby, Dolores. Do you hear me?!" She sat down, still struggling to stay calm. But when she looked in the mirror and saw the anger and contempt on Billy's face, she burst into tears.

"You're going to have an operation, Dolores! Do you understand?! You can have it here or back in Washington, but you're not going to have this baby! You're not!"

He walked over to the dressing table now and stood over her. He was furious, and at first she dared not look at him. But after confronting herself in the mirror, she found the courage, stood up and faced him. Struggling and succeeding to overcome her natural modesty, she loosened the towel and let it drop to the floor. She stood there naked before him.

"Look at me, Billy," she said, placing her hands on her belly. "I'm carrying your child, your child, your own flesh and blood. How can you turn your back on us?" She hoped he still had a heart, that he'd be touched by the image and come to realize what she'd realized just days before, that to destroy the innocent life in her womb was an unthinkable, evil act.

"Get dressed! You disgust me!" was Billy's only response. Dolores didn't move.

"I said get dressed!"

"Get out, Billy! Get out!" she shouted.

He stepped back slightly, unaccustomed to her assertiveness and anger.

"Get out!" she shouted. "Get out!"

He glared at her but headed for the door. As she watched him leaving, she was gripped by a wave of sadness and despair. Naked still, she sat down, laid her head on the dressing table and began to sob. Billy, too, had a change of heart, and he walked back over and touched her gently on the shoulder. But it had come too late, and Dolores raised her head, tears streaming down her face, and screamed one last time: *Get out!* This time Billy did get out, and as he tried to slam the door, Sofia thwarted his effort by entering the room.

Billy rushed down the stairs, almost tripping as he passed the portraits on the wall. He hurried out of the Main House and rushed down the garden path to the patio bar. A slave woman came over, and he ordered a brandy. When she brought the drink, he quickly drank it down, then told her to bring the bottle. He sat there drinking and thinking, suddenly recalling his father's fateful words years before, that *if he married a nigger, his children would be niggers.*

"Well, look who it is, Billy McHugh! Welcome to *La Dulce Gardenia*! I heard you were visiting," said Arturo de Castilla.

Arturo smiled and offered his hand. Billy shook his hand and tried to smile, but failed miserably.

"We were all so happy to hear that Dolores is expecting your second child!"

Billy was not about to respond to that and simply held up his glass of brandy.

"Won't you join me?"

"Well, maybe just one," said Arturo, who called the slave woman and told her to bring him a glass. "I'm on my way to the *Notario's* office, and that reminds me, Billy. You being a lawyer and all, I'm sure you will be happy to know that we are going to begin distributing the assets of my father's estate. Dolores, of course, is entitled to a one-fifth share."

"Thank you Arturo, and please keep me informed"

Later that afternoon and after drinking more than a half-bottle of brandy, Billy returned to the Main House and went directly to Dolores's quarters. Carmen told him that Dolores had gone to church with Sebastián, and Billy decided to wait for her in her quarters. He was drowsy from the brandy, and when he lay down, he soon fell sound asleep.

He's in the hallway. He goes over to the door and knocks. The midwife opens the door and announces that Dolores has given birth to a healthy baby. He walks in the room. He sees the doctor leaning over the water basin washing his hands. He walks over to the bed and finds Dolores holding another dark-skinned mulatto baby. He turns and backs away, startled to the point of disbelief, when he sees senior partners, Henry Phipps and Joseph Bartlett, standing nearby.

"Look papá! Look what I have!" said Sebastián as he ran to the bed, clutching the horseshoe and thrusting it at Billy, who awakened with a start.

"Don't do that," Dolores cried, calling then for Carmen to come and take him to the other room.

Billy got up slowly, rubbed his eyes, and went to the water basin to wash his face. Dolores went to her armoire and removed her shawl. Neither spoke. When Billy finished drying his face, he walked over and put both hands on Dolores's waist, startling her.

"I'm truly sorry, my love. I don't know what got into me. It's my fault that you're pregnant. It's not your fault, you..."

"It's nobody's fault, Billy," interrupted Dolores. "We're man and wife, and it's a perfectly natural thing, a joyful event in a couple's life. What is unnatural is your reaction. For you, it's a tragedy."

Billy was about to speak, but Dolores held up her hand to show she had not finished.

"I spoke with Father Juan Pablo this afternoon. I told him I was pregnant and that my husband did not want the child and told me to destroy it. Father was shocked and said we could both be ex-communicated. He also said that I have valid grounds for the annulment of our marriage. Is that what you want, Billy? Is that really what you want?"

"No, no, my love! I don't want that! I love you, Dolores. I have always loved you. Surely, you know that. It's just the terrible shock of how I learned you were pregnant.

"Be honest Billy. That is not what shocked you. What shocked you was the thought that you might be the father of another mulatto child, and that it might harm your precious career opportunities. You should be ashamed of yourself! You could not find a sweeter, more darling little boy than Sebastián anywhere in the world, and yet you deny him the love and affection he needs because of the color of his skin. How can you be so heartless Billy? The child in my womb is your own flesh and blood, and yet you are willing to destroy it before it is born. If I had known you were so heartless, I never would have married you..."

Before he left Havana, Billy tried to soften his position and reconcile with Dolores, suggesting that she have the baby, and turn it over to an orphanage. Dolores did not mention that Sofia had expressed interest in adopting the baby. There was no resolution of the problem.

Billy departed Havana aboard a steamer bound for New York with a stop in Charleston, providing an opportunity to visit his mother, Bonny, whom he had not seen since before the War.

CHAPTER XIX

Charleston in Ruins

Charleston harbor was littered with the sunken remains of sailing ships and ironclads, causing some difficulty for the steamer to navigate its way to the few remaining wharfs. As he walked down the gangplank, Billy could scarcely believe it. There was desolation as far as the eye could see. Few of the stately mansions that lined the exclusive section of the Battery were still standing. The reports had been true; Union naval vessels and Army artillery had been continuously bombarding Charleston since the summer of 1863. From the outbreak of the War, Union forces had sought to capture the city, but they were repelled every single time. Charleston had stood like the impenetrable bulwark of the Confederacy, and the South was exceedingly proud of that. However, on 15 February 1865, General Pierre G. T. Beauregard, who had initiated the conflagration four years earlier by bombarding Fort Sumter, saw the inevitable and evacuated the last of the Confederate forces. Three days later, the mayor of Charleston surrendered the city to General Alexander Schimmelfennig and his predominately-black troops.

There were more than a few passengers disembarking with Billy, all of whom looked shocked and in a state of disbelief at the extent of the destruction.

Billy walked up to what he recognized as King Street, passing the remains of houses shelled to rubble. Many were left with only their battered brick chimneys that stood like scarecrows amidst a vast fallowed wasteland. Weeds, grass, and thistle sprouted in the streets. Union troops on horseback rode past, a stark reminder that Charleston was now under Martial Law. At one point Billy had to scurry out of the way of a wagon, loaded down with furniture, mattresses, and every conceivable variety of household goods, salvaged or scavenged from the ruins. No sooner had he done so when a buzzard swooped down from above, alighting on the carcass of a dog, probably the last of the carrion on the streets of Charleston after all the carcases of decaying horses and oxen had been picked to the bone. Billy walked farther north and soon found himself at the College of Charleston, where he had studied as a youth. The building appeared to be intact, but when he walked up the steps and tried to enter, he found it locked. There was a sign on the door saying *Classes not in session*, and when he turned and walked back down, he saw a Union corporal with a fixed bayonet standing on the walkway.

"What's your business here, mister?"

"Oh, hello," Billy said. "I grew up here in Charleston and I'm a graduate of this College. I came to Charleston to visit my mother, whom I haven't seen since before the War."

It seemed to satisfy the corporal.

"Say, you wouldn't happen to know where I might hire a carriage, would you?" Billy asked.

"Your best bet would be the Citadel. They sometimes sit out there in front."

Like the College, the Citadel appeared to be undamaged, and Billy was able to procure a carriage.

"Where can Aah take ya, suh?" asked the coachman.

"Do you happen to know the road leading north to the Pringle Estate?" The coachman nodded. "There's a house, at least there used to be, just before the entrance road. That's where I want to go."

"Aah knows dat road, suh, and ya need not worry 'bout da house. Yankee shellin' neva did reach way up der. And Genral Sherman neva did come dat way either like everyone done sposed he would."

"I'm glad to hear that," Billy said. "That's my mother's house, and I haven't seen her since before the War. Tell me, what was it like here during the War?"

The coachman turned and looked at his passenger. "Ya don't wants ta know, suh, bad, real bad! Course we negroes are now free men, so Aah spose it was all wuth it. And dey givin us rations now at da Freedmen's Bureau, so we's not starvin no mo."

It started to look familiar as they rode past the sites he had known as a boy: the stony creek that ran down to the river; the cotton fields that lined the dusty road; and the negroes sitting beneath the large oaks draped with Spanish moss.

"There it is, I see it," Billy said as the coachman pulled back on the reins and they slowed.

"Aah told ya, suh, it was still standin," said the coachman.

They rode up the gravel path to the house. Several negroes, men, women, and children, were sitting on the front steps. Billy jumped down and walked over to them; one of the women got up and went inside the house.

"I'm looking for my mother, Mrs. Patrick McHugh. I'm Billy McHugh."

"She don't live here no mo," said a stout negro man rather defensively, as he took off his hat to swish away some insects that were buzzing about his face.

"Do you know where I can find her?" Billy asked.

"She ain't been here in some time since da house been allocated ta us unda Genral Sherman's Orda 15."

Billy recalled how Julius had asked whether he and Becky could acquire some land in Charleston under such an Order. By now, the negroes all wore expressions conveying challenge and derision, and Billy's better judgment told him to find his mother first, before thinking about contesting their right and title to his mother's house. So, he bid them good-bye and yelled for the carriage driver to wait, thinking he might get some information about his mother at the nearby Pringle estate."

"Do you know if the Pringles are still living here?" Billy asked.

"Last Aah heard dey was," said the coachman.

They set off down the road, and when they approached the entrance, Billy thought he recognized a young black man walking there. He told the driver to stop. As it turned out, it was one of Julius' sons, and Billy spoke to him for a few minutes. After advising him that his parents were doing fine in Washington, Billy asked him if he knew anything about Mrs. McHugh. The young man told Billy he heard she had gone to live and work in the Orphan House.

The ornate Orphan House occupied an entire city block near the corner of King and Calhoun Streets. It was surrounded by a six-foot high stonewall. Two black soldiers dressed in immaculate Union Army uniforms stood guard at the entrance. Billy explained that he was there to find his mother, and they waved him through. He walked through a garden to the building entrance. He asked a woman in a white uniform leading a troop of young boys, if she knew where he could find Mrs. Bonny McHugh. The woman did not know, but she directed him to the administrative office. One of the counselors there told him that Bonny McHugh worked in the infirmary, which was on the second floor. He found the infirmary and spotted his mother at a desk. He walked over slowly so as not to startle her and stood there right in front of her.

"Billy? Oh, Billy! Is that really you! Tell me I'm not dreaming!" Bonny stood up, burst into tears and embraced her long-lost son."

"It's been more than four years, and I, I…" Her crying choked off her words. "I prayed, Billy oh, how I prayed that you would survive your imprisonment!"

She took out a handkerchief and tried to dry her tears, but they continued to flow down her face.

"I thank God that you've returned!"

"I thanked God that you survived, mama. I tried hard to reach you during the War, but it was just impossible. And when I learned about Dad, I was deeply saddened and wanted so to be with you."

"I've been waiting so long to meet your wife and child, Billy. Your father, God rest his soul, told me all about them. He had mellowed in those last years, Billy."

"Dolores and Sebastián are in Cuba, mama. I hope you'll be able to meet them soon. But mama, what happened to our house? I rode out there today looking for you and discovered a family of negroes living there. I was worried that something had happened to you. But thank God you're safe."

"Oh, Billy, let's not talk about that now. I just want to be with you."

The orphan girls on the bench were becoming restless.

"I must finish up with these girls, Billy, so why don't you go down and wait for me in the garden, and I'll be down shortly?"

Billy made his way to the garden and sat down on a bench. Bonny joined him shortly thereafter.

"You remember the Becketts, Billy? Certainly Constance Beckett. Well, Emily Beckett is on the Board of the Orphan House, and thank God, she got me this position after they forced me out of our house under the supposed authority of that Military Order. As hard as it's been for me to adjust to this life, at least

I have a roof over my head and a small salary, which has been enough to keep me out of the poorhouse."

"I'm familiar with that Military Order, mama, and don't think it will hold up under legal scrutiny. Trust me, we're going to get your house back, and in the meantime, I'll supply whatever funds you need."

Bonny smiled warmly and reached for his hand, whereupon her eyes became misty.

"You'll be all right now, mama. You'll be all right," Billy said.

"If we get the house back, I won't ever need any help, Billy." She looked around, leaned over and whispered, "I buried your father's cache of gold, silver and Yankee greenbacks in the green house, and I'm sure that no one but me would be able to find it."

The management excused Bonny from her duties for the rest of the afternoon, and she and Billy talked for another hour. Bonny then suggested they find a carriage and ride out to the Becketts' house. She told Billy how they had helped her during the war years and that they were her closest friends and confidants. They too, had been forced out of their house. Fortunately, they had enough gold and Yankee greenbacks to acquire a modest little house in the northern part of the city

"It's been almost a year now, since we learned that Constance's husband, Travis, was killed at Petersburg. Poor little Felicia, who is just three-years-old, will now have to grow up without her daddy. It's such a tragedy and such a shame. What did this War accomplish, Billy? What did it accomplish? Nothing but death, destruction and pain! The South will never be the same, and we will never be the same."

2

Bonny lifted the brass doorknocker and knocked several times. A moment later the door opened, and though Billy had not seen her in more than a decade, he recognized the woman standing there as Constance Beckett, the girl who had once been so fond of him, the girl his mother had so fervently urged him to court.

"Well, hello, Bonny. And glory be, don't tell me, this must be your son, Billy. What a wonderful surprise. Do come in and make yourselves at home," Constance said, a wide smile on her face, a face still quite pretty for a woman of her age, which Billy guessed was her early thirties.

"I was just as surprised when he showed up at the Orphan House a few hours ago," Bonny said. "And I can tell you that it warmed my heart like never before. I waited four long years for that moment."

"I'm trying to think of how long it's been since I saw him," said Constance, motioning for them to have a seat.

Billy sat down in a wing chair, noticing a tear in one of the seams.

"And I'm trying to remember when I saw you last, Constance," Billy said. "I think it might have been at your eighteenth birthday party."

"Well, glory be! Has it really been that long? The sweet days of our youth," Constance said with a sigh. "We were so innocent and idealistic. The years and the War have changed all that, haven't they?".

"How's your mama holding up?" Bonny asked.

"As well as you could expect, given this Yankee occupation, but you just missed her. She went down to the Orphan House a little while ago. And Dad's working down at the Union Headquarters.

I'm sure not proud to say it, but he's been working for the Yankees."
Just then, a young negro woman appeared on the stairs, carrying
a little girl who was crying.

"Excuse me, y'all, but lil Felicia here be needin her mama.
Won't stop cryin and fussin no how."

"Bring her down here, Nancy, I'll take her," said Constance,
as the little girl continued to cry.

The negro girl came downstairs, walked over and placed the
little girl in Constance's lap.

"You're in luck, Billy," said Bonny. "This is Felicia, the most
adorable little girl in all of Charleston, maybe in all the South for
that matter."

"And your description doesn't even do her justice," Billy said,
admiring her dewy-white complexion, big blue eyes, and curly
blond hair.

"There now, Felicia, there's no need to cry, mama's here."

"Isn't she the most precious little girl you've ever seen?" Bonny
said. Constance kissed her daughter lightly on the neck, tickling
her and eliciting a cute little giggle from the three-year-old.

"You remember Mrs. McHugh, Felicia, and this is her handsome son, Billy."

Felicia looked at them shyly, and then started staring at Billy,
reminded perhaps of her daddy, whom she had seen for the last
time months before when he was home on furlough.

"She misses her daddy," Constance whispered softly.

"May I serve y'all some tea?" Constance asked. "I believe we
have a little left that father got down at Union Headquarters. His
position does have some benefits. He is paid in Yankee greenbacks,
and gets good benefits in addition to the tea and other supplies. So,
if you can put aside your pride, you can do all right working for
the Yankees. Of course, he did have to take the oath of allegiance

to the United States of America. The Occupation Forces insisted that we all take the oath, but so far I've managed to avoid it."

"I had to take it too," said Bonny, "or I wouldn't have gotten the work at the Orphan House."

"Y'all pardon me a minute," said Constance. I'll go out and see how Nancy is doing with our tea." Billy watched closely as she walked out of the room, noticing her slender figure and graceful gait, and recalling once again that anticipatory coupling in her bedroom many years before.

"When are you and Dolores going to have another child, Billy?" Bonny asked.

Billy nodded his head slightly, acknowledging that he had heard his mother, but he did not directly respond.

"Are you a soldier, Mister Billy?" Little Felicia asked, looking up at him.

Constance now reappeared in the parlor, followed by Nancy carrying a tray of tea and sweet rolls.

"No, Felicia, I'm not a soldier. I am a lawyer. I do a different kind of fighting."

Felicia now came over to Billy, looking up at him admiringly.

"You're certainly in the right profession at the right time," said Constance. "After four years of war we're going to need a regiment of lawyers here in the South to get things back in order." Constance sat down now and watched as Nancy poured the tea.

"You were one of the smart ones, Billy. You didn't go to war. I begged Travis to give up the fight and to stay home with Felicia and me, but he would not listen. What did all his honor, valor, and patriotism get him? What did it get Felicia and me?"

"I want a sweet roll, mama," said little Felicia.

"You may have half of mine," said Constance. Felicia slipped away from Billy and got half a piece of her mother's sweet roll, after which she returned to Billy, taking her place again between his knees.

"Your mother told me about your imprisonment, Billy. We were all so relieved to hear that you'd been released," Constance said.

"I spent six months in Confederate prisons, the last one at Castle Thunder in Richmond. By a strange coincidence, my old friend, Charlie Flynn, was also imprisoned there. You remember Charlie, don't you Constance? The State Department was able to arrange a prisoner swap and got me released, but Charlie never made it out of there. He was shot and killed when he tried to escape..."

Billy lowered his head, still feeling the pain and loss of his dear friend.

They continued talking for another hour or so, drank all the tea and finished all the sweet rolls. Shortly thereafter, they heard the sound of carriage wheels on the gravel driveway.

"Oh, that must be mama and papa," said Constance. They'll be very happy to see y'all."

"But I must be going," said Bonny. "The Orphan House doesn't allow me to stay out at night. It's the house rule for the counselors."

"Mama and papa will insist that y'all stay for supper," Constance said. "Nancy's husband, Roy, can drive you back down to the Orphan House."

The door opened and in walked Emily and Richard Beckett. They did indeed insist that Bonny and Billy stay for dinner. And since Billy had no place to stay for the night, they also invited him to bed down on their couch.

Though the Becketts' couch was somewhat worn and lumpy, Billy had had a long journey from Havana, and he fell into a deep sleep. He awoke sometime in the wee hours of the morning when he felt someone pulling his hair. At first he thought it was part of his dream, but when he opened his eyes, he saw little Felicia standing there.

"Daddy let me sleep in his bed," she said, then climbed up on the couch and snuggled up close to him.

"All right, Felicia, but just for a little while. Your mama will be worried if she wakes and finds you missing."

"Mama's asleep, Mister Billy." But in fact, Mama was not asleep, which suddenly became apparent.

"Felicia, you skedaddle back upstairs right this minute," Constance said, standing there in her nightgown. "I'm terribly sorry she woke you, Billy."

"She didn't wake me. I was already awake" Billy fibbed. Felicia hesitated.

"You get up and go back to bed right this minute, young lady." Constance said.

This time Felicia got off the couch and ran up the stairs.

"She still misses her daddy. I do too," said Constance. "It hasn't been easy without him."

Billy was now wide awake, and he shifted over slightly on the couch, hoping Constance would sit down. When she did, she positioned herself on the edge of the couch. By then, Billy's eyes had adjusted to the dark, and he could see the outline of her slender body through the sheer material of her nightgown. He leaned up, and her long blond hair brushed lightly against his cheek, her sensual feminine fragrance sending a surge of desire pulsing through his being. He had resisted the constant temptation in Costa Rica, saving himself for Dolores. But there had been no love making in Cuba, and he could resist no longer and gave in to his lust.

CHAPTER XX

New Years Baby

Carmen handed Dolores the light blue muslin dress that she had just finished sewing.

"I hope it's not too tight, Dolores."

Dolores slipped out of her sack-like shawl and tried it on.

"It's lovely, Carmen, and not too tight." Dolores smiled and kissed her favorite servant on the cheek. "You're not just a seamstress, Carmencita. You're an artist, and I can always count on you for perfection."

"I'm so happy you like it, señora, but let me see the back," Carmen said, motioning for Dolores to turn around. "Yes, I thought so. I would like to make one small adjustment to the waist. It won't take long."

Dolores took off the dress, but before she could wrap the shawl around her, Sofia walked in with Sebastián. His little face took on a look of astonishment. It was the first time he had really seen his mother's pregnant condition, and he ran over and put both hands on her belly. Dolores was now in the final days of her second trimester, and she could no longer conceal her condition, nor did she want to.

"Mamá, why are you so fat?"

"I'm sorry, Dolores," said Sofia, chuckling. I'll take him back to my quarters."

"It's all right, Sofia. He can stay," Dolores said, deciding right then and there that it was time to talk to him.

"Mamá is going to have a baby, Sebastián," Dolores said, smiling and placing her hands on her belly. "You will have a little brother or maybe a little sister, Sebastián. The baby is growing here inside of me."

That did not satisfy Sebastián, and he tried to lift up Dolores's undergarments to get a better look, whereupon Dolores stepped away and began wrapping the shawl around her.

"You can't see him now, Sebastián. He is not ready yet to come out, but he will be soon enough." Sebastián looked more perplexed than ever.

"But where did you get the baby, Mama?"

"Take him back to your room, Sofia," Dolores said. Sofia turned to Carmen.

"Take him, Carmen. I need to talk to Dolores." Carmen picked up the blue dress, took Sebastián by the hand and started for the door.

"Come with me, Sebastiánito," she said, tugging him toward the door, his head turned all the while, staring at his mother.

"Where did you get the baby, mamá?"

"God gave him to us, Sebastián."

2

The next afternoon Mario Luis delivered two letters to Dolores. One was from Mister Thomas Meadows of the Congressional School in Washington and the other was from Billy. She chose to open the one from Mister Meadows first.

October 20 1865

Dear Mrs. McHugh:

I am sorry to have to tell you that we had to fill the teaching position previously reserved for you with another candidate. We would, however, like to know if you would be available to fill a position for the next academic year. Please contact us no later than two months before the next academic year, which begins in September 1866.

We highly value your contribution and service to the Congressional School, and hope you will be able to rejoin our faculty. In any event, we wish you success in your future endeavors.

Sincerely,
Thomas V. Meadows, Headmaster

Dolores now turned her attention to Billy's letter.

16 de octubre de 1865
Avenida de las Flores
San José, Costa Rica

My dearest Dolores:

I cannot tell you how sorry I was that we quarreled when I was in Cuba. I am ashamed of my words and my actions, and I beg you to forgive me. I miss you, my love, and think of you every minute of every waking day. But I beg you to try to understand the shock and anxiety I felt when I learned that you were pregnant again.

I am being considered for a partnership in one of the country's leading law firms, and you know how much this means to me. I understand your strong maternal instincts, but there are times when a wife must sacrifice for her husband and his career. This is one of those times, Dolores.

I have given a lot of thought to this matter, and I am convinced that it would be best for all of us that you have the baby but give custody to your family in Cuba. I know that your sisters, Sofía and Constancia, will love and care for the child as their very own. Trust me, my love, this is the best solution for everyone concerned.

My workload in Costa Rica and Washington continues to be heavy, but as soon as it eases, I will come to Cuba and we will be together again.

Your loving husband

She put the letter down and walked over to the bed where Sebastián lay asleep. She stood there for a moment looking down at him, a warm smile on her face. Sebastián stirred, opened his eyes and then sprang out of bed.

"Mamá, I had a dream. Papá and I were playing with the baby, and..."

"Come closer, Sebastiánito. Mamá wants to hug you." She wrapped her arms around her dear little boy with the *acanelado* skin and smothered him with hugs and kisses. Her eyes immediately turned misty, and she tried but failed to hide her tears.

"Why are you crying, mamá?"

"I'm crying because I'm happy, Sebastián, happy that you are my little boy."

"When will the new baby come, mamá?" He asked, touching Dolores's belly.

"Soon, Sebastián, very soon now." There was a knock on the door and Sofia came in, looking concerned.

"I need to talk to you, Dolores."

"And I need to talk to you, Sofia," said Dolores, clutching Billy's letter in her hand. "Tell Carmen to come in and take Sebastián." Sofia left, returning a moment later with Carmen.

"Sit down, Dolores. Arturo's lawyer has filed an action, challenging the validity of papá's new will, and denying your right to inherit any part of his estate. I knew all along that his show of compromise was nothing more than a masquerade. He is a greedy, conniving man, Dolores, and he cannot be trusted."

"I don't understand," Dolores said. "I thought they were going to start distributing the assets."

"They were, but they can't now because of this suit. I am terribly sorry for you, Dolores.

You do not deserve this. It's hard to believe that my own brother is such a scoundrel, but he truly is."

"Sofia, can't we talk about this later? I received a letter from Billy, and I…"

"This is urgent," interrupted Sofia. "You only have another week to file an answer to the complaint. We will have to go to the *Notario's* office. Constancia and I will go with you. Ricardo and Constancia were planning on buying their own *finca*, and they cannot now, because the distribution will be delayed for God knows how long. Felipe, too, is deeply concerned. He begged Arturo not to go ahead with this action, but Arturo wouldn't listen."

"I don't understand," said Dolores. "Papá recognized me as his rightful daughter, and he signed a new will. How can Arturo now say that I'm not entitled to share in the estate?"

"Arturo is arguing that the new will is invalid because it thwarts mamá's intent under their original joint will. To be valid, he argues, both mamá and papá would have had to execute it."

"How could mamá have signed a new will? She had already passed away," Dolores asked.

"That will be part of our answer to the complaint," Sofia said.

Dolores handed Sofia Billy's letter. Sofia read it and handed it back to her.

"Thank God he has dropped his insistence that you have an *operation*. And if you were to agree to give up the child, I can't argue with his suggestion that you entrust the baby to me. If that's what you decide to do, dear sister, I will raise the child here in Cuba, loving it as my own. But I must be frank and honest with you, Dolores. Billy's character is in doubt here. He is clearly more concerned about his career than he is about you and your unborn child."

"Yes, Sofia, but is he that much different from other men who are committed to pursue their careers above all else?

"Yes, Dolores, his position and actions are much different than other men. Other men might ask their wives to sacifice for the benefit of their husbands' careers. But Billy asked you, indeed ordered you, to destroy your innocent unborn child. That's more than simply a sacrifice, Dolores. That's an evil act; it is in fact murder. What does that say about the man, my dear sister?" Sofia saw the tears now streaming down Dolores's face.

"Now, now, Doloresita, I'm afraid I've been too hard on you," said Sofia, who embraced and kissed Dolores. "But it's only because I don't want you to be hurt any more than you've already been hurt by Billy."

3

The final months passed, and Dolores's time was at hand.

Sofia rushed down the stairs and ran out to the plaza, where a carriage stood waiting. She shouted excitedly to the coachman:

"Go to Doctor Morales' clinic and tell him to come immediately. Doña Dolores's time is near."

The coachman raised his whip, bringing it down hard on the two black horses, and the carriage set off at a fast pace. Sofia stood watching until she was sure it was well on its way before rejoining Constancia, Daisy and Soledad, who were gathered at Dolores's bedside.

"The messenger left, and Doctor Morales should be here soon," Sofia said, reaching for Dolores's hand. "How do you feel, Doloresita?"

"I'm all right," she said, forcing a weak smile.

"It won't be long now," said Constancia. As if Nature had been listening, Dolores grimaced at the onset of another contraction.

"They're much stronger now than the earlier ones," Dolores said.

"It will all be over soon, Dolores," said Constancia. "We were all hoping for a Christmas baby, but a New Year's baby will be just as wonderful and blessed."

Just then the door opened, and little Sebastián rushed into the room. Carmen was right behind him, but before she could grab him, he ran over to his mother's bedside

"Mamá, I want to see the baby," he said as he tried to lift up the sheet covering Dolores.

Sofia pulled him away.

"The baby has not come yet, Sebastián," said Dolores. "When he does come, I promise you can see him."

Carmen took Sebastián by the hand and began tugging him out of the room, but he resisted.

"Don't worry, Sebastiánito," said Constancia. "We'll tell you when the baby comes, but for now mamá needs to rest and prepare for the baby's birth."

Sebastián went reluctantly with Carmen. Moments later, there was a knock on the door. It was Panchita, the corpulent kitchen slave. She was carrying a pitcher of cool water, which she had just drawn from the well.

"Oh, thank you, Panchita. I have a terrible thirst," said Dolores.

Sofia filled a glass of water for Dolores and propped her head up to drink it. Then she fluffed up Dolores's pillows. As they waited for Doctor Morales, the frequency and duration of Dolores's contractions increased, and it soon appeared that her time had arrived. Fortunately, within minutes they heard a carriage pulling up to the plaza. Sofia ran to the window.

"He's here, Dolores," said Sofia, watching as Mario Luis helped Doctor Morales out of the carriage and escorted him into the Main House. They walked up the stairs, and Doctor Morales entered the room, went directly over to Dolores's bedside, and asked about her contractions.

"I am going to need two basins of water, one hot and the other cold," said Doctor Morales.

Soledad and Carmen were dispatched to the kitchen as Doctor Morales opened his black satchel and began setting out his instruments on a nearby table. But as it happened, Dolores's contractions suddenly eased, and when Doctor Morales lifted the sheets and examined her, he determined that the baby was not yet ready to be born. Another hour passed in which all they could do was wait and try to ease Dolores's discomfort. At one point Carmen left the room to check on Sebastián, and through the open door they heard the clock in the hallway striking twelve o'clock midnight.

"It's going to be a New Year's baby, Dolores!" said Sofia.

It was then that her contractions began anew. These were undeniably the birth pangs, and within moments and seemingly effortless, Dolores gave one final push and the baby emerged into the world and the waiting arms of Doctor Morales; whereupon he cut the umbilical cord and began wiping the baby clean.

"It's a girl!" said Doctor Morales.

"She's white!" exclaimed Sofia, "as white as a gardenia!"

"Are you sure? Let me see her! Let me see her!" Dolores asked, excitedly.

"I'm sure, dear sister!" said Sofia.

Doctor Morales leaned over the bed now and gently placed the newborn baby girl in Dolores's outstretched arms.

"Look how beautiful, Dolores!" exclaimed Constancia.

"Oh, thank God!" said Dolores, smiling, overwhelmed with joy as she nestled her newborn baby daughter in her arms.

"My congratulations, señora McHugh and Happy New Year! I can't think of a better way to begin the new year than with a new life," said Doctor Morales, smiling broadly.

"She's so beautiful and so fair!" exclaimed Sofia. "What will you call her?"

"'Felicidad,'" responded Dolores without hesitation, as she lovingly kissed her infant daughter. "It's the name my mother had chosen for me, but it will go instead to her grandchild."

At that, baby Felicidad began to cry, and Dolores began gently rocking her in her arms.

"It's drafty in here. Maybe she's cold," said Daisy.

"I'll close the window," said Soledad. Doctor Morales was putting his instruments back in his satchel and looked up.

"Newborn infants are very susceptible to colds and other illnesses, señora McHugh, so try to keep her warm," said Doctor Morales. "Still, you're fortunate to have given birth in winter.

Summer babies are susceptible to the cholera and are often too weak to fight it. In any event, you seem to have come through it in fine form, señora McHugh, and the baby is certainly robust and healthy. I have another patient to visit, so I had better be on my way. I will say good night, and again congratulations to you, señora McHugh! I will come back the day after tomorrow to check on things. I wish you all a very Happy New Year!"

It must have been the draft because soon after Soledad closed the window, Felicidad stopped crying and went back to sleep. It was then that Dolores too fell asleep.

As Dolores lay sleeping there with her newborn baby daughter, Sofia noticed that Carmen was still in the room.

"You may go if you wish, Carmen," said Sofia. "I'll watch over them."

As Carmen was leaving, she closed the door a little too noisily, and Dolores opened her eyes, looked at her newborn baby girl and smiled.

"Happy New Year, Felicidad!" she whispered.

"Look how beautiful, how fair! Just like you said, Sofia, as white as a gardenia."

Just then little Felicidad began to whimper and stir. Dolores leaned up and Sofia positioned the pillows behind her neck and back. Much to Dolores's delight, there appeared to be an abundance of mother's milk, and Felicidad caught on quickly. Dolores's face took on a look that would have graced the finest work of religious art.

Sofia sat there mesmerized, her eyes turning misty, hoping that one day she, too, would get to experience this maternal moment of bliss. Soon Felicidad stopped nursing and went to sleep. Dolores too drifted off again

Sofia got up and left, and the room fell silent and still.

4

Billy stepped down from the carriage onto the elegant granite plaza of *La Dulce Gardenia*. He wondered whether Dolores had received his letter, informing her of the time and date of his arrival in Havana. When he looked up, he saw Mario Luis approaching.

"Bienvenido, señor McHugh and Happy New Year!"

"Thank you, Mario Luis, and a Happy New Year to you as well." The coachman stepped forward now with Billy's luggage and stood waiting as Billy dug into his purse and shook out some silver coins to pay the fare.

"Doña Dolores will be very happy to see you, señor," said Mario Luis. Billy wondered whether she had given birth, but did not want to ask Mario Luis. As they entered the Main House and walked to the staircase, Billy spotted Felipe de Castilla coming down the stairs.

"Oh, it's you, Billy! Bienvenido and Happy New Year!" Billy remembered the shock and dismay he'd experienced, when Felipe revealed Dolores pregnancy before she herself had had the chance to tell him. *Don't tell me, Felipe. I don't want to hear it from you like the last time.*

"Happy New Year, Felipe. It's nice to see you again," Billy said. They stopped on the stairs and shook hands.

"How have you been?" Felipe asked. "I understand you've been working hard on a railroad and banana venture in Costa Rica. You know, I was thinking that we might be able to collaborate on some other projects in Central America, once we clear up some of our estate problems."

"Well, I've now successfully completed the negotiations in Costa Rica, and I'll be returning home to Washington, so I'll have more time for that. And tell me, how is Arturo? He too mentioned he had some interest in some Central American projects."

Felipe smiled and shrugged his shoulders.

"Arturo is Arturo. He does things his way and his way only, so it might not be so easy. He is very independent minded, that is, except when it comes to Cuba. For that, he is a monarchist, a monarchist to the very core. But I must be going. I have some papers to file with the *Notario*. I'm sure I'll see you tonight at dinner and we can discuss things."

"I look forward to it, Felipe." Billy turned and continued up the stairs. He heard a door close and spotted Carmen, who had just come out of Dolores's quarters.

"Why, Massa Billy! How nice to see you and Happy New Year!" Carmen smiled and then walked away. Billy stood for a moment, trying to gather his thoughts. He knocked, and Sofia opened the door.

"Billy! Billy's here, Dolores!" said Sofia.

"Billy, you're here at last! Come and see our new baby girl!" Sebastián suddenly appeared and ran over to Billy excitedly.

"Hello, papá, look what I got!" He held up a little book with horses on the cover.

Billy patted him on the head, then walked over oh so slowly to Dolores's bed. He was tense and apprehensive, afraid of what he was about to see. He leaned over slightly now, but his vision was obscured by the blanket, partly covering the baby's face.

"This is your newborn baby daughter, Billy. Look how beautiful," Dolores said as she pulled back the blanket.

"She's white!" Billy exclaimed. "She's white!" he repeated, staring at her wide-eyed.

"Yes, my love, as white as a gardenia. That's what Sofia said the moment she was born.

I want to name her Felicidad, Billy. I hope you agree."

461

Billy didn't respond and kept staring with amazement at his beautiful, white baby daughter.

"Why is the baby so white, mamá?" Sebastián asked, as he moved closer and appeared to be about to touch her face.

"No, dear, we must not wake her," said Dolores as Billy glanced at him.

"I want to hold her, my love?" Billy said, with the widest smile that Dolores had seen from him in years.

"She will be waking soon, my love, and you can hold her to your heart's content."

"I'm hungry, mamá," said Sebastián, circling around the bed and beginning to fuss.

"Now, now, Sebastián, please behave. You will wake the baby," said Dolores.

"I will take him in the other room," said Sofia. "Come with me, Sebastián." She reached for his hand, but he resisted and ran to the other side of the bed, where he began tugging on Billy's trousers. But Billy was oblivious to everyone and everything, totally captivated and enamored of his adorable, fair-skinned baby girl.

"Mamá, I'm hungry," Sebastián said again, and in a rather loud voice. The baby began to stir, moving her lips as though she were nursing.

"May I hold her now?" Billy asked.

"You can hold her to your heart's content, Billy," said Dolores, smiling lovingly at her husband.

Billy reached down and gently picked up baby Felicidad. His smile would have lit up the darkest of rooms, as he rocked her gently back and forth, cooing with her all the while.

"How did you get to be so beautiful," he mused, nuzzling her lovingly. "I like the name Felicidad. It fits her perfectly, my love. I can already tell that she is a happy child. It almost looks like she's trying to smile."

"Will you take me riding, papá?" Sebastián asked, staring up at his father. "Please papá, please!," he said in a loud and insistent voice. It startled baby Felicidad and she began to cry.

"Now, now, my princess, don't cry," but baby Felicidad only cried harder.

"I'll take her, Billy. She's hungry." Billy carefully passed her back to Dolores.

Sebastián began tugging again on Billy's trousers.

"Go along now with Auntie Sofia, Sebastián," said Dolores. "Carmen will get you something to eat. Hurry now."

"Let's leave Dolores alone, Billy so she can nurse the baby," said Sofia.

"I won't be long Billy," said Dolores. Billy leaned over and kissed his wife on the cheek, then followed Sofia out of the room.

"Billy, there are some issues about papá's estate that I need to discuss with you," Sofia said. "If you will come to my quarters now, I can bring you up to date."

"How long will it take?"

"I promise you that I will try to keep it short. I know you are anxious to get back in there with your new baby girl, but this is important."

Sofia occupied a large section of the second floor of the Main House. Her quarters contained a good-sized study and library. There were comfortable armchairs, and the walls were lined with mahogany bookcases filled with books, most of which appeared to be legal texts. But there were also novels, including Miguel de Cervantes' *Don Quixote*.

"Have a seat, Billy. May I get you some tea or brandy?" Sofia asked. Billy declined, and Sofia got right to the point.

"Arturo has filed a lawsuit, challenging the validity of papá's will and denying Dolores's right to a share of the estate."

"On what possible grounds?"

"Well, we talked about this before. He is arguing that papá's second will could not legally change the joint will, which he and mama executed years before; because, it would thwart their joint intent, which was to exclude the illegitimate Dolores from any inheritance. The suit maintains that at the time they executed the joint will, papá had not yet recognized Dolores as his rightful daughter. Arturo argues that mamá never would have intended to include the illegitimate Dolores in the estate."

"Didn't you tell me some time ago that there was a Spanish Civil Code provision prohibiting the disinheritance of offspring?"

"Yes, I did, and we will certainly argue that. I should also tell you Billy that Constancia and I are deeply opposed to this suit and will do everything we can to ensure that Dolores gets her fair share of the estate.

"I think I'll take that brandy after all, if you don't mind," Billy said.

"Yes, of course," Sofia said, reaching for the cord chain on the wall to signal the servants. A moment later Mario Luis appeared. "Mario, bring Mister McHugh a glass of brandy, and a glass of sherry for me, please."

"Right away, doña Sofia." Sofia noticed that Billy was staring at Mario Luis, who was limping badly. When the old house slave left the room, Sofia turned to Billy.

"He is eighty-eight years old, and we don't know how much longer he'll be with us, Billy"

"That's a ripe old age for anyone," Billy said, "but especially for a slave."

"Well, these Africans all tend to live long lives as long as they are treated well, and Mario Luis has always been treated well."

"We've had a similar experience in the United States for the most part," Billy said.

Mario Luis returned with the drinks, and as Billy sat and

talked more about the lawsuit, his mind wandered, and he could think of nothing else but his newborn baby girl in the next room.

"When are you planning on leaving, Billy?"

"I can only stay another few days, Sofia. I need to get back to Washington soon. I found out that there's a steamer to New York leaving next week, and I'm hoping that Dolores and the baby will have recuperated enough to come with me."

Sofia appeared surprised. She had assumed that Dolores would stay in Cuba at least until the baby was a few months old.

There was a knock on the door. Carmen opened it and peeked in.

"Doña Dolores told me to tell you that she's finished nursing the baby." Billy took another swallow of his brandy and then stood up.

"We can talk about this later, can't we?"

"Yes, of course," said Sofía. Billy immediately went back to Dolores's quarters, where he saw that baby Felicidad was asleep in the crib next to Dolores's bed.

"She's asleep, my love," said Dolores.

"How are you feeling, Doloresita?" Billy asked, as he bent down and kissed her tenderly on the cheek. She smiled warmly and reached for his hand.

"I'm feeling much better today Billy, but I miss you. We have not had much time to talk. You haven't told me what you think of our newborn baby girl, though I believe I already know."

"When I look at her, my love, it's hard for me to believe. She is so adorable, so precious and she is ours. I was tortured with anxiety and worry during your pregnancy, and I took it out on you, my sweet Doloresita. Every time I think of what I ordered you to do..."

"Let's not talk about it, Billy!" interrupted Dolores. "It's over and done with."

"I'm so sorry, my love! Can you ever forgive me?"

"I forgive you, Billy." She grasped his hand, pulled him closer and kissed him on the lips. "You were upset, my love. I understand, and I think you were working too hard. It was the strain, but that is all in the past, and that is where it belongs. We need to concentrate on the future, the future of our children and the future of our family. We have a darling baby daughter, Billy, Sebastián has a baby sister and we have all the makings of a happy family…"

Just one week after the birth of their second child, Billy, Dolores, Sebastián and baby Felicidad departed Havana on the steamer *Trade Winds*, en route to New York, their final destination, Washington.

CHAPTER XXI

Triiumph and Tragedy

On June 1 1866, William Calhoun McHugh was named a partner in the prestigious law firm of Henry Phipps & Partners. The vote was unanimous, which Senior Partner, Joseph Bartlett, disclosed to Billy during the celebratory dinner given in his honor. Within weeks, Billy and Dolores purchased the lovely southern colonial house on Connecticut Avenue that they had been admiring for some time, and Dolores undertook the task of making it a home, furnishing and decorating it with great care and enthusiasm. It was a three-story house with five bedrooms, a large kitchen and a combination library and study. There was a large backyard, filled with fruit trees and a swing for Sebastián. It had a large playroom adjacent to his bedroom, which was filled with toys and stuffed horses, some of them fashioned by Julius, who along with Becky, took up employment again for the McHugh household.

Dolores contacted Thomas Meadows of the Congressional School, and he offered her a substitute teacher position for the September term, with assurances that it would likely become a full-time teaching position.

The 4th of July dawned sunny and hot, and as the McHugh family prepared to depart for the picnic grounds, Felicidad began to cry and fuss.

"Maybe we should leave her here with Becky," said Dolores, but Billy would not hear of it. He wanted his Partners to see her.

"Let's go, papá!" Sebastián said. "I want to ride the ponies."

"Here, let me hold her," Billy said. Dolores passed Felicidad to his waiting arms, and he began gently rocking her. "There, my little angel. Papá has you now," he cooed. It was not long before Felicidad was living up to her name, smiling and looking up at her papá, her big blue eyes all aglow.

"Carry her, my love. You have a calming effect on her, and vice-versa."

The first time Billy saw baby Felicidad, he was truly smitten. He adored her and sought to meet her every need, even feeling jealous that he could not feed her like Dolores. He often intervened with both Becky and Dolores, believing that he knew better how to care for her. He would pick her up, smiling, hugging, kissing and cooing with her, evoking in her little baby smiles of delight and the first signs of laughter. He loved to stand over her crib when she was asleep; admiring her, delighting in her, planning all manner of activities he would do with her as she grew up. It was obvious that little Felicidad was just as smitten with her papá as he was with her.

"Let's go, papá! I want to ride the ponies." Sebastián said again.

Billy did not respond, continuing to rock Felicidad and delight in her presence.

Becky glanced at Sebastián, knowing that he would not be getting the kind of love and attention that Billy gave to his white baby girl. Becky knew, however, that Dolores would give him the love and attention he would need without showing favoritism or depriving Felicidad.

When they arrived at the picnic, there was already a large and lively crowd. The law firm's management committee had chosen a delightful spot in Rock Creek Park with a bubbly stream as a backdrop. Julie and Brad Mitchum spotted Billy and Dolores. Joseph Bartlett, who was talking to Minor Keith, also spotted Billy and was the first to greet him.

"Well, here's our newest partner," Bartlett said, putting his arm around Billy, and reaching out with his other to shake his hand. "How does it feel, Billy, to come to the firm's 4th of July picnic as a partner of Henry Phipps & Partners?"

"It feels wonderful, Mister Bartlett," Billy said, smiling and feeling quite proud of himself.

"Please call me Joseph, Billy. You have certainly earned the right to."

Minor Keith, who was standing next to Joseph Bartlett, reached out and shook Billy's hand.

"Henry Phipps & Partners has got one fine young partner here in Billy McHugh," said Keith. "Those contracts he negotiated were the best I've ever seen. If he does as well with the railroad construction contracts, we'll have the finest railroad in Central America, better even than the Panama Railroad."

"Thank you, sir," said Billy. "I thoroughly enjoyed the work, and I'm very happy you're pleased." Billy signaled for Dolores to come over. "You haven't yet met the new addition to the McHugh family, Joseph."

Dolores approached holding Felicidad. Sebastián, meanwhile, had spotted Jackie, the Mitchums' little boy, and ran over to him.

"This is Felicidad," said Billy proudly.

"Oh, she's a little doll! Congratulations, Billy!" said Bartlett, his admiration echoed by Minor Keith.

"How old is she?" Keith asked.

"She's six months," said Billy and Dolores simultaneously. "She was born in Havana on New Year's Day."

"So this is little Felicidad," said Bartlett. "I've heard all about her, but this is the first time I've had the pleasure of seeing her in person. She's a beautiful child, and I can see why you're both so proud of her."

"What did you say her name is?" asked Minor Keith. "It sounded Spanish to me, and as you well know, I don't speak a word of Spanish."

"Her name is FE-LIC-E-DAD," Billy said, pronouncing each syllable slowly and clearly. "It means happiness in Spanish." At that Felicidad began to cry, frightened perhaps by the strange voices.

"I'll take her," said Billy. "There, now, you're not living up to your name" he said as he nuzzled and kissed her. Minor Keith had to laugh at the irony, but a moment later, Felicidad stopped crying. "There now, my little angel, you're happy again," Billy said with a smile.

"She really loves her papa, doesn't she?" said Bartlett.

"And it looks like it's mutual," added Minor Keith. Just then, Sebastián ran over to them.

"Papá, Jackie is going to ride the ponies," he said in Spanish, tugging on Billy's pants leg. "Take me, papá, hurry!" he continued, this time in English.

"Hello there, Sebastián, do you remember me? I visited you once," said Joseph Bartlett. Sebastián didn't respond and continued to tug at Billy's pants legs.

"Say hello to Mister Bartlett, Sebastián," said Dolores. But Sebastián still did not respond. "He remembers you, Mister Bartlett. He's too excited now about the pony rides."

"Of course, Mrs. McHugh. I remember when I was his age," said Bartlett.

Minor Keith stared at Sebastián, surely noticing his dark skin in sharp contrast to that of his baby sister.

"How old is your boy?" Keith asked.

"He will be four on the first of August," Dolores said, looking then to Billy. "Why don't you take Sebastián to ride the ponies, Billy? He's been waiting all week for this."

Billy was not quite ready to leave Bartlett and Minor Keith, but he complied, passing Felicidad back to Dolores.

"I'll be back shortly, gentlemen. Let's go Sebastián." He walked away with his little boy with the *acanelado* skin.

Dolores excused herself and joined Julie Mitchum, and the two of them decided to go down and watch their little boys ride the ponies.

Billy joined Brad Mitchum, and they walked down to the pony pen with their two little boys. There were four ponies for the children to ride, but at least four times as many children. So, a line had formed, and Billy and Brad stood with the boys, waiting their turn.

"I want the black and white pony!" Sebastián said in a loud voice.

"I want the white one!" said Jackie.

"They're all nice ponies," said Brad Mitchum, "so don't be disappointed, Jackie, if you don't get the white one." The line moved forward.

"I want the black and white one, papá," Sebastián said again. "He looks like Francis' horse but not as big."

"You will just have to wait and see," said Billy, as he rubbed Sebastián's curly top head of brown hair.

"I guess Sebastián has ridden before," said Brad. "I understand that he's has spent a lot of time in Cuba."

"Yes, he has Brad, but as far as I know, he's never really ridden a horse, have you, Sebastián ?"

"Auntie Constancia let me sit on a horse, papá, and I wanted to ride." Sebastián started jumping up and down excitedly, anticipating his turn to ride. as a tall negro stable hand led the white pony over to be mounted.

"I get the white one!" cried Jackie excitedly, as Brad led Jackie over to the pen. The negro picked him up, put him on the pony and they began walking around the pen.

Now it was Sebastián's turn. Another stable hand led a shiny black pony up to the stand and called out, "Next."

Billy took Sebastián by the hand and started walking down to the pen, but Sebastián resisted.

"No, papá not the black pony," said Sebastián, seeing the black and white pony right behind the black one.

"Who's next?" the stable hand called out.

"Hurry up," said a woman with a little girl behind Billy. "Go ahead! You're holding us up!"

Billy did not like the tone of her voice, but he tried nonetheless to hurry Sebastián.

"Come on, Sebastián. There's nothing wrong with that black pony. We're holding others up who want to ride."

"I want the black and white pony, please papa." The woman behind them continued to fume, as the stable hand lifted Sebastián up and placed him on the black pony.

"That negro boy shouldn't even be here. Don't want to ride the BLACK pony! Why not? Birds of a feather by my mind!"

Everyone heard her, including Sebastián, who was crying as he sat atop the black pony. Billy turned, looked at the woman and was about to say something, but he let it pass.

Later that afternoon Billy saw Minor Keith and Henry Phipps at the refreshment stand. Standing next to Minor Keith was the woman who had made the racist remarks about Sebastián.

"Billy, I'd like you to meet my daughter, Madelyn," said Minor Keith. "Madelyn, this is Billy McHugh. He is the newest partner in Henry Phipps & Partners. He did all the negotiating for us in Costa Rica. We couldn't have gotten all we got without him."

It was unclear whether Keith's daughter recognized Billy from the pony rides. There was no doubt on Billy's part.

2

As the September school term neared, Dolores was concerned that Sebastián was having difficulty transitioning back to English, and she wanted to enroll him in a nursery school where he could improve it. She inquired of Mister Meadows at the Congressional School, and he recommended the Friedrich Froebel Institute, which had pioneered the concept of kindergarten education in Germany. Dolores discussed it with Billy, and he had no objection.

Dolores made an appointment with a Miss Helga Mueller and visited the Froebel Institute to discuss the curriculum and its appropriateness for Sebastián. Dolores was very impressed with Miss Mueller, with the school's physical plant, and especially with a Miss Chambers, whom Dolores met and learned would be teaching the class. Miss Chambers assured Dolores that Sebastián would likely have little trouble reacquiring a facility with English. Dolores was quite pleased and enrolled Sebastián for the September term.

On the first day of classes, Billy left early for his law firm as usual, and Dolores got ready to take Sebastián for his first day of kindergarten.

"Ya be a good lil boy, Sebastián," said Becky, smiling and holding Felicidad.

Dolores kissed Felicidad good-bye, took Sebastián by the hand and walked with him out to the street. She had made previous arrangements with Francis to send one of his carriages.

"Good mornin, Mizz McHugh," said the driver. "Sho is a pretty monin, ma'am.

Where can Ahh take ya dis monin?"

"Good morning, we're going to the Friedrich Frobel Institute, the German School," said Dolores.

The driver helped her into the carriage. Sebastián broke away and ran up to the horse, which had just let loose with a large load of horse dung in the street.

"This horsie poops a lot," he said in broken English, heavily accented.

"Hurry, Sebastián or we'll be late," cried Dolores.

"Aa'll get 'im," said the driver.

He picked Sebastián up, carried him back and placed him on Dolores's lap. And they set off for the Friedrich Froebel Institute. When they arrived, there was a cluster of carriages parked in front of the school, and the mothers were walking down to the entrance with their children. Dolores could not help but notice that everyone was white. Standing at the door, greeting the children and their mothers were Miss Mueller, the Headmistress, and Miss Chambers, the kindergarten teacher

"Good morning, Mrs. McHugh!" said Miss Mueller.

Her face then took on a startled look as she spotted Sebastián, who had been standing behind Dolores fooling with another little boy.

"Oh, is this is your little boy? We need to talk a moment, Mrs. McHugh. Come inside with me, please."

Miss Mueller turned to Miss Chambers.

"Martha, watch her little boy a moment while I talk to Mrs. McHugh."

"His name is Sebastián," said Dolores, already guessing what the problem was.

"Yes, Sebastián, thank you, Mrs. McHugh."

Miss Chambers took hold of Sebastián's hand, and Dolores followed Miss Mueller into her office.

"Have a seat, Mrs. McHugh. I must say I did not know when

you enrolled him that Sebastián was of mixed race. I am so sorry to have to tell you that the Friedrich Froebel Institute cannot accept children of mixed race. Please understand, Mrs. McHugh. I have nothing against negro children, but it is the policy of the Institute. I would recommend that you seek to enroll Sebastián in the Frederick Douglas School for Coloreds. It has a fine reputation, a good faculty, and I am confident they can provide a good foundation for your boy's education. We, of course, will refund your payment in full. Again, Mrs. McHugh, I'm truly sorry if we caused you and Sebastián any inconvenience."

Miss Mueller smiled officiously and extended her hand. Reluctantly, Dolores reached out and shook it. Miss Mueller then led Dolores back outside, where Miss Chambers was holding Sebastián's hand and greeting the last of the new kindergarten children.

"You have a delightful little boy here, Mrs. McHugh," said Miss Chambers, not yet aware that the School had rejected him because of his race.

"Come along, Sebastián; we're going home," said Dolores

"But you said school starts today, mamá"

"Good luck, Mrs. McHugh," said Miss Mueller. "I'm sure you will find the Frederick Douglas School to your liking."

Miss Chambers looked disappointed and watched as mother and child walked slowly back to the street.

"Why are we leaving, mamá? You said Jackie Mitchum is going to this school. I want to go too," Sebastián said in Spanish."

"There are some problems with this school, Sebastián. I will explain it to you later. We will find you a better school. Don't worry."

Out on the street, Dolores noticed that the carriage she had arrived in had left. As chance would have it, she looked up and spotted Francis' carriage passing by and called out to him.

Since returning from Cuba, and in spite of Billy's admonitions, she had ridden with Francis on several occasions. He just always seemed to be there when she needed a carriage.

"Good morning, Mrs. McHugh, where can I take you?" Francis asked, as he stepped down and greeted her and Sebastián.

"Good morning, Francis. We're going back home."

"Mickey, mamá," Sebastián cried, as he ran up to pet his favorite horse.

"Are you planning on teaching at this German School?" Francis asked.

"No, and I certainly would not want to," Dolores said, as she glanced at Francis, judging that Sebastián was out of earshot. "I thought I had enrolled Sebastián in kindergarten, but they informed me that they don't admit negroes or children of mixed race."

Francis frowned, nodding his head in sympathy, acknowledging that he was familiar with the school's policies regarding negroes.

"I want to feed Mickey, mama!," said Sebastián quite loudly.

"Come back here now. We're going home," said Dolores

Francis helped Dolores into the carriage, then turned to Sebastián.

"I just happen to have an apple for Mickey, young man. You can feed it to him when I get you home."

Sebastián smiled, and Francis picked him up, carried him back to the carriage and placed him on Dolores's lap. As he drove off, he opened the small window behind the driver's seat so he could talk to Dolores.

"I am glad to hear that you are not going to be working at that school, Mrs. McHugh. I can assure you that they are not your kind of people."

Dolores looked at Sebastián, wondering if he had understood what had just occurred at the German school. She put her arm around her dear little boy with the *acanelado* skin and hugged him.

When Dolores told Billy that the German kindergarten refused to admit Sebastián and had suggested that she enroll him in the Frederick Douglass School for Coloreds, Billy reacted angrily and forbade it.

"Now it's the schools rejecting him, and in doing so they're rejecting us. I'm sure there will be other incidents like the one at the 4th of July picnic. Please understand, Dolores, I feel sorry for Sebastián. I know it's not his fault, but it's not my fault either, and…"

"Well, whose fault is it then," Dolores interrupted, "mine? my family's? my mother's? my grandmother's?" She was noticeably upset.

"I know that's what you're thinking, Billy."

It was the same old issue—*sangre de negro*—and it remained contentious and unresolved.

3

Becky walked into the room carrying Felicidad.

"She jest now wake up, Mizz McHugh, but Aah has ta go shoppin fo groceries, so ya needs ta take her. Sebastián can come long wid me."

Dolores motioned for Becky to bring Felicidad to her, but Billy said he would take her.

"There, now, my sweet princess, papá has you now."

Billy rocked her and cooed with her lovingly, touching her little pink fingers. Dolores felt compelled to tell him.

"I know how very much you love Felicidad, Billy. I love her just as much, but Sebastián also needs your love and attention. He needs it even more now because he sees you showering so much of it on Felicidad."

Billy did not meet Dolores's eyes and kept cooing with Felicidad.

"It's cruel what you're doing Billy."

Billy still did not respond, and Dolores's tone changed from one of scolding to one expressing pain and despair.

"We must protect him, Billy. We must!" Dolores said.

"And how do you suggest we protect him without harming ourselves? I suggested that we turn him over to Becky and Julius or that you take him back to Cuba and let your family raise him, and you accused me of being cold and cruel. I still believe it is worth considering. You can always visit him. Race and color are less of a problem in Cuba. You know that better than I do. It would solve the problem, and it would be better for us as well."

Dolores looked at her husband with disbelief. She had heard it all before, but the fact that he brought it up again meant that he was still deadly serious about it.

"You are not the man I married, Billy. I remember how you used to be. You were protective of black people and people of mixed race. You taught Julius how to read and write. You left your home and went north, because you did not believe in slavery. You brought Julius with you and gave him his freedom. And yet you can sit here now and suggest that we abandon our dear sweet son, our own flesh and blood, because his skin color might reflect poorly on you and might damage your precious career. How could you, Billy? How could you be so cold and so cruel?"

Billy had heard it all before, and he sat there silently, judging that it would only make it worse to say something more. He looked at Felicidad, who suddenly started crying.

"There now, my little angel," you're with papá now," he said, kissing and nuzzling her. She calmed down some, but then started crying again. Dolores took her.

Dolores normally nursed Felicidad in the bedroom, seeking

privacy and solitude. But this time she did not. She sat down across from Billy, unbuttoned her blouse and exposed her breast. Billy watched as Felicidad's little mouth sought and found Dolores's large, brown nipple and began to suckle. Billy was immediately transfixed and could not take his eyes off them. Before long, he felt the first signs of arousal. There came a point when Dolores gently pulled Felicidad off that one breast and moved her to the other, which tantalized and titillated Billy all the more. There came a point, however, when Dolores looked up and met Billy's eyes, instantly bursting his erotic fantasy like a child's summer soap bubble…

Julius called out now from the kitchen.

"Billy, Aah needs ta talk wid ya." Dolores stopped nursing Felicidad and covered her breasts.

"I'm in the living room, Julius,"

Julius walked in and began telling Billy about the carriage house he had been working on in the back yard.

"Aah pretty much done finished er, Billy, but think ya should have a look jest ta be sho."

Billy got up now and went out to the backyard with Julius. He had decided to acquire a carriage, wanting to end their dependence on carriages for hire, and especially those belonging to Francis, the mulatto carriage driver.

When Julius left for the day, Billy returned to the house and found Dolores in the bedroom with Felicidad slung over her shoulder. She was pacing back and forth, patting her on the back, trying to get her to burp.

"Oh, Billy, I need to make plans for returning to Cuba. I received a telegraph from Sofia, and there are some documents concerning the estate and the lawsuit that require my signature. At first they thought they could send them, but now they say that I must appear in person."

"What about your commitment to the Congressional School? Aren't they expecting you to teach a class this semester?"

Dolores stopped pacing and turned to Billy.

"They're starting me off again as a substitute teacher, and I've already notified Mister Meadows that I will be gone for the first few weeks of the term."

"What about the children?" Billy asked, his expression reflecting his disappointment.

"They will come with me, of course."

"Couldn't you take Sebastián and leave Felicidad here with me? Becky can take care of her."

"Becky can't nurse her."

Billy had no argument for that.

Dolores resumed her pacing with Felicidad, trying to get her to burp.

"Would you like me to help you, my love?" Billy asked, his smile acknowledging the silliness of his offer.

"Come on, Felicidad just one more burp," said Dolores. No sooner had she said it than Felicidad burped and loudly so. "There it is. Now she's done."

Billy smiled and put his arms around Dolores's waist.

"How about if you put her down for a nap, my love?"

"I don't think she will nap now, Billy. She's not tired."

"Well, why don't you put her down anyway, so you and I can take a little nap?" She knew exactly what he had in mind and put Felicidad down in her crib.

During the course of their marriage, Dolores had rarely denied Billy his physical needs. It was something deeply embedded in the Spanish and Cuban culture. So, in spite of their having argued rather seriously just minutes before, Dolores grasped Billy's outstretched hand and walked with him over to their marital bed.

5

Dolores closed her valise and breathed a sigh of relief.

"Hurry, Sebastián. We do not want to miss our train. The steamer won't wait for us, and if we miss it, we'll have to wait another week."

"I'm ready, mamá," he said as he picked up his little satchel.

Felicidad was napping, and Dolores tried to wake her as gently as possible.

"There, Felicidad, we must leave now," Dolores said as she picked her up and kissed her tenderly. Sebastián ran over.

"Why does she sleep so much, mamá?"

"She's a baby, Sebastián. Babies sleep a lot. You slept a lot when you were a baby. Hurry now, go look in your room to make sure you have not forgotten anything."

He ran off, returning a moment later.

"Mamá, I looked out the window, and the carriage is there. Francis is feeding Mickey. Can I go out and wait in front?"

"All right, but take your satchel. I will be right out." Dolores nursed Felicidad for a fast few minutes.

"I will give you more later, sweet child."

Dolores picked up her valise and went outside, where Francis stood waiting with his carriage.

Sebastián petted Mickey, talking to him excitedly, as though he were expecting a response.

"Good morning, Mrs. McHugh," said Francis, smiling broadly. "I am driving my new carriage today, so you will be riding to the B&O Station in style, ma'am."

"Good morning, Francis. Yes, I can see that it is a shiny new carriage. How very nice of you!"

He took their luggage and secured it atop the carriage.

"And how is your pretty baby girl this morning? Oh, she is noticeably bigger than the last time I saw her!"

"Yes, she's growing very fast, Francis."

Dolores then called out to Sebastián.

"I'll get him, ma'am."

Francis picked him up and put him into the cab.

"Mamá, I want to ride a horse in Cuba. I'm old enough now, even Auntie Constancia said so…"

Francis climbed up to the coachman's seat and urged Mickey with a light touch of the whip and a loud giddy-up. As he was wont to do whenever Dolores was his passenger, Francis reached back and opened the little window so he could talk to her.

"How long will you be in Cuba, Mrs. McHugh?"

"Several weeks, as best I can judge, Francis."

"Blanche has been asking about you, ma'am."

"Please tell her that I hope to meet with her again when I return."

"I will tell her. Oh, and have you found another school for Sebastián? I would strongly recommend the Frederick Douglas School for Coloreds, ma'am. I know some of the teachers and they are excellent, just as good as the white schools, maybe even better."

Dolores was disappointed that Francis had mentioned that, because Sebastián reacted immediately.

"Mamá, why can't I go to Jackie's school? Is it because I am not white? Is it mamá, is it?"

Dolores knew now that Sebastián had understood why he was not admitted to the German school, and it deeply troubled her.

"Sebastián, dear, I promise you that I will find a good school for you, a school where you will be happy, have lots of friends and receive a good education."

From the expression on Francis' face, it was clear that he was impressed with how Dolores had handled Sebastián's sensitive question, but he surely regretted having triggered it in the first place.

They rounded a corner and had to slow down as a large crowd of people, both white and black, were marching in the street, heading for the White House. They carried placards and banners, denouncing President Andrew Johnson. Francis brought the carriage to a stop, as all they could do is sit and wait for the crowd to pass. When finally the way was clear, he drove off. However, there was another crowd surging onto the street heading their way. This one was even larger, louder and more unruly than the last. They, too, were carrying placards and banners in support of states' rights, and against the "unconstitutional" fourteenth amendment.

Sebastián stuck his head out the window.

"Keep your head inside the carriage, Sebastián," said Dolores, "It's not safe."

Francis knew that Dolores had a train to catch, and he was becoming concerned with these delays. Once the crowd had passed, he applied a strong whip to Mickey, and they set off at a fast clip, eventually entering Massachusetts Avenue. They were a few blocks from the station and crossing the intersection of Massachusetts and New Jersey Avenues, when Francis suddenly cried out "Whoa, Whoa, Mickey!" He pulled back hard on the reins, trying his best to avoid the fire engine that was rushing to a warehouse fire near the train station. But it was too late, and the fire engine plowed broadside into the carriage with a thunderous roar of crashing metal, wood and horseflesh. The impact split the carriage in two, sending the cab section tumbling over again and again before coming to rest upside down a half-block away, the doors open and the wheels spinning. Passers-by who had witnessed the terrifying collision rushed to the carriage, horrified. They looked inside the wreckage and saw Dolores and Sebastián pinned up against the side of the carriage by several thick metal support members from the carriage frame. They were covered in blood and there was no movement.

"There's a woman and child trapped in the carriage," shouted one man. "Hurry, someone please go and summon an ambulance. The Naval Hospital is close by. I'll try to get the woman and child out of the wreckage."

"Oh, my God! There's a baby here beside the tree!" yelled an elegantly dressed woman carrying a parasol.

She bent down and looked more closely.

"It's a baby girl," she said, a look of horror on her face.

Several firemen rushed over to the carriage wreckage.

"That was one horrific collision!" cried one of them. "But the carriage certainly got the worst of it."

The fire engine was virtually undamaged and the horses escaped with minor injuries.

"Oh, the poor little thing is not moving," said the elegantly-dressed woman, who was obviously horrified by the death-like appearance of the baby.

A husky fireman rushed over to help, noticing a deep wound on the side of Felicidad's head. His countenance expressed a profound sadness, and he made the sign of the cross but said not a word.

Dolores and Sebastián were trapped in the twisted wreckage of the carriage, and it took some strenuous efforts with crowbars to finally free them. They were both unconscious and covered with nasty cuts and gashes all over their bodies, but they appeared to be breathing. One of the firemen retrieved some blankets from the fire engine and laid Dolores and Sebastián down on them. The elegantly dressed woman who had discovered baby Felicidad, picked her up and gently put her down on the blankets next to them.

The ambulance arrived, and a doctor, a nurse and two assistants jumped out. They rendered first aid to Dolores and Sebastián as best they could, then placed them on stretchers and loaded them into the ambulance.

"Are there any other injured?" the doctor asked.

"You saw the baby, didn't you?"

"Yes, we put her in the ambulance with the woman and the little boy.

"There's a colored man layin' over there in the street," said one of the firemen, pointing to the body. "It's probably the carriage driver. From the looks of things he's not going to make it."

"Let me be the one to determine that," said the doctor, who rushed over and felt for a pulse. He then signaled to his assistant for another stretcher, and they loaded Francis into the ambulance.

6

By the time the ambulance arrived at the hospital, Francis had taken his last breath and was pronounced dead. Dolores and Sebastián regained consciousness a few hours later. The doctors' initial diagnosis was that Dolores had suffered a collapsed lung and a concussion. Sebastián had two broken legs and a deep cut close to his carotid artery, which would not stop bleeding. The little boy's pain was apparently excruciating, and he screamed in agony. In spite of his age, they believed it was necessary to administer morphine.

Though seriously injured, doctors were hopeful that both Dolores and Sebastián would make a full recovery. The doctors were silent and subdued as to Felicidad's prognosis. Witnesses at the scene of the collision stated that the baby was thrown from the carriage on impact. When Dolores regained consciousness, she was wracked with pain and frantic with worry over her children. The doctors informed her of Sebastián's injuries and diagnosis but said little about Felicidad's condition and diagnosis. When she questioned them, they were evasive in responding. Dolores pleaded with them to bring Felicidad to her bedside, but the doctors said it was not advisable.

The ambulance crew found Dolores's name and address from the steamship ticket in her purse, and the hospital sent a messenger to the McHugh residence to inform them of the accident, and that the woman and her two children were being treated at the Naval Hospital.

Billy had left the office early that day and was home by six o'clock. Becky was in the kitchen preparing his supper, when there came a knock on the door.

"I'll get that, Becky," Billy said.

He opened the door and saw a man in a white frock.

"Are you Mister William McHugh?"

"Yes, I'm William McHugh."

"I'm sorry to have to tell you this, Mister McHugh, but there's been an accident. Your wife and children have been taken to the hospital, and—"

"What! What kind of accident? Are you certain! Are they all right? Is the baby all right!"

Billy's face turned pale.

"It was a carriage accident, sir. However, I am not aware of their injuries or present condition. If you will come with me to the hospital…"

"Are you sure you've got the right person? McHugh?" interrupted Billy.

"Yes, I'm sure, Mister McHugh."

"Becky, Becky! Come in here right away!" Billy became frantic as Becky rushed into the parlor.

"There's been an accident, Becky! Dolores and the children are in the hospital," Billy said, a terrified look on his face, as images of his beloved Felicidad flashed before him

"Oh, ma God! Don't tell me!" Becky said

"I'll wait for you in the carriage," said the messenger.

"I'm going to the hospital, Becky, and I want you to come with me."

Billy sat in the carriage, gripped with worry as they rode to the hospital. His mind was spinning frantically, lurching back and forth from one terrifying possibility to another.

We're sorry Mister Mchugh, but the baby did not make it. We did all we could.

No, Lord, please! I beg you!

We did our best to save your wife. We're so sorry, Mister Mchugh.

God in Heaven, don't let them die!

We were able to save your little boy, Mister Mchugh. He is strong and will make a full recovery.

"Aah knows what ya thinking, Billy, but da Lord ain't gonna let 'em die," said Becky. She then turned to the messenger. "Do ya. know how Mizz McHugh and da chillren are doin'?"

"No, I did not see them, and I'm not aware of their condition," said the man.

"Where da accident happen? Becky asked, as she continued to question the messenger.

"At the intersection of Massachusetts and New Jersey Avenues," he said.

At that, the coachman, who had been catching snippets of the conversation, blurted out:

"They should station a police officer there to direct the carriages and slow them down. They go too fast in that intersection."

When they arrived at the hospital, Billy jumped out of the carriage and ran inside, leaving Becky to find her way. He inquired at the desk and was told his wife and children were in the second-floor ward. The nurse behind the counter pointed to the stairs, and Billy ran up and rushed over to the doctors and nurses, who saw his distress and tried to calm him down.

"I'm Billy McHugh. My wife and children were in an accident! Are they all right? Where are they? Take me to them! The baby is just eight-months old! Is she all right?" he asked in a loud, insistent flurry of words and staccato-like voice.

"We understand your distress, Mister McHugh. But please try to stay calm," said a rotund nurse.

"Your wife and children are being treated, Mister McHugh," said one of the doctors, who had come over from his desk. "We'll take you to them in just a moment. But please try to calm down. We are doing everything we can to care for them."

Becky now appeared at the front desk on the second-floor ward, but the nurses at the desk would not let her enter. She tried to explain that she was the trusted servant of the McHugh family, but the nurses still refused to admit her.

Becky persisted and got rather loud, whereupon Billy heard the ruckus and rushed out to vouch for her. They walked back to the ward together.

"The nurse will take you to your wife and children now, Mister McHugh," said the doctor.

They followed the nurse over to Dolores's bedside. Billy's heart sank when he saw Dolores lying there motionless, her head wrapped in bandages. He reached for her hand, trying to hold back tears.

"*Soy yo, mi amor. Soy yo.*" Dolores opened her eyes.

"Oh, Billy! You're here! And Becky too! Thank God!"

She paused, having obvious difficulty breathing and talking.

"Are the children all right?" She asked in a barely audible voice.

"I don't know, Dolores. I begged them to take me to them. Did you see them, Dolores? Did you see Felicidad? Is she all right?"

"I didn't see them, Billy. They wouldn't let me."

Dolores moved her arm and grimaced.

"They told me you had a collapsed lung and a concussion," Billy said. Are you in pain?"

"When the drug wears off, it hurts a lot," said Dolores. "And it's beginning to hurt right now," she said, grimacing again.

"My wife is in pain!" Billy shouted. "Hurry, please. She needs more pain reliever medicine."

The nurse was reluctant to administer morphine without the doctor's consent. Billy insisted, and the nurse got the doctor's consent. Before long Dolores fell asleep, but not before urging Billy to go and find the children. Moments later, a man in a white frock approached Dolores's bedside.

"Is this Mister McHugh?" Billy looked up and the nurse nodded.

"I'm Doctor Fletcher from the children's ward, Mister McHugh. I will take you to see your children now."

Billy and Becky followed him out past the front desk and into a small adjacent ward. Lining the perimeter were hospital beds containing children of various ages with various maladies. The doctor walked over and stood by Sebastián's bed. Becky followed him, but Billy did not, rushing instead to the center of the rectangular ward where there were several rows of bassinettes.

"Where is she?" Billy shouted. "Where's our baby girl!"

"I'm going to take you to her, sir but first come over here and I'll advise you of your little boy's condition." Billy persisted in checking every bassinette for Felicidad but to no avail.

Only then did Billy go to Sebastián's bedside.

"Your boy is resting now, Mister McHugh. He broke both legs, but we set them and they are stabilized. He was in severe pain, and in spite of his age, we had to administer morphine. We also gave him a sedative and he is sleeping now. We expect him to make a full recovery."

"Thank da Lord," said Becky, reaching down and touching Sebastián's hand. The doctor gave her a stern look.

"Where is our baby girl, Doctor Fletcher? Where is she? Take me to her now!" Billy repeated, sounding more and more alarmed.

"I'll take you to her in just a moment," said the doctor.

"Is she all right? Please, doctor, tell me the truth!"

The doctor did not respond and avoided Billy's pleading eyes.

"Aah knows it's hard fo ya, Billy, but ya jest gotta try not ta worry too much. Dey say Sebastián gonna be all right, and with da Lord's help, Felicidad can be all right too."

Becky tried her best to comfort Billy, but her effors were in vain. He was frantic with worry and his eyes began tearing up in anticipation of just what he feared.

Why won't they take me to her? Why isn't she here? Is she alive? Dear God, please, I beg you! Don't let her die!

Doctor Fletcher led Billy and Becky to a door on the other side of the ward. There was a sign on the door: CRITICAL CARE ONLY. They entered the small room and saw two bassinettes. Billy rushed over and saw baby Felicidad in one of them. She was deathly still with no sign of life. This time Doctor Fletcher looked directly at Billy.

"She suffered a traumatic brain injury, Mister McHugh, and she's in a deep coma." Billy's face contorted in pain. His eyes closed, his head sank, and he burst into tears which turned to sobs.

"I'm truly sorry, Mister McHugh."

Billy sobbed mournfully now, struggling to catch his breath, trying but failing to speak. He looked up at the doctor, pleading, begging for a hint of hope, the merest word, the slightest sign, but it never came.

"I must be frank and truthful with you, Mister McHugh. It would not be ethical of me to be anything less."

Billy reached down and touched Felicidad's little pink fingers, as copious tears flowed from his eyes and dripped down upon the face of his precious baby girl. He sobbed even harder now and began to shake, looking as though he might collapse. Becky propped him up and steadied him, whereupon Billy turned and looked directly at Doctor Fletcher.

"Is she going to die?" Billy asked plaintively.

"She is not going to wake up, Mister McHugh."

"Not ever?"

"Not ever," said Doctor Fletcher, noticeably moved himself by the overwhelming pain and sadness of this father at the loss of his beloved child.

"Lil Felicidad gonna be wid da Lord, Billy," Becky said, crying in sympathy with her former master and benefactor. "Dat's da only consolation fo us right now."

Becky opened wide her arms and Billy sought refuge within them. Doctor Fletcher left them alone, and they stayed there together with baby Felicidad and cried long and hard.

7

A leaden-grey sky hung over the gravesite as the priest presided.

"...We therefore commit this child of God to the earth from whence she came—ashes to ashes, dust to dust."

Billy stood there, his head hung low, tears streaming down his cheeks as he struggled to endure the unendurable. Dolores and Sebastián were still in the hospital recovering. The funeral had been postponed several times, but their condition had not improved enough to permit their release from the hospital.

As they lowered the little white coffin into the grave, Billy collapsed, and if the priest had not partially blocked his fall, he might have tumbled into the grave. Joseph Bartlett and Brad Mitchum rushed over and lifted Billy to his feet, but he remained unsteady. They stayed there with him as the priest said the final prayers and the last of the mourners dropped flowers upon the coffin. When they urged him to leave the gravesite with them, he refused. He stayed there alone, peering down at the coffin, sobbing as the cemetery crew began shoveling the dirt onto the grave.

"...Aah ain't neva seen a man faint befo," Julius said as he and Becky walked away from the burial site.

"Dat's cause ya ain't neva seen a man hurt like dat," Becky responded. "He maybe loved dat white baby girl mo den Nature and da Lord would allow."

Several months passed and Dolores made a full recovery. Sebastián's broken bones mended, and the casts on his legs were removed. Billy had no physical injuries, but his emotional pain and suffering showed no signs of easing. Indeed, it only seemed to worsen. The death of Felicidad left him a broken man. Senior partners, Henry Phipps and Joseph Bartlett, were alarmed at the depth of Billy's deterioration. He was arriving late to their law chambers, often not arriving at all. He was sullen, withdrawn and disheveled in his dress, and the quality and quantity of his work product rapidly declined. Bartlett had to relieve him of several important projects, including Minor Keith's Central American projects. Bartlett, however, was not yet willing to give up on Billy and urged him to take some time off. He also suggested that Billy consult a neuro-physiologist friend of his, a Doctor Malcolm Turner, whom Bartlett described as a specialist in the treatment of *neurasthenia*.

Dolores, too, was devastated by the loss of Felicidad. The fair-skinned baby girl had brought her closer to Billy, strengthening their marriage. But unlike Billy, Dolores's injuries healed, and she eventually regained her equilibrium. She had to, for both Sebastián and Billy needed her loving care.

Sebastián was troubled and confused by the death of his baby sister. He repeatedly questioned his mother, asking why God had allowed her to die.

"Mamá, why don't you ask God to send us another baby girl?"

Billy wondered whether they could have another child. Dolores was not past her childbearing age, but there was just too much uncertainty, too much risk. There was no way of knowing whether the child would be white like Felicidad or brown like Sebastián. That was totally in the hands of Nature and God Almighty. There was another problem, an immediate problem. Billy had become impotent, and he had not had intimate relations with Dolores since the eve of the tragic carriage accident.

Though Dolores was very reluctant to leave Billy at a time when he was consumed by grief, circumstances arose that made it imperative. She received a telegraph from Sofia, announcing that she and Eugenio Andrés Montserrát were engaged to be married and the wedding date was just weeks away. The telegraph also stated that the lawyers and *Notarios* required Dolores's presence and signature on several new pleadings in Arturo's suit, challenging the validity of don Fernando's second will.

On the eve of her departure, Dolores had another heartfelt talk with Billy.

"I'm deeply worried about you, Billy, and about us. I know how much you loved Felicidad and how difficult it has been for you, but we simply cannot go on like this. She has gone forever, but Sebastián and I are still here, and you must not let her death destroy our marriage and our lives. I am your wife. Sebastián is your son. You must not shut us out of your life. We do not deserve it, and we cannot live like this. I am very worried about Sebastián. His teacher told me last week that he's been moody and withdrawn and hasn't been playing with the other children."

"And you're blaming me for that?"

"Yes, I am! You are pulling him down with your terrible moods and your lack of love and affection. He feels ignored and unloved and so do I. If our marriage is to survive, you have to be my husband and Sebastián's father again. You need to go back to your law practice before you lose your position and your career. I want to be proud to be your wife again, Billy, and I want us to be a family again."

"Do you really think we can be a family again after what's happened?"

Billy turned away from Dolores's fervent look.

"I hope and pray to God we can, but it depends more on you than on me, Billy."

"Oh, is that right? And how so?" Billy asked, now sounding antagonistic.

Dolores looked away.

"You're not the man I married Billy, not the man you portrayed yourself to be. You abhor your son, your own flesh and blood because of the color of his skin..."

"I don't abhor Sebastián," Billy interrupted, "but he's out of place here. He would be better off in Cuba. We would all be better off if he were in Cuba."

"And how about me, Billy? Would you be better off with me in Cuba? Would you be better off without me?"

Her stark question startled him, and he looked away.

"Do you love me, Billy? Do you really love me, knowing now what we know about each other? Do you love Sebastián or are you only capable of loving that darling little *white* child who was tragically taken from us? Tell me the truth, Billy! Tell me the truth," she repeated and loudly. "We must be frank and honest with each other. It's too important not to be."

"I loved you, Dolores. I loved you dearly, and you gave me the most precious baby girl, for which I loved you even more."

"But she's gone, and no one can bring her back! You have to accept that, as difficult and painful as it may be. You've got to accept me and accept Sebastián, accept us as we are for better or worse."

"Maybe we can have another child," Billy said, his voice shaky and lacking confidence.

"And what if it's another child like Sebastián ?"

"It won't be, it can't be," he said, his voice a mere whisper, his eyes filled with tears.

Dolores got up now and tried to comfort him. But Billy turned away. Just then, Sebastián came running down the stairs.

"Mamá, I am finished packing."

"That's a good boy, Sebastián." She tenderly embraced her dear little boy with the *acanelado* skin and watched as Billy walked out of the room.

The next day Dolores and Sebastián departed for Havana. Sebastián was frightened during the carriage ride to the railroad station, and Dolores directed the coachman to avoid the intersection of Massachusetts and New Jersey Avenues.

CHAPTER XXII

Descent into Darkness

It was Saturday. Two weeks had passed since Dolores left for Cuba. Billy sat in the kitchen of his five-bedroom house on Connecticut Avenue. The shades were drawn and the house was dark and dreary. The noon hour had not yet tolled, but the bottle of brandy on the kitchen table was nearly empty. He reached for it again, pouring the last of its contents into his badly soiled glass and swigging it down. In the months following Felicidad's death, sadness, despair and desperation hung over Billy McHugh like a heavy black shroud of death. His physical health was in serious decline, and he suffered from a nervous stomach, weight loss and insomnia. More than once he had considered taking his life.

Billy had consulted Doctor Turner, whom Joseph Bartlett had recommended. In fact, he was to have seen him this very week. But he didn't go; he'd given up on the so-called nerve doctor, concluding that the good doctor had done nothing more than ask questions.

Becky continued to prepare meals for Billy, but he had little appetite and often left them on the plate untouched. He had not shaved, and his beard had taken over his face. He had no energy to shave or even bathe. The few times he'd left the sanctuary of his house, he was unrecognizable, having shunned his suits and cravats, adopting shabby shirts and work pants, some of which he borrowed from Julius. He had not set foot in the law chambers of Henry Phipps & Partners for weeks on end. That was just as well, for he was incapable of any meaningful work. He drank and drank heavily, starting often in the morning and continuing throughout the day.

I don't need her. I hope she stays in Cuba. She was responsible for Felicidad's death. I told her not to ride with that mulatto carriage driver. I'll never see my darling baby girl again. Why was she the one who was killed?

He reached again for the bottle of brandy, brought it to his mouth and sucked out the last few drops.

Just then there was a knock on the door. He could not bear to see anyone, but the knocking was insistent. He got up and peeked out the window. It was their neighbor, Mrs. Appleby. She was holding a pot of something. Unbeknownst to Billy, Dolores had asked her to stop in from time to time to check on him. She was not the only one Dolores had asked. Joseph Bartlett and Brad Mitchum had also agreed to check on him. Reluctantly, Billy walked out to the living room and opened the door.

"You'll excuse me, Mister McHugh for dropping in unannounced, but I've prepared a pot roast and potatoes and thought maybe you'd like some. I know that Mrs. McHugh is traveling and your servants are off today."

He tried to smile, but it was half-hearted, and he did not invite her in, which may have been a blessing, for he had not bathed and smelled of alcohol and body odor.

"Well, that's very nice of you, Mrs. Appleby, but I'm not at all hungry. Our house servant cooks for me. But thank you, anyway," he said, suddenly sorry he had been so curt and unfriendly. She was a nice woman, an attractive woman in her late twenties. He continued to stare as she stepped over a small hedge onto her property, remembering a time when a pretty woman brought a smile to his face, a twinkle in his eye and a stirring of his blood. In his present condition, neither Dolores nor the fair sex in general excited him; nothing did, and that realization only seemed to increase his sadness and despair.

He walked back to the kitchen and picked up the bottle again, but this time it was truly empty. He needed another, but he would have to leave the house to get it.

He walked a block or two down Connecticut Avenue, eventually flagging down a carriage. Julius had always purchased the wine and spirits for the McHugh household, and Billy did not readily know where to go. He asked the coachman to recommend a spirit shop, and the coachman dropped him at a place called Lin Chou Spirits and China House. Billy entered, and immediately noticed a strong, pungent, and sweet-smelling odor. An Oriental man in a red and black Mandarin gown appeared from behind a curtain.

"Welcome to Lin Chou's China House. My name Sam. How may I serve you?" Billy looked around but did not see any spirits.

"I was told I could purchase some brandy here."

The Chinaman smiled and beckoned for Billy to follow him. He led him off to the side and through an elaborately painted, multi-colored curtain and into a room filled with all manner of bottled spirits.

"We have finest French, Spanish and Portuguese brandy." Billy picked up a bottle from a wooden case with Chinese writing on it.

"This *baijui*. Not for you. Need acquire taste," said the Chinaman as he walked over to a stack of cases filled with brandy.

Billy selected two bottles of French brandy, paid the man and looked for the exit, not wishing to linger there any longer. But as they were walking back to the main room, another curtain opened, revealing a pretty, young Chinese girl wearing a bright yellow robe. She smiled, and as Billy looked into the room, he smelled that same pungent, sweet smell, only this time it was much stronger. The Chinese girl paused, waiting for Sam and Billy to step out of her way. Meanwhile, the curtain remained open, and Billy got a good look inside, where he saw Chinese and Caucasian people lying on cots smoking long thin pipes.

"You have this experience, sir?" asked the Chinaman.

"No," Billy said as he stole another look before the curtain closed.

"Perhaps you wish try some? Smoking make you feel good, have more energy, ease yo pain, help you relax."

He looked at Billy as though aware that he needed those promised benefits.

"We give you pipe and lamp. Girls instruct you how to smoke, make you velly comfortable," Sam said, smiling and revealing a mouth full of brown-stained teeth. He then handed Billy a brochure made of red silk paper with bold black writing in English:

Opium banishes melancholy, begets confidence, converts fear into boldness, makes the coward eloquent, and dastards brave. Nobody, in desperate circumstances, and smiling under a disrelish for life, ever laid violent hands on himself after taking a dose of opium, or ever will. (John Brown 1735-1788)

"Five dollar, good price. You stay, smoke long as you like." Billy nodded, his muted response mirroring a conflict. He was in dire need of what the Chinaman and the brochure offered, but he recalled having read that opium was terribly addictive. But that brochure and the words of the Chinaman were persuasive, and

Billy said he would like to try it. Hearing that, the Chinaman clapped his hands and called out: :

"Guo lai, Hong! Guo lai Hong!"

And a moment later the slender, young Chinese girl in the yellow robe reappeared. She smiled at Billy, whereupon Sam looked to see if he approved. Billy nodded his head.

"You pay now. Jade take you, show you how to smoke."

Billy produced the five dollars, then followed the girl to that back room. The fumes inside were so thick that he questioned whether it was even necessary to smoke his own pipe. Jade said it was, and walked him over to the only vacant space, where there was a bed, or more accurately, a small cot. Alongside the cot was a little table with a tray on top, containing a long, narrow, black pipe and what looked like an oil lamp made of brass and glass; except this one had a distinctive funnel-like chimney. Jade picked up a little glass bowl, which was about the size of an egg. Billy, meanwhile, was nervously looking about the room. With his ragged, disheveled appearance, he was not readily recognizable, but he was still wary of being seen here, knowing now what was going on. The other patrons, however, paid him no mind, seemingly lost in their drug-induced state of sweet, joyful bliss and cogitation.

"Your name, what?" Jade said.

"What?" Billy asked, not having understood her language. She tried again.

"How they call you? You French man, maybe?" This time he understood.

"Billy," he said in a muffled voice.

"My name Jade. You lie down. Jade show you how to smoke."

She was an attractive, petite girl with exotic dark eyes and long, jet-black hair pulled back and fastened with two clasps made of jade. Billy guessed that she was no more than sixteen or seventeen, but he could not be sure, since he had had no previous experience with Orientals.

"Lie down on side. I prepare pipe."

She picked up the pipe and attached the little glass bowl, after which she opened a little silver box with steam emerging out the sides and extracted a white globule about the size of a pea. She inserted it into the glass bowl, then guided the pipe-bowl over the stream of heat rising from the oil lamp's little chimney. Seconds later, she drew on the pipe, inhaling the vaporized opium fumes. She repeated the process then passed the pipe to Billy.

"Now you smoke. Will not take long. You feel leally good."

Billy drew on the pipe but immediately started coughing. He had never been a tobacco smoker, so it took a little while before he was able to do it without coughing.

"Hold inside then blow out," said Jade, who was sitting on a pillow next to the bed.

It did not take long before Billy began feeling loose and very relaxed, and as he drew more of the vapors into his lungs, a delightful floating sensation came over him. It brought a smile to his face, a genuine smile, the first in many months. He stretched his legs out now and felt every muscle in his body loosen and relax.

"Oh, look, now you smile!" said Jade. "See? opium good for you."

Billy passed the pipe back to her, and she drew the vapor deeply into her lungs. However, it did not seem to affect her the way it was affecting him.

"You want me cut your hair, trim beard? Then I know how you look." She laughed and laughed hard, drawing again on the pipe. "Never know, maybe you handsome man," she said, laughing and making Billy laugh.

They passed the pipe back and forth, but increasingly Billy

kept it longer, drawing on it repeatedly before passing it back. Soon, the globule of opium in the pipe bowl was consumed.

"How you feel? You want smoke more?" Jade asked.

"Yes, I want smoke more", he said, playfully imitating her broken English, smiling and tugging her over closer to the cot.

"Wait, Billy. We need clean pipe first."

Jade took the pipe and began cleaning out the glass bowl with a knife before inserting another globule, which she extracted from the silver box.

Billy was now in a state of bliss, a divine feeling of joy unlike anything he had ever experienced in his life. Other intense feelings arose, each taking on a different color in his mind's eye, changing rapidly yet smoothly like a magical kaleidoscope, a rainbow of happy, sweet, wonderful feelings, flashing, surging throughout his mind and body alike. He felt alive again. A powerful sense of well-being lifted his fallen spirit, banishing his pain and melancholia. He looked at Jade and smiled, experiencing an overwhelming joy at her presence, a desire to become one with her. He reached for her hand, tugged her over to him and lifted her up to the cot. She smiled, settling into his embrace. He delighted in her slender, delicate body, feeling now a passion in his loins. He wanted her; he wanted more of that divine state of opium bliss, and he did not care now if the entire world was watching and knew his identity. He began kissing her tenderly, yet with abandon until Jade abruptly broke the spell.

"No, Billy, we go upstairs, my apartment on second floor."

With her limited English, she explained to him as best she could that she was now on her own time and no longer working for Sam. Then she stood up and tugged at Billy's hand. He stood up, but staggered. In spite of her smaller, delicate size, she steadied him. They walked out arm in arm to the main room, and she led Billy up the stairs to her apartment. They entered and

Jade immediately walked to the little table by her bed and lit the opium lamp. Quietly and calmly, they took off their clothes and got in bed, where periods of intense lovemaking alternated with interludes of peaceful and philosophical contemplation. They were spiritually and physically intertwined and oblivious to the passage of time. Billy had visions that this was how it was in heaven. He hallucinated and saw his darling Felicidad, finding her in peace. He had suffered through more than six months of extreme grief, pain and debilitating melancholia. He had been impotent. He had been living in hell, but it was all finally over; at least that is what he believed.

2

In the days and weeks that followed, Billy returned to the Lin Chou Spirits and China House to smoke opium. He joined Jade in her apartment, and she cut his hair and trimmed his scruffy beard, discovering that he was indeed a handsome man, though much too skinny. The fact that she was a prostitute did not seem to bother Billy nor diminish the pleasure and benefit he derived from her.

They smoked opium and made love, and those two ingredients seemed to be the medicine that Billy needed to ward off his dark demons of despair. But the more opium he smoked, the more it took to achieve the desired effect. And before long, he found himself in need of the opium pipe on a daily basis. He had heard about opium's addictive tendencies and was now beginning to find that the reports were true. But he deemed his addiction preferable to the unbearable pain and despair that had been consuming him.

One morning he awoke and discovered that he was unable to urinate. He was forced to visit a doctor, who diagnosed his condition as gonorrhea. He knew, of course, that he had contracted it from Jade, and he was forced to end their physical relationship at least for the time being. She, too, sought medical attention and was eventually cured. All the while Billy continued to see her and smoke with her. Indeed, he was compelled to smoke, and his usage increased, exacerbating his dependency on the seductive, curative, pain-relieving opium.

Becky and Julius knew of Billy's suffering first hand, but they did not know that he was addicted to opium; not until that morning when a Good Samaritan found him lying in the gutter near the Capitol Building and brought him home. As luck would have it, the man was a physician who worked the night shift at the Naval Hospital. He flagged down a carriage, rendered aid, and when Billy regained consciousness, he was able to get his address.

As Julius helped the doctor carry Billy into the house, Becky explained that she and Julius were the McHughs' house servants and that Mrs. McHugh was away in Cuba. Julius and the doctor placed Billy on a sofa, and the doctor washed and bandaged the cut on his head. When Billy opened his eyes, the doctor noticed that his pupils were inordinately small, his breathing was shallow, and his hands were cold and clammy—the telltale signs of opium addiction.

"Is he a veteran?" the doctor asked.

"No, suh, he's a lawyer and he wuk fo one a da best law firms in the Uniad States."

"The reason I ask is because so many veterans, both Union and Confederate, were treated with morphine for their injuries, and morphine is derived from opium. By the time they returned from the War, they were addicted to it. Opium addiction is so common today that they refer to it as the 'soldiers disease'."

"Ta tell da truth, Doctor, Aah figured somethin like dat was botherin him. Aah watched 'im go from terrible sadness and pain to what look like peace, calm and happy times, and it seem ta happen almost ova night. He come home one day wid his hair cut real nice and his beard all trimmed, lookin real good, like his old self. Took off dem old clothes and put on his suits and cravats. Becky and me done complemented 'im, 'couraged 'im ta take up his law practice again, din't we, Becky?"

"Yeah, we sho did, and Aah took dem old ragged clothes he'd been wearin and hid 'im real good, hopin Aah'd nevaa see 'im again wearin'em, but he done found 'em. A fine lawyer like Billy McHugh shunt be seen like dat no sir, shunt nevaa be seen like dat."

"Aah had a friend o mine once who done lost his wife and chillen." Da massa sold 'em off inta slavry. He tried ta fight off da pain and sorrow wid opium, and befo long it killed 'im. So, Aah'v seen dis opium thing befo."

"These troubled souls see opium as an escape, a cure," said the doctor. "The trouble is the cure is worse than the disease itself. But, there's nothing much more that I can do for him now, and it's getting late, so I must be going."

Becky and Julius thanked him for all he'd done. As the doctor was walking toward the front door, Becky asked him.

"Can ya tell us how we oughta care fo him, doctor?"

"I'm afraid there's not much more that you or I can do at this time, except try to see that he eats three meals a day and gets enough sleep. He is going to have to come to grips with his habit and break it. And it is not going to be easy. It may be worth trying to persuade him to come and see me at the Naval Hospital."

When Billy fully regained consciousness, he was embarrassed and disoriented and told Julius and Becky that he had been beaten and robbed. Billy had never been a liar, but that was beginning to change.

"Ya stay right der on da couch, Billy, and Aah'l fix ya some eggs and grits," Becky said. Billy tried to stand but sank down again on the sofa, covering his face with his hands.

"Yo jest take it easy and rest, Billy," Julius said. "We gonna take good care o ya."

Billy asked for coffee, but otherwise kept quiet. His head pounded, and he barely had enough energy to sit up. At one point he looked up at Julius as though he was about to say something, but then lowered his head again, apparently embarrassed and humiliated that they saw him in this condition.

Becky came into the living room with a plate of eggs and grits.

"Aah wants ya ta eat dis, Billy. Aah knows ya done lost weight, cause Aah can see it."

Billy drank the hot coffee and asked for more. He started slowly eating the grits and picking at the eggs.

"When ya done eatin, Aah'm gonna take ya upstairs, clean ya up and put ya ta sleep. Look ta me like ya really need it."

Julius had received a message for Billy the day before, but in Billy's present condition, he was reluctant to give it to him. It was a letter in an unsealed envelope signed by Joseph Bartlett, which Julius dared to open and read. Though Julius was not totally literate, he understood that Mister Bartlett wanted Billy to report to the law chambers "without delay." When Julius showed the letter to Becky, she was alarmed, fearing that Billy was going to lose his position, which would put her and Julius at risk of losing theirs.

Becky took Billy upstairs, cleaned him up and got him into bed, when there came a knock on the door. She went down, opened the door and saw a young Oriental girl standing there holding a little wooden box.

"Billy McHugh live here?" Becky nodded. "My name Jade. I am friend of Billy. Have package for him."

Julius rushed over and yelled at her to go away, suspecting that she was the source of Billy's opium problem. But seconds later Billy appeared on the stairs.

"Let her in! She's my friend!" Billy said.

Becky and Julius backed away, and Jade entered the house.

"Bring her here!" Billy shouted.

Becky led her up the stairs. Julius went back to the kitchen, where he reread the letter from Joseph Bartlett, knowing full well that he had better deliver it and soon.

3

The next morning when Becky and Julius arrived for the day, they discovered that the Chinese girl was still in the house.

"Oh, how it pains ma heart ta see what's become of Billy McHugh!" Becky said. 'He's not da Billy we done known all dese years, Julius. Ta bring anotha woman inta dis house when his sweet wife is away. Der's somethin terribly wrong wid dat. Aah nevaa woulda believed it, Julius, iffen Aah din't see it wid ma own eyes."

"She ain't no woman, Becky. She can't be no mo den sixteen years o age. He oughta be shamed o hisself. And Chinese! Why, dey don't come any lower. Dey lower den da lowest niggaa slaves in Charleston. Dey all use dat opium. Aah seen it befo, it's part o der culture."

They heard someone coming down the stairs, and a moment later Billy appeared in the kitchen.

"Good morning," he said curtly. "I want you to prepare some sausage and eggs and bring them upstairs, Becky."

He stood there in his bare feet, wearing the raggedy old clothes that Becky thought she had hidden for good.

"Billy, Aah got a letta fo ya. Woulda give it to ya yestaday but Aah jest plum fogot." said Julius.

He opened the cabinet, took out the letter and handed it to Billy. The envelope was clearly Henry Phipps & Partners stationery. Billy took out the letter and began reading it. When he had finished, he said nothing, but his worried expression said it all.

Jade came into the kitchen, wearing one of Billy's robes. It was open at the neck and revealed her pert little breasts. As the early morning sun streamed through the kitchen window, Julius noticed the small pupils of Jade's eyes and recalled the doctor's words from the day before. Billy's eyes bore the same telltale sign.

"What for breakfast?" asked Jade, a silly grin on her face.

"Go back upstairs. There'll be eggs and sausage shortly," Billy said. But she hesitated, maintaining the silly look.

"You hear me! Go back upstairs!" Billy said.

This time she obeyed, but she tugged on his shirt for him to come with her.

"I'll be up in a minute," Billy said, turning to Becky. "When you're finished making our breakfast, I want you to iron my black suit, including the vest."

"Yes, suh," Becky said, glancing at Billy with sadness in her eyes, unaccustomed to being spoken to so coldly.

With the exception of Patrick McHugh, Becky had never heard it before, not in all the years she had served the McHugh family. Billy said nothing more, then turned, walked out of the kitchen and climbed the stairs to the master bedroom.

That afternoon Billy dressed in his freshly ironed black suit, his cravat and his top hat. Jade prepared a small and measured amount of opium to settle his nerves and fortify his courage, Billy smoked it and left for the law chambers of Henry Phipps & Partners.

"Well, well, good aftanoon, Mistaa McHugh," said Percy the

doorman, smiling broadly, as Billy entered the law firm. "Sho is good ta see ya, suh."

Billy said hello and handed Percy his hat. The other lawyers, including Brad Mitchum, who occupied the open area of the firm's offices, looked up. Brad got up, came over and greeted Billy.

"Good to see you, McHugh. How are you feeling?"

Brad smiled through his surprise at the sight of Billy's pallid complexion and loss of weight.

"Not too bad," said Billy. "How have you been, Brad?"

"Working hard as usual. How is Dolores doing? Julie's been asking for her."

"Well, hello, Mister McHugh!" said Millie, the attractive young mulatto intern. "It's so nice to see you again. We've all missed you."

The door to Joseph Bartlett's office opened, and a woman walked out. Bartlett looked up, and seeing Billy, got up from his desk.

"Billy, I've been expecting you. Come in and have a seat," Bartlett said, calling out then for Millie to bring them some tea.

"How are you feeling, Billy?"

"I wish I could tell you that I'm fully recovered, sir, but I'm not," Billy said, shifting uncomfortably in his chair. Bartlett managed a polite smile.

"Doctor Turner told me that you stopped seeing him. That was not a good idea, Billy. He's an expert in the field, and we thought he could help you."

There was a knock on the door. Millie came in with a tray of tea and biscuits.

"Put it right here, Millie," said Bartlett, moving files out of the way. "You take it with lemon and sugar, don't you?" Bartlett said as he poured the tea.

"Yes, that's right," Billy said

"Have a biscuit. They are nice and fresh. Have several in fact. It looks to me like you have lost more weight. Have you been eating?"

Billy tried but failed to muster a firm and confident look at his boss, hoping to get him to stop the curt manner and tone in which he was addressing him.

"My appetite hasn't fully returned, but it's better than it was."

"Are you sleeping?" Bartlett asked. "Doctor Turner said you were suffering from insomnia."

"I still am," Billy said.

"Henry and I are deeply concerned about you, Billy. I will not beat around the bush. We believe that your condition has deteriorated over the past few months. We know about your opium use."

Bartlett's words startled Billy.

"Doctor Turner said he suspected it, but we wanted to be certain, so we retained a Pinkerton man to look into your activities. I have his report right here in my desk, and I am going to ask you directly. Have you been frequenting an opium den near the Capitol and cavorting with an adolescent Chinese girl?"

Billy lowered his head, avoiding Bartlett's eyes.

"Tell me the truth!" said Bartlett. "Is this Pinkerton report accurate? I want to hear it from your own lips."

Billy reached for his tea, nervously spilling some into the saucer.

"I'm sorry, sir, but it's the only way I've found to deal with my pain. Without it I might as well be dead," And…:"

"Come now, Billy!" interrupted Bartlett. "I lost my son at Shiloh. You didn't see me smoking opium. You have had the benefit of expert care and treatment, though you have not used it properly. And you've had ample time to heal and to resume your work and your career."

Bartlett paused and refilled the two teacups.

"No one can deny that the firm has been understanding and

patient with you, Billy. And I personally have supported you more than anyone, but we're not going to continue paying your salary, and particularly not to finance your opium addiction."

Billy continued to look down, avoiding Bartlett's gaze.

"Did you ever stop to think of the damage to our client base that would result, if the word gets out that our top young partner was an opium addict? Then throw in the fact that you have been cheating on your pretty wife and sleeping with some adolescent Chinese girl! Why, I have no doubt that Minor Keith would take his business to another firm. And he would not be the only client to do so. We keep telling Keith that you've developed a nervous condition from the tragic death of your baby daughter, but Billy, how long can we continue to keep him in the dark?"

"I've tried my best to put it behind me, sir, and I'm still trying."

"Do you think that smoking opium is going to cure you?" Bartlett asked.

Billy looked directly at Bartlett this time.

"I don't know if it will cure me, Joseph, but it has helped to keep me out of the terribly dark abyss that I was living in, the sadness and despair..."

A nervous tic suddenly appeared in Billy's eye, and then his right hand began to twitch. He tried to tuck his hand under his leg, but Bartlett had seen both the tic and the twitch.

"I wish you could see yourself now the way others see you, Billy. You are a mere shadow of the brilliant young lawyer whom we hired five years ago. Look how your hands shake. You are thin and gaunt, and I suspect dreadfully undernourished. Your confidence and self-esteem are gone. You have been avoiding my eyes. I know you are ashamed of yourself. You've got to pull yourself together, stop the opium smoking and get back to your law practice before it's too late."

There was a knock on the door, and Henry Phipps walked in. He came up behind Billy and put his hand on his shoulder.

"How are you feeling, Billy?" Phipps asked.

Billy turned, looked up and met his eyes for just an instant.

"I'm a little better, thank you, sir." Bartlett looked at Phipps disapprovingly.

"I'm not finished with him, Henry."

Phipps turned and headed for the door, placing his hand on Billy's shoulder once again as he passed.

"Take care of yourself Billy," Phipps said and left the room.

Silence prevailed for a moment, broken by the sound of Bartlett opening his desk drawer. He took out an envelope and held it in his hand. Billy's head hung down, his countenance one of overwhelming sadness, which seemed to move Joseph Bartlett. He was reminded of Billy's agonizing months in Confederate prisons awaiting his execution. He had sent him to Mexico. Yes, it was at the request of Secretary of State, William Seward, but it was he who had agreed to send him. And no sooner had Billy recovered from that dreadful period in his life, than tragedy struck with the devastating carriage accident and the loss of his infant daughter. It was just too much to bear, too much for any man to bear. Bartlett asked himself, were they being too hard on Billy McHugh? Should they give him more time to recover? But the decision had already been made, and it was Bartlett who had to deliver it.

"Billy, we're terminating our partnership with you effective today. It is the consensus of all the partners in the firm. The terms and conditions are those stated in this letter."

Bartlett handed the letter to Billy.

"This check will be your last. If and when you stop your harmful opium habit and regain your health and your moral rectitude, we will consider reinstating you as a member of Henry Phipps & Partners."

4

Billy left the law chambers and returned home, where he broke down and cried like a baby. Things became worse when he discovered that he had no more opium. The little he had smoked before the meeting with Joseph Bartlett had worn off, and in addition to the shock and pain of having been sacked, he was experiencing serious withdrawal symptoms: painful stomach cramps, nausea, vomiting, and diarrhea. And that was just the first wave. There followed a second wave with cold sweats, a pounding headache and dizziness.

He lay on his bed writhing in pain, screaming, beseeching God Almighty to relieve him of his misery or take his life. Becky and Julius were frantic, deciding that they must get him to a doctor. But in his brief moments of lucidness, Billy shouted that the only way to relieve his pain was to get him more opium. The two loyal servants tried their best to reason with him, begging him to make an effort to pull himself together and break the habit, but to no avail. Billy yelled at Julius and pleaded with him to go down to the China House and tell Jade to bring him some more opium. Finally, Julius relented. Billy gave him the money and begged him to hurry, saying he didn't know how much longer he could stand the pain.

Becky continued to try to comfort and console Billy, but he was inconsolable. He would not and could not listen to anyone, not Becky, not Julius, not senior partners Phipps and Bartlett, not even his sweet wife, Dolores. He heard only the screaming urgency of his addiction, compelling him to get some opium and assuage the excruciating physical and mental pain of withdrawal. However, while Becky was applying cold presses to his pounding head, she said something that he listened to, something that he really heard.

"Ya oughta go on down ta Charleston, Billy, and visit yo mama. Would do ya both a world o good."

5

The train ride to Charleston was slow and uneventful, that is, until he ran out of opium. Jade had only been able to give him a small amount as the "soldiers disease" was becoming an epidemic. And the military and civilian authorities enacted serious measures to restrict the supply.

The moment Billy stepped off the train in Charleston, he looked down the platform, and the image of Charlie Flynn flashed before him: those last few minutes of Charlie's life in Richmond's Castle Thunder prison, when the two old friends said good-bye. Billy had added:

I'll see you in Charleston, partner.

A profound sense of guilt and sadness swept over him, quieting for a brief moment the all-compelling craving for opium.

He walked out of the station and hailed a carriage.

"I have a terrible toothache," he told the coachman. "Do you know where I can buy some opium?"

"Well, used ta be ya could find it down der wid da Chinese on the wharfs. But evaa since da Yankee Army been occupyin Charleston, not even the Chinese can get der opium. Da Yankee Army conductin a campaign right now, tryin ta fight opium addiction. Dey puttin' a lot o pressure on da city fathaas ta stop da opium supply. Dey got hundreds, maybe thousands, of rebel soldiers comin back from da War as addicts. Dey don't need no mo addicts, dat's fo sure. Ya gonna see signs all ovaa da city. Dey been postin'em fo weeks, tellin people not ta take opium, sayin it's a dangerous drug."

"What about the doctors and pharmacists? Aren't they still using opium to treat tooth aches, headaches and other maladies?"

The coachman shrugged his shoulders and said he didn't know one way or the other.

Billy was worried, knowing that if he did not find some opium and find it quickly, he'd be thrown back into the living hell of withdrawal. The only thing he could think of was to wait until the onslaught of withdrawal, then go to the hospital, and beg for it. He did not have to wait long, and the coachman agreed to take him to the hospital. When they arrived, he had already begun to foam in the mouth, exhibiting the signs of an epileptic fit. The doctors were familiar with the symptoms and were sympathetic. They administered a small dose of opium, but only after getting his promise to enter treatment. His demons temporarily subdued, Billy decided to go to his mother's house, assuming that she had gotten her house back.

When Bonny saw Billy walking up the gravel path to the front door, she couldn't believe her eyes and rushed out of the house to greet him.

"Billy, Oh Billy, you're home again in Charleston. My prayers have been answered."

She threw her arms around him and smothered him with hugs and kisses. Then she took him inside and made him a delicious roast beef dinner with all the trimmings, lamenting the fact that he looked so thin. They talked for hours. She told him how she had gotten her house back through the efforts of James Hamilton, the law partner of the late lawyer and political leader, James Petigru. Bonny was no longer impecunious. She had dug up the stash of gold, silver and Yankee greenbacks, which she had buried under the greenhouse. It was a sizeable fortune amassed over the years by her late husband, Patrick, from his slave trading and blockade running. Bonnie had more than enough now to live comfortably for the rest of her life.

Billy did everything he could to hide his addiction from his mother. It was inevitable, however, that she would learn of it sooner or later. It happened in fact in the first few days of his return. He had exhausted what little he had gotten at the hospital, and once again was beset with terrible withdrawal symptoms. He was in his room on the bed when he began shaking. He shook so badly that he fell out of bed and began screaming and writhing with stomach pain and convulsions.

Bonny heard him and rushed to his room. Billy faced his mother and confessed that he was addicted to opium. The next day Bonny sought the aid of Father O'Brien of Saint Mary's Roman Catholic Church, who gave her the name of a Doctor Richard Barnes, a captain in the Union Occupying Army. Billy was still in the throes of intermittent withdrawal, and Bonny took him to see him.

Billy hoped, if nothing else, to at least get a dose or two of opium. It's not that Billy didn't try. He pleaded with Doctor Barnes, but the good doctor was not about to feed Billy's habit, at least not until one frightening counseling session when Billy slipped into a convulsive fit, forcing Doctor Barnes and his orderly to restrain and gag him, fearing he might bite off his tongue. The good doctor then decided to alter his tactics, concluding that Billy was not able to tolerate a total withdrawal from the drug. He undertook now to administer small amounts of opium, gradually decreasing the dosage until Billy was able to tolerate total abstinence. It was a long and painful road to recovery, but he finally succeeded in overcoming his addiction.

Opium, however, was not Billy McHugh's only problem. He was without a job, without resources, and totally dependent upon his mother for food and shelter. It was a hard pill for him to swallow. As for Bonny, she was thankful to have her long-lost son back home, and she spared no effort and expense to help him get back on his feet. Her overriding goal, however, was to convince him to remain in Charleston.

"You don't belong up there in Washington with all those Yankees, Billy. Of course they're down here now too, but they're doing some good. They're rebuilding the city, and it's going to be a good place to live, to work and to raise a family once again. You can prosper here, Billy..."

Bonny used more than words to convince her son that his life would be better in Charleston. She arranged dinner parties and outings with the Becketts. Constance Beckett was the kind of proper southern girl whom Bonny had always hoped Billy would marry. Constance and her little girl, Felicia, presented a strong attraction for Billy, but Bonny had a big hurdle to overcome. Billy missed Dolores; he missed her terribly. He tried many times to sit down and write that heartfelt letter, the letter that would spark their reconciliation. But every attempt ended up in the fireplace. He hoped that she would somehow learn that he was back in Charleston, and every day he anxiously awaited the postman; just as he'd done as a youth, hoping for a letter from his beloved Dolores. But the letter never came.

PART VI

Spring/Summer 1867

CHAPTER XXIII

Victorio Arquídez

It was early Sunday morning as Dolores and Sebastián walked along the garden path towards the patio bar. The sun was rising, and the gardenias were in full bloom, their sweet scent filling the air all about them, their brilliant whiteness spreading forth upon the land like a vast field of cotton. Mother and child walked along hand in hand, as heavy raindrops from the nighttime showers dripped rhythmically from the tall palms and mango trees. Colorful birds had begun their morning serenade, adding to the joy and delight that Dolores felt to be home in the verdant lushness of her native Cuba.

"Don't step in that puddle, Sebastián" cried Dolores

But it was too late, as he had already begun to tramp through it, stamping his feet, which playful and spirited little boys of his kind find simply irresistible.

"I can wear other clothes later, mamá," said Sebastián, laughing, breaking her grip and running off to the patio bar and right past his Auntie Sofia and Uncle Eugenio, who were eating their breakfast.

"Good morning, Sebastián," they said.

Sebastián ran to the slave hut, where the two slave women were preparing breakfast for their masters and mistresses.

"*E Ku Aero, E Ku Abu,*" they said in their native Yoruba tongue. They had taught Sebastián a few greetings, and he answered back, using the same words with a perfect accent and a devilish little smile.

Sebastián had been spending time at the patio bar, playing with the slave women's offspring, one of whom was a seven-year-old boy by the name of Adebayo.

"Come back and say good morning to your Auntie Sofia and Uncle Eugenio," said Dolores as she sat down with them.

The two slave women came out of the hut now, carrying pots of coffee and tea. Sebastián followed behind them, running over to Sofia, who stood up, picked him up and kissed him on the lips.

"Good morning, Sebastiánito," said Sofia. "He's gotten very heavy, Dolores. Has he been eating again over in the slave quarters?"

"No, he knows he's not allowed to," Dolores said. Eugenio asked him to sit down beside him, but Sebastián saw Adebayo and ran back to the hut.

Adebayo was tall, rangy and very black, and just like Sebastián, full of energy and mischievousness.

The slave women brought out the breakfast of eggs, pork, bread and fresh fruit. Sebastián ran back with Adebayo tagging along behind him. Sebastián sat down at the table, and Adebayo, who knew his place, sat on the ground next to a large mango tree. Sofia began telling Dolores about an experience they had on their honeymoon in Tuscany, and when she finished, her expression turned more serious.

"I forgot to tell you, Dolores, we have some news on the law suit. We filed an affidavit with the Appellate Court attesting to papa's conversation with Constancia and me just weeks before his death, in which he told us that mamá had had no objection to your sharing in his estate. We discussed it with the lawyers, and Eugenio and I are both of the opinion that it should carry some weight, because, well, here, I'll let Eugenio tell you." Sofia turned to her husband.

"Yes, that's right, Dolores, the affidavit should carry some weight because it can be seen as contrary to Sofia's and Constancia's best interests; because if you are not deemed to be a legitimate heir, Sofia's and Constancia's share in the estate will then be greater." Surprisingly, Dolores frowned and shook her head.

"Papá must be turning over in his grave. Why can't all this be settled amicably? Our dear papá would not want us to be fighting with each other like this."

"It was going to be settled amicably until Arturo chose to file that suit," said Sofia. "It's Arturo's insatiable greed and quest for total control and power. But let's not talk about it any more. It's such a glorious Sunday morning, and I'm sorry I brought it up in the first place."

"How about if we all go riding after breakfast?" said Eugenio. "I know Sebastián would like that very much, wouldn't you little man?"

Eugenio smiled, reached out and patted Sebastián on his curly top head.

"No, Uncle Eugenio, I don't want to ride today, and besides, Fresco is sick. Adebayo and I want to play."

Adebayo, who'd been listening attentively, looked up from beneath the mango tree and smiled at them.

"Are you sure you're feeling all right?" Dolores asked in disbelief. "What could you possibly enjoy doing more than riding?"

Sebastián had a mouth full of food and remembered his mother's command not to talk with his mouth full.

"We're building a fort," Sebastián said, smiling and turning to Adebayo triumphantly.

"And just where are you building this fort?" Dolores asked.

"Down by the stream, in back of the tobacco barn, said

Sebastián We can fish there also when it's finished." Dolores still had her doubts and looked to Sofia for assurance.

"It should be all right, Dolores, but I'll ask Flora, who works in that building, to keep an eye on them."

"Well, Eugenio and I are going riding," said Sofía, why don't you join us, Dolores? It should be fun."

"I can't right now, Sofia, I want to attend mass and then I'll have to read those documents the lawyers sent me."

"What an awful way to spend such a delightful Sunday, and all because of our own greedy brother. He should be ashamed of himself for tearing our family apart. I know papá would be ashamed of him, if he were still alive."

Sofia turned to her law professor husband.

"Have we considered everything, mi amor? Is there anything else we can do at this point?"

"Yes, win the case, and as to that, I think our chances are quite good."

"I just want it to be over," Dolores said. "It's so disruptive and contentious…"

2

As Sebastián and Adebayo walked back to the Main House, Adebayo suggested that they pass by the slave quarters. It was Sunday, and he knew that there would be lots to see. But Sebastián was hesitant, because Dolores had ordered him to stay away from the slave quarters.

"Don't worry, Sebastián, nobody see us. We jest hide in di bushes and see what we can see. It will be fun. Let's go!"

They made their way to the path leading up to the slave quarters and scurried behind a patch of palm trees, high grass and wild gardenia bushes. Now, as the two youngsters hid there, two slaves walked past speaking Yoruba. Adebayo listened.

"Di Chief Overseer come to di slave quarters, and he gonna rape a woman," said Adebayo.

Not surprisingly, Sebastián did not understand.

"Jest you watch and you see," said Adebayo.

At that moment, Adebayo peeked out and caught sight of the devil himself, staggering up the path towards the slave quarters, a bottle of rum in one hand and his bullwhip in the other. He passed perilously close to where the boys lay hidden, sending cold chills up their spines.

In the past, a light-skinned Kongo girl with the Spanish name, Graciela, had been a favorite of the Chief Overseer. Graciela had arrived more than a decade earlier as a ten-year-old in the hold of *The Wandering Maiden*, captained by Patrick McHugh. Victorio had noticed her immediately and followed her physical development closely, choosing to deflower her at the first sign of pubescence. Following that first time, he continued to. take her on a regular basis. There came a time, however, when he grew tired of her and divided his inexhaustible sexual energy amongst other desirable slave women. That freed up Graciela, who took up with a towering Lucumi Chief named Teodoro, known for his strength and prowess. Teodoro and Graciela became a couple and had two young children. Although slaves rarely entered into Catholic marriages, they did form couples, which were recognized and respected by masters and slaves alike.

The drums were beating and the slaves were dancing as Victorio Arquídez approached the slave quarters. Sunday was the slaves' one day of rest, and they were seeking to extract the last bit of enjoyment from it. The Chief Overseer burst right into the crowd, scowling, cursing, cracking his bullwhip and clearing a path through the masses to an earthen-fire pit, where the slaves were roasting a pig.

"You better cook it well," Victorio said, callously placing his filthy jackboot on the pig and pushing it over on its side.

"Cut me a big hunk from the other side," he said, removing his foot.

"Sí, don Victorio, I cut it for you," said one of the cooks, reaching then for his machete and hacking off a good-sized piece dripping with juice.

When the cook went to give it to him, Victorio grabbed it out of his hand and stuffed it into his mouth, slurping the juice all over his mustache and beard. Then, he burped, took a large swallow of rum and staggered off to seek a woman.

"Where's my little *puta*, Amana? I don't see her. Where is she?" he yelled to no one in particular.

He questioned several slaves, but none of them had seen her. Then he grabbed one hapless little slave by the throat.

"You go find her and bring her to me right now," he yelled.

The little slave ran off, a terrified look on his face. Victorio then began searching for his other favorite women, shouting out their names. "Flor, come over here, now! Palomita, where are you, you little bitch? Daisy!" He rushed around, looking everywhere, but the women were nowhere to be seen. He went up to one of his usual sources, grabbed him by the neck and shouted.

"If you are hiding them, I swear I'll skin you all alive."

Meanwhile, the little slave who'd run off to search for Amana returned without her, infuriating Victorio, who began flogging him hard, turning his whip then to any and all slaves who strayed within range. The Chief Overseer staggered around, cursing, swigging down the rum and cracking his bullwhip, furious that he couldn't find his women. Still undeterred, he headed for the ramshackle dwelling that was the slave quarters. He went inside, finding it deathly silent and deserted. He walked down the putrid corridor, largely immune to its foul odor, past the empty cots, then broke the silence.

"Where are my *putas*? Where are they?" He screamed.

"Ay, don Victorio."

The voice was weak and barely audible, coming from the last cot in the ramshackle quarters. She leaned up in her filthy cot, her expression one of fear and revulsion at the sound and sight of the Chief Overseer. It was Angelina, who was in her ninth decade, the oldest slave on *La Dulce Gardenia*.

"You're still alive, you disgusting old hag! I should have fed you to the dogs along with that worthless old Bartholomew. You're just like him and can't earn your keep."

Angelina would never forget that day when the Chief Overseer turned his vicious bloodhounds on her dear friend Bartholomew and stood there watching as they tore him to pieces.

"Where are my *putas*? Where are they!" he shouted, staggering against Angelina's cot, almost knocking her out of it.

At that moment, he heard sounds coming from the back yard. He opened the door and went outside. Much to his delight, he saw Graciela. She was there with her mate, Teodoro, and they were tending their yam garden.

"Graciela! I have missed you," he said, his leering, lecherous smile conveying his evil intent. Graciela began trembling and turned to Teodoro for protection.

"Try to stay calm," whispered Teodoro. He turned then to the Chief Overseer, hoping not to provoke him.

"Graciela is my wife, don Victorio, and we ask that you please respect that." Teodoro's words could not have been more provocative to the Chief Overseer."

"So, she's your wife, is she? You filthy black scum! She is a slave and the property of *La Dulcet Gardenia*. Get over here, you little bitch", shouted Victorio. "I'll take her whenever I please. You hear me! Whenever I please!"

Graciela didn't move. Victorio was seething with rage and raised his bullwhip, swinging it down hard at Graciela. The whip encircled her torso like a boa constrictor squeezing its prey, and Graciela screamed. Teodoro tried to hold on to her, but Victorio pulled hard on the whip and yanked her over to him. Teodoro was in a quandary, wanting desperately to protect his mate but endeavoring to avoid a fight, which he knew he could not win.

"I beg you, don Victorio, turn her loose and leave us at peace. Please, she is my wife."

Victorio's answer was to squeeze Graciela's buttocks and scowl at Teodoro. Teodoro's face flushed with anger, and he took a few steps towards the Chief Overseer.

"Back off you filthy African scum or you are going to be very sorry you did not." Teodoro took another step toward him, and Victorio reached into his pocket and pulled out his pistol.

"You take one more step and I'll blow your black brains out." That stopped Teodoro in his tracks.

Meanwhile, the Sunday celebration out front was beginning to wind down, and some slaves had found their way to the back yard, including a few of Victorio's subordinate overseers.

"Take them out front. Tie this *cabrón* to that large royal palm, and tie the *cabrona* to one of those smaller palms facing him." His subordinates did as they were told.

By now, a crowd of slaves had gathered to watch.

"So, she's your wife, is she? She's a slave, the property of *La Dulce Gardenia* and my *puta*. You hear me. My *puta*! Watch me now, watch how I'm going to enjoy her, you filthy black scum."

He ripped off Graciela's soiled white garment and dropped his trousers. Then, he put two fingers in his mouth and retrieved some spit, after which he spread her legs and rubbed it on her private parts. Graciela screamed and looked like she was about to faint. Victorio turned and with an evil smile on his face, thrust his large penis inside her, pumping furiously and taunting Teodoro all the while.

"You see? Your '*esposa*' loves my *pinga*," (Your 'wife' loves my dick) Victorio shouted then laughed hard. Meanwhile, Sebastián began slowly rising from the bushes, looking like he was about to flee.

"Stay down," whispered Adebayo, pulling him back. "I tell you when it safe to leave."

Victorio raped Graciela repeatedly for another hour, during which he drank another full bottle of rum before passing out.

3

The Kongo Chief, Teodoro, sat on the bank of the stream that ran through the grounds of *La Dulce Gardenia*. His brother, Osunlade, and a trusted comrade, Babatunde, later joined him.

"That Catalán *cabrón* has raped his last woman on this plantation," said Teodoro, anger flowing from his every pore.

"Let's cut off his *cojones*!" said Babatunde, a powerful brute of a man whose muscular body was the result of years of hard labor on the plantation railroad. "We'll make a eunuch out of that *hijo de puta*."

"I'd like nothing better than to castrate him, but even as a eunuch he could still hurt us. No, I want that cabrón dead, and I want him to die a slow, painful death, the kind he has inflicted on so many of our African brothers and sisters over these many years."

"Listen, I have an idea," said Osunlade. "Victorio Arquidez has his bloodhounds, but we have an even fiercer species."

"And what is that," asked Teodoro, as he looked at Osunlade with great interest.

"Our crocodiles. You know the ones I'm talking about? They live down where the stream enters the swamp. They are big, strong and fearsome. You remember that British veterinarian who came to the plantation last year to help us breed the oxen? He told me that our crocs are unique to the island of Cuba, because they can jump. I have seen them jump high out of the water, five, six feet or more, and snatch those furry *hutias* right out of the trees. I've also seen them leap up and snatch an egret or a flamingo right out of the air." They all smiled in unison.

"I like the idea," said Teodoro.

They met again and worked out a plan. Teodoro enlisted the Chief Overseer's housemaid and cook, Teleayo, who had suffered untold abuse and humiliation at the hands of the hated Chief Overseer. She agreed to prepare an herbal potion and slip it into his water that would cause him to fall into a deep, zombie-like sleep.

Osunlade set the plan in motion by going to the swamp and selecting a large tree with strong branches that hung out over the water. He slung a rope over a thick branch and fashioned it to function as a pulley. In the early morning hours of a full-moon night, they slowly made their way to the Chief Overseer's cottage. Teleayo was waiting and assured them that she had given the Chief Overseer the potion and that he was in a deep sleep.

They crept into Victorio's room and found him deathlike still in his bedclothes. They picked him up, carried him outside and placed him in an oxcart. Then, they began making their way down the rugged path that ran along the stream and led to the swamp.

"Wait," said Babatunde. "I stashed some pork in an iron pot behind those bushes."

They waited while he retrieved it, then started off again. The wheels of the oxcart were squeaking loudly, and they became alarmed. Although it was the wee hours of the morning, kidnapping the Chief Overseer was a brazen and highly risky operation that could cost them their lives and the lives of their families, if discovered.

A hundred meters from the swamp, the path took an increasingly steep, downward slope, and at one point, the old ox lost its footing and the cart skidded, knocking Victorio out of the cart. They panicked, but amazingly he didn't wake up.

"We better leave the oxcart," said Teodoro. "We can carry him the rest of the way!"

"All right, but we better tie him up. We don't know how much longer that potion will last," said Teodoro. They quickly tied him up, then carried and dragged him the rest of the way. Osunlade led them to the tree he had prepared, and they laid Victorio Arquídez on the ground.

"Tie that pork on him; tie it on his feet, his legs, his arms, tie it everywhere," said Teodoro. "Now, throw the rest of it in the water to attract the crocodiles."

Next, they tied the rope to Victorio's waist, making sure it was very tight.

"All right now, let's hoist him up. Everybody pull! He's a fat pig, so we need to pull hard."

"Wait, someone needs to slide the rope all the way out over the branch, so we can swing him over the water," said Osunlade.

"I'll do it," said Babatunde." He climbed the tree and slid the rope out to the ideal spot; then, they hoisted the Chief Overseer up and swung him out over the swampy water. Only then did he wake up, twisting and turning about like a marionette ineptly played. He must have thought he was having a nightmare, because it was just too horrible to be real. But he soon realized that it was real, whereupon he let loose with a blood-curdling scream that would have awakened and shaken the dead. Fortunately, the swamp was in a remote area of the plantation, and no one could hear it, except the three African slaves who had sought, planned and were well on their way to achieving their long-awaited revenge.

"Cut me down you filthy black scum," Victorio screamed. "I swear that you and your families will pay for this with your lives." He screamed and threatened them with all manner of horrible punishments, but to no avail.

"Here they come" said Osunlade.

They slid silently across the water, a large male in the lead, gliding slowly and coming to rest directly below where Victorio Arquídez was dangling and twisting on the rope. The large croc raised its head, opened wide its mouth and gazed up at him. It then jumped up some three or four feet and clamped shut it's jaws with a terrifying **clap**, coming within a hare's breath of Victorio's ankles and feet.

"Pull him up! The filthy cabrón is too low. Pull him up!" cried Teodoro. "We don't want him to die so soon. Let's tease the crocs into a feeding frenzy, then we'll lower him down a little at a time."

Victorio twisted and turned, struggling to find some way to escape the horrible death that surely awaited him.

"Cut me down, cut me down you filthy black scum," changing then his tactics.

"Have mercy on me," he now cried pitifully, aware that his aggressive threats were to no avail.

"I swear that I will never again touch your women. I will be a friend and protector of you African slaves."

He pleaded and begged their forgiveness for all the vile and evil acts he had committed over the years, promising to bestow upon them all manner of favors and benefits, if they would just cut him down and let him go.

"Oh, so now you will repent, will you? Well, it's too late,

cabrón. You sealed your fate years ago, and there is no escaping it now," said Teodoro defiantly.

"Lower him down now a little more, boys."

The big croc jumped again and this time higher. With its mouth agape and its sharp white teeth illuminated by the full moon, it clamped its jaws down hard on Victorio's foot, tearing it off at the ankle and swallowing it whole. Victorio screamed in agony and then blacked out.

"Pull him up again! Hurry! Hurry," cried Teodoro, but it was too late. The large croc jumped even higher this time, tearing off Victorio's right leg just above the knee. As it thrashed about, biting and swallowing, pieces of human flesh slipped out of its mouth, attracting several smaller crocs intent on getting their share. Victorio somehow came to, seemingly aware that there was no escape and that his time was up.

"Shoot me! Shoot me; I beg you," he pleaded as a copious stream of blood ran down from the stump of his right leg. His pathetic pleas were met, however, with a stone cold silence; that is until Babatunde spoke up.

"Maybe it is time to put him out of his misery, Teodoro. What do you think?"

"He does not deserve our mercy, but the sight of the filthy *cabrón* is beginning to sicken me. So, all right, let's put him out of his misery. But we're not going to do it with a bullet. Lower him down boys; lower him down all the way."

It was all over in a matter of seconds as the violent thrashing and gnashing of jaws and teeth of Cuba's jumping crocodiles put to death the evil Chief Overseer of *La Dulce Gardenia*, granting its slave population their long-awaited vengeance.

When the sun rose over the swamp that morning, there was no sign of Victorio Arquídez and no sign of what had occurred there the night before. The de Castilla brothers made some initial inquiries into the Chief Overseer's sudden disappearance. There were, of course, rumors, one of which gained credence over time and gradual acceptance. When questioned, Victorio's housemaid, Teleayo, stated that the Chief Overseer had acquired a fortune over the years by stealing slaves consigned to *La Dulce Gardenia* and selling them in Puerto Rico and Jamaica; and that he likely fled to Catalán with his ill-begotten fortune.

CHAPTER XXIV

The Beach at Marinanao

The lawsuit was still in the Appellate Court. Arturo had won the suit at the trial level by bribing the judge, and it appeared that he intended to spread money around in hopes of winning at the appellate level as well. Bribing appellate judges was, however, more difficult, and it was not clear that he could get away with it. Felipe continued to be Arturo's passive ally, but was showing signs of tiring of the disruptive litigation that had split the family apart.

One morning Mario Luis slipped a letter under Dolores's door. She had not had a letter from Billy in months, nor had she written to him. She was reluctant to open it and placed it on her night table. She walked past it numerous times that day, staring at it, aware of the painful irony. Back when their love was fresh and new, a letter from Billy would send her heart fluttering with joy. She would open them immediately, swooning over every sweet word.

Finally, she opened the letter.

May 3 1867
15 Riceland Road
Charleston,
South Carolina

My dearest Dolores,

As you can see from the address on this letter, I am back in Charleston living with my mother in the house where I was born and raised.

I miss you terribly, my love, and long to be with you and Sebastián once more. There is so much I want to tell you, so much I need to say to relieve my troubled heart; so much for which I beg your understanding and forgiveness. I have decided to come to Havana and have booked passage on the King Neptune scheduled to arrive on May 15.

I pray that you and Sebastián are well, and that God may bless and keep you now and forever.

Your loving husband

As the weather turned warmer, Dolores and her sisters began going to the beach at Marinanao, a nearby seaside villa. They would pack a picnic lunch for the day and sometimes spend the night in a nearby rustic farmhouse. It was a new experience for Sebastián, who had seen very little of the sea other than the view from a steamship. Unlike Sebastián, Constancia's two children had been going to the beach for years and were perfectly at home in the water. Sebastián had not yet learned to swim, Dolores wanted to teach him and sought the help of Sofia and Eugenio. Dolores knew and told the others that they would have to watch him closely, because he liked to venture off by himself.

Sofia peeked into Dolores's room.

"Hurry Dolores, the carriage is waiting."

It was a beautiful morning, a perfect day for the beach. And no sooner had they pulled up to the beach at Marinanao, than Sebastián jumped down from the carriage and darted for the water. Eugenio chased after him and caught him just before he reached the surf.

"Sebastián, you mustn't go in the water by yourself," yelled Dolores. "One of us will go with you until you have learned to swim well."

"But I can swim now, mamá. Uncle Eugenio said so, didn't you, Uncle Eugenio?" Eugenio smiled, attempting to please them both with his response.

"Yes, Sebastián, you are learning to swim well, but your mamá wants to be sure that you become even better, so she won't ever have to worry about you…"

They spent a pleasant day at the beach, and that evening enjoyed a delicious dinner of *pargo* (red snapper), black beans, rice and fressly baked bread at a local restaurant. They decided to stay the night and retired to the nearby farmhouse. Dolores and Sofia shared a bedroom. They had just gotten into bed, when Sofia turned to Dolores.

"I saw Mario Luis slip a letter under your door, Dolores. Was it from Billy?"

Dolores looked away and did not respond.

"I know you are finding it difficult to talk about Billy and your marriage, Dolores but…"

"I was going to tell you, Sofia, but I wanted to wait until we got back home. Billy is coming to Havana next week."

"Next week? Are you sure?"

"Yes, he is arriving next week."

"Do you miss him, Dolores? Tell me the truth." Dolores looked away, but Sofia pressed her for an answer.

"Do you still love him?"

"He's my husband, Sofia."

"But do you still love him? Tell me the truth!" asked Sofia.

Dolores laid her head down on the pillow and began to weep.

"I'm so sorry, Dolores. I did not mean to upset you, but you know how I feel. Billy has mistreated you and Sebastián. You cannot go back to Washington with him. You belong here in Cuba and so does Sebastián. I am telling you this, dear sister, only because I want what is best for both you and your son."

2

Dolores was awakened in the wee hours of the morning on May 15 by a howling wind and a heavy rain pelting her bedroom windows. It was somewhat early in the season for a full-blown hurricane, but that was what this appeared to be. Dolores woke Sebastián and brought him into her room. Only then did her thoughts turn to Billy, who was to arrive this day in Havana. She had planned to meet him, but with a hurricane raging, she knew that Havana was out of the question. The roads would be blocked and the railroad shut down.

Dolores heard the sound of the door opening. It was Sofia and Eugenio.

"Dolores, are you all right?"

"I think so," she said.

"It's Auntie Sofia and Uncle Eugenio, mamá," Sebastián said.

A moment later Constancia appeared, then Carmen and Mario Luis. All of them were carrying candles and stood there for a moment casting ominous-looking shadows on the walls.

"Where are Felipe and Arturo?" Constancia asked. At first, no one responded, and then Mario Luis spoke up.

"They left last evening. They were very quiet and rushed off in two carriages. It almost seemed that they knew a hurricane was coming."

"How could they possibly know that a hurricane was coming?" Sofia asked.

"Arturo has some ship-captain friends," said Constancia. "They know a lot more about storms than we do. I've heard tell that some sailors can smell a hurricane long before it strikes."

"Wouldn't they at least have shared that information with us?" Eugenio asked. "They are not that hostile, are they?"

"You don't know Arturo," said Sofia.

They all huddled together in the library until the break of dawn, when the wind died down, the rain slowed and the sky cleared.

The city of Havana escaped the brunt of the storm, and the *King Neptune* arrived in port as scheduled. Billy stepped off the gangplank, expecting to find Dolores there to meet him. He waited and watched while the other passengers met their loved ones and friends, but still there was no sign of her. His heart sank, and he tried to console himself, thinking that maybe she had not received his letter. He hailed the last remaining carriage, directing the coachman to take him to the railroad station. The coachman said there had been a hurricane that passed southwest of Havana, but Billy saw no sign of a storm during the train ride to *La Dulce Gardenia*. It was only when they were within a kilometer or two of the depot that he saw the signs.

There were vast stretches of uprooted sugar cane, overturned wagons and oxcarts and battered storage facilities. The depot itself had taken a battering, witnessed by the blown out windows and the barrel tiles strewn about the ground. It was deserted and it was a long walk to the Main House, but it looked like that was his only option. Then he remembered that the overseers would sometimes leave a horse and carriage behind the depot for late arriving guests.

He walked back and looked around, but there was no carriage, just an old mare without a saddle. He untied her and used the rope to secure his luggage atop her back. Then he mounted the beast bareback and rode off at a slow and cautious gait. It was difficult and tiring without a saddle, but eventually he made his way to the long entrance road to the Main House, passing slaves bent over clearing rubble from the storm. They looked up at him, their faces expressing surprise at the sight of a white *Massa* atop a tired old horse without a saddle.

The black wrought iron gate was unbolted, the door to the Main House unlocked and all was quiet. He entered and called out several times: "Anyone home?" But he got no response. He walked over to the spiral staircase and began climbing up to the living quarters. When he reached the crystal chandelier, he stopped and gazed upon Dolores's portrait there on the wall. He had viewed that portrait several times over the years, but this time he was struck like never before by her incomparable beauty and her sweet simple nature, portrayed so masterfully by the Spanish artist.

I mustn't lose her, for I could not live without her.

Suddenly, he heard someone coming down the stairs, and when he looked up, he saw Panchita carrying a large water jug.

"Oh, señor McHugh, I didn't know you were here. We had a hurricane, sir."

"Is doña Dolores upstairs?" Billy asked.

"Yes, señor, they are all asleep upstairs. No one slept last night in that terrible storm."

Billy climbed the stairs and went directly to Dolores's quarters.

He paused a moment, wondering whether to knock. But when he found the door unlocked, he entered.

"Papá, we had a hurricane." Billy picked up his little mulatto son and kissed him on the cheek.

"Is your mamá all right?"

"We go to the beach, papá, and I know how to swim. I have a nice school, and the teacher likes me. Auntie Sofia says mamá and I should stay here in Cuba."

"Sebastián, who are you talking to? You are supposed to be resting. Now go back to—Billy! How did you get here? I did not think you could possibly make it in that hurricane." He rushed to her side and threw his arms around her.

"Oh, how I've missed you, my love," he said, as he went to kiss her on the lips. Dolores turned her head, offering only her cheek.

"Go to your room and go back to sleep, Sebastián," said Dolores. breaking Billy's embrace and walking over to the water basin. She poured herself a glass of water, still somewhat startled at seeing him there.

"Didn't you get my letter, Dolores? I wrote and told you I was coming."

"I got your letter, Billy, and I was going to meet you, but I did not think you could possibly get here with that hurricane."

"There was only a light rain in Havana, and the railroad was running. I didn't see any damage until I got close to the plantation, and that's when I got worried about you."

Dolores poured another glass of water and offered it to Billy. He drank the water, then moved closer to her, but Dolores moved away.

"What's wrong, my love"?

"There's nothing wrong, Billy. I'm just very surprised to see you."

But there was something wrong, surely there was.

"You must be very tired, Billy. I'll have Carmen fix you a bed in one of the guest rooms."

She pulled the servant's cord, and just then, Sebastián ran back to the room. Billy picked him up and kissed him on the cheek.

"How is your horsemanship coming along, young man?"

"I ride every day, papá..."

Billy awoke just before noon with sore legs and a sore rump from the hard ride on the saddle-less mare. He asked Carmen to draw him a hot bath.

He had come to Cuba to take Dolores and Sebastián back to the United States with him, but as he sat there soaking in the comforting bathwater, he recalled Sebastián's words from the night before

Auntie Sofia said mamá and I should stay here in Cuba.

Billy knew that Dolores loved, trusted and looked up to Sofia. She was a lawyer, a university professor and a smart, practical woman, who had always been there for Dolores when others had not. He knew that he would have difficulty in convincing Dolores to reject Sofia's advice.

As he walked down the garden path and the patio bar came into view, he saw Dolores and Sofia sitting there with a man he did not recognize.

"Billy, how nice to see you! Please sit down and join us," said Sofia.

Billy kissed his sister-in-law on the cheek.

"Dolores told me that you arrived last evening. How in God's name did you make it through that terrible storm? Oh, and Billy, forgive me, this is my husband, Eugenio, whom you have not met."

They shook hands. Billy sat down next to Dolores, kissed her on the cheek and reached for her hand.

"I thought I'd see Sebastián here with you, my love," Billy said, raising his coffee cup for the slave woman.

"He's in school now," Dolores said, smiling, but withdrawing her hand. "He's going to a very good school run by Sofia's colleague, He has many friends, and there is a good racial mix of students. We're all very pleased with his progress. The term is about to end for the summer, and he doesn't want it to."

"Why don't we leave these two alone Eugenio", said Sofia. "I'm sure they have lots to talk about. Oh, but Dolores don't forget that we have to visit the *Notario*."

"I was going to ask you, Sofia, how is the lawsuit coming along?" Billy asked.

"Well, we lost at the trial level, and the case is on appeal."

"You lost? How could you possibly lose with that Spanish Civil Code article you showed me?"

"We were all shocked by the decision, Billy. We filed an appeal, of course, and the case could come up before the Appellate Court as early as next week."

"I thought that article of the Civil Code prohibited disinheriting one's offspring?" Billy said.

"It does, but the trial judge was bribed and simply ignored it. That is how justice is rendered here in our Spanish colonial courts. The decision is a travesty of justice, but it is what it is, and we will have to deal with it," said Sofia. Billy glanced at Dolores but saw no reaction.

Billy's reception the night before was a chilly one at best. Dolores had avoided his attempts to embrace her. So, the moment Sofia and Eugenio left, he moved closer to her, wrapped his arms around her and went to kiss her on the lips. Again, she turned her head and offered only her cheek.

"What's wrong, *mi amor*?" he asked, though in truth he knew and had known for years.

"Please try to understand, Dolores. When we lost our precious Felicidad, my life became a living hell. You had left and I was all alone. I had no energy, no appetite and suffered from unrelenting insomnia. I began to drink heavily, but that only made it worse. Then, I tried smoking opium, and at first it seemed to be a miraculous cure. It lifted me out of my extreme pain and despair and I felt alive again. I began smoking it on a daily basis, but before long it took over my entire life. I spent every hour of every day craving and seeking more opium. I hit rock bottom and became a hopeless addict. Henry Phipps & Partners sacked me, and I lost my partnership…"

She was moved by his words, and his countenance mirrored the terrible pain and suffering he had endured.

"I decided to take…I decided to, to take my own…my own life." He broke down and cried, pleading with her to have pity on him, imploring her to forgive him. She was deeply moved, her eyes filled with tears and the hardness in her heart melted away.

"We have both suffered terribly, Billy. No one could have foreseen the carriage accident, but God must have had his reasons. Things will be better now. I know they will. I tried not to love you. Billy. I tried very hard, but I just can't"

She reached for his hand, brought it up to her lips and kissed it tenderly. Now came the sweet embrace, the tender kisses and the healing forgiveness that he so desperately needed.

The next thing he knew Sebastián was standing there in his blue and white school uniform. Billy hurried to dry his eyes with his napkin.

"Mamá, papá, Teacher Menéndez said I was the best writer today. She said all my letters were perfect."

"That's wonderful, Sebastián," Dolores said. "Come here and give me a kiss."

"I'm proud of you, Sebastián," Billy said, smiling and patting him on the head.

"Papá, will you come riding with me? I can ride Fresco very fast now!"

Billy looked to Dolores, who smiled and nodded her approval.

Father and son rode together for more than an hour, and for the first time in years, Billy showed a genuine interest in his mulatto son. He showered him with attention and affection, complimenting him on his riding ability and praising him for his fluent Spanish and English. He promised to take him to the beach to help him with his swimming and to go fishing. All that week Billy devoted his time and attention to Sebastián. He waited each day for him to come home from school. They took long walks together, and he told him stories and anecdotes about his grandfather, Patrick McHugh, the sea captain. They laughed and played together, and Billy tried hard to make up for the times he had mistreated him in word and in deed.

Sebastián was thrilled with all the attention, and by Friday it almost seemed as though he had forgotten about that other hurtful papá in Washington.

On Friday evening after dinner, Billy, Eugenio, and Ricardo went off to the library to sip brandy and smoke good Cuban cigars. Dolores and Sofia went up to Sofia's living quarters and sat down in her comfortable armchairs. Mario Luis brought them a glass of sherry, and they talked long into the night.

"...A bright future awaits you and Sebastián right here in Cuba, Dolores." Dolores shook her head.

"I told you Sofia that Billy and I had a long talk. He has changed, Sofia, and we have reconciled."

"Come now, dear sister. Do you really believe that he is changed? Is his sudden interest in Sebastián real and sincere, or just a charade to fool you into thinking he has changed?"

"Oh, dear sister, it's so unlike you to be so suspicious and cynical. I love Billy, and I know that he still loves me."

"And just how do you know that he loves you? What has he done to prove that he loves you? From what you have told me, he has done everything to disprove it. And furthermore, how do you know that he didn't suddenly appear here in Cuba because he appreciates that you are about to become a very wealthy woman?"

"But Sofia, Arturo and Felipe bribed the judge and won the judgment, didn't they? Couldn't they bribe the next judge?"

"It won't be so easy this time, Dolores. Eugenio and I are confident that we will win the appeal. You are going to be a one-fifth owner of *La Dulce Gardenia* and all its vast resources. Billy is no fool. He's a lawyer and he's aware of that."

"I'm surprised at you, Sofia. Billy is not that kind of person, and he does not need my money. He is a brilliant lawyer and commands a very good salary. He bought us a big beautiful house in Washington." Dolores caught herself now, recalling that Billy himself admitted that Henry Phipps & Partners had sacked him.

"I don't think you or I know for certain what kind of person Billy is, but the way he's treated you and Sebastián is some evidence of his character. You and Sebastián can have a very good life here in Cuba. You can get a teaching position at one of the local schools. Billy is not worthy of your love, Dolores. Let him go back to Washington or Charleston or wherever else he wants to go. You and Sebastián belong here in Cuba."

3

Early Saturday morning, Dolores and Billy mounted a carriage and rode to the Church of the Little Flower. They held hands and chatted contentedly. They talked now of the happy memories when they had first met and fallen in love; they talked about the future. They laughed and exchanged sweet little kisses until they neared the church, where they became more sedate and serious.

They entered the church, dipped their fingers in the Holy Water font and made the sign of the cross. After which, they genuflected and walked down to a pew on the Virgin Mary side of the nave. They knelt and said a short prayer. There were several penitents standing in a queue behind the confessional, and they walked over hand in hand and stood behind them. Billy lovingly placed his hands on Dolores's slender waist, admiring her long, lustrous, dark brown hair. Soon, it was Dolores's turn, and she smiled sweetly at Billy, walked up and entered the confessional.

"Forgive me, Father, for I have sinned. It's been two weeks since my last confession."

"What are your sins?" asked the priest.

It did not take long for her to confess her sins, all of which were venial. She then fell silent.

"Are there any other sins you need to confess, señora?"

She did not respond immediately, and a tense silence took hold, until finally:

"I don't believe so, Father."

"Has there been any improvement in your marriage, señora?" The question startled her, for the priest obviously recognized her, and Dolores knew then that it was the young priest, Father Joseph behind that screen.

"Yes Father, there has been some improvement," she responded with a quivering voice.

Though she had complete trust in Father Joseph, she felt uncomfortable nonetheless.

"Does your husband still blame you for the death of your child, señora?"

The priest's question was even more startling, and it produced another awkward silence.

"I don't know, Father."

"Is there anything else you need to confess, señora?"

"No, Father."

"In the name of the Father, the Son and the Holy Ghost, I absolve you of your sins. For your penance, I want you to make an offering to the poor, and say two Our Fathers and two Hail Marys. Go in peace, my child, to love and serve the Lord, and try not to sin again."

"I will try, Father."

Billy watched as Dolores exited the confessional and entered a pew to pray her penance. Billy now entered the confessional.

"Forgive me Father, for I have sinned. It's been more than a year since my last confession".

The priest shifted in his seat, and though Billy could not see his face, he could see the outline of his frame; and having heard his voice, he concluded that he was a young priest.

"What are your sins, señor?" Billy hesitated, then haltingly:

"I, I, was unfaithful to my wife, Father." He felt more comfortable now that he had gotten it out.

"Have you committed adultery?" asked the priest calmly and matter of factly, indicating to Billy that though he was a young priest, he was accustomed to hearing confessions of adultery.

"Yes, Father."

"Is your wife aware of it, señor?" The question startled Billy.

"No, Father."

"Are you going to confess to her?"

"I, I, don't know, Father. Isn't it enough to confess to you?"

The priest leaned forward, closer to the screen.

"If you are truly repentant, contrite, and resolve not to repeat your sin, señor, I can grant you absolution. But I would advise you to listen to your conscience and ask yourself whether your failure to confess to your wife will poison your relationship and lead to the destruction of your marriage."

Stone cold silence ensued as the priest waited for Billy's response, but it was not forthcoming.

"How many instances of adultery were there, señor?" The silence continued. Finally:

"There were three women, Father, but there was only one for whom I had some feelings."

"Are you still involved with this woman for whom you say you had some feelings?"

"No, I am not," Billy said.

"And what is the present status of your relationship with your wife, señor?"

"My marriage was in deep trouble, Father. We lost a darling baby girl in a carriage accident. It was a terribly painful and devastating loss, one from which I still haven't fully recovered, and don't believe that I ever will."

The priest cleared his throat, shifted in his seat and moved closer to the screen as Billy continued.

"I was so disconsolate and depressed that I no longer wanted to live. I sought relief by smoking opium and became addicted to it. I lost my health, Father, my partnership in a fine law firm, and my self-respect. It was then that I sinned, Father."

The lawyer in him had stepped forth in his defense, the need to present arguments, reasons and excuses to justify, or at the least, to mitigate the sins.

"My wife had returned here to Cuba, and I was all alone, Father, suffering profound grief and pain. I'm not trying to excuse what I've done. I know what I did was wrong. I am only trying to explain how the tragic loss of my precious baby girl brought me to the brink of suicide and caused me to commit those terrible sins. I'm ashamed of myself, Father, and I'm truly sorry for my sins."

"Your wife is a kind and caring woman, señor. I have no doubt that if you confess to her and tell her how truly sorry you are, she will forgive you and your marriage will be saved."

He knows who I am; I've said too much.

"Are there any other sins you need to confess, señor?"

"No, Father."

The priest leaned back again from the screen, producing a squeak from his seat.

"In the name of the Father and the Son and the Holy Ghost I absolve you of your sins. For your penance, make a generous contribution to the poor and say two Our Fathers and two Hail Marys before you leave the sanctuary."

"Amen," Billy said, making the sign of the cross.

He exited the confessional and entered a pew to say his penance.

As they left the church, Dolores turned to Billy.

"I always feel so much better after I make my confession, don't you, my love?"

"Yes, I do also, said Billy," though he wanted to leave it at that.

They mounted the carriage, and the coachman set off for *La Dulce Gardenia.* They held hands along the way. Dolores was ebullient. Billy was somewhat pensive as the priest's advice and admonishment echoed in his mind.

"It's such a lovely day, Billy. Why don't you take Sebastián to the beach at Marinanao? Eugenio took him there recently and they had a wonderful time. Sebastián became fascinated by something he called the flattop rock, and he's been wanting to go out there again and climb it."

"That's a great idea, my love, but why don't you come with us?"

Dolores smiled, moved closer to Billy and reached for his hand.

"You need to be alone with him, my love, just the two of you as father and son, so he can get to know you better, trust you and feel confident that you will be there for him. That is what has been lacking between the two of you. Please, my love, it will be good for you both. I'll tell Panchita to pack you a delicious picnic lunch."

4

In spite of the warm, sunny day, the beach was not overly crowded. Billy may have discovered the reason why, when he swatted a sand fly on his neck, blaming it on the direction of the wind. Fortunately, by the time he and Sebastián walked down the beach and planted their blanket and umbrella, the sand flies had disappeared.

"Papá, look. There's nobody out on that flattop rock," Sebastián said, pointing excitedly. "Can we go out there and fish, papá? Can we? Uncle Eugenio took me out there last time, but he said the tide was in and the water was too deep. Maybe the tide is out now, papá. Can we look and see? Can we, papá?"

Billy smiled and put his arm around him.

"Wouldn't you like to take a swim first? Mamá told me that your swimming has gotten very good. We can go out on the jetty later and fish. I heard you caught some really big *pargo* the last time. Here, let's put your life vest on, and we'll take a swim."

"I don't need the life vest, papá, and it hurts my arm. I'm a good swimmer, even Uncle Eugenio thinks so."

"I'm sure your uncle is right, but it's better to wear the life vest," Billy said, as he helped strap it on.

"All right, now let's go, little man. The water looks very inviting."

They ran to the water. Sebastián was all smiles and went to jump in by himself, but Billy grabbed his hand and pulled him back.

"Wait for me," Billy said.

"Let me show you how I can swim, papá!"

Sebastián broke Billy's grip and swam off some ten feet or more, quite impressively. Billy watched as he swam back, feeling more confident that Sebastián had indeed learned to swim.

They swam together, laughing, joking, frolicking and delighting in the horseplay that little boys love to do with their papas. When they swam back to shore, Sebastián asked again if they could go out and fish on the flattop rock.

"Look, papá. There's still no one fishing there. So maybe the tide is coming in. Let's go and see how high the water is."

"Let's eat lunch first. Aren't you hungry?" Billy asked.

"Yes, papá, I'm very hungry, and Panchita packed us some chocolate cake."

When they reached the shallower water, they stood up and Sebastián started giggling and running.

"I'll beat you papá! I'll beat you!" he said, scampering out of the water and running up the beach toward the blanket. Billy took off after him but let him win the race.

"I beat you, papá! I beat you!"

"Yes you did, you beat me easily. I didn't know you could run so fast."

"I even beat Adebayo once, papá, and he's a fast runner."

They dried off, sat down on the blanket and reached for the picnic basket.

"I see a vendor over there, papá. Can we buy some lemonade?"

"All right, go over and tell him to bring his cart." Sebastián ran off, returning moments later with the vendor, who poured them two tall glasses of lemonade. Billy paid for it with a silver coin, tipping the vendor generously.

"All right, Sebastiánito, what will it be, a breast or a leg?"

"A leg, papá. I like the dark meat. It's juicier and tastes better."

"All right, a leg for you and a breast for me," Billy said, handing Sebastián a chicken leg and receiving in return a cute little grin.

Sailboats passed by offshore as they ate their lunch. Sebastián pointed to them excitedly, smiling, laughing, and looking genuinely happy to be with his papá. Billy, too, felt happy to be with his son, glad that he had taken Dolores's suggestion to spend the day with him, just the two of them.

As they ate their lunch, Billy looked at his little mulatto son, who was about to turn five. It was as though he saw him for the first time. He focused at first on his natural good looks—his bushy, curly brown hair, his big brown eyes and yes, even his *acanelado* skin. He was a mulatto all right, but a fine looking mulatto at that. However, it was not just his good looks. Sebastián was a delightful little boy, full of fun, adventuresome and devilishly charming. And as Billy continued to admire him he was struck with pangs of guilt.

You must never again be unkind to him and mistreat him, Billy, never again!

They finished the chicken and began eating the chocolate cake, when Billy noticed a bump, a prominent bump, on Sebastián's right leg just below the knee. He reached over and touched it.

"Where did you get that bump on your leg?" he asked, though he certainly should have known.

"That's from the accident, papá, but it doesn't hurt anymore."

Sebastián's words were innocent and devoid of blame, but they stung even more, for Billy had had little if any sympathy for Sebastián after the accident. His only concern had been for his fair-skinned Felicidad and to a lesser extent for Dolores. Sebastián had suffered two broken legs and had endured excruciating pain. He spent months recuperating with two thick, cumbersome casts on his legs.

"I finished my lunch, papá. Can we go out to the flattop rock now?"

"Let's go over to the fishermen's hut first and see if we can rent a couple fishing poles."

They rented two poles, bought some bait and began walking over to the jetty. Just then, they saw a young couple walking down the beach with a fair-haired little girl between them. Apparently, she was just learning to walk, and she giggled and beamed with delight as her father and mother held her hands and helped her along. Sebastián stared at them then looked up at Billy.

"Papá, why don't you ask God to send you another *white* baby girl?" He had asked Dolores that same question, but without the word "white."

Billy chose not to respond.

As they walked along the beach, heading for the jetty, Sebastián urged Billy to hurry.

"We better walk faster papá, because lots of people want to fish on the flattop rock."

No sooner had they climbed up on the jetty, when two fishermen walked past them, talking animatedly. They stopped, however, some twenty feet from the end of the jetty, set down their gear and began to fish.

The site that had so completely captured Sebastián's attention, was a massive rock formation separated from the jetty by a fifteen foot gap. When the tide came in, the gap would fill with water and the flattop rock was inaccessible. But when the tide went out, the water level in the gap would drop, and the flattop rock would then become accessible from the jetty. One had only to jump down in the gap, walk through the shallow water and climb up to the flattop rock.

When they reached the end of the jetty, Sebastián was all smiles as he stared at the flattop rock, wanting more than ever to stand atop it triumphantly.

"The water doesn't look very deep, papá. Can we get out there now papá, can we?"

"Not yet, Sebastián. The tide hasn't gone out yet and the water is still too deep. Let's fish for a while, and we'll come back later and check the water level."

Father and son caught several nice-sized red snapper. From time to time, Sebastián would run and check the water level in the gap.

"The water is getting lower, papá. Hurry, come and see."

"Yes, I see it," said Billy. He also saw the two fishermen, who were about to jump down in the gap.

"Excuse me, señores, but would you mind if I took my little boy out there for a while? Since he first set eyes on that flattop rock, he's been wanting very much to get out there."

"Go right ahead, señor.," said one of them. "We have often fished there, but the fishing is just as good right here on the jetty."

"Thank you so much, señores, you're very kind," Billy said.

"Let's go Sebastián." Billy took him by the hand, and they stepped down in the gap and made their way through the shallow water to the flattop rock. Billy climbed up, then pulled Sebastián up.

"Look how far we can see from here, papá. I want to come here all the time."

They put their gear down, Billy baited their hooks and showed Sebastián how to cast out his line.

The wind was calm, and seagulls flew overhead, followed by a flock of pelicans. One of them suddenly dove down in the water and came up with a fish.

"This must be a good spot, Sebastián because Pelicans always know where to find the fish."

"Look, papá, that other pelican got a fish too. Oh, look papá there's a ship. Is it as big as *The Wandering Maiden*?"

"It's hard to tell from this far away," said Billy. "Oh, but, see the smoke? It's a steamship, so it's probably bigger."

They fished for more than an hour, encouraged by the two friendly fishermen to take their time on the flattop rock. Father and son laughed, joked and succeeded in filling their basket with fish.

"I only need to catch two more fish to have more than you, papá"

"Are you sure your Uncle Eugenio didn't teach you how to fish?" Billy joked.

"No, papá, this is the first time I have ever fished."

"You learn quickly little man, Oh, but let's not forget to check the water level in the gap, so we know when to make our way back to the jetty..."

Suddenly, Sebastián was jolted by a powerful strike that bent his fishing pole down to the breaking point. But he somehow held on.

"Look papá! I caught a big fish," Sebastián exclaimed. It was an enormous creature with a long, pointy bill, and it leaped high out of the water making spectacular acrobatic twists and turns.

"It's a blue marlin!" shouted the fishermen. "He's too big for your boy, señor. Hurry, take the pole and bring him in!"

Billy rushed over, reaching for Sebastián's pole, but the marlin leaped again, crashing down with its great size and weight, pulling Sebastián off the flattop rock and into the sea.

"Sebastián!" Billy screamed, horrified as he kicked off his shoes and dove in after him.

"Hurry, Miguel!" shouted Joaquín, the other fisherman. "You go after the boy! I'll go after the father."

They dove off the jetty and swam quickly out to the flattop rock. Miguel swam to the spot where the marlin had pulled Sebastián in. He dove down, searching frantically for him. Joaquín made his way to where Billy had dived in. He swam down, and when he came up to take a breath, he spotted Sebastián bobbing to the surface, behind where Miguel had been searching.

"I see the boy, Miguel!. He's right there behind you," shouted Joaquín.

"I see him now! I see him," yelled Miguel, who swam back and found Sebastián lying facedown and motionless in the water. Miguel turned him over on his back, noticing with alarm that his face had turned blue. He took hold of him now and began rapidly swimming toward shore.

Meanwhile, Joaquín swam off some distance from the flattop rock and began diving down again, this time in the deeper water. He found Billy on the sandy bottom and raised him to the surface; whereupon he wrapped an arm around his torso and began swimming toward shore.

When Miguel reached the shallower water with Sebastián, he picked him up and ran to shore and up the beach, placing him down on a blanket. A crowd of curious onlookers quickly surrounded them.

"We need an ambulance! Somebody, hurry, go to the Centro and tell them to come right away!" An adolescent boy immediately ran off, while a flurry of commands, prayers and sympathetic advice reverberated through the crowd.

"Turn the boy on his stomach!"

"Put this pillow under his chin!"

"Try holding him up by his feet so the water can drain out of his lungs."

Desperate and not knowing what else to do, Miguel picked up Sebastián by his feet and began shaking him. Just then, someone shouted:

"They found the father! They found the boy's father!"

The crowd turned and saw the fisherman Joaquín, struggling

through the shallow water, towing Billy toward shore. Several men ran down to help, and they dragged him up to the beach and laid him down on a blanket.

At that point, a tall, thin man in a stylish white swimsuit began pushing his way through the crowd to where the victims lay.

"Let me in there," he said. "I can help him. I saw them save a little girl last summer at Varadero Beach. We need to turn him over on his stomach and compress his back to a steady count of one-two-three to flush the water out of his lungs."

The man bent down now, straddled himself over Sebastián and began the compressions. After a minute or two, however, he stopped, apparently struck with fear and indecision when there was no water seen escaping from Sebastián's mouth.

"I'm a doctor. Let me through," shouted another man close by."

He made his way through the crowd to where Sebastián lay and got into position, administering the compressions at a faster pace and with greater force. Several minutes passed, but still there was no water to be seen escaping from Sebastián's mouth. Cries of alarm rose up from the crowd, and several women began praying the rosary, beseeching God, the Blessed Mother and all the saints in heaven to intercede and save the little boy.

It was early afternoon, and Dolores was in her quarters when she heard a carriage pulling up to the plaza. Moments later, there was a knock on her door. She opened it and saw Sofia standing there smiling broadly.

"I have some very good news for you, Dolores. I have just come from the lawyers' office. They are not usually there on Saturday, but they were today. The Appellate Court has ruled. The decision came down late Friday evening, with all three judges ruling in our favor. I'm certain that Arturo won't appeal any higher, because he knows now that there is no way to get around that provision of the Spanish Civil Code, not even with bribes." Sofia was simply ebullient.

"That's wonderful news, Sofia!" Dolores said, as she embraced her sister.

"Wonderful, indeed!" said Sofia. "You are going to be a very wealthy woman!"

"You don't know how happy this makes me, Sofia. But it's not because of the money, though that certainly is welcome news, but because it's what papá wanted. He loved me, Sofia, of that I am certain. He accepted me as his rightful daughter, bestowed upon me the de Castilla name and made me a part of the family."

"Constancia and I have known that all along, Dolores, and papá's intent was implemented by the Appellate Court's decision. Papá is now smiling down on all of us."

"Oh, this is simply wonderful. I must go out to Marinanao and give Billy the good news." Dolores waltzed over to the floor-length mirror, smiling happily, beside herself with joy and relief.

"Billy is in Marinanao?"

"Yes, he took Sebastián there for the day. I wanted them to have some father and son time together. It's something they both need." Sofia's smile noticeably diminished.

"You are not still thinking about going back to the United States with him, are you, Dolores?"

"I love Billy, Sofia. He's my husband. We have reconciled, and he's made a solemn pledge to me and to God Almighty that he will never again mistreat us. And I believe him, Sofia. He has changed. He is a..."

"Don't be a fool, Dolores!" interrupted Sofia. "He hasn't changed, and he never will change. Of that I am certain."

"You are mistaken, Sofia. Billy has changed. We had a long,

heartfelt talk. He has accepted Sebastián, accepted him for who he is, a child of mixed race, a child with African blood."

Dolores spoke with passion and conviction, but Sofia's expression revealed her skepticism.

"You are making a big mistake, dear sister, a very big mistake; and I am sure you will live to regret it." Sofia paused, waiting for Dolores's response, but it never came.

"Did you tell Sebastián that you are going to return to the United States? He is only five, but I am sure by now he knows the difference between life in Cuba and life in Washington. Why would you want to subject him again to the racism and discrimination he suffered in the United States?"

"Cuba too has its racism, Sofia, and you know that as well as I do."

"Maybe so, but it's nowhere near as bad as in the United States. Besides, you are going to be a very wealthy woman, a woman with power and influence. You can prevent and avoid much of it here in Cuba, but you cannot in the Unites States. Your family and your roots are here in Cuba, Dolores. This is where you belong. This is where Sebastián belongs."

"Billy is my husband, Sofia. Could you leave Eugenio?

"I think it's safe to say that Eugenio would never treat me the way Billy has treated you, Dolores. And besides, Billy can't go back to Washington. You yourself told me that he lost his job and acquired a reputation as a ne'er do well and opium addict. So, where is he going to go, and where is he going to take you and Sebastián, Charleston, South Carolina? If you thought Washington was racist, what do you think you will find in Charleston, South Carolina? South Carolina was the first state to secede from the Union. It is the heart of the Confederacy, where the Civil War began.

"I'm tired of this conversation, Sofia, and I don't wish to talk about it any more."

"As you wish, dear sister," said Sofia, persisting nonetheless with some final admonitions.

"Just ask yourself, why has Billy come here now to take you back to the United States? He's a lawyer, and he has known all along that you would ultimately prevail in the litigation over papá's will, and that you would become a very wealthy woman."

"You will have to excuse me, Sofia, but I am going to Marinanao to be with my husband and my son." Sofia walked over, kissed Dolores on the cheek then left the room.

The coachman helped Dolores into the luxurious black carriage with the silver trim, and they set off down the long entrance road of *La Dulce Gardenia*. They rode past the field slaves tending the grounds along the entrance road. As was their custom, they looked up from their labor and waved as the carriage passed.

Dolores could not quite believe how happy she felt. Her heart and her mind danced with joy and delight as she contemplated her new life together with Billy and Sebastián. And before she knew it, she was in Marinanao.

As the carriage made its way along the beach road, Dolores looked out upon the beautiful blue waters of the Caribbean. Seagulls sailed overhead, and the tall coconut palms lining the beach road swayed in the balmy breeze. A wave of exhilaration swept over her, and she couldn't wait to share her good news with Billy and Sebastián.

Dolores knew that Billy would have set down their blanket near the jetty to be close to Sebastián's prized flattop rock, and she directed the coachman to pull up to the jetty. As he helped her out of the carriage, she instructed him to return in the late afternoon to take them to their favorite restaurant and then on to the farmhouse, where they would spend the night.

She began walking along the jetty, looking out to the flattop rock, but there was no sign of Billy and Sebastián. Looking now up the beach, she saw a throng of people huddled together and an ambulance drawn by two black horses, pulling up on the beach road. Two men jumped out, removed a stretcher from the back, and hurried down the beach. A terrifying premonition took hold of her and shook her to the bone. She started running down the beach toward that crowd, slipping and falling in the loose sand, struggling then to her feet and running again.

"Billy, Sebastián where are you?" Her heart pounded, and she prayed she would find them amongst the crowd of onlookers and not the objects of their morbid curiosity. She kept running, calling out: "Billy, Sebastián, where are you?"

The crowd kept growing and milling about.

"What happened?" Someone asked.

"Maybe another shark attack. I heard last week that a man lost his leg and his dog…"

"I heard that a little boy hooked a huge blue marlin and it pulled him into the sea." The words struck Dolores like a dagger to the heart as she slowly approached the crowd.

"Let me through! Please let me through! It's my little boy! Please, let me through."

"Back off and let her through," shouted a tall man holding a bible.

He grasped her hand and began leading her through the unruly crowd. When they finally broke through, it was not Sebastián she saw lying there on a blanket; it was Billy. He lay on his stomach, and there was a man straddled over him pressing down on his back. Dolores collapsed in the sand, and her eyes filled with tears.

"It's my husband," she cried, her face contorted in shock and pain.

"We're trying to expell the water from his lungs, señora," said the fisherman, Joaquín. "He had a weak pulse when we dragged him from the water. He dove in to save your little boy and may have hit some jagged rocks. If he is to survive, I must expel the water from his lungs."

Dolores closed her eyes and prayed to God that her dear Billy would be saved. She was terrified to ask about Sebastián, but Joaquín saved her the effort and the pain.

"Your little boy is over there, señora," said Joaquín, pointing to the throng of curious onlookers, as he continued to administer the compressions to flush the water from Billy's lungs.

"Come with me, señora, I will take you to your boy, said a corpulent woman who lifted Dolores up from the sand and led her by the hand. "There's a doctor with him now, señora."

"It's the boy's mother. Let us through, please. Let us through."

Dolores's heart pounded as they struggled through the crowd, making their way to the spot where the fisherman, Miguel, had placed Sebastián after dragging him from the sea.

Tears streamed down Dolores face as she dropped down in the sand, reached out and tried to touch Sebastián. Miguel held up his hand.

"You mustn't disturb the doctor, señora. He is trying to expel the water from your boy's lungs."

Two women standing there lifted her up and urged her to join them in praying the Our Father. Dolores, however, reached out to the Lord with her own silent, desperate prayers.

The doctor continued the compressions, but there was no water to be seen escaping from Sebastián's mouth. Dolores looked on, still sobbing pitifully, praying as she had never prayed before. A chorus of Hail Marys rose up from the crowd, beseeching the Blessed Mother to intervene and save the little boy's life. However, in spite of the doctor's efforts, there was no water to be seen emerging from Sebastián's mouth.

An ominous silence took hold and several minutes passed. Hope was beginning to fade. Dolores sobbed, trembled and it appeared that she was about to collapse and pass out. But alas, that was just when that first little trickle of water emerged from Sebastián's mouth. The doctor was encouraged anew and increased the speed and strength of his compressions. Another trickle emerged and then another, each one a little bigger than the last. Finally, water spurted from Sebastián's mouth, and he coughed and opened his eyes. Dolores looked to the heavens, made the sign of the cross and gave thanks to God.

The crowd responded with a loud "Amen," and the doctor stood up to a rousing round of applause. Now, she could touch and embrace her dear little boy with the *acanelado* skin. And she bent down and enveloped him in her arms. She continued to cry, but these were tears of joy and relief.

Sebastián looked up at her, a querulous look on his cute little face.

"I caught a big fish, papa," he said."

"It's me, Sebastián; it's me, mamá."

"I caught a big fish, papá" repeated Sebastián, staring at his mama and eventually recognizing her.

"But mama, where is papá?" Dolores smiled and kissed him tenderly on the forehead.

By then, the crowd was dispersing, and when Dolores looked over, she saw Billy sitting up on the blanket.

"I see your papá, Sebastián, and I'm going to take you to him right now."

She picked him up, and as she began walking over to Billy, Sebastián squirmed out of her arms and ran to his papá, smiling all the while. Dolores watched as Billy hugged and kissed him lovingly. She gave them a moment together, then walked over and embraced them both.

"My precious Dolores and Sebastián," Billy said, as tears of joy ran down his face.

"I caught a big fish, papá! Did you see it, papá? Did you?"

"Yes, I saw it, Sebastián. It was the biggest fish I have ever seen, and I'm so proud of you and how you were able to hold on to it."

Billy got up now. Sebastián took his place between his papá and his mamá, and they began slowly walking up the beach.

"Will you take me riding when we get home, papá?" Sebastián asked.

Dolores and Billy looked at each other and smiled, confident that Sebastián was going to be just fine.

"I'm sure that your papá will take you riding once he gets a little rest, Sebastián."

As they walked up to the beach road, they saw the two fishermen approaching. Joaquín and Miguel waved, then walked up to them, exchanging *fuertes abrazos* with Billy and warm greetings with Dolores.

"We are so happy to see the three of you together," said Miguel. "There were moments when we feared the worst, but with God's help we were able to do our part."

"I remember looking up, Dolores, and seeing this kind and courageous man, Joaquín, smiling down at me. The doctor told me how he rescued me and saved me from drowning, and how you, Miguel, rescued and saved our son, Sebastián."

Dolores looked at the two humble fishermen, feeling an overwhelming sense of gratitude and respect for them.

"I'm Dolores de Castilla, señores. My family and I are the owners of *La Dulce Gardenia*. We are eternally grateful to you and want to host a special dinner in your honor and reward you for your heroic acts."

Billy glanced at Dolores and smiled, realizing that the Appellate Court must have ruled in Dolores's favor.

"We will be greatly honored to attend the dinner, señora," said

Joaquín. "But our greatest reward is that with God's help, we were able to save your little boy and your husband."

As they rode back to *La Dulce Gardenia*, Sebastián fell asleep. Billy and Dolores recounted their blessings and talked of the future.

Epilogue

The Decade 1867--1877

A week after that fateful day at Marinanao, Dolores and Billy held a celebratory dinner for the two fishermen, Miguel and Joaquín. They welcomed and honored the two heroes for their extraordinary acts of bravery and self-sacrifice. Pancho and Panchita prepared a feast that surpassed even their famous Christmas fare, with *lechón*, prime Argentine beef, lobster, shrimp, select veal and lamb dishes with choice wines and Champaign. A marvelous Spanish gypsy guitarist and the most popular group of Contra Step musicians in the City of Havana, supplied the music. After dinner, they gathered in the library for brandy and cigars for the men and pastries for the women. They had a wide-ranging conversation, in which they learned a lot about the two honorees.

Miguel and Joaquín were not the simple, humble fishermen that Dolores and Billy had assumed. Indeed, they had held long-term positions as subordinate overseers on *La Buena Cosecha*, the neighboring De Wolf plantation. It so happened that the Chief Overseer had recently sacked them both for refusing to carry out his order to impose a cruel punishment on several slaves, who were accused of staring inappropriately at one of the pretty, young De Wolf daughters. Miguel and Joaquín explained that the real reason why they were sacked was their emerging progressive views on the role of an overseer. Miguel and Joaquín were suffering from the loss of income and were fishing that day at Marianao to earn a little money by selling their catch to local restaurants. It was clear that they would have been working as usual at *La Buena Cosecha* had they not been sacked. And God only knows who would have, or whether anyone would have, rescued Sebastián and Billy. Dolores truly believed that it was God's intervention and not a mere coincidence that Miguel and Joaquín had been there that day.

Dolores and Sofia wanted to reward Miguel and Joaquín monetarily, which they did, and quite generously. However, Dolores wanted to do more and saw an opportunity to do so. She recognized that Miguel and Joaquín were a different breed of overseer, who were seeking to implement a more progressive and less hostile relationship between the overseers and their African charges. Dolores saw the need to reject the long legacy of cruelty, terror and intimidation left by the likes of Chief Overseer, Victorio Arquídez. She realized that *La Buena Cosecha*'s loss could be *La Dulce Gardenia*'s gain. And before Miguel and Joaquín departed that evening, Dolores, Sofia and Constancia agreed to offer them positions as subordinate overseers at *La Dulce Gardenia*, knowing full well that they would be opposed by Arturo and Felipe, but resolving to find a way to handle that. The offers were made, and Miguel and Joaquín gladly and enthusiastically accepted them.

That summer day at the beach in Marinanao in 1867 was a critical turning point in the lives of the McHugh family. Billy and Sebastián nearly drowned that fateful day. Dolores believed that God had saved them for a reason, and she and Billy resolved to embrace a new life, a life of love and devotion. They came to reflect long and hard on their lives in the United States, on the racism and discrimination that they had been forced to endure. They concluded that in spite of Emancipation and the end of the Civil War, conditions in the United States were unlikely to change, and might even get worse under the strains of Reconstruction. They were not willing to return to that toxic environment that had almost destroyed their marriage, and they decided to spend the rest of their lives in Cuba.

It was early Sunday morning as Dolores and Billy walked hand in hand down the garden path to the patio bar. The sun was rising over the lush verdant grounds of *La Dulce Gardenia*. Multi-colored tropical birds had begun their early morning serenade. The air was thick and moist, and heavy raindrops dripped rhythmically from the tall palms and mango trees. They walked past the large patch of gardenias, marveling at their sweet scent and brilliant whiteness, spreading forth upon the grounds like a vast field of cotton.

As they neared the patio bar, a female slave attendant saw them approaching and began wiping the moisture from the chairs.

The happy couple sat down, continuing to hold hands. They were in a playful mood, launching *piropos* back and forth---those flowery and charmingly exaggerated compliments so loved and admired in the Spanish-speaking world. Later that morning they attended mass at the Church of the Little Flower. In the afternoon, they went to the neighboring De Wolf plantation and watched Sebastián play baseball.

The couple's decision to spend the rest of their lives in Cuba was the right decision for Sebastián. Though born in the United States, he was in essence a child of the tropics, and it was clear that he would thrive in the vibrant racial and social fabric that was Cuba. *Sangre de negro* was not the problem in Cuba that it was in the United States. When Dolores and Billy told Sebastián that they would not be returning to the United States, he practically jumped for joy. Just as his Auntie Sofia had often said, Sebastián knew the difference between his life in Cuba and his life in the United States. He was at home in Cuba and needed no period of adjustment. Dolores was able to enroll him in *La Escuela Diplomática*, a special school for the children of diplomats and consular officers serving in Cuba. The advanced curriculum of the school challenged him and he excelled under its tutelage. Equally important, he was popular with his schoolmates and teachers and had many friends. It was evident that he was a happy and well-adjusted little boy, who was to become a happy and confident adolescent and young man.

Remaining in Cuba was the right decision for Dolores as well. She was born in Cuba and had spent most of her life there. She was back home now with her husband Billy, the Billy whom she dearly loved; the Billy whom she knew in her heart had always loved her. Contrary to Sofia's belief that Billy would never change, Billy had changed, evidenced by the fact that there was a new addition to the McHugh family. A year after they had made their decision to remain in Cuba, Dolores gave birth to a beautiful baby girl with dark brown hair, blue eyes and *acanelado* skin. She bore a close resemblance to her brother, Sebastián, and the couple chose the name Beatriz, after Dolores's mother. Much to their delight, they learned that the name Beatriz had Latin origins and carried the meaning, "Brings joy" or "Brings happiness." Baby Beatriz lived up to her name and brought much joy and happiness to the McHughs.

Thanks to the Appellate Court's decision on Don Fernando's second will, Dolores had become a very wealthy woman, capable of providing every benefit and luxury for herself and her family. Wealth, however, was never Dolores's goal in life. She never forgot her humble origins and remained as always a kind and sweet woman, a Christian woman who truly lived a Christian life. She resolved to do some good with her wealth and embarked upon a campaign to build and support orphanages throughout the island. She did so while remaining anonymous. In time, however, people learned that she was the benefactor, and she was recognized and celebrated for her good works and generosity.

Dolores maintained her striking beauty well into middle age. People marveled at how she seemed to defy the normal effects of aging. Her long and lustrous dark-brown hair remained free of gray, and her *cintura de avispa* (hourglass waist) remained as stunning as it was in her youth. Sofia would often say that Dolores had discovered the Fountain of Youth that had eluded Spanish Conquistador, Ponce de Leon. Dolores, however, always attributed her youthful appearance to her *sangre de negro*, which she inherited from her Yoruba mother, Beatriz.

Remaining in Cuba was also the right decision for Billy. However, unlike Dolores and Sebastián, he needed time to adjust to his new life. Billy faced another obstacle--his skeptics and especially Sofia, who believed that his "change" was based upon Dolores's newfound wealth. But the skeptics were mistaken. Billy's decision emerged from his heart. He had come very close to losing his precious Doloresita, and when she forgave him and they reconciled, his love for her became eternal.

Before his tragic addiction, debauchery and fall from grace, Billy had been a brilliant and successful young lawyer, achieving a partnership at a very young age in one of the finest law firms in the United States. He longed to resume his legal career. Billy had practiced law under the Common Law System in the United States. The Common Law was borrowed from the British and was based upon the doctrine of *Stare Decisis*—that the decisions of courts of law constitute precedents and are to be applied in subsequent cases of a similar nature. Billy now faced the challenge of learning and practicing under the Civil Law system in Spanish Colonial Cuba. The vast majority of countries in the world are Civil Law countries. Common Law countries constitute a distinct minority. The Civil Law is based upon the written law, the law enacted by a country's parliament and codified as the basic codes that govern and regulate the legal relations of its citizens, i.e., the Civil Code, the Commercial Code, the Mineral Code, etc. The decisions of courts do not constitute precedents and do not play the important role that they do in Common Law countries.

Billy began taking courses in Civil Law at the University of Havana to further his goal of practicing law in Spanish Colonial Cuba. Sofia and Eugenio were aware of Billy's extensive legal practice in the United States, and once he had progressed in his studies, they suggested that he might wish to teach a course in the Common Law as practiced in the United States. Billy responded enthusiastically and put together a course in Comparative Law. He began teaching and interacting with his students and discovered that he enjoyed teaching and had a knack for it. His course quickly became popular, and the word soon spread in the legal community about this American professor, William C. McHugh, also known to be a highly experienced, bilingual international lawyer. As a result, offers poured in from Havana's premier *bufetes de abogados* (law firms) and Billy eventually joined the highly regarded Havana law firm of *Bustamante* & Crespo.

Billy was determined to clear the air and put his painful and shameful dismissal from Henry Phipps & Partners behind him. He opened a correspondence with Joseph Bartlett, informing him of his new life and career in Cuba. Bartlett was delighted and congratulated him on behalf of the entire firm of Henry Phipps & Partners. They continued to correspond and eventually met again at a convention in Philadelphia, where they discussed establishing a correspondent relationship between their law firms.

Billy went on to have a successful career practicing law in Cuba and teaching Comparative law at the University of Havana.

Sofia was delighted with Dolores's decision to remain in Cuba. Indeed, she had always urged her to do so, and to let Billy return to the United States and live his own life. It took some time, but Sofia came to realize that she had been wrong about Billy. She observed his actions now and not just his words: how he related to Sebastián; how he rejoiced at the birth of Beatriz, who like Sebastián, had *sangre de negro*. Sofia came to see and trust that Billy truly loved Dolores and could not bear to be without her.

Sofia was a law professor at the University of Havana. The academic life satisfied the intellectual needs of this highly intelligent professional woman. However, it was not enough to quench her powerful and unrelenting thirst for Cuban independence and the abolition of slavery. The seeds of those idealistic and patriotic aspirations were planted early in her student years and were nurtured by her relationships. One of her early relationships was with her student friend and *novio*, Carlos Santiago. Young Carlos was a radical, revolutionary zealot, who had attempted to assassinate the Captain General. He failed and was executed by garroting in the *Plaza de Armas*. Sofia, however, did not choose to take such drastic measures, at least not yet.

Sofia's weapon was the pen. She began writing articles in liberal journals and other publications, discovering that she had a talent for arousing passionate feelings with her words; so much so that the Office of the Captain General brought pressure on her and prohibited the publication of her articles. Sofia, however, continued writing, increasing the temper and tone of her words while obtaining publication in Mexico and Argentina. "Why," she wrote in one of her most passionate and widely acclaimed articles, "do we Cubans remain a subservient Spanish colony when the rest of Spain's possessions have long since become free and independent?" She went on to write--"Why does slavery continue to exist and thrive in Cuba when the rest of the world has long since abolished this inhuman and evil practice?" The article, bearing the stark one word title "Why?" caused a stir, reverberating amongst all the local intellectual groups in Cuba and throughout Spanish America. The Monarchy in Madrid and its Captain General in Havana, Francisco de Lersundi, reacted quickly and strongly, undertaking surveillance and harassment measures against Sofia and her husband, Eugenio Andrés Montserrát. Sofia, however, was undeterred and continued to advocate "all necessary measures" to achieve independence from Spain and the abolition of slavery.

After the Appellate Court's decision upholding the validity of don Ferrnando's second will, Arturo de Castilla confronted a new challenge to maintain his role as the general manager of *La Dulce*

Gardenia. The three sisters, and especially Sofia, now challenged Arturo, and he soon learned that he would have to deal with them to maintain stability in the operation of the plantation. Ironically, what they finally agreed upon was a variation of Arturo's earlier proposal that they had rejected years before. They formed a corporation and assigned to it all the assets of *La Dulce Gardenia.* Dividends would be declared and distributed in accordance with a *Fideicomiso.* (A Trust). An independent *Fiedecomisario* (Trustee) would decide the frequency and the amount of such dividends. Like Arturo's previous proposal, this new structure would eliminate the need to sell the assets and break up the operations of the *ingenio.* The arrangement functioned for a time, but it eventually broke down, and the inter-family strife worsened. Surprisingly, and soon after, Arturo declared that he had had enough and proposed that his four siblings buy him out. His three sisters and his brother, Felipe, were only too happy to accept his proposal. The assets were appraised, and they allocated a portion of them to be sold. The proceeds were paid to Arturo in full settlement of his one-fifth interest. Soon after, Arturo purchased a mid-sized *ingenio* some forty kilometers southwest of *La Dulce Gardenia.*

Over time, Felipe de Castilla lost interest in the operations of *La Dulce Gardenia.* As long as he received his dividends, he was happy to allow the three sisters, and the professional managers whom they ultimately hired, to run things. Even after Arturo was bought out, Felipe showed no interest in asssuming an active role in the management. Indeed, he took on a new life, flaunting his wealth by adopting an ostentatious, luxurious lifestyle. He moved out of the Main House, bought an elegant mansion in the heart of Havana and became a "bon vivant." Before long, however, he developed serious drinking and womanizing problems. His wife and children moved out and returned to live in the de Castilla Main House. Felipe's sexual adventures led to multiple romantic entanglements and love triangles. One such episode cost him his life, when he was caught *In flagrante delicto* by the cuckolded husband, who shot and killed him. The three sisters later bought out Felipe's wife's inherited interest, thus becoming the sole owners of *La Dulce Gardenia*.

Dolores's hiring of the "two fishermen," Miguel de Jesús and Joaquín Espinosa, was a brilliant move on her part. With Dolores's urging, the three sisters implemented meaningful reforms to replace the horrid practices and abuses of Chief Overseer, Victorio Arquídez and his like-minded subordinate overseers. In just a few short years and with the blessing of the acting Chief Overseer, Miguel and Joaquín were able to plant the seed and nourish the growth of a more cooperative relationship between overseers and slaves. In so doing, they were able to improve productivity. When it came time to appoint a permanent Chief Overseer for *La Dulce Gardenia*, the sisters agreed that either Miguel or Joaquín would be the perfect choice. It was a difficult decision, but in the end they chose Miguel de Jesús, agreeing nonetheless to pay Joaquín Espinosa a salary on a par with Miguel's.

Within a few short years, the three sisters decided to expand their business interests and purchased a small *ingenio* that offered good opportunities for growth and profitability. They were proud of the reforms they had instituted at *La Dulce Gardenia* and expressed that pride by choosing the name *Las Tres Hermanas* (The Three Sisters) for the plantation. They appointed Joaquín Espinosa the Chief Overseer.

Sofia and Dolores had long since advocated the abolition of slavery, and they decided that the time was ripe for establishing a new kind of workforce. They resolved to test the policy first on the slave workforce of the smaller *ingenio, Las Tres Hermanas*. They "freed" the slaves and hired them as workers for a wage. The slaves enthusiastically embraced the new arrangement. However, the sisters were not yet prepared to implement the policy at *La Dulce Gardenia* with its massive slave workforce, as conservative interests strongly opposed the movement and threatened violence. However, the policy gradually gained a measure of acceptance throughout the island, and the three sisters achieved recognition as forerunners in transforming Cuba's *ingenio* workforce from slave to free.

The New Decade 1877- 1887

Cuba is entering a new decade, and the question on the mind of every patriotic Cuban is whether Spain will continue to deny Cuba its rightful place in the world of free and independent nations. At present, Spain shows little sign of granting Cuba independence. Indeed, there are many leaders who predict that Cuba will not achieve its independence in this century. Cuba, Puerto Rico and the Philippines are Spain's only remaining colonial possessions. Cuba is without a doubt the jewel in the Crown, and Spanish pride is at stake. More importantly, Cuba provides *La Madre Patria* with very substantial revenue each year. Therefore, it seems clear that the only viable option for the freedom-loving people of Cuba is to fight for their freedom as their sister countries in the hemisphere had done decades before. It will not be an easy fight. Spain will continue to do everything in its power to hold onto Cuba...

www.ingramcontent.com/pod-product-compliance
Lightning Source LLC
Chambersburg PA
CBHW030741030726
47497CB00001B/83